Drop & Hook

Russ Ainsworth

American Literary Press
Five Star Special Edition
Baltimore, Maryland

Drop & Hook

Copyright © 2008 Russ Ainsworth

All rights reserved under International and Pan-American copyright conventions. No part of this book may be reproduced, stored in a retrieval system, or transmitted in any form, electronic, mechanical, or other means, now known or hereafter invented, without written permission of the publisher. Address all inquiries to the publisher.

Library of Congress
Cataloging-in-Publication Data
ISBN-13: 978-1-934696-20-0

Library of Congress Card Catalog Number:
2008907163

Published by

American Literary Press
Five Star Special Edition

8019 Belair Road, Suite 10
Baltimore, Maryland 21236

Manufactured in the United States of America

Special thanks, in Baltimore, to dispatcher Phil Shanks, truckers Ralph McNeill and Art Gray, and Ed Staniewicz, for his Polish; and, in St. Louis, trucker and dispatcher Mark Kohring, warehouse owner Richard Kerns, and Dr. Lonnie Frei. This book is dedicated to Elmer Kraemer, a great Lutheran, editor, mentor and friend.

Credits to *Pedal to the Metal (The Work Lives of Truckers)* by Lawrence J. Ouellet; David Butler's *The Fall of Saigon*; *Abandoning Vietnam*, by James H. Willbanks; *Battle for Hue* by Keith William Nolan; Mimi Gleason's *The Tet Offensive; January-April 1968*; Brian J. Cudahy's *Box Boats: How container ships changed the world*; Mark Levinson's *The Box: How the Shipping Container Made the World Smaller and the World Economy Bigger*; *U.S. Marines in Grenada*, by Ronald H. Spector; and *Urgent Fury; The Battle for Grenada*, by Maj. Mark Adkin.

Illustrations by Alison Thiemann

Kenny Wisniewski, a rugged young man of twenty-nine, walked around the 1989 Freightliner conventional tractor with a Caterpillar motor—425 horsepower—looking for leaks from oil lines, grease seals, axles. He found none, and he reached up to open the door and stepped up into the cab on the lot of Sam Zaleski, a truck dealer in southern Baltimore's industrial zone.

Kenny settled into the well-worn seat and moved it back two clicks to accommodate his six-foot-two height. He rubbed back his sand-colored hair and pulled down an Orioles baseball cap.

The steering wheel felt right, and he studied the instrument panel, noting that Zaleski hadn't misled him about the mileage. The three-year-old tractor had 434,000 miles on it, 434,387 to be exact.

Wisniewski found no chips in the windshield on his side, a couple smaller ones in the corners of the right side, likely caused by truck tire debris. He saw where he would hook up his CB and small fridge, when he bought them. Truckers pull out this kind of equipment when they trade in their tractors.

And that was what had happened to this tractor. Phil Mulhaney, an experienced over-the-road driver, had purchased this rig only three years ago, and had decided to buy a new one.

Wisniewski inspected the fuse box and determined that no one had messed with the wiring. He found no water leaks yet, at least none around the windshield, doors and molding areas. The mirrors were all there; none were broken or cracked.

He looked over his right shoulder to take note of the single sleeper, something Mulhaney apparently preferred. Most OTR (over-the-road) truckers choose a double sleeper, for they might sleep in their cabs three to five nights (or days) a week, but Kenny wanted to specialize in pulling containers; in other words he wanted to become an inter-modal trucker, driving from pier to warehouse and back, and that usually meant no overnights for someone based in Baltimore. And, more importantly, that meant he could be home each night.

Also, in inter-modal trucking, he would need only the tractor, and not a trailer or refrigerated trailer, called reefer. The steamship lines, like Maersk of Denmark and Orient Overseas Container Line, would supply the chassis, on which he would place a container.

As an owner-operator, he would contract with a trucking firm but remain independent himself, and non-union, although that was not a real goal of his, having grown up in this working-class city, in a working-class neighborhood with a tradition of organized labor and Democratic politics.

But he was thinking not only of his own first truck since completing two four-year stretches in the Marines but also of his intended marriage, soon he hoped, to Mira Kowalski. He had known her since second grade at St. Casimir's Church school in Canton, still in 1992 a heavily Polish-American section of Baltimore. He wouldn't want to be away from Mira for more than a night at a time, if that.

Sam Zaleski climbed into the tractor as Wisniewski prepared to drive onto the interstates around Baltimore on a trial run. "Like it?" Sam asked, as the door gave a solid crunch as it closed.

"So far, Sam. So far," Kenny said. "Let's see how she perks."

"Just so you know, the brakes were replaced at 300,000 miles or thereabouts, Phil Mulhaney told me—he showed me the paperwork—and we replaced the clutch. . . . Give it a good test, Kenny. I want you to be fully satisfied."

"So everyone tells me, Sam. You're a good man."

"If you want truckers to trust you, Kenny, you've got to be honest with them. There're no better folks on earth."

Wisniewski started the engine, and it sounded like it should. He took note how the gauges responded—the air compressor pumped up the air pressure; the oil pressure showed about forty pounds—just right.

He felt that the clutch had about the right amount of free play as he depressed it to shift into reverse, a gear well into his right side and forward. The tractor moved back easily. He stopped, and shifted down into granny low—named for grandma, it was so slow—and then shifted up and down sequentially into second, third, fourth and fifth as he drove up Broening Highway, turned left onto O'Donnell Street, and climbed an access road onto I-95. He then shifted from the low range to high range, flipping a lever as he moved through neutral and into sixth, seventh, eighth, ninth gears while doing fifty-five miles an hour, and finally to tenth when he reached seventy miles an hour, the speed he suspected he'd be using most of the time when he drove on the interstates.

The tractor zipped along until Wisniewski angled onto I-695, which forms a ring around Baltimore. Kenny thought to himself, 'she's handling beautifully,' but to Sam he said, "Seems pretty good, Sam, a lot more response than I'm used to in the tractors we drove in the Marines."

"I wouldn't know, Kenny. I just hoofed it in the Army, infantry, you know."

"Oh, we did a good deal of that, too. You never walk too much in the Corps."

About fifteen minutes later, he dropped a couple gears as he turned south onto I-83, the Jones Falls Expressway, heading back into the city, slowing down to sixth gear when he came to the streets in Canton, his neighborhood.

There were no funny noises, no grinding, no clunking as he shifted. There were some rattles, like with the windows, but the truck had almost 500,000 miles on it, and that was par for the course, Zaleski assured him.

Kenny Wisniewski got hooked on trucking while driving big rigs in the Marines. He had enlisted after graduating from Mt. St. Joseph High School, wearing the purple and cream just like his idol, his uncle, Stanislaus Wisniewski, commonly called Stach, and sometimes Whiz. Stach was a lieutenant in the Baltimore Police Department. Kenny hiked most of his first enlistment in the Corps, but was allowed to get into trucks after he re-enlisted.

The greatest excitement of his first four years was when he saw limited action in the invasion of Grenada in 1983, helping secure Pearls Airport. He re-enlisted hoping that he would get to drive trucks, and was assigned to Fort Leonard Wood in Missouri where he got his Military Commercial Drivers License (MCDL) after mastering ten-ton Heavy Expanded Mobility Tactical trucks. He then handled MK16s, pulling semi trailers. After eight years in the Corps, he came home to Baltimore to drive for two years for UPS, putting aside all the money he could to fulfill his dream of driving his own truck. At first with UPS he drove the familiar brown trucks, and then moved up to UPS tractor-trailers.

"Well?" Sam asked, as Kenny slowly drove the bobtail (tractor without trailer) through Canton.

"I like it, Sam. But I got to get some financing."

"Polish-American?"

"You bet. My Uncle Stach and me, well, we are supposed to go down there pretty soon. The family has been dealing with Polish-American bankers for generations."

"Best to stay Polish."

"Yep."

But Zaleski continued: "You know, Kenny, and I'm suggesting this only because I like you, and I do think this truck would be a good buy. But a lot of truck drivers that I've visited with start as company drivers, handling a company truck. That way they get experience, and they can put aside some money, without the fuel and maintenance bills. It's just a suggestion, you know."

"Sam, I've thought about that, and I'm going to be talking with the family, my dad and three of my uncles, and I'll put that on the table, too."

"Let me know pretty soon, okay?"

"Absolutely. And thanks," as Kenny guided the truck into its previous space, and reached across to shake hands with Sam.

Sitting on the front steps

Capt. Daniel Russo, forty-two, head of the detective bureau in Baltimore's Northern District, got off work late. Another drug raid in the district had yielded a couple of low-ranking runners, and he had worked overtime debriefing the two detectives who made the arrests.

Russo drove his six-cylinder gray '90 Ford Taurus up Keswick Road to 36th Street, over to Falls Road, and down the Falls Expressway. He hesitated getting into traffic as a tractor without a trailer roared by, and noticed two tractors headed north pulling containers, likely to Pennsylvania, he guessed.

'Pretty late in the day for that,' he thought to himself. 'Must have some delays, accident or something, over on I-695. Probably have a cache of drugs on board. Maybe the feds were checking out containers on I-695. Not very likely,' and he chuckled to himself and discarded the thought.

He reached home on South Exeter Street in Baltimore's Little Italy about 6:45. His wife, Tina, had already fed the boys, Lou, eleven, and Jerry, nine, and they were off to watch a show on their great Uncle Antonio's big color set. Tina brought out the lasagna she had kept warm in the oven and joined Dan for dinner.

When Dan finished and went outside, Antonio, known as Tooky, was holding forth on his front steps with Rocco, Dan's cousin, about the brand new Orioles Stadium at Camden Yards. Dan carried out his beer and folding chair. Tina cleaned up in the kitchen, delaying her arrival on the front steps. Most nights she would come out for only a few minutes, make some excuse for returning to the house, and then dive into her latest book heavy on politics and/or environment.

Every one else in the immediate family gathered on or about the front steps of Aunt Angela's house. Nales, her husband, died eight years ago, and her son Rocco and his wife Betty's younger daughter, Sue, and her new husband, Jasper Mottola, had moved in with Angela. Sue's sister, Maria, was attending Trinity College in Hartford, Conn., and calling home for money at least once a month.

The talks on the front steps were a tradition in Baltimore, a tradition that was dying, undercut by television and air conditioning. But there were still some here and there in the ethnic sections of Baltimore, like Little Italy, butting up against the Inner Harbor tourist attraction, and Canton, farther out and heavy on Polish-Americans.

Antonio: "It's really beautiful, Rocco. You seem to be right on the field, even when you're five or six rows back."

Rocco: "That's what other folks have told me, Tooky." Almost everyone in the ethnic sections of Baltimore had a nickname.

Angela: "Oh, were you at the ball game today, Tooky?"

Antonio: "Sure was. The old timers from St. Leo's were on an outing there, Ange. It's really a nice ballpark." He paused to sip his Bohemian National. "Seats 48,000, they tell me."

Jasper: "Wasn't the bar run by Babe Ruth's father in there somewhere?"

Antonio: "I don't know, but I'll bet Schooch does," referring to Dan, who inherited that nickname from his father, Luigi, who had been a terrific bocce player. He had lost part of a finger on his right hand in a fish-market accident, and he had a trick of rolling the ball in such a way that it would "schooch" around the other balls to rub up against the pallino, the target. His three teammates would shout "schoochone!" "schoochone!"

Dan: "Stach Wisniewski told me they have a marker in center field. And something else he said. They have a statue of Babe Ruth right there near the entrance."

Antonio: "Right, we saw it, Schooch."

"And what was wrong with that statue, Tooky?"

"I don't know. I didn't see anything wrong with it. Kinda looked like the pictures you see."

"He's holding a right-handed glove. But he was a lefty, you know."

"Really? I knew he batted left. I didn't ever know he threw left, too."

"Yep. And one hell of a pitcher."

Jasper: "Well, I'll be. You'd think they'd fix that statue, wouldn't you?"

Rocco: "Where were you sittin', Tooky?"

"Left field. When we were going in, someone said there was a 410-foot marker on the outfield wall. And a pretty tall wall comes in from the side; that kinda breaks the outfield up some."

Jasper: "Don't they have a complicated name for this field?"

Dan: "Orioles Park at Camden Yards."

"That's what I meant. Why two names?"

"Well, the club owner wanted to call it Orioles Park, and the former mayor, now the governor, wanted to call it Camden Yards, so they compromised."

Rocco: "So how'd the Os do?"

Antonio: "We won, of course, but with the new stadium we win every time."

Angela: "How many of there were you?"

Antonio: "Pretty good group, oh, probably twenty-five to thirty, I would guess. Kept those beer sellers hustling."

Dan: "Was Father Mike along?"

Antonio: "You couldn't keep him away."

When Daniel Russo, then eighteen, got his draft notice in the summer of 1967, he elected to enlist into the Marines, hoping he'd get a better deal than he might have in the Army. Surprise: He got the Tet offensive, which began in Hue, South Vietnam, on January 31, 1968.

He was a grunt in the undermanned Marine units that fought house-to-house and block by block into and out of the Citadel, a walled fortress in Hue, for about a month, alongside the poetically named Perfume River, before driving off the North Viet forces. He was wounded at least three times, but elected each time to stay with his platoon.

The third time, with shrapnel wounds in his arms, he begged off being lifted out by helicopter. The choppers brought in ammunition and took out body bags and those too injured to argue. Dan was treated later.

His left arm still shows the wounds and won't lift as well as his right. He has a slight limp from other wounds.

The same day that Captain Dan Russo talked baseball with his relatives on South Exeter Street, Lt. Stanislaus "Stach" Wisniewski, thirty-seven, Kenny's uncle, finished his work on stadium control at the new ballpark. He dropped by the Cajun Gumbo, one of the restaurants on the ground floor of the eight-story, 1,000-foot-long old B&O warehouse just behind the outfield walls of Orioles Park. Stadium control required forty officers at the old Memorial Stadium, now abandoned, but forty-eight at the new park, plus, in the beginning, as many as fifty-six officers working near the stadium, plain clothes and regular.

The warehouse was restored as part of the ballpark's construction. The Camden Club was on the seventh and eighth levels; a 1,200-person banquet hall on level six; the owner's private suites on five; the main kitchen for the ballpark's club level on four; Orioles' offices on floors three and two, and retail outlets on the first floor, including Bambino's Pub, an Orioles' baseball stuff store, and Cajun Gumbo.

This outlet was already known for great take-outs. Stach studied the menu over the counter, passed on the house crab cakes, and chose some crawfish tails, enough for him, wife Stephanie, and two of the children. Stella, the five-year-old, would turn up her nose, so he'd have to stop at a burger and fries outlet for her.

"You want some special sauce?" asked the clerk, a middle-aged woman whose nametag read Doris.

"Yeh, sure, why not," Stach said, remembering his brother-in-law George's endorsement.

"Six tubs?" the woman said.

"Oh, no, that's way too much," Stach returned. "Three or four will do." And he paid for the meal. "We wouldn't know what to do with all that sauce," he added for some reason, and the woman, apparently noticing his uniform for the first time, flushed, and glanced back over her left shoulder to a mustached man in the window.

"Oh, sorry," she said as she picked out four of the tubs for him. Stach filed away the incident.

Stanislaus Wisniewski had been a grunt in the Marine Corps who saw action in Vietnam, very limited action. He was in a platoon put aboard one of the ships in the flotilla sent to bring out as many Americans, government-related and not, as possible in the last days before America withdrew totally from Vietnam. The flotilla would also receive compromised South Vietnamese, and some South Vietnamese pilots flew copters loaded with their families out to the ships.

Wisniewski's platoon—with no experience in Vietnam, combat or otherwise—was flown by CH-54 choppers to Tan San Nhut airport serving Saigon, dumped on the tarmac and ordered to take up defensive positions around "Dodge City," the evacuation center, to cover the South Vietnamese and others fleeing. The Marines also watched as South Vietnamese pilots took off in their fixed-wing craft to safety in Thailand.

Later, Stach's platoon coptered over to the U.S. Embassy in Saigon, and the only action he saw there was helping push away some South Vietnamese trying to climb the wall, and, as the evacuation played out, locking and bolting doors while he and the other Marines climbed to the rooftop to board CH-46 copters as morning broke on April 30, 1975, and returned to the rescue flotilla. They were the last of the 7,100 U.S. and South Vietnamese personnel evacuated by air. Another 70,000 plus evacuated by ship.

The rest of Stach's Marine service was spent stateside.

Peanuts and Cracker Jack

Baltimore's new ballpark opened this spring, on April 6, 1992, when Rick Sutcliffe shut out the Cleveland Indians

2-0, giving up only five hits, before 44,569 people, including President George Bush, who bounced in a curve as the official first pitch.

Oriole Park at Camden Yards came about because the Baltimore Colts, worshipped by area football fans for such heroes as Johnny Unitas and Raymond Berry, had just upped and left town in 1984 for Indianapolis.

Baltimore's popular mayor, William Donald Schaefer, who had been an opponent of public spending on sports stadiums, immediately became the lead booster of a new park for the Orioles. In 1986, he was elected Maryland's governor and helped push through two state-run lotteries with sports themes to fund construction not only for a new Orioles ballpark but also one for a professional football team, when and if one could be found.

The Os' park was built immediately west of the Inner Harbor on the Baltimore & Ohio Railroad's old yards, replacing such companies as Parks Sausage and Southern Seafood. Contractors took about two and a half years to raze buildings in the way and build the stadium.

Where center field is today, George Herman Ruth Sr. operated a saloon. His son, who became the Babe, worked there as a kid before hitting the streets and finally being rescued by the good brothers of St. Mary's Industrial School: One of the artifacts uncovered in the construction was the Ruths' outhouse. They had lived over the saloon; the outhouse was out back.

Incidentally, the house where the Babe was born is only a couple blocks west of the new stadium, and has been converted to a museum tourists frequent in droves.

Oriole Park at Camden Yards cost $110 million. The grass is real, the bricked walls around the park are real, and the outfield is not symmetrical like the modern stadiums at St. Louis and Cincinnati. Oriole Park is more akin to Brooklyn's Ebbets Field, Boston's Fenway Park or

13

Chicago's Wrigley Field—without all those pillars.

When Oriole Park opened, the fans came out in record numbers, and the Os did great. By May 5, they had won ten of their first eleven home games—they lost to the Cleveland Indians 4-0 on April 9, the first night game at home—and were in first place.

The New York Times reported that by July 15, 547,637 more fans had entered Oriole Park than the previous July at Memorial Stadium, or 2,035,897 so far this year to 1,468,360 at Memorial Stadium last year. By the same date, the St. Louis Cardinals had drawn 80,125 more folks this year than last, with 1,267,894 to 1,186,879. The Cincinnati Reds attracted 32,237 more this year, with 1,158,855 compared to 1,136,618 last year. By comparison, both those National League clubs generally outdrew the Orioles.

About a week after Lt. Wisniewski had that encounter at the Cajun Gumbo outlet at the ballpark he suddenly recalled it. For he had this knack—people said one of his nicknames, Whiz, came from his last name, but many men on the force thought it was from his genius of filing away seemingly unimportant happenings like those Cajun Gumbo sauces and then bringing them back up at just the right time. He let these remembrances gnaw at him.

For example, his remembrance of an unusual smell at an auto accident scene—it turned out to be baking soda used to purify crack—had led him and then detective, now captain, Dan Russo to their first big arrests, a crack dealer and one of his top runners, about fifteen years ago.

A second result of Wisniewski's "chewing his cud" resulted from Stach stumbling onto a drug operation by people in wheel chairs as the runners, most of them faking their handicap.

Since 1976, when all that happened, Wisniewski's cud had acted up many times, leading to major and minor arrests. Detectives throughout the force thought he had a sixth sense for solving crimes and sought his counsel.

So, about five weeks after his encounter at Cajun Gumbo, Stach stopped by there again, this time in plain clothes, and ordered a similar meal to go. He asked for four half-orders of Shrimp Diane. "I'll have some special sauce," he added.

"With shrimp, we offer tartar or cocktail," the same woman, Doris, having looked him over, replied tersely, glancing back at a Latino with a small black mustache and a scar on his left cheek, who Stach thought might be one of the owners or the franchisee himself. "I better have a couple of each," Stach said, and paid his bill, but filed away the face of the man in the window.

Mow down those duckpins

"What do you think, Schooch?" he asked Dan Russo as they waited to bowl a week or so later at the Patterson Bowling Center on Eastern Avenue. Stach was referring to the two incidents at Cajun Gumbo.

The alleys, though antiquated, were still going strong in a Canton area that was beginning to feel what would become a surge of revival.

Dan: "You need a vacation. Been down the ocean lately?"

"Last year we took the kids. You know that. But don't you think it was strange to offer me so many tubs of some special sauce?"

"Mebbe you look like you need it. Has it got some special sex enhancer?" And Dan got up to bowl.

Wisniewski and Russo developed their friendship not only through joint work on the drug bust in 1976 but also through their common interest in duckpins bowling at the Patterson Bowling Center on Eastern, about halfway between their homes.

Stach got Dan onto the high-powered team of five by promising that Dan would work on improving his average, and he did, from a shaky 90 to an usually reliable 140, which is a tremendous improvement for duckpins. Dan moved from the second position on the team, regularly reserved for the worst bowler, to fourth, which is the third best after the anchor and leadoff. Stach himself had become anchor when Casimir "Casey" Zielinski died of a heart attack.

Zielinski was sixty-five, a year from retirement on the railroads, but he really had no future planned, so the folks at the wake at Zielinski's home on Potomac Street said it was only fitting that he went out on a high—his last scores at the Patterson Bowling Center were 210, 142 and 170, terrific in duckpins. Some friends were collecting funds for a plaque for the alleys and pressing the owner to put up Casey's bowling shirt on the wall.

Duckpins, born at the Diamond Lanes in Baltimore, reportedly got their name because their bouncing around on the alleys looked like a bunch of ducks taking off from Chesapeake Bay. The balls are five inches in diameter, have no holes, and weigh no more than three pounds twelve ounces. A bowler gets three balls to knock all ten pins down, and an average in the low 100s is pretty good.

"Not bad, not bad, Schooch," Stach said. "You may yet learn this game. On the way to a 145?"

"Don't jinx me." He lit up a Camel, and saw Stach grimace. "I know, I know, but I only smoke here, not at work, not at home, only here, and only three Camels every Thursday night. What's the harm in that?"

"Why not cut back to two, and then one, and . . .?"

"Why bug me? Don't you harass your brother-in-law enough? And it hasn't stopped him, either."

"Oh, one day it will, one day it will. . . . So, how about this Cajun Gumbo place? That's got to be an outlet of some sort, maybe just small potatoes, I don't know."

"Because it's you, we'll check it out—deliveries and all that. I'll have to get the Central District involved, you know. But when I tell them you're engrossed in it they'll jump in to help."

"Engrossed? Big word. But do I have that kind of a reputation?"

"The word gets around. The word gets around. And how about getting one of the department artists to do up a mug of this suspicious guy in the window."

"Yeh, that's a good idea," and glancing at the alleys, "You're up."

Pop the question?

On a Tuesday night when both Stach and Kenny were free—Kenny was driving for UPS at the time—they met with Stephanie, Stach's wife, and Mira Kowalski, Kenny's girlfriend, at Captain James Restaurant at Boston and Aliceanna. After ordering, Stephanie, a slender brunette with a slightly pinched face, who disarmed many men by staring them down when she talked to them, turned to Kenny, "Well, young man, are you ever going to ask this young lady to marry you?"

Stach: "Hon, that's too much."

Stephanie: "I'm waiting."

Kenny: "One day, Aunt Stephanie, but you gotta remember that Mira's folks are intensely Polish. They love traditions, and I guess I'll have to deal with them."

Mira: "We'll have to put up with them, honey. But, Stephanie, how did you and Lt. Wisniewski get engaged?" hoping to divert Stephanie from pressuring Kenny further.

"I'm afraid I was a little forward, Mira. But I'll let Stach tell the story. Kenny already knows it."

Stach, after a questioning, not-very-happy look at his

wife, which she met without blinking: "Not just a little forward, Steph." He paused. "Anyway, remember, Mira, this was 1976, the year of the Tall Ships in Baltimore, and we were all sitting outside, you know, on the front steps.

"Anna and the women were up at Hawk's house, and the men next door outside my parents', and the talk was just going on as it usually did, with my dad and Kenny's dad arguing over whether they should warsh the walls before painting. Did you know they had their own painting company?"

Mira nodded. "Kenny mentioned it."

"Well, anyway, they were going at it pretty good, and the women were discussing something else, whatever, but I can remember real good when my sister Anna recognized Steph walking down South Kenwood opposite us. Anna invited her over, and next thing everyone knows that Steph Kerenski and I were going out together.

"First, Anna introduces Steph as Nick Kerenski's niece. He runs the hardware store on Dillon, you know. And then Anna goes through the whole darn family, including my parents. And the women get a buzzing, you know. And everyone's talking all at once, so I thought I just had to stop all that, dumb me."

"But loveable," Stephanie cut in.

"Oh yeh. So I decide to fess up that, yes, I knew Steph, and we had gone on dates and all, and I was thinking that I might just want to buy that hardware store her uncle runs—he really wanted to retire and travel—and yes, I could find something for Steph at the hardware store."

"Oh, yes, Mira, he was saying he would take me on as the bookkeeper, imagine that. I am a CPA, you know."

Stach: "Oh yeh, we had to get that aired for everyone. And so I tried to explain that I would like to have Steph work at the hardware store, and I got going pretty good, even explained that I had been studying this Urban

Homesteading Program, and for one dollar we could buy a vacant, rundown house in the city, fix it up to building code, live in it for eighteen months and then sell it. Now, that was certainly clear, to me, you know.

"But she comes back with a one-two punch, saying something about me making a marriage proposal, you know."

Mira: "Sure sounds like one to me."

Stephanie: "Certainly does, doesn't it?"

Stach: "In retrospect, I suppose you might interpret it that way, but that wasn't what I meant."

Stephanie: "Whatever he meant, what he said was he wanted me to live with him for eighteen months and . . ."

Stach: "I guess I had talked myself into a corner on that one, so, not to disappoint her, . . ."

Stephanie: "Oh, yeh."

Stach: ". . . I figured I might as well marry her as anyone else, her being a CPA and all."

Wham! "Ouch," Stach said, rubbing his left arm.

Stephanie: "Stick to the script, Stach. You said in front of all your folks on the steps in front of your house that you were sure you wanted to marry me. Cause, then I just . . ." leaned over and kissed him, and Stach held Stephanie in a vice grip, kissed her back and let her loose.

Stephanie: "And, what happened next, Kenny?"

Kenny: "Well, Aunt Stephanie, it seemed like everyone up and down South Kenwood clapped and whooped."

Mira: "What a beautiful story. Thanks for telling it, Stach."

Stephanie, surprised at Stach's public demonstration, blinked and turned to Mira: "So that wasn't quite the traditional way to get engaged, was it? We did our own thing."

Kenny: "I was there. That's the way I remember it, Mira."

Mira: "But you know how my dad's so involved in St. Casimirs (she pronounced it Casmers, as did most of the neighborhood) and he's so intent on keeping up all the old Polish traditions."

Kenny: "I know, I know. And one of these days I just might go along with them. We'll see." And he sounded very much like his Uncle Stach.

A week later, Stach accompanied Kenny to a Polish savings bank in Canton to see whether he could get a loan to purchase the truck tractor, and asked for Ted Lewandowski.

Lewandowski, a tall lanky man with graying hair—what there remained of it—was a top official in the bank, a man in his low sixties, thoroughly experienced in home loans but equally proficient in finding money for businesses, especially Polish-American ventures. He smiled on meeting Stach: "Stach Wisniewski, or is it Lt. Wisniewski now?"

"Stach will do, Stan. How are you? This is my nephew, Kenny, and he's looking for some suggestions, much like I got from you, what is it, sixteen years ago? That was when Steph and I bought Kerenski's Hardware?"

Lewandowski: "Was it that long? You're probably right. Kenny, good to meet you." They shook hands.

"Didn't I hear you were getting married? That Mira Kowalski is a beauty."

Kenny: "Well, we haven't actually got engaged, sir, but I'll agree with your description of her."

"So what's up? Buying a row house already?"

Stach: "Kenny's in the market for a truck tractor, but I'll let him explain."

"I need help in buying a tractor, sir, a big truck tractor, so I can pull containers out of Baltimore to Philly, Wilmington, Hampton Road, Virginia, and back. I drove big trucks in the Marines, and I'd like to get into the business. Right now, I'm doing pretty well with UPS. You know those little brown trucks." Lewandowski smiled. "But I really want to get my own rig."

"You have a license for big trucks?"

"Yes, sir. Got my MCDL, sorry, the military's commercial driver's license when I was in the Marines. It just transferred to a regular CDL, commercial driver's license. I didn't have to go to any special school. A lot of truckers, older men, just grandfathered in their licenses when everyone had to get new ones with their Social Security numbers."

Lewandowski admitted, "I'd never even try to back up one of those tractor trailers. Get it all messed up."

"It's a lot like pool, sir. You have to visualize your shot before you make it. Backing up, you just have to think

21

backwards. Like when you're backing to your right . . ." He turned his head to the right as if he were actually backing up. ". . . pretty soon your mirrors will be showing you only the trailer," his hands were working away ". . . and then you either have to guess, and that takes a lot of experience, or get someone on the outside helping you."

"Well, the country needs more trucks and more drivers, I know that, Kenny. What are we talking about?"

Stach: "Kenny's done his homework, Ted. Been to a couple dealers. Well, he'll tell you."

Kenny: "I did go to three dealers in the area—most truck sales are done through dealers, you know—and I think I got a very good deal on a used tractor only three years old. It's got only about 435,00 miles on it, and . . ."

Lewandowski cut in: "That's a lot of miles."

"Not for a truck that will likely run for a million, a million and a half miles, sir, and at $42,000, maybe we can get him down to $40,000. That's a lot better than a new one costing a lot more. It's too tough a business for a new driver to get a new truck."

Lewandowski nodded thoughtfully.

Kenny: "I'd also want to put in a CB radio, a small fridge, stuff like that for the road, all for less than $500. I can cover that. The previous owner just pulled out his personal gear for his new truck—which is normal—and I want to install mine."

"A fridge? Come on, Kenny. What next, a microwave?"

Stach: "I laughed, too, Stan, but there are good reasons."

Kenny: "The fridge is for Cokes, the caffeine, you know, and I probably wouldn't need the microwave. But a lot of drivers do have 'em to heat up their pastries and such."

"Really?"

"The over-the-road drivers need those when they're waiting at a gate for a container, or waiting to pick up or dropoff. Murphy's Law says there'll never be a place nearby to eat when you know you have to sit still for a while."

"I guess that makes sense for a trucker. . . . What kind of truck are you looking at?"

"A 1989 Freightliner conventional, with a single sleeper."

"Un huh?"

Stach: "Kenny doesn't figure on doing more than sleeping in his cab but one night per week, if that, and then he's back home, unlike the over-the-road truckers who go out for four, five days, weeks or more. They'd prefer what's called a double sleeper—gives them more room to get some solid sleep."

Kenny: "What I'm looking at, Mr. Lewandowski, is more of a regional truck, with a shorter wheel base, for we have to get into smaller places."

"I see. . . . Well, let's see. You say you think the dealer will come down to $40,000, and how much can you put together?"

"I've put aside about $10,000, and I'm hoping my uncles will cough up $5,000 per . . ."

"Adding up to . . ."

Kenny: "I'm hoping to put together $20,000 to $24,000."

Lewandowski: "Then you don't need me or our agency, Kenny Wisniewski." Kenny looked surprised.

"Oh yes, we could consider giving you a loan. But many could construe that we were using you. You could build up what you need simply by setting aside funds." He turned to Stach. "It was good seeing you again, Stach," and extending his hand to Kenny, "Kenny, when you're ready to buy a home, whether it's a row house or not, just come on back. We'll take care of you then. And good luck with your tractor."

A family affair

About two weeks later, the extended Wisniewski family gathered on a Saturday to consider Kenny's dream of buying a tractor. Anna, ably aided by Aunt Sophia, Mira, and even Aunt Irene, who stirred the soup from time to time, adding a little salt each time, provided a well-done ham, boiled potatoes, peas, carrots, lettuce and mushrooms with cream, with cake and ice cream for dessert, and coffee for the older folks. The younger ones got their caffeine from Cokes or Pepsis.

Junior and Betty, Kenny's parents, who lived down South Kenwood Avenue, arrived early, and she unwrapped the desserts she had prepared. He helped with the chairs and tables.

Fred and Marta Wisniewski, Kenny's uncle and aunt, drove up in their '91 Ford Mustang, and Les, also an uncle, and Isobel Wisniewski arrived in his still running '72 Ford pickup, which was working on its second motor and probably had 350,000 miles, although the speedometer showed only 47,000-odd. Les could repair the motor as well as he could do rough or finished carpentry.

He popped out of his pickup to ask his brother, Fred, "Where's that pretty Thunderbird you had?"

"Traded it in for this beauty. You like it? Five-liter, eight cylinders," he explained as he popped the hood. "Prettiest car I've ever seen." Fred was vice president for sales of a major Ford dealership in Baltimore County, and could pick and choose exactly what he wanted.

"Looks mighty nice, Fred, mighty nice. Now I got old Pauline still going strong, only 47,000 miles, you know," and Les chuckled. He had always called his vehicles by women's names, and Isobel never asked why. She figured they were old girlfriends, and didn't want to know for sure, and was happy that this worn-out, banged-up pickup truck was not named after her.

Fred: "Well, we didn't need the big car anymore. The grandkids are all busy, with the CYO and school groups. Steve's off on some hiking adventure in West Virginia, and Nadine, well, the twins never let up on her."

John, Fred and Marta's oldest, was forty-four, a doctor working in Delaware, who rarely came down to see his parents; his wife, Ruth, did not get along with her in-laws. They had two children, Bob and Jimmy, who were developing athletes, active in the CYO.

Steve, thirty-two, Fred and Marta's other son, and a computer whiz, was still single, and loved to ski in the winter and hike in the summer; it was doubtful whether he'd ever marry.

And their daughter, Nadine, thirty, had the twins by Harold, a realtor in Pennsylvania who had deserted her for a new mate. Fred and Marta no longer spoke of him.

Les: "I actually got Greg (his son) to promise to stop by, and to pick up his sister at College Park. Well, now, here they are." And Greg, his wife, Kathy, and their son, Lester, seven, drove up in a Honda, along with Mary, now twenty-five, in her first year of graduate work at the University of Maryland. Greg was an accountant who frequently told Kathy that he should just get out his set of tools, passed along by his father, and do some jobbing. Each time she would have to talk him out of it.

Greg: "Uncle Fred, you have new wheels. Let's see, '91 Mustang, eight cylinders?" Fred

Kathy: "Hello, everyone." She hugged Sophia, Irene, Mira and Anna. "It's so good to see you all.

nodded. "Yep, well, good luck with it."

Fred: "Good to see you, Greg. How's work?"

Greg: "Great. But one day I'm going to team up with Dad and do some real work."

Les: "You're always welcome, son, but the women say you'll make more money doing what you're doing now."

Greg: "Yea, I know. They're probably right. Still…"

And, what do you think of our big boy?"

Irene: "Looks a little scrawny."

Anna jumped in to cover that remark: "That's quite a compliment, Lester. She means you have lots of muscles."

Irene: "I do?"

Sophia: "Yes, he's a handsome young man, all right."

Lester didn't say anything. He didn't trust the old women.

Anna: "Okay, everyone. Time to come in for dinner. Let's eat."

George, her husband, who had just come down from a short nap to recoup from a few too many beers the night before: "Well, hello all. Got to do what the wife says. We're all set up in the living room."

Like most of the row houses on South Kenwood Avenue, Anna and George's house measured only fifteen feet wide and twenty-one feet deep, so the rooms were pretty small. When the family gathered, the kitchen table was extended by two borrowed card tables and one stored in the basement. The tables then stretched into the parlor to get everyone seated. The parlor was rarely used, only when the priest came to call or when a casket was placed there for a wake.

The house was pretty decent to live in, compared to many row houses in Canton. Some were eight feet wide; many were nine feet. How small were they? The standard answer was: "You sneeze. You hit your butt on this wall, and your head on the other."

George, though host, turned to Stach: "Whiz, probably you should say a prayer."

"Be happy to." And he began in Polish, "*Poblogoslaw Panie Boze nas I te dary, ktore z Twojej opatrznosci spozywac mamy. Przez Chrystusa Pana naszego. Amen.* And I'll let Kenny translate."

Kenny: "Bless us, O Lord, and these thy gifts, which we are about to receive from Thy bounty, through Christ our Lord," and he paused for a second as everyone said with him, "Amen."

George: "Well done. Let's eat," which was said a little too quickly after the prayer for Anna, who scowled at her husband. For his sister's sake, Stach raised one hand to stop the platters from moving and said, "How many of you—perhaps all of you—remember the greetings at St. Casimir's School?" He looked about as everyone studied the ceiling in an attempt to remember. "Well, here comes the priest, . . . "

Anna cut in ". . . or the nun . . ."

Stach and several others: "*Niech bedzie pochwalony Jezus Chrystus.*" Stach: "In English?"

"Praise be Jesus Christ," everyone including George responded.

Stach: "And the nun or priest would respond, Aunt Irene?"

"*Na wieki wiekow. Amen.*"

"Meaning?"

Most everyone with broad smiles at Aunt Irene's memory: "Now and forever. Amen."

The extended family meal properly begun, family chatter took over as the huge plates were passed. When the talking died off as folks tackled the food before them, Stach spoke a little loudly: "Probably, we should get down to business. Kenny here has a plan we'd like the family to consider." Actually they all had a pretty good idea of what he was seeking.

Kenny swallowed down a chunk of potato: "Great food, Anna, Aunt Sophia, Aunt Irene. Thanks to all of you for coming. What I'm thinking about is buying a tractor, a truck tractor so I can become an owner-operator and pull containers from here to Philly, Wilmington, other cities in Pennsylvania."

Les: "I'm told that's a wide-open field, Kenny, with big demands for both trucks and drivers."

"Yep, and most of the men in inter-modal trucking are owner-operators."

Les: "I hear about a lot of owner-operators just barely getting by, or getting into deep debt, 'cause they can't come up with another load to pick up and deliver. How about that?"

"It's a problem, but the answer is to get a contract with a firm that handles containers, either as a company driver or as an owner-operator. And one suggestion I've had from several sources is that I could start as a company driver and put aside what I can so I can buy that tractor."

Stach: "And I've got some pull with a firm here that has both short hauls and long hauls delivering these containers."

Fred: "Rex Rossler?"

Stach: "Yep."

Fred: "Figures. He owes you."

Stach: "Better explain inter-modal, Kenny."

Kenny, who accented his points with half a bread roll: "Well, it means that a big container, or box, once filled and sealed in some other country like Germany, gets loaded onto a truck, driven to a pier where it's loaded onto a specially designed ship to cross the Atlantic, then put on a train or a truck, like mine, and delivered to a particular warehouse in a particular city, where it's likely stored for a while, and then trucked to whoever ordered the goods."

Greg: "Don't you need something behind the tractor, Kenny?"

"You mean a trailer, Greg? Nope, the steamship lines provide the chassis, the trailers they set the containers down on. The containers are all parked on chassis in a pool at the terminal. We just pick out the one that's got our load."

Fred: "Got the tractor picked out?"

"Yep, an '89 Freightliner. Would you like to see it?"

Les: "By golly, if we're going to put up some big money, then I sure would." Nobody blinked around the tables, not even Marta, Fred's wife, who sixteen years before had balked when Stach and Stephanie, not yet married, had asked for help to buy a hardware store in Canton.

But this time, Kenny and Mira breathed easier, and the conversation switched to Canton rehabbers, politics, Orioles baseball. Junior spoke quietly to Les, saying: "We'll commit for $2,500. I'd like to do more, but my painting company just doesn't make that much."

Les: "You're doing the best you can, Junior. We understand, and we're real thankful for what you can do. We have a lot of confidence in your son."

After dinner, the men went off to see the tractor, Stach's brothers happy that they hadn't had to weather any withering stares by Mira the way they had had to with Stephanie sixteen years before when she sought help on buying the hardware store. George, Les, Junior and Fred took a turn around the dealer's lot with Kenny driving. They came back persuaded that the deal was doable.

When they returned and gathered around the tables for coffee, Stephanie asked, with a penetrating stare: "How long do you think that tractor will last, Kenny, or, maybe a better question, how long do you think you'll stay with this one before trading up?"

"As I told the men," Kenny said, turning to Aunt Marta, knowing that she could influence her husband either way, "the dealer is asking $42,500, but I think we can wheedle that down to $40,500. A new tractor would run $80,000, possibly as much as $90,000. And Aunt Stephanie, I would hope to keep this one for three, four, maybe five years, depending on the mileage."

Isobel: "That is a saving."

Mira: "Kenny has to start somewhere."

Irene: "Will he be gone a lot?"

Kenny: "I hope not, Aunt Irene."

Sophia: "Well, I hope not, too, Mira. Keep the men out of temptation, I say."

Several women: "Amen to that." And the men smiled and looked at the ceiling.

Traditions, traditions, traditions

It was only two weeks later that Kenny induced John Sokolowski, who years before had promised to be Kenny's best man, to conduct an engagement ceremony in Mira's home, with both extended families present. John had not expected that part of the deal, but he swallowed hard and agreed. There would be no surprises like Stach and Stephanie's engagement.

So on April 12, for the couple had to give six months notice for the wedding, the Wisniewski and Kowalski families gathered at Mira's parents' row house on Ellwood Street for a ceremony in the parlor—with the extended families pushed into the living room and kitchen.

Mira's father, Emil, went back and forth in the parlor to a little table already covered with a cloth, to put down a crucifix, a bowl of holy water and the engagement ring. The crowd pressed forward into the parlor, and John, glancing at an index card in his left hand, asked Mira and Kenny in sequence: "Are you here of your own free will? Have your families consented to your coming here?" The answers were foregone, of course, and John then blessed the ring by sprinkling holy water on it and saying, "In the name of the Father, the Son and the Holy Ghost."

Kenny picked up the ring and put it on Mira's finger, to applause by the men and sighs by the women.

But Mira's parents weren't through. Emil brought out a loaf of bread that his wife, Danuta, had baked special, and he had Kenny and Mira hold their hands over the bread, and he bound them together with a special cloth Danuta had knit, commenting, "Two hands joined together . . . " and he faltered ". . . until death do them part," his wife whispered loud enough for everyone to hear, and he smiled, saying loudly, "until death do them part." Everyone applauded once more.

The wedding was set for September 12 at St. Casimir's, of course, for both families belonged to the great old church.

Now Kenny and Mira didn't actually set the date by themselves, nor did Emil throw his weight around. What happened was that the couple met with Father Miczelowski and decided on a nuptial mass, meaning there would be readings of scripture, by members of their bridal party if they so chose, and they did, a homily by Father

Miczelowski, the exchange of vows, the eucharistic prayer and Holy Communion, which meant to those invited to the wedding that a priest would indeed be conducting the service. And they set 2 p.m. Saturday, September 12, for the wedding. Other couples would have the choice of 10 a.m. or noon for the other weddings at St. Casimir's that day. The 2 p.m. time allowed for photos afterward and preparations for the reception, beginning at 7 p.m.

And Mira had enough courage to tell her father and mother that she and Kenny had set the date. The parents were surprised that they hadn't been consulted, but they acquiesced while showing without saying that they would have liked to have compared notes.

There's a less formal service, by the way, without Communion, and a deacon can handle that. Mira knew her folks would prefer having Communion, but she also was aware that the Wisniewskis were very close to Father Miczelowski and would want him to preach the homily.

Now, besides all these arrangements, the Baltimore Archdiocese required its young people considering marriage to attend a formal program of preparation. Because both Mira and Kenny had grown up active in St. Casimir's, and continued their attendance—despite his working weekends for UPS—Kenny somehow got to one of the several masses scheduled by St. Casimir's each weekend—they had little trouble getting through the program. They also had Catholics as best man and maid of honor, although that was no longer required by the archdiocese. Several other members of the bridal party were Protestants of various colors.

"What's your beef?"

The police surveillance of the Cajun Gumbo outlet next to the stadium was beginning to pay off. Far from the fish outlet, detectives picked off several low-level runners—kids, really, just beginning their careers in drugs, and now interrupting their lives with jail terms. The teens were merely pawns to the organization.

Not particularly athletic nor brainy, these teens, some white, some black, had convinced themselves that they had no future in Baltimore besides drugs, and they enjoyed believing that they had the protection of the "Big Knife gang," so called by the police because all the teens picked up had so identified the leader. But detectives could not pin down who "Big Knife" was. Gangs dealing drugs were known by nicknames, and the nicknames frequently changed.

But the detectives were about to be refocused, because Lt. Stach Wisniewski, in civvies walking along Eastern Avenue to the Patterson Bowling Center, almost stumbled over a spaced-out, young black man sitting on the curb, full of curse words, shooting off his mouth about not having enough to sell, and somebody wanting too much of his take.

"Hey, man, what's your beef?" Stach said, sitting down beside him on the curb, hoping the young man would keep talking and would keep looking at his feet and not at Wisniewski.

"Wha' you say? I gaugh a whole hell of a beef, man, a whole hell. Hey, man, I does my job, I picks up the stuff, and I brings mos' the money to the man, but, shi', he wans every damn, damn bi'. An' I gaugh big debts, you know. Hell, he's not givin' me notin', man, notin'."

"Notin'," Stach said, trying to copy the young man's accent.

"Yeh, shi', notin'. Fo' months I be workin' for 'im, and 'e give me shi'. He makin' thousans on dos' rocks, and I gettin' hundreds, and not even tha' sometime."

"Li'e today?" Stach said, guessing.

"Yo damn righ', bro," the young man said, still concentrating on his shoes.

"Mebbe I should talk to 'im, real clear like?" Stach suggested. "He roun' here?"

"His stash house right up that damn Patson Par' Avnue. Yo jest ask fer Big Knife two shi's, I's call him. Him real name Farens. He a mean batard," with the emphasis on the second syllable.

Stach figured he had pushed his luck well beyond the limits, patted the young man heavily and rose up, leaning on the young man's shoulder and turning behind him so the young man would not see his face, and saying, "I got to go, bro. I see this batard, and I see you later. Righ'?"

"Yeh, man. You take care of him, OK?" And the young man still studied his shoes, never looked up, and within minutes, so stoned was he, he had forgotten the encounter. But two other young men, one black, the other white, had been watching and listening to the exchange from the shadows of a nearby sally alley. However, they had not heard much, except the words "Big Knife two shi's."

Stach, unaware that he had been spotted, quickly walked to the bowling alleys and entered, smiling broadly. "You swallow the canary?" asked Dan Russo.

"Damn righ', bro," Stach said, in a poor imitation of the young man on the curb. "I got a name. I got a name for Big Knife, and I'd suggest you pick up a stoned-out grunt who's sitting on the curb two blocks down Eastern bemoaning his world. He tells quite a story, and probably needs some quick protection."

Dan pulled out his cell phone, stepped outside because of the bowling alley noise, and called two detectives to pick up the man. About fifteen minutes later, Dan's cell phone rang.

He again stepped outside.

He came back to the lanes. "Damn it all. They found who I would guess was your man face down in a sally alley off Eastern, his throat sliced and pockets empty. It could have been unconnected, but, well . . . Imagine that on this heavily trafficked street! But we still got a lead. I'll call Sylvester."

The third man

Sylvester Reed, a police lieutenant in the Southwestern District, was born in a row house on Collington Avenue in eastern Baltimore, and grew up in the Hartford Road-Darley Avenue area.

He went to Mergenthaler Vocational Technical High School, where he took all the mechanics courses, which benefited him when he enlisted for a four-year hitch in the Navy, serving as one of the gunners on the reactivated battleship Wisconsin. The sixteen-inch guns could fire 2,700-pound projectiles more than twenty miles, landing them within sixty yards or so of targets called for by Marine units under pressure from North Vietnamese troops north of the city of Hue.

Coincidentally Capt. Russo and Lt. Reed could have determined that the shells Reed fired benefited Russo as one of the Marines who drove the NVAs out of Hue, but the two men had never discussed their time in Vietnam.

Reed, his hitch served, declined re-upping and enrolled at Baltimore City Community College with the police department paying for it. As a cadet, he trained for six months at the Police Academy in the Baltimore Police Headquarters on Fayette Street, doing much of the training at Owings Mills.

He worked first in the Eastern District, and then in the Western, which was as rough if not rougher.

When Captain Russo called, Reed said he knew the

name Big Knife, of course, but didn't know any Farens. On the other hand, after checking in at the city morgue, he found that he did know the victim, a minor punk named Willie Mason, known as Peeseoff, who never had a chance to grow up right. And Reed knew Peeseoff's woman—girlfriend, mother of his child, whatever—and he surmised that she might be eliminated, too, if she could identify Big Knife. Reed knew he had to act quickly.

The word travels fast in the ghetto, and, when this young woman heard that her Peeseoff had been murdered, she bolted from the putrid room she had shared with Willie Mason, his real name, and their four-year-old daughter, Keeyse. Dragging the girl along, the woman headed toward the Inner Harbor hoping to run into a policeman, any policeman, to get protection. She caught up with Aunt Emily, a black woman who had managed to raise four sons and had seen all of them through high school and community college, Catonsville for three of them and Dundalk for the fourth. She still lived along North Kendall, and was hurrying along to her Wednesday-night prayer meeting at First Apostolic Faith Institute on Caroline Street.

"Lawsy me, Lateischa, it be a long time since I feasted my eyes on you all. And you look scared, as if you'd seen the devil, hisself. What the matter, child?"

"Auntie Emily, I's scared to dea'h. They gaugh Willie, my man," but Aunt Emily didn't seem to know him. "Peeseoff," the young woman explained, causing the older woman to nod her head and comment, "He a man heading into hell, girl. It better not to follow him, no way."

"He already 'dere, Aunt Emily, and I's no idea where to go. I's 'fraid dey kill me, too."

Aunt Emily slowly shook her head: "What can I do?"

"Maybe you be good luck for me and Keeyse. Maybe I go with you?" she pleaded.

"Suit me fine, child. Yo both be better in church, where I'm goin', than most any place I know."

"But I don't believe any of that stuff, you know."

"I knows, but you needs help, and that's what the church is here for, girl. And maybe you will believe," she said in a hopeful manner. "Maybe I find someone to help you."

They headed into First Apostolic Faith Institute, past some women tidying up the pews and into Brother Ben's office, where Aunt Emily explained the young woman's immediate problem.

Brother Ben: "Well, Lateischa, you just relax. I got a great friend—name's Sylvester Reed—and he can do miracles for you. I know. He helped me, got me into this job. And he can help you, too. You just sit down in that chair, and mind the little one."

Brother Ben dialed the detective bureau at the Southwestern District station, and was transferred to Lt. Reed's voice mail on his cell phone. "Brother Ben here, Syl. I need your help in a big hurry, here at the church. Got a young lady whose man has been killed, probably by some gang or other, and she thinks they're after . . . Oh, there you are."

Sylvester: "I'll be there as soon as I can, Brother Ben. But right now I'm tied up. Should I send over a couple cruisers?"

"She's real certain they're after her."

"OK. They're on the way." And he signed off.

Brother Ben put the phone down and turned to Lateischa, when he heard someone crashing through the front door, yelling, "Whar is tha' whore? Whar is tha' whore?" And the women in the church screamed.

Brother Ben quickly strode to the door, locked it. He pointed to a closet on the right, motioning the woman and child to hide in there. When she was hidden, he unlocked and opened his office door to see six women, including Aunt Emily, standing in front of two wild-eyed youths waving pistols and shouting: "You tells us, old women, or you finds ou' wha's on the other side, like now!"

Brother Ben said loudly but calmly: "Whoa, brothers. No sense scaring these sisters; they're good women, and they'll pray for you." The two punks swung their pistols over to point at him.

No. 1: "Well, lookie who we got here, a revrand. OK, revrand whoever, we's looking for a Lateischa, Peeseoff's woman. Now either you gots her, or we gonna waste you."

Brother Ben: "Or neither, man. I don't have any Lateischa, and . . . " he paused as he heard the sirens of approaching patrol cars, ". . . I think you had better . . ." He dove behind a pew as the second punk appeared ready to fire his weapon. The two men rushed forward toward the door of Brother Ben's office—as the sirens wound down—shot the lock to pieces, crashed through the door, fired shots into the desk and into the closet, hearing a scream and a thud, and smashed through the back door. Shouts were heard behind the church. A volley of shots followed.

The several women in the church ran to see if Brother Ben was all right, just as he peaked his head over the pew. "I'm fine, sisters. But I hope we haven't lost our young woman." He rose, as first one officer and then another carefully entered from the rear, and then two more from the front of the church.

"Were there only two of them, pastor?" the first officer said.

"Yes, just two."

"Well, you might want to pray over them, now, out back. Was anyone hurt here?"

"Yes, I'm afraid so. They fired into a closet where I had a young woman hiding."

Just then Lt. Reed walked into the church. "Everyone

OK here? Oh, hello, Brother Ben. I'm sorry I couldn't get here sooner." He turned to the police sergeant: "Courtney, what happened?"

"There was shooting inside here when we pulled in, so we went around back as Simpson and Prentice came in the front. Two punks came out the back firing wildly at us, so we brought them down. They're out back. But the reverend believes they might have killed a young woman he was hiding in a closet."

"And they have, lieutenant," Cpl. Alfred Prentice said, as he carried out a trembling and bloodied child. "But this tyke survived, with only a flesh wound, it appears. Pastor, you want to look? Women, I'm not sure . . ."

Aunt Emily, as she led the other women past the police officer: "I brought this woman into the church because I thought she'd be safe. And now she is. I want to pray over her, if that's all right, officers."

Lt. Reed: "Go right ahead, Aunt Emily, but don't disturb anything. Sergeant, you want to call in the crime scene people. Have you checked the cars out front? Did either of the punks have car keys on them?"

Prentice: "Nope. No ID of any kind—even the numbers on the pistols filed off—but I think I know one of them. Member of the Blood Curses, I believe."

Brother Ben: "One of the worst in the city. We've tried to reach them . . ." And he broke off.

Sylvester took Aunt Emily by the shoulder, as they and the other women, along with Brother Ben, peered into the open closet, seeing the crumpled body of the young woman puddled in blood, her head down—much as she had lived her short life.

Aunt Emily: "Will you pray over her, Brother Ben? Then, I pray over her, too, Lt. Reed, if that's all right?"

"Certainly, Aunt Emily. You're the best prayer I ever met."

Brother Ben: "Dear Gawd. Take this poor sister into your heart. Give her life in heaven that's so much better than she ever had here. Help us remember her as one of the legion of poor people marching here in hell, but thinking of those better days to come, not only in heaven, but also here on earth."

Aunt Emily: "Amen, brother. Amen. . . . I pray now, but I do it to God and myself." And she and the other women knelt in a half-circle just outside the puddle of blood, and Aunt Emily wept as she prayed silently, and some of the blood got onto her dress, and she didn't back off. And the officers and Brother Ben teared up.

Lt. Reed, returning to the church proper after the women rose from their praying, took the child from a woman officer who was holding her: "Well, now, maybe this young tyke can have a better life than either her mother or father. How would you like that, little one?"

Aunt Emily: "She called Keeyse."

Reed: "Well, you know, Aunt Emily, that Jasmine and I have not had any luck having children, and this youngster just might need a couple parents like us."

"I knows you, Sylvester, and I knows Jasmine, and you two be great. Chillen today has no future here. This little one need love, lots of it." And she took Keeyse into her arms, and the little one settled down.

The crime scene officers arrived, taking photos, studying the bodies of the young woman and the two hoods outside. The pistols were carefully wrapped for analysis, especially to see if they could be tied to other killings.

Regular officers kept the crowd that was building up outside the church at a distance, saying the church would open as soon as the bodies had been removed. Brother Ben assured would-be rabble rousers that the two men shot to death had come firing into the church and had fired into the closet, killing the young woman, before they rushed out the door and fired, first, at the officers. His word was accepted. The crowd settled down. The coroner arrived.

For it's one, two, three strikes

About a month later at Oriole Park at Camden Yards: "How's it going, lieutenant," asked Patrolman Don Skimmer as he walked by Lt. Stach Wisniewski en route to the upper deck.

"Not bad. You?"

"This beats driving with the duty sergeant in the Western District, sir."

"No doubt. But you gotta learn. You never know what's around the next corner, and the duty sergeant can respond immediately and effectively, no matter what."

"Yes, sir. I'm learning."

"Good. . . . Get along."

"Yes, sir."

Wisniewski watched the young patrolman climb the steps. No doubt he was taking some experienced patrolman's place, because new men rarely get good duty at the ballpark, with its perk of extra pay. Patrolman Skimmer was climbing to the higher level when Stach stopped following him with his eyes and returned to a face he thought he recognized, and looked away in an attempt to recall who that was.

He walked away down the aisle of the stadium and up some steps to look at the familiar face, now in a better profile for he was turning to talk to the man next to him. Both were in casual wear, expensive casual wear. Still no recognition.

The other man he had not seen before. He had a Latino look about him. A third man joined them, and the lieutenant immediately recognized former Deputy Mayor Patrick Sorensen. Thoughts coalesced in Stach's brain.

He walked farther along, now pretty well across from the three men, still keeping them in view. They were very animated in their conversation, with hands going all the time. They glanced from time to time at the action on the field. They stopped a beer vendor, and two of them drank. Not Sorensen.

Lt. Wisniewski was looking for a camera, a good camera, and he came upon a fan who was sitting with a woman, probably his wife, but, more importantly, was aiming what looked like a pretty expensive camera. Stach waited until the man finished shooting left-fielder Brady Anderson, who struck out.

"Excuse me, sir," Stach said leaning over the fan.

"Something wrong, officer?"

"No, no way," Stach said as he crouched down beside the fan. "I do have a favor, though. Might I ask you to take one or two photos with your camera and, when they are developed, would you send me the pictures, or copies. It's police work, incidentally. I'd be happy to buy you a roll of film."

"My grandfather was a policeman, lieutenant. I'm Andrew Greenings. My grandfather was Sgt. Richard Greenings, Southwest District. Shoot away," and the man handed his camera to Wisniewski. "It's a fancy German-made camera. You know what you're doing?"

"Yes. Mind if I sit down so I'm not so obvious?" Greenings jumped up and stood beside Wisniewski, who said, "I'm looking through this viewfinder, and to focus I play with this part here, right?"

"Right." And Greenings took note of where the officer was shooting.

Stach took two pictures and returned the camera to Greenings. "Actually I took two photos. Here's my card," and he passed his business card to the fan.

"You want these right away?"

"No hurry, but whenever you can. Thanks, both of you, and enjoy the game."

"Thank you, Lt. Wisniewski," Greenings said, reading from the card. "I hope these help."

Stach stopped. And standing in front of Greenings so that he would cover him from the three men, Stach said: "There is one thing you, or your wife . . . ?"

Greenings broke in, "Martha."

"Very good. Well, there is one thing you could do. First, zero in on that section where I was shooting, and look for three men sitting together. One man has a blue shirt on, the second, light red, almost pink, and the third, dark green. If you check out that sign on top of the visitors dugout, Oriole Park at Camden Yards, and you pick out the R, and then follow it up about four rows . . ."

". . . Sorry, lieutenant. There are three Rs on that sign to pick from."

Stach chuckled. "I meant the first one, in Orioles."

"OK. I've got them."

"Good. Now, put the camera away. I'd like you to walk over close to that section I was shooting, and without raising any suspicions just check what row and seats the three men are in. The photos might give a clue to the general area, but having someone actually give me the seat numbers would be extremely helpful."

"You're going for finger prints?"

"Your grandfather's genes carried through to you. Yes."

"I'm on my way."

"Pick up a beer or a dog on the way."

"Good idea. Martha?"

"Oh, I'm too worried. Please be careful" "

I will. No sweat." And Greenings was off on his mission.

Lt. Wisniewski excused himself, assured Greenings' wife that her husband would be all right, promised to be back after an inning or two and wandered off. He also suggested that Mrs. Greenings not stare after her husband.

"I'll try not to," she said.

Playing cop, Greenings took a roundabout route through the stadium, climbing up one side of his targets and coming down on the other side, first checking them from in back and then from the side. He then walked down the other side of the three men, noted the row, and then, throwing all caution aside, actually strolled along the aisle in front, counting off to himself and not looking directly at the three.

He then took an equally circuitous trek back to his seat, stopping to make some notes, and surprising his very worried wife by coming down from a different direction.

"That was fun. Did the lieutenant say when he'd come back?"

"In an inning or two. But I don't want you playing cop anymore. Do you hear?"

"It's in the genes, darling. Didn't you hear him say that?"

"You heard me. Now I'm off to the ladies room. I was so worried."

"Don't be a hero."

"Enough of that," and she didn't smile as she hurried away.

Meanwhile Stach had drifted along, checking on stadium security, some officers watching the action on the field, some, their backs to the diamond, watching the fans. All straightening up a bit when an officer came by, either nodding to him or commenting.

"Pretty good game, today."

"Yep. Any problems?"

"No, sir."

"Good."

Lt. Wisniewski then descended to the stadium offices, looking for someone responsible for the cleaning crews. He found Jim Balzone, a husky Italian-American who had been boss of the cleaning crews at Memorial Stadium for five years before it closed, and had transferred over to Oriole Park.

"You're Jim Balzone?"

"Yes, officer. You have some trouble?"

"Nope. But I have a few questions for you."

"Shoot."

"How soon after the game do your work crews start cleaning the seats?"

"Usually about forty-five minutes, which gives the fans time to wend their way out without feeling that we're pushing them. We have seventy-five people, and they do a quick sweep of the stadium in an hour. Then we return an hour or so later, or the next morning if it was a night game, and give a thorough cleaning, which takes about two hours.

"That's fine. Right after the game ends, I'll have some detectives paying special attention to some seats behind the visitors' dugout. If you'll just keep your workers away from seats in the third, fourth and fifth rows behind the visitors dugout, for fifteen minutes or so, we'll be out of your way."

"Anything we can do to help, lieutenant."

"I was hoping you'd say that. I appreciate your help, Jim," as he shook hands with Balzone."

"Glad to do it," and he left to instruct his workmen.

Stach walked off, took note that the game was now in the eighth inning, and glanced over to the stadium seats where the three men were seated. And they were gone. He thought to himself that he should have had a sergeant trail them, but then thought there was no big deal. If his suspicions were correct, they'd be found and identified pretty soon.

He returned to the Greenings. The husband stood up. "Here are the seat numbers and row number, lieutenant."

"Thank you, very much, Andrew. I really appreciate that."

"Well, Martha was a little worried, you know."

"What do you do for a living?"

"I'm a head-hunter. Ever heard of us?"

"Try to find the right person for such and such a job?"

"Precisely."

Martha: "And he does very well at it."

Lt. Wisniewski: "Then you found the right job for you."

Andrew: "I love it."

Martha: "He really does. He comes home beaming all over, at least once or twice every week."

Lt. Wisniewski: "Well, when I need a good detective, I just might have to consider giving you a call. Thank you, folks. You've been a great help. I'm sorry I can't tell you yet how much of a help."

Greenings stood up again; the two men shook hands, and Wisniewski nodded to Martha, and walked away.

He had phoned the district's detective bureau, and two detectives were sent to the stadium to take fingerprints from the three seats as soon as they could without alerting fans. When they got to the stadium—the game had gone into extra innings—the two were briefed by Lt. Wisniewski and wandered into the vicinity to keep the three seats under observation in case anyone else chose to sit there. Fortunately no one did.

Once most of the fans left this section of the stands, the cleaners stepped aside to watch as the two detectives quickly took over the three seats, sitting in the next seats to dust the seats and the arm rests with powder, photograph the seats and rests and then lift what prints there were with tape.

When the detectives returned to headquarters, they found that they had partial but passable prints from the three persons. Copies of these prints were then sent to the FBI's national fingerprint file.

Their report came back fairly quickly and was reviewed by Capt. Dan Russo. They confirmed the identity of Patrick Sorenson, the former deputy mayor and now Customs official, dating back to when he was putting in his two years service as a draftee in the Army. He was a public information office instructor at Fort Slocum, N.Y., an island college campus base off New Rochelle. The other two partial prints lifted had no twins on file with the FBI.

A couple nights later Stach was sitting down to dinner, when Stephanie asked him to pick up the next day's dinner on his way home. His daughter Stella chimed in: "And don't buy no more sea food for the rest of us. I hate it. It smells terrible!"

Something snapped in Stach's brain, and he brought his fist down on the table, startling everyone, especially Stella, who assumed she had pushed her father too far, but he said: "That's who that was. That's the guy in the window at Cajun Gumbo. That's the same person."

Stephanie: "What are you talking about?"

"First, let me thank Stella," and he got up and walked to the end of the table and gave her a big kiss on her forehead. "You, young lady, have just solved a mystery."

Stephanie explained: "Daddy's knack for remembering something. You just brought it back again, Stella."

"And you deserve a treat," Stach said. "Tonight, you and I will go down to O'Donnell Street and get some ice cream."

"Whee!" Stella yelled, smiling at her older brother and sister, who, after making a logical case for favoritism, were invited along. And Stach filed away the face and the place for another day.

He was tempted to go over to Northern District headquarters immediately, but he had promised Stella her ice cream. And he didn't explain to the kids what help Stella had given, and not to Stephanie until the children were fast asleep.

What's your work experience?

As soon as Kenny had put down the deposit and gotten provisional title to the '89 Freightliner, he stopped by Rex Rossler Lines, on a tip from Capt. Russo, and asked to talk to Ralph Wickham, the safety manager, who had a small, functional office in the firm's warehouse. Wickham shook hands with Wisniewski, and, sitting down behind his desk, commented, "I have a series of questions for you, young man.

"Are you over twenty-one?"

"Twenty-nine, sir."

"And you have your own tractor?"

"Yes, sir."

"And it's . . ."

"A 1989 Freightliner."

"How much mileage?"

"440,000 miles."

"You'll need $300,000 insurance."

"That's working, sir."

"You have at least two years' driving experience?"

"Yes, sir. I started driving a truck in the Marines, and drove for about three years, and when I got out three years ago, I started driving for UPS."

"We also want to know your work experience, and your Marine Corps service counts, as does schooling. We're looking at the last ten years."

"Yes, sir. Three years with UPS, eight years in the Corps. Graduated from Mount St. Joseph's High School before that."

"Any lapses in there?"

"No, sir. Entered the Corps the week after I graduated from St. Joe's. Started working for UPS a week or so after I got out."

"Fine. The U.S. Transportation Department requires all this, incidentally, and you'll have to go through a physical for them. You look like you'll have little trouble with that.

"You have your own tractor, or do you want to come aboard as a company driver?" Before Kenny could answer, Wickham explained, "As a company driver, you can put aside more money than you would as an owner-operator, you understand." When Kenny looked curiously at Wickham, he continued: "There are fuel bills, the truck note, the insurance, for example, and they will be yours to pay.

"Company drivers park their company trucks on Friday, and maintenance is the company's responsibility. As an independent you'll be doing that maintenance on your truck—oil changes, tire repairs, clutch adjustments—over the weekends."

Kenny: "Thanks, anyway, but I got some great help from my family, and I want to have a say in what I do and when I do it."

Wickham: "That's true. As a company driver, you don't have a choice, and it could be that you would have to make a late run in the afternoon that, because of traffic, would get you home late. An independent can choose his loads and his schedule, but he has more bills.

"At Rex Rossler Lines we have fifty-two drivers in all, thirty-two owner-operators and twenty company drivers. There are some jobs that an owner-operator usually will not do, for example take a 5 p.m. job that means he will take five hours to accomplish what could be done in three if the container was ready to go in the morning or early afternoon. So, to satisfy some of our customers who often schedule late pickups, we have the company drivers take those jobs."

Kenny: "I'd still want to be an owner-operator, Mr. Wickham. I'll want the chance to say I don't want that particular load, if I believe it wouldn't pay enough or it cut into plans that Mira, my wife-to-be shortly, has made."

Wickham smiled, thinking to himself that this was a very determined young man. But he said, "Just wanted you to know. Now we'll contract you as a subcontractor to the company, meaning you work exclusively for us. In effect, your truck is leased to us."

The safety manager looked up to see whether Kenny understood.

"We pay 67 to 70 percent of the line haul, meaning, for example, that if you're taking a container to Wilmington, and the line haul is $300, well then, you can work out your percentage. The line haul is what we charge the customer based on the weight and miles transported. Plus the fuel, of course. You understand?"

Kenny nodded.

Wickham: "You get paid when you turn your paperwork in. We also charge the customer for the diesel fuel, so you keep records of that."

The safety manager, looking through some notes: "You a relation of Lt. Stach Wisniewski, by the way?"

"Yes, sir. My uncle."

"And a friend of Capt. Dan Russo?"

"Yes, sir. But I know him mainly through Uncle Stach."

"Well, they both recommended you. And they have fine reputations. I checked with some police contacts I have." He rose from his chair, stuck out his hand, and they shook hands. "Good luck, Wisniewski. I'll see you from time to time. Welcome to Rex Rossler Lines."

Kenny almost saluted, but smiled and said: "Yes, sir. I mean, thank you, sir."

Wickham: "Now you need to see our dispatcher,

Brandon Stacy. His office is just down the corridor. And take along this copy of the questions I asked you."

Kenny found the dispatcher behind a big counter, identified himself and handed over the report. "You're the new man?" Stacy asked.

"Yes, sir."

"Well, Rex Rossler Lines are mainly short-haul, picking up containers from the piers and dropping them off within 125 miles of Baltimore. You'll often make several trips a day, back and forth, taking containers to, oh, York or Lancaster in Pennsylvania, or Wilmington in Delaware, where you'll drop off a filled container and pick up an empty—drop and hook, all day long.

"If you're going only twenty-five to thirty miles, you might make as many as eight trips in a day. And most of those trips will be picking up a container from the piers and dropping it off at a warehouse and picking up an empty and dropping it off back at the piers, drop and hook, drop and hook.

"But it's not boring," Brandon stressed, "because there are different obstacles every day. If one steamship load is slow or backed up, we allow the drivers to switch to another ship load. Almost every day, we assign truckers to drop and hook, and sure enough they'll have at least three changes from the schedule—a different pier, maybe a different warehouse because of a fork-lift breakdown. And sometimes we pick up from trains, and there will be changes there, too.

"You still interested?"

Kenny nodded, and stood as Brandon rose, and they shook hands over the high counter. "We'll start you with short runs and then go for the longer runs. Let's see. I have your phone number here. I'll likely start calling you in a couple days. Good luck."

The expanding Cajun Jumbo file.

It took less than a week for Lt. Stach Wisniewski to receive two large prints of the three men at the stadium, sent along by Orioles fan Andrew Greenings. They were sharp, and Stach confirmed his earlier decision that the man he had seen in the window at Cajun Jumbo was the man on the left with the black mustache and the scar on his left cheek, and that the man on the right was the former deputy mayor.

As to the man in the middle, Stach posted the photos in the roll-call room at his district, asking for identification. It took three days to get a response, only because the officer who recognized the third man had just returned from special assignment. When Sgt. Tom Breckenridge saw the photos, he immediately went to Lt. Wisniewski's office.

"Sir, I know who the middle man is in the photos you posted," he said as he stood in the doorway.

"Come in, Tom. Sit down."

"I joined the force after working for about ten years in security at the World Trade Center, and the middle man is the boss of Sanchez Importers, located on the fourteenth floor. Believe his name is Sanchez. Seems to be a regular guy. Always treated security well. If the number of customers he gets in his office is any indication of his business, he's raking it in.

"I think I recognize one of the other guys, too. Wasn't he the deputy mayor?"

"Yes, he was. He's over in Customs now."

"Sounds a little cozy, no?"

"Yes, it does. How about the third man?"

"No clue. I would have remembered the mustache and the scar, for sure."

"Thanks a million, Tom. That really helps."

"Glad to help, sir," he said as he stood up. "I'm pretty familiar with that building, if you need any interior help."

"I'll make a note of that, Tom. You may well be called on. And thanks for that, too."

Breckenridge left, and a smiling Stach Wisniewski sat down and added some notes to his expanding Cajun Jumbo file.

Keeyse's adventure

About a month after a welfare agency took over custody of Keeyse, the girl orphaned when both her father and mother were murdered the same day, and no living relatives having produced themselves, the agency released her to the temporary custody of Sylvester and Jasmine Reed. Jasmine had welcomed the chance to have a child but questioned her husband and the agency staff very closely about the child's genes. "Will she have a penchant for running with the rabble? Will her genes compel her to go bad? Will she be as worthless as her father, as useless as her mother?"

Now, Jasmine did not phrase the questions in just those words, but the staff members knew what she meant. They contended, as did her husband, that the Reed home would be just the right place to overcome the child's beginnings, and that she had as good a chance of enjoying a worthwhile life as any other youngster, that she was young enough to forget what little she had learned so far.

And they were probably right, but her short-term memory was strong. It took Keeyse about a week to get used to her new home. Jasmine Reed put in for a three-month leave from her job as a computer programmer at a downtown firm, planning on her mother to baby-sit most days after the leave expired. Sylvester helped her on Thursdays, his day off, and on one such special Thursday he took the tyke down to the Inner Harbor, Baltimore's tourist treasure.

Keeyse was awed by the place and the people, mostly tourists, but also young adult joggers, and more whites than she had ever seen before, and that frightened her some. Keeyse and Sylvester walked about, with she firmly squeezing his hand, and he stopped at a tourist's store to purchase a doll that resembled Whitney Houston, at a souvenir shop for a "crabby" T-shirt, and at the fudge store, the busiest of this chain in the nation, where Keeyse giggled and sang along with the help hustling the candy.

As they boarded a water taxi to Fells Point, she held her new treasures in her left hand and kept a strong, sticky grip on Sylvester with her right hand. She was wide-eyed and bubbly as the boat backed off, tooted its horn, and putted away from the dock. She giggled and bounced around, pointing at the tall buildings, and the small craft coming and going—a tall ship with its sails furled; privately owned yachts docked, some from other countries; yachts as long as 180 feet; a police launch she saw at a distance, heading out past the Domino Sugars plant; a sailboat tacking; and even kayaks slithering through the calm, twenty-eight-foot-deep waters.

'Big Knife, Big Knife'

About halfway to the Fells Point dock their water taxi passed another going the other way, and as Keeyse pointed to a man standing in the back, her face tightened, and she said quietly, as if remembering something hideous, "Big Knife, Big Knife."

Sylvester followed her finger, took note of the man, and diverted her to the other side of the boat to see some mallards swimming along, some sea gulls patrolling about five feet off the surface, while he fished out his cell phone and alerted the Baltimore Police Department's tactical squad to cover the Seaport Taxi's docking in the Inner

Harbor. He wanted to commandeer immediately the water taxi he was on and send it in pursuit of the other, but he had to have someone watch Keeyse and he had to take into account the other civilians on board, many of them children. If the arrest got out of hand, he would not want the tyke or any of the other civilians, especially the children, in harm's way.

He had to wait until the craft reached the Fells Point dock. Then he scooped up the child and her goodies in his arms and walked swiftly toward a bar, having spied a police officer standing outside. His fortune held; it was a woman officer, just watching over the tourists. He quickly explained why he was dumping the child on the officer, and ran back to the dock, showing his badge and ordering the young driver to offload the passengers who had boarded, along with the announcer, who protested in vain. The craft then took off after the other taxi, which was more than half the distance to the Inner Harbor dock.

The chase was on, with Reed's commandeered craft quite a ways behind. The water taxis are allowed to do only six knots in the Inner Harbor, but Lt. Reed pressed the driver of his taxi to push its twin ninety-horsepower engines up to fifteen knots.

Reed's craft might have closed more stealthily if the announcer on the pursued water taxi hadn't glanced back to see the other boat coming out. "Now that's unusual," he said out loud, causing the man Keeyse had called Big Knife, a tall, muscular black man, about thirty years old, still standing and watching ahead, to question him, "What funny?"

The announcer, later identified as Bob Heusing, responded, "Well, the taxis usually wait until we're docked before they come out, and that one is definitely leaving, and it looks like they just got most of the passengers off. And they're supposed to be making a series of stops on their route. And they are going way faster than we're allowed to do here. So that's what's funny."

Big Knife fingered a 44-caliber revolver in his side pocket, nudged men standing on both sides of him, and studied the Inner Harbor for anything unusual. "Somethin' smell lie' shi'," he said to his two aides, his best enforcers. "Look 'roun'."

They saw lots of tourists walking about, some young men and women jogging along the harbor's edge, and folks seated at tables on the balconies overlooking the harbor—all normal.

But then one of the two aides noticed a couple tourists pointing to two police officers armed with what looked like heavy weapons who had fallen into a prone position aiming at this water taxi.

"SWA' team," Big Knife said out loud, and the two bodyguards fingered their 38-calibre pistols.

Big Knife turned back to see that the other water taxi was coming on, and that the police launch had reversed course and was coming into the picture. By nature, Big Knife pulled out his revolver, causing one woman to scream, "He's got a gun!" Whereupon, the other men brought out their pistols, and Big Knife pushed his weapon to the driver's head, saying sharply, "You listens, boy, and you do 'xac'ly wha' I says."

The driver mumbled his acquiescence, confirming by the pressure against his temple that he had no alternative.

"Firs' you turns this here boa' tha' a way," pointing with the revolver to port and docks.

The Seaport Taxi turned, the chasing boats altered their direction to intercept, and the three gang members stiffened as six policemen rose from their prone positions and began walking along parallel to the water taxi, their heavy weapons still pointed at the taxi. Other policemen were running down to the waterfront from different directions.

The tactical squad usually numbered ten men plus their commanding major, and they were all on scene now, having sped with lights flashing but no sirens blaring from the Eastern District.

A crowd was gathering, many tourists believing that this was some act staged for their benefit—as many were in the Inner Harbor—and cameras popped and camcorders began chronicling.

Big Knife said loudly to all those on board his craft, "Y'all stan' up, stan' up, git on this here side of the damned boa', hear me, and look at dem damn buildings," pointing to the Leggs Mason Building and its smaller neighbors.

The fourteen on board, besides Big Knife, his two bodyguards and the driver—two old men, two middle-aged men, three young mothers with children, and a young couple also with children—did exactly what they were told, in effect becoming human shields for the gangsters. The mothers put their children in front of them, away from the hoods' guns. The fourteen were all standing on one side of the water taxi, a light load for a craft that could squeeze in forty-nine passengers, the announcer and the driver.

A loud speaker sounded from an officer who had just come down to the levee. "This is Major Russell Schroeder of the Police Department's Tactical Division. Water taxi, hove to, and dock here!" pointing to a point ahead of the taxi. There was no change in its course, so he added, "You three men are outnumbered and outgunned! Throw your weapons overboard! Put your hands up!"

Numerous firearms—revolvers, M-14 rifles and small machine guns—in the hands of men trained to use them were now aimed at the water taxi, and other officers were running down to the Inner Harbor, but most of these were there to urge the tourists to take cover. Those already on the dock who realized that this may not be an act after all began backing off, but their camcorders kept running.

Meanwhile, Lt. Reed and his scared-to-death driver were closing from the back. Big Knife was momentarily stymied, but he knew he had two bodyguards who would give their lives for him, and they had fourteen hostages, fifteen including the water taxi driver.

"Keep away, coppers, or we start blasting these hostages, hear!" shouted Big Knife, who later was identified as Wilson Aimes, key man in a high-volume drug cartel, who had a record three pages long but had spent only twelve years behind bars.

Police never uncovered any reference to Farens, who Willie Mason, a.k.a. Peeseoff, had mentioned. At this moment Big Knife would face all sorts of time for breaking parole by carrying weapons—and a number of other charges.

"Shu' the hell up!" he said to his bodyguards as they asked what to do. "I gaugh to tink." He thought for about thirty seconds. "Kill the bastards," he said. "They all die . . ." he shouted to the policemen on the landing, ". . . less youse back off!" And he fired point blank into the back of a young woman from St. Louis, and the bullet went through her and into her son, and they both fell as the other women screamed. Big Knife slipped behind another woman before the snipers could zero in on him.

Because of the human shields, the tactical unit found it extremely difficult to get off shots, but Lt. Reed in the other water taxi could, and did, bringing down one of the enforcers. Aimes's other sidekick and Big Knife himself then whipped about to blast the trailing water taxi, methodically firing up and down the side. "Aim at the front," Big Knife yelled, and the driver was hit at least four times, but Reed scampered back and forth along the floor and behind the dividing seats, and miraculously survived with only a graze wound on his left arm. The boat slowed and fell aside, the driver no longer conscious.

Several of the shots fired by Aimes and his aide had penetrated the bottom of Reed's water taxi, and it began taking on water. He slithered around, trying to stuff towels into the holes, and succeeding somewhat. At that very moment, the two old men on board Big Knife's water taxi seized the opportunity to battle with the punks. They died as heroes, both shot to death, but all that commotion allowed the police snipers on shore to bring down the second bodyguard, who collapsed in a heap, hit at least twice in the chest, but still breathing.

Aimes was wounded, too, but still standing. He waved his weapon in the air and cried for mercy.

"Drop the weapon overboard!" Major Schroeder shouted on his loud speaker. When Aimes did, two middle-aged men, whose children had been threatened, immediately began pummeling and kicking him, and Lt. Reed fired into the air. "Stop, stop! We'll take it from here!" And they backed off.

Big Knife stumbled against the side of the boat but brought out a huge knife—akin to a Bowie knife, and likely the reason for his nickname—and grabbed for one of the women standing. A soggy Lt. Reed, slipping against the side of his water taxi, fired along with a policeman on board the police launch, and two snipers on the dock cut loose. Aimes slumped to the floor of the boat, the knife clanking about as it fell. The shootout had ended.

The police launch came alongside to push and pull the two Seaport Taxis toward the dock, and police officers and medics rushed on board as the craft bumped into the dock. They found one of the bodyguards dead, but both Aimes and the second enforcer still breathing. The medics who followed the officers on board put oxygen masks on both men and began intravenous feedings.

Three of the six others wounded also were given oxygen and IVs; the fourth had a wound on his right arm and was bandaged. Five of the fifteen people unlucky enough to have been on this particular run by the water taxis had been killed—the two men who had intervened, the mother and son from St. Louis, and Aimes's aide—plus the driver of the water taxi Reed commandeered. And six people, adults and children, on the two boats had been wounded in one way or another, including Aimes, his other aide, and Lt. Reed. Three people, including the driver of the boat Aimes was on, miraculously escaped injury.

An assassin on the loose

Three Maryland State Police medivac helicopters that had hovered out of range of the firearms, swept in, landed on the dock, and the medics and police officers carried the wounded to the copters.

The watching tourists applauded, no one any longer suspicious that this had been a publicity stunt.

The choppers lifted off, and two flew to the landing pad at the University of Maryland Hospital Shock Trauma Center off Pratt, the third carrying wounded children and their parents to the pediatrics center at Johns Hopkins Hospital at Monument and Broadway. The copters unloaded and returned to the scene, picking up those less seriously wounded.

At dockside, Major Schroeder ran up to shake Reed's hand. "That was a mighty fine action on your part, Syl. I'm putting you in for a medal, I'll tell you . . . " But noticing the wound, added, "You better get your arm checked."

"You have all this under control, sir. I'll have a doc check it later. I gotta get back to Fells Point to pick up my little girl. She's the one who IDed this Big Knife guy. But let's keep that secret. Her mother and father have already been killed by his gang."

"I'll cover for you with the media. Here they come,"

the major said as a woman TV reporter and her cameraman came rushing up. Reed just looked away and walked by them.

Bob Gilhooey, a *Baltimore Sun* reporter coming up behind the TV crew, saw and stopped Reed. "You look like you've been soaked. Were you directly involved in this shootout, lieutenant?"

"In a small way, Bob. Check with Major Schroeder. He has all the details."

Syl skipped taking a water taxi back to Fells Point, electing to walk along the docks. He desperately needed to breath deeply in the fresh air off the water and to cool down before he recovered Keeyse, and hopefully to be somewhat dryer. He heard several "well done's" from tourists who had seen him get off the water taxi or assumed he had been in the water battle. He just nodded and walked quickly on.

When the choppers landed at the hospital, the surgeons quickly sized up each patient's condition, and, in four of the cases, including both Aimes and his still-breathing aide, put in chest tubes. That was all Aimes needed. The four bullets fired by Lt. Reed and the police snipers had somehow passed through his body without hitting any crucial organs. He would not even go to the operating room, as most of the other wounded would.

Aimes' surviving bodyguard, later identified as Courtney Ballou, had taken two hits from tactical squad sharpshooters, and those had done major damage. One round went through the lungs, the other through his esophagus, and he required heavy surgery.

A news blackout on Aimes and Ballou had been ordered by police, and no information was forthcoming. Reporters could only speculate. However, certain people knew who Aimes and Ballou were, and where they were.

While the tourists were applauding the tactical squad's

success in ending the confrontation, one person watching was extremely upset.

It turned out that one of the best seats for taking in all the action on the waterfront was on the fourteenth floor of the World Trade Center, where Felipe Sanchez, president of Sanchez Importers, had looked out his window to see something developing in the Inner Harbor, and then had focused on the action with a powerful set of binoculars. The phone rang with a call from Patrick Sorensen, the former deputy mayor and now a Customs official.

Sorensen: "I just heard about a bunch of shooting down on the waterfront, with police involved. Have you any idea what it's all about?"

Sanchez: "It's not good news. I glanced out the window to see one water taxi chasing another, and the police launch getting involved, and a bunch of cops lying down on the wharf with rifles pointed out at one of the water taxis. Next thing, there's shooting, and . . ."

"And . . ."

"I'm not certain, but I'm pretty sure Willie Aimes, a.k.a. Big Knife, and two of his key aides have been brought down. It looked like the three of them on the one taxi. But they all may have survived. As I say, I'm not sure. Some people on the boats got it, too."

"Wasn't Aimes one of your key men?"

"One of the three top dealers, yes. He put together about twenty-five to thirty runners in the neighborhoods. And he kept that group in line. Got his payments, passed on the cream to me. He knew his job, had a real passion for it."

"Tough man to replace?"

"Yes, but I don't think the police will link us. He's been the longest of the three main men, about seven years or so. But I don't think the police will link anything."

"I sure as hell hope not," a comment Sorensen regretted making the second he uttered it.

Sanchez hung up, miffed at Sorensen, dialed a number, and spoke quickly and quietly: "Find out which hospital Big Knife and his men have been taken to and eliminate them. They just left the Inner Harbor on helicopters."

"How do we kill them?" a young woman's voice answered.

"I don't give a damn how. Just do it," Sanchez said and, not hearing anything further from the other end, added, "immediately."

"I'll be back to you with a price," and she hung up.

Hospital calls

Aimes, a.k.a. Big Knife, had been taken to a private room on the eleventh floor of the University of Maryland hospital, accompanied by Patrolman Spencer Lodge, a new member of the tactical squad. Ballou, the other suspect, was gurneyed straight into surgery in the shock trauma operating room on the ground floor, and a police guard was stationed outside the entrance to the operating room, screening anyone coming in by checking his or her photo ID.

But the woman who had taken Sanchez's call was as busy as the hospital staff. She called sources at the three likely hospitals and bought information on both Aimes and Ballou. She found out that they were both at the University of Maryland Hospital, and her sources deduced from the placement of police guards that one was being operated on and the other had been taken to a private room on the eleventh floor, with the guard inside. She obtained the room number, and then called Bo Jager on his cell phone.

Jager was a brilliant killer for hire, whose seventeen murders—for which he had been paid thousands of dollars—had all gone unsolved by the police, mostly because they were small fries.

He answered the call in his seven-room suite in a condominium overlooking the Inner Harbor, with the latest in entertainment technology, kitchen equipment—he was a gourmet cook—and clothes, closets stuffed with them. One of these yielded a hospital nurse's uniform, identical to the ones worn at the University of Maryland Hospital. The male nurse had been one of Jager's strangulation victims for reneging on a drug debt, as were most of his other victims, though many were of much greater worth, including one city ward boss. Jager had taken the male nurse's second set of clothes on the chance that they might come in handy.

Now he placed the clothes in an overnight case, along with a sealed test-tube of potassium, a Coke from his refrigerator, a small club and a mini-Uzi machine pistol with a silencer.

Jager drove his blue '92 Acura Legend coupe to Pratt Street near the hospital, parked, put the maximum number of quarters into the meter, and walked through a public entrance. He hurried on to a public bathroom to change, and waited in the hallway until he spied someone who looked somewhat like him, offered him the Coke, which was tainted and guaranteed to propel him toward a bathroom in minutes, and trailed him in, silently strangling the man as he urinated, shoving his body into one of the stalls. Jager removed the man's nametag and placed it on his own uniform.

He took the elevator to the eleventh floor and found Aimes's room and knocked, the sound cushioned by the skin-colored, light gloves he was wearing. Someone inside challenged him, and Jager responded that he was a nurse checking the IV.

The door opened. Patrolman Lodge wrote down the name on the nametag and hesitated on the likeness in the photo.

"It's an old photo," Jager explained. "I need to get it updated."

Lodge let him in.

Jager never looked at the patient. Aimes was unconscious—luckily for Jager, for Aimes might have recognized Jager and screamed. Jager looked over the IV assembly, replaced the bag, and, turning back to the officer, but still ignoring the patient, said simply, "Have a good day." Jager left quickly as Aimes's body began responding to the potassium.

Jager was around the corner in the corridor before he heard Patrolman Lodge burst open the door and shout, "Someone get in here quick!"

Jager walked along hurriedly and right between two officers from the Central District, Ben Husley and Ernesto Capillo, who were checking out the security. They immediately responded to Lodge's shouting, and learned from the first nurse on the scene that Aimes apparently had been poisoned by something put into his IV assembly. Hulsey alerted hospital security.

"What now?' Capillo asked. "Where's the other guy?"

"In surgery, I believe," Hulsey answered.

"Where the hell is that? We got to get there in a hurry."

Hulsey stopped a passing nurse. "Where is surgery? Where they'd be working on someone flown in by copter?"

The nurse: "Ground floor. Elevators that way, stairs this way."

Hulsey: "I'll take these stairs. You find the elevator."

"Can we alert anyone on the way?"

"We have a man outside the operating room."

"If he's still alive," Capillo hollered as he ran down the stairs.

Hulsey pushed the button for the elevator, but all cars were floors away from his and headed in the wrong dircction.

65

The two officers reached the door to the operating room at the same time, partly because Capillo turned the wrong way off the elevator. But they found the police officer slumped in his chair outside the operating room, dead from a bullet wound in his chest, his .38-caliber pistol in his left hand partway out of its holster.

Then came screams from the operating room. Dan looked around to locate the button to open the door, and on entering the two officers discovered the hospital personnel taking cover, and one male nurse bursting out through the door on the other side of the room. Capillo chased after him as Hulsey took note of what had taken place.

Ballou was bleeding badly from two holes in his head, and was either dead or would be momentarily, a woman doctor said, as she regained her footing and checked out her patient. "We had no chance to protect him, or even ourselves," Dr. Sylvia Turnwill explained hurriedly to officer Hulsey. "I believe one of our nurses has been seriously wounded," she added, pointing to the side where Hulsey now saw a nurse sprawled on the floor bleeding from a bullet hole in her chest.

Dr. Turnwill quickly organized her team to begin treating the downed nurse, while another doctor came over to examine Ballou. "He's dead, officer," the doctor explained to Hulsey.

"We'll have investigators up here in minutes," Hulsey said. "Can you tell me where that door leads?"

"To the cafeteria. I hope your fellow officer gets him. We just can't have this."

"Thanks," and Hulsey ran off in chase of both the killer and Capillo.

But Jager had eluded the officers simply by dropping his uniform blouse into a wash gurney and donning a face mask and white jacket that an orderly would wear, flipping on some glasses, keeping his head down and pushing the gurney along, adding a limp to the act and allowing Capillo, gun drawn, to charge right past him. When Jager turned the corner, he discarded the gurney, face mask and jacket, ran along a corridor toward an emergency exit, and banged open the door, which sounded an alarm throughout the hospital. Jager walked quickly toward the front of the hospital, put on an Orioles baseball cap he had in his pocket, stuffed the gloves, marked by the emergency alarm, into his pants pocket, walked out the front door and, turning to a sidewalk, knelt down to pick up some pages he had dropped along the sidewalk.

Two patrolmen came running down the walk. "Hey, you see anyone coming out of that door there?"

"Someon' wen' off tha' way. Tha's all I see," Jager answered in a heavy Southern drawl.

"That way!" one of the patrolmen shouted as they both charged away, corralling a young Indian doctor who was going off duty and getting into his car.

Jager walked, again not hurriedly, to the hospital's main entrance, pocketed his cap, entered, ambled up to the information desk on the first floor and asked a middle-aged woman volunteer, "Where is the gift shop, please?"

"Right there," she pointed to her left. "You can't miss it."

"Thank you," Jager said, returning her smile, and strolled into the gift shop as two officers came by heading for the front door. Jager looked over the teddy bears while he listened to one officer saying to the other, "I think he got away from us."

"He might still be in here somewhere," the other responded.

Jager chose a cuddly purple teddy bear, paid for it and took an elevator to the seventh floor, a patient floor, and found the men's room, where he took the stall and applied makeup, mustache and thick glasses, checking out his changed features in a mirror. He then sat down in a waiting area, putting the teddy bear beside him as he read through a *Readers Digest*. Various security personnel came by, but none stopped to question him.

After two hours and six magazines, mostly sports, Jager got up to take the elevator down. "You don't want to forget your teddy bear," said a frail teenage girl in a white smock.

"Oh, sorry," Jager said. "I was going to give it to my nephew, but he was sound asleep when I visited, and he already had three. Would you like it?"

The young teen smiled. "Thank you, mister," she said, and she cuddled the teddy.

Jager smiled back and caught the elevator down, struck up a conversation with a young couple taking their new baby home, the mother in a wheel chair, and left the hospital with them through the main entrance, with watching police officers assuming he was part of the family group.

Jager walked with the couple and child for a while, and then returned to his car, started it up and drove back to his condominium. He would not have to call the woman contact. She would read of the killings in the papers and would make another large contribution to the anonymous trust fund that Jager maintained.

The shootings and deaths in the Inner Harbor had an immediate negative impact on tourism, with a few tour companies canceling hotel and event reservations for the next two weeks. Also, as many as fifty parties called to say they would not need the hotel rooms they had requested. The Baltimore Visitors Center handled a few calls, assuring folks that the city was safe, that these shootings were an aberration.

The two men who had taken on Big Knife on their water taxi and had paid with their lives, but in doing so provided clear targets of Aimes and his right-hand man, were hailed as heroes in the churches they attended, with both funeral services heavily attended.

The Baltimore Sun reported that Aimes's aide, who was shot to death on the water taxi, had been kicked out of the Army and had an extensive police record.

The most sympathy went out to the father and daughter of the woman and her son from St. Louis, who were shot to death by Big Knife on the boat. The father, a real-estate agent in St. Louis, and his daughter, a third grader in a suburban elementary school, flew back to St. Louis, with the mother and son in coffins in the cargo hold. The family was seen off at BWI by Baltimore officials and, because the family is Lutheran, the pastor of a Lutheran church in the city.

The man and his daughter were not on the water taxi because she had come down with a cold. They were planning to meet for lunch near their hotel. Their pastor in St. Louis and a number of parishioners met the plane.

Here comes the bride . . . and groom

Kenny and Mira's wedding finally took place on September 12. About an hour and a half before the ceremony, all the women in the bridal party gathered at the Kowalski home on South Ellwood to get ready. Finally, Mira in her finery stepped out the front door to walk down the four steps to the sidewalk, and a saxophone player and accordion player, both from the six-member band that would play at the reception, started up Polish music, prompting the bridal party and all the neighbors who had gathered to dance in the street.

The dancing continued for nearly twenty minutes, with Mira applauding as the two players switched from familiar tune to familiar tune. It was a relatively short hike to the church, but Mira, her maid of honor, Danuta, Mira's mother—who carried the marriage license—the bridesmaids and the flower girl, the daughter of one of the groomsmen, climbed into a limousine for the ride to St. Casimir's.

The service began with Father Miczelowski approaching the altar and standing there as Kenny and three friends came up to wait for Mira and her girlfriends. First a young woman and then a young man, both members of the wedding party, read scripture from the Old and New Testaments, respectively. Another young man and young woman read appropriate prayers they had written and had cleared with Father Miczelowski.

Father gave a short homily, noting the kind and wholesome nature of both participants, mentioning Kenny's work and Mira's, and their loyalties to St. Casimir's. He also didn't neglect the families, stalwart members of his congregation.

The priest then wrapped the long strings of his stole around the bride and groom's clasped hands, blessed them and sprinkled them with holy water. He then led the exchange of vows and rings and declared the new couple as one under God. He invited applause, which was quite deafening.

Father Miczelowski proceeded through the eucharistic prayer into offering Holy Communion, first to the couple, then to her and his parents, the wedding party and finally the congregation—as many as 180 friends and relatives. The ceremony ended with Mira and Kenny kneeling and praying before the main altar, and then moving to a side altar to kneel in prayer before the Virgin Mary. Mira placed her bouquet on that altar, and the two returned to the center aisle, and, to Mendelssohn's "Wedding March," walked swiftly to the rear of the church to shake hands with each of the guests.

The reception took place at the Polish Home hall on Broadway, and traditions took over. The newly married and photographed couple were met at the door by Mira's mother again checking her crib card: "*Co wolisz: chleb, sol czy pana mlodego?*" meaning, "Do you prefer the bread, the salt, or the groom?" and without cribbing Mira replied in Polish, "All three. May the groom earn the money to pay for the bread." Kenny sprinkled the bread with salt and handed it to Mira to kiss. And everyone nearby applauded.

"Let the fun begin!" shouted George Mihok, who was the master of ceremonies for the evening.

Mira and Kenny took seats at the head table, and their godmothers—Wieslava Sokolowski, Mira's, and Cynthia Zielinski, Kenny's—stepped up behind the seated couple and began "*Serdeczna Matko,*" a hymn to the Blessed Mother.

The godmothers removed Mira's veil and replaced it with a *czypek*, something like a doily, on her head, and a string of tiny babies, tied with pink and blue ribbons, around Kenny's head. And they pulled down over his head a tall, goofy hat, which he suffered agreeably as the godmothers led everyone in "*Spashnabitchie,*" (a merrily song) with the accordion player joining in, and everyone singing or banging on their plates.

The dolls signified prospective happy and healthy children, and the hat that the bride and groom might have a happy marriage.

George Mihok, or "Hawk" to most everyone, then welcomed by name the parents, the bridal party, and "Mr. and Mrs. Kenneth Wisniewski," which drew a mighty cheer. Then the band hired for the evening struck up the "Polish Wedding March," while the newly married couple danced around the hall, ending back at the head table.

Hawk then described the special wine the parents of the bride had brought, Denaturat, and Emil poured a glass for his daughter and new son-in-law. Everyone cheered as Mira sipped and Kenny gulped, and Hawk explained that the parents hoped the couple would never thirst, and would have good health. "And many children," Danuta said loud enough for most everyone to hear and to cheer as well. The band led a chorus of "*Sto Lat*," or "May you live 100 years."

After special toasts by the best man and others, everyone lined up behind the bridal party at the tables piled with foods. Most folks had caterers supply the food, but the Kowalskis insisted on home cooking, so the near relatives had pitched in.

There was kielbasa with sauerkraut, pierogis, beet soup, roast pork, baked potatoes, and such succulent items as ham and chicken for non-Polish Americans, the few who were there, such as Capt. Dan Russo and his wife, Tina, and some friends of the couple, classmates from high school. After the main meal, folks would work through the cold cuts.

"Let the dancing begin!" Hawk boomed, and the band switched from a waltz to polka after polka, oberek after oberek, to schottische, to tango and even the Chicken Dance, with five circles assembled by the younger people and the old-timers who still felt young, but were a movement or two behind, and who, after a few rounds, wheezed off to a corner or a table for a breather and some beer.

Last came the apron dance, as the bride danced first with her father, Emil, her new father-in-law, Junior Wisniewski, and then with every man at the reception—including some old grandfathers who struggled to make one turn—after each had placed his generous offering into an apron held by Wieslava Sokolowski, Mira's godmother. Kenny, before sweeping his bride away in a polka, was the last to dance with Mira, and he threw into the apron his wallet, well, actually a wallet his Uncle Stach had loaned him stuffed with dollar bills. He had enough money put aside for the honeymoon; the money collected would go toward fixing up and furnishing the row house on South Kenwood Avenue where his grandparents had lived. It had been rented out for three years.

The couple left after changing into relaxed clothes and hugging their parents—it was just a little after midnight—for an undisclosed hotel "down the ocean." Dan and Tina Russo weren't too much later, but the Wisniewskis and Kowalskis didn't silence the band nor usher out the final dancers until nearly 5 a.m. And the two families agreed as they did that it had been a fabulous wedding and reception.

Under a tradition called *'popavenie,'* everyone at the wedding was invited to stop by the Kowalski and Wisniewski homes, only a couple blocks apart, for the leftovers from the wedding, and most, especially relatives and close friends, took advantage of the chance not only to eat but also to visit, and the food and the talk lasted for three nights.

Hawk on the final night again had too much to drink, as he did at the reception and the first two nights of *popavenie*, but he did not become obnoxious. And he slept it off the next morning, getting off to work late each day.

Downfall of a salemen

Most of the time Mihok was a good worker and a great "player." But on the road, and when he relaxed at something like this wedding, he enjoyed partying. He liked to meet people, and he was intense, persuasive, a great salesman who could move the slot cars and other toys sold by a Baltimore firm, Folks Inc., in a thirteen-state area—when he was sober.

But his brother-in-law Stach suspected that George's problem stemmed more from smoking than from drinking. Two instances impacted Stach, and he chewed them over later:

They were having kielbasa at Glava's bar off Eastern Avenue three or four months back, and George had just put out his second Pall Mall when their sausages arrived. He took a bite, began chewing, appeared to shake his head and then swallowed with an unusual effort.

"Anything wrong, Hawk?"

"No, I'm a little dry, that's all." And he ordered another beer, and waited to take a deep draught before returning to his kielbasa. "Once in a while my throat gets a little dry," he explained between bites and sips, "and I just have to water it down a little."

When Stach thought about the incident a while later, he decided that the smoking was tensing George, or drying up his throat, or something like that. The problem would only get worse, Stach suspected.

About a month later, Stach tried to put his thoughts into words for Hawk, who was driving I-83 north, giving Stach a ride to Northern District headquarters. "Bull," was George's response. But then, his nerves on edge, he turned the side-view mirror away, and the rear-view mirror askew, because he couldn't keep out of his peripheral sight the broken lines marking the highway's lanes, nor, in the rearview mirror, the cars coming up behind them.

George lit up another Pall Mall, took a deep pull and felt better, confidently telling Stach, "Anytime I want, I can quit drinking and smoking, just to test your theory."

And he actually did, for four days, and his sudden, inexplicable bursts of temper caused Anna to break down in tears for the first time in their marriage. Then he chewed out the boys for some minor matter—and rushed off to buy a carton of Pall Malls to regain control of himself.

Anna, stymied by his unforeseen change of moods—she hadn't noticed that he had stopped smoking, for the house and his clothes still smelled—confessed that there were problems in their marriage when Stach noticed that his sister was very upset. He invited Hawk to lunch at the Sip & Bite at Hudson and Alacea.

"You been having some problems lately, Hawk?" Stach said after ordering the calories-loaded blue-plate special.

"Sometimes I just get blue, you know," George responded. "Salesmen have off-days."

"Smoking, drinking getting you down?" No answer. "I think, Hawk, that you drink because you smoke. It's a big problem, but I love Anna, and my nephews, and I could like you a lot better if you'd stop smoking and drinking. I think you drink because you smoke. That smoking is affecting your throat and ears and mind, just burning them up somehow, and the drinking is strictly to get you through meals without choking, just like you're doing now. . . . Now that's what I think."

George took a long draught from his second bottle of Budweiser. "I don't see the connection, but one day I'll just stop one or the other, and you'll see how wrong you are."

Stach: "It's gonna take both."

George: "Why not." And he snuffed out his cigarette and crunched up the pack in his pocket. But he finished the last of his Bud.

And Stach, realizing that this was just a demonstration for his sake, asked how the boys were doing in school.

About three weeks later, Anna picked up the phone, saying sleepily: "Yes?"

"Anna, Stach here. We got a problem."

Anna snapping awake: "Whaaa! Has something happened to Hawk?"

75

"Yeh, but he'll be OK. Got into an accident on the Falls Expressway."

"Was he drinking again?"

"Afraid so. He's been taken to Mercy Medical Center, at St. Paul and . . ."

"Yes, I know that hospital. But he must have been hurt pretty badly. Oh, I just wish he had stopped that damn drinking."

"He will now."

"He didn't hurt anybody, did he?"

"Nope. Just himself. Ran into the back of a tractor trailer. We think the driver was pulling a container back from Harrisburg, or maybe Cleveland. The driver might have been shook up a little, but he wasn't hurt that I could tell. But I better get over to the hospital, OK?"

"Yeh, OK. Thanks, Stach. Will I see you there?"

"I'll be there."

Anna walked into the emergency room at Mercy Medical Center.

"I'm Anna Mihok. My husband, George . . ."

Nurse: "Oh yes. He's in the recovery room now. Just a minute."

"Thank you."

Anna shifted from foot to foot, looking around the room as doctors, interns and nurses scurried about, even at this hour, tending patients, answering family members. She had thrown her clothes on and didn't feel well dressed or groomed. A large clock on the wall read 2:35.

"This way, please," said the nurse.

Anna tagged along, and entered the recovery room. She looked over the shoulder of a young Indian doctor.

George: "Oh, hi, babe. What brings you here?"

"Don't you know? Are you still drunk?"

"No, babe. I just had one too many. It's tough out

there, you know."

Doctor with a heavy British accent: "He's been talking for a while now . . . about some type of little cars. Not making a great deal of sense. But the head wounds have been treated, and the rest of him appears all right. We'll be doing some tests still."

Stach, who had entered the room right after Anna, gave his sister a shoulder hug: "He hit the windshield, Anna. No seat belt on."

"Were you there?"

"Yeh, I got a call from the investigating officers. Apparently Hawk asked them to call me."

Anna, turning away from George: "What do we do now, Stach?"

"You'll have to take him home whenever he's ready. He'll be charged, of course, but it's a first offense, nobody but him got hurt, so he shouldn't see any jail time. But now's the chance to get him off the beer, the bottle, whatever, and off those damn cigarettes. He's gotta quit them too, or he'll be back drinking."

"I've fought him so hard on this . . ." as she broke into tears and nestled on Stach's shoulder.

Stach, holding her close: "You're gonna have to be real nasty now. No smokes. No beer. No liquor. Never. . . . And believe it or not, he'll be back. He's one hell of a salesman."

George: "You got that right! You got that . . ." and he just seemed to drop off into sleep.

Doctor: "Some of the sedatives are taking hold—he really didn't need much. The nurses will be taking him to a room for an overnight stay. He should be ready to go home in the morning. . . . But I'd strongly urge you to get him into treatment of some sort, nothing less than Alcoholics Anonymous. That group appears to get results for those who are serious about quitting."

Stach: "Were he awake, he'd probably argue with that."

Anna, angrily: "He goes, or he's out of the house. I've had enough."

As they began following the gurney to the semi-private room, Stach, his arm still around Anna's shoulders, said, "You OK for tomorrow?"

"I'll drive the boys over to Mt. St. Joe, and I'll go to work, for a while—I have to—and come back here for Hawk. Is the car a wreck?" Anna worked as a dental assistant-receptionist downtown, having earned her certificate in dental assistant from Community College of Baltimore.

Hawk's car, a '90 red Mercury Sable with 45,000 miles on the speedometer, was "pretty well gone," Stach told his sister. "Doubt you can salvage it. He sort of ran up along the retaining wall, and that slowed him down some before he swerved across a lane to nail the container the truck was pulling. He had to be out by then. There weren't any skid marks."

"Thank God he didn't hurt anyone, but himself."

"Amen to that."

George woke up about 10:20 a.m., stretched and felt the pain, in his head, shoulders, even his knees.

Anna, who was seated in a chair next to the bed: "Ready to tell me about it?"

"Oh, you're here. Did they call you or something? Ooooh, that hurts," after struggling to roll over on his pillow.

"I'm waiting."

"I can't tell you much." Long pause as he thought back. "Last I remember I kinda staggered out of this sports bar in Shrewsbury."

"Where?"

"Shrewsbury, Pennsylvania, just across the state line."

"One of your favorite haunts?"

"Yeh, you could say that. Anyway, someone was arguing with me about driving, but I said I felt fine. I don't remember much after that, though."

Anna, as an older doctor different from the night before entered the room: "So you drove stone drunk from the Pennsylvania border to Baltimore, a half an hour or more?"

Doctor, to Anna: "The effects of alcohol increase quickly in a half-hour. It's amazing. Had he slept for four or five hours, he might have driven home without an accident."

Anna to the doctor: "So, someone could walk out of a bar and think he's capable of driving, and a half-hour later . . ."

Doctor, looking at the patient sheet on a clipboard: ". . . run into a tractor-trailer on I-83, as it says here? Yes."

George: "Is that what I did?"

"So Stach said."

"Was he here? Oh boy."

"He got a call from the investigating officers—seems you had told them about Lt. Wisniewski—and went right to the scene. He called me."

"And you were here last night?"

"And you were sloshed, sloshed and bleeding, and wondering why I'd come."

George grimaced and turned to the doctor: "Do I get any pain killers?"

"There's enough in your system for now. I'm going to look at the tests, check your reactions and probably let you go home in an hour or so."

Anna: "I'll call Stach to help."

George to the doctor: "Is it all right to smoke?"

Anna fiercely: "Never again! Not one drag! Never again. Did you hear that?" And she looked through his pockets on his clothes on a rack to pull out the remains of one pack, crumpled them up and propelled them toward a waste basket, missed and walked over and stamped on them.

On the front steps of South Kenwood Avenue that night, George came out shakily, his head wrapped in bandages under an Orioles cap.

Aunt Irene: "So how're you feeling?"

"I've been better, Aunt Irene."

Aunt Sophia: "I could say something, but it's too obvious, Hawk."

"I can guess, Aunt Sophia. I can guess."

Irene: "And amen from me, Hawk. Doing that to your wife and boys. Well, I never . . ."

Stach interrupted: "It's tough to stop once you're hooked, but you gotta stop the cigarettes and the booze, Hawk. One supports the other."

Irene: "Well, the air will be more pleasant around here. I'm sure that tobacco smoke just fires up my 'ritis," and she gave her left elbow and knee a little twist.

"Will I be charged, Stach?"

"Oh, yes. Nothing I can do about that, Hawk, but you shouldn't get any jail time or anything like that—if you go to Alcoholic Anonymous." Turning to Anna, Stach added: "Has his boss called yet?"

"He's been fired. All we need."

"He gets rid of the smokes and the booze and then, three, six months down the road he'll get another job, or maybe his own back. Hawk, if you can do that, I'll go see this Folks guy myself," referring to the president of the firm.

George, humbled, cleared his throat: "I'd really appreciate that, Stach."

Welcome to AA

Three weeks later, George swallowed deeply as he entered the basement of St. Casimir's Church, fearing that many of the folks there for the AA meeting would recognize him. He was wrong. He knew no one; no one appeared to recognize him. He breathed easier.

There were about thirty-five people present, he guessed, and almost every one of them was smoking. 'Oh, great,' he thought to himself. The air was so heavy with smoke that he would have a hard time convincing Anna that he hadn't started smoking again. His clothes would give him away.

Actually, he didn't mind the smoke. It would take him at least two years before he would start to move away from smokers, and it wouldn't be too long before such places as St. Casimir's decided against allowing smoking in their basement rooms and the AA meetings would recess at least once to allow the smokers to light up outside, and the butts would pile up in the outside ashtrays.

A salesman to the core, George studied everyone, not staring at the floor as a nervous few there did, obviously newcomers like himself. One of the patriarchs of this AA group came up and introduced himself.

"Hello, I'm Bill, and you are . . .?"

"George, George Mihok. I didn't get your last name," George said, flashing his salesman's smile and offering a firm handshake.

"We only use first names here, George," Bill cautioned. "Good to have you with us."

"Yeh, well, the judge didn't give me any choice, you know. I got to get this form signed," and he pulled out a paper from his inside jacket pocket.

"No problem. You can get that signed after the meeting." He didn't stress "after." "Just see me. There's a few here with those forms."

"There are?"

"Sure, even that older woman, Barbara, over there. Too many pain killers," Bill said as he nodded toward a grandmotherly type. "It's good to have you here, George. It will get easier, you know."

"So they tell me," George said, with obvious doubt.

"Come on, let's meet a few folks. Barbara, this is George, and he has a form like yours."

"Welcome to AA, George. You'll make it, if I can," she added, with more than a shred of doubt in her voice. He would hear that particular sentence often.

"And Bill," Bob continued to a well-suited middle-aged man who stood up to shake hands with George.

"Hello, how are you," he said mechanically, but he averted his eyes, George noticed.

Bob let George find a seat as Bob moved to the front of the room: "Well, let's get started, OK?" he said in a commanding voice. "I'm Bob, and I'm an alcoholic," . . . and everyone said, some shouted, "Hello, Bob!" . . . "and I'd like to introduce our newest guest, George, here."

Everyone almost on cue: "Hello, George!" which embarrassed him, as well as Bob's almost prideful confession that he was an alcoholic. George just nodded his head left and right and sat lower down on the metal folding chair.

"Is there any business?" Bob asked.

Someone in the back row. "Hello, I'm Sue, and I'm an alcoholic."

Most everyone: "Hello, Sue!"

"We are a little short in the coffee fund, Bob, so if anyone could help a little . . ."

Bob: "Thank you, Sue. Any other business? . . . Our speaker tonight is Stan."

A smallish man, perhaps forty, came forward to stand by Bob. He was smoking a Camel and was extremely nervous, either looking to the ceiling or the floor as he stumbled through his talk.

"Hello, I'm Stan, and they tell me I'm an alcoholic." He said that with the sense that perhaps "they" were wrong.

"Hello, Stan!" most everyone said in encouragement. George just listened.

"I don't talk much, you know." Stan paused, looked at his shoes for a minute or so. "I used to work on the railroad, loadin' and unloadin' freights, freight cars. And it was a good job. . . . We had them forklifts, you know, and, well, it was good work. But the railroads, well, you know, they aren't doin' very much any more—they're usin' more and more of those damn containers comin' in from overseas . . ." He looked down for a minute or more," . . . and we don't load so many cars anymore."

He paused, looked at the ceiling for a while, and then brought his head down to study the table, not really looking at anyone. "So there's lots of times we don't work for mebbe two, three weeks at a time, you know. And I sort of sit and . . ." He paused, looked out the window for more than a minute. "There ain't much I know how to do, 'cept loadin' freight, I guess . . . and you can't watch TV all the time, so I'd have a beer now and then, and then mebbe the TV shows would look better, and my wife said I'd be laughin' at the dumbest shit, oh 'scuse me, . . . stuff."

He paused, looked at the ceiling for a while. He snuffed out his Camel and lit another one. "And, well, you know, I just kept drinkin' those beers, and den I finally got back to work, but I couldn't work so good as b'fore for some reason, and I banged up some pallets with that fork lift, and then I banged up the fork lift, and I got sent off by the union for treatment." He paused, pursed his lips, and nearly cried. "Them was rough days, but I got through."

"Good for you!" three or four people almost shouted.

"So here I am now, and . . ." Stan stopped, and went back to his place and sat down, and everyone applauded.

"Good for you, Stan," someone said. "You'll make it if I can," another added, while Stan studied his shoes and drew on his Camel. He didn't look like he would make it, George thought.

Bob: "Thank you, Stan. You just got to remember that you're still an alcoholic, but a recovering one. But you got to hang in there, and keep away from that beer."

Then he turned to someone next to him for comment on Stan's talk, and several people spoke as Bob turned from one to another, saying what George would suspect after several meetings that they had said many times before, fitting it to this person, and George just waved his hand and they passed him over, and he was happy about an hour and a half and three coffees later when Bob signed George's form and he could go home. "I'll be back next meeting," he said. He had no choice. He had to have that form signed three different times.

The Pittsburgh Connection

Dan, at Patterson Lanes about a week later: "So your brother-in-law tried to drive through a container being towed on I-83?"

Stach: "Yep, really smashed up his car. No doubt he totaled it."

Dan: "Well, this much you might want to know, you son of a gun, dumb Polack, or whatever. We did have one of the canine guys check out that container, like you suggested, and sure enough his dog went crazy. There had been cocaine in there at one time. Nothing left but the smell. We did a real thorough search."

"You checking that container's history?"

"Trying to keep ahead of me, are you? Apparently

that's not an option, not yet, any way. If it weren't for a DIA agent who just happened to take down the container's numbers on the trip out to Pittsburgh—sort of a hobby of his—and they just happened to be the same as this one. Now that's coincidence."

"And the driver?"

Dan, after pulling out a notebook: "On both the outbound and the homebound, a fellow by the name of William C. Schmidt, southerner, of course, like most over-the-road truckers for some reason. Driver's license from Montgomery, Alabama, but I'll bet he grew up in some little town nearby. Got a little sharp with one of our detectives. But no record."

"Who's he drive for?"

"You guess, Whiz."

"You put it that way, and I'd say Rex Rossler Lines."

"Bingo! How'd you guess? You win every time. That container was driven to Pittsburgh to a well-known clothing store, in fact. One of the people unloading the container could have taken out the stash, or the driver might have helped unload the container and put aside the stash, or it could have been picked up by someone who came in the store to buy a particular item that had the cocaine in it."

"So?"

"I'm going up there shortly to check out in depth with the Pittsburgh P.D. I'm even going to suggest we cooperate in some way, like exchanging key personnel."

Wisniewski looked up curiously.

"It's just an idea I've been mulling over," Russo said, "and I got clearance from Major Bentzen to approach the Pittsburgh department. We were hoping to get some help from the DIA into the history of this container. So far, they say, there's no system for trailing them."

Stach: "In truth, these caches of drugs could be inserted without the knowledge of the drivers, the shippers, the steamship lines, the stores or even warehouses receiving shipments, just some crime family taking care of business."

Dan: "Seems like we could do something. . . . I got something else that will make your day."

Stach turned to him, but said only, "You're up."

Dan got up to bowl; Stach followed.

Dan: "Good spare."

Stach: "Should have been a strike. So, what's the other surprise?"

"The DIA did provide a little help. A fairly recent shipment in that container was to the O's Stadium warehouse."

"That could have been Cajun Gumbo . . ."

"Yep, the Whiz's cud strikes again. And guess who the driver was?"

"This same guy, Smith?"

"Schmidt."

"You know, here's an idea. Since you're thinking of a personnel switch with Pittsburgh, if either side would welcome that . . . my nephew recently started pulling containers over to Philadelphia and back, but he's new enough that he only gets a call here and there, now and then, and he's not that busy. Perhaps if we leaned on our old buddy, Rex Rossler, to step up Kenny's calls and maybe have him assign Kenny to drive along with this Schmidt guy, you know, and keep his eyes open . . ."

Dan: "He'd have to be careful, but we could brief him. I wouldn't want him all alone with a real drug runner, you know, if our suspicions hold water. . . . Maybe I could have Sylvester Reed somehow shadow your nephew, just to keep him out of trouble. Let me work something up, okay?"

"Sure."

"But maybe we might just want to coordinate with the feds."

"Lunch at the Sip & Bite that they'll blow us off."

"You're on. And you're probably right. But I owe you anyway for suggesting we get the dogs out there on your brother-in-law's accident."

Salesman on a short leash

Lt. Stach Wisniewski lived up to his promise to his brother-in-law, after he went a month without smoking or drinking, and Hawk got his job back at Folks Inc. on a trial basis. The president-owner helped Mihok acclimate to life without smokes or booze by giving him short runs and slowly extending the trips from one day to up to six days, and still, via phone, kept his number one salesman on a short leash.

Within the second month Hawk was ringing up orders for slot cars at a pace that pleased Henry A. Folks so much that he boosted Mihok's commission 10 percent and his spending allowance on the road by 15 percent. Hawk was pleased. Anna was grateful, and the boys found their father ready to play catch, bowl, or jog a little, activities he had never done with Lou and Jerry before.

Anna started washing all the walls to try to get rid of the smoke, but George, making better money now, had Junior Wisniewski come over to paint the walls, and the smoke smell ebbed room by room, with Hawk moving the furniture around as Junior needed.

George even got some videos of an exercising guru and began to work out in the living room, wearing sneakers to avoid getting harassed by the neighbors. Anna watched from the kitchen in pure disbelief. They went out to dinner occasionally, and Hawk didn't need alcohol to get him through. And their sex life and their sleep improved greatly, especially for Anna, who no longer had to worry about his driving home.

Cocaine crisis in Baltimore

On Thursday, June 16, the federal Drug Investigations Agency called a meeting to address the cocaine crisis in Baltimore, inviting officers from all the districts in the city and from the near suburbs.

Bob Hampton of the DIA opened with a status report on illegal drug traffic in and through Baltimore, especially cocaine. He said his office had over the last three years seized more than $130,000 in marijuana and $1.4 million in cocaine. He said cocaine accounted for most of the drugs netted, which likely was 25 to 30 percent of the cocaine brought into the city. Some of the people there, including Capt. Dan Russo, would estimate that only 10 to 15 percent of the cocaine moving into and through the city on I-95 had been seized.

Hampton said some crime group—it was assumed to be Colombian—was somehow bringing cocaine into the city in considerable quantity, storing it somewhere and repackaging it, probably in a warehouse, and moving it onto the streets.

A detective from the Eastern District raised his hand, got recognized and said: "We're seeing young punks working in teams, one taking money at one corner, who walks to another corner to pick up the drugs, and then reconnects with the customer on a third corner."

Hampton: "I'm told you can make the complete deal on one corner, now," and several heads nodded knowingly.

He mentioned the popularity of crack for five dollars a rock, its instant high, its almost immediate addiction. He returned to his notes, saying that cocaine purchased wholesale in New York for less than $20,000 can be sold on the streets of Baltimore for as much as $50,000. He added that the DIA was trying to monitor communications among known top-level traffickers, with some initial success, and would expand these efforts in the Baltimore area.

He described the inventiveness of the cartels nationwide by commenting, with a smile, "We even found some cocaine in air shipments of Mother's Day flowers from Colombia." He looked up to see whether that impressed anyone, but the sixty or so local officers and even his own fifteen agents seemed unfazed.

"We stopped that cold when we got Customs to order those 747s bringing the flowers in to land in Miami, and to be unloaded, and dogs sniffed through the whole lot before the planes were reloaded and sent along." That appeared to impress his audience.

"Colombia exports textiles, pharmaceuticals, coffee, bananas, printed materials, tobacco and 400 to 500 tons of cocaine every year, maybe more," Hampton said. "We know that container ships, yachts and fishing boats carry a lot of this cocaine into the states. Speaking of containers, the cartels prey on containers dropped off and ignored for extended periods of time. That gives the cartels the opportunity to pick up drugs in those containers, if there, or to simply profit by selling off the legal cargo in those containers. And there is a network of criminal importers, shippers, truckers, even dock hands who can be bought." He picked up papers off the podium as he said, "We know that these networks create their own paperwork and just drive off with containers, or else they break into containers, taking what they want, and then reseal them. And we're penetrating those networks, some of them Russian—and eastern European—originated.

"We have found containers stolen off storage lots, and with your help we're tightening security on that. Some of those containers sit around for a while until they're broken into and the drugs removed. And the criminals know how to get around the seals, believe it or not," and he looked up to see some of the officers taking notes.

"We know for certain that some of the stuff stolen is repackaged at some area warehouse or warehouses." That perked interest among a number of officers. A major from the Southwest District asked, "Any particular warehouse?"

Hampton: "No, I'm sorry. But, since you brought it up, I'd like you to listen to one of our agents, Tomas Estafan, who was just assigned to our jurisdiction from southern California. Tomas."

A litany of drug trafficking

A short, lean man with a trimmed beard, likely in his late twenties, who was born in the Dominican Republic, wearing jeans and T-shirt, came to the podium, speaking good English with a Caribbean accent,

"Yes, sir. I was along on several raids on warehouses in and around LA, ah, Los Angeles, and here's what we discovered. Let me insert here that you better have good cause to make one of these raids, for we stirred up a hornet's nest over two of the seven we targeted. But here are some concealments we uncovered:

--"Nowadays they ship paint pigment in huge sacks, and the cartel people somehow insert into those huge sacks little bags with no more than ten pounds of cocaine. You look at those sacks and you just can't see anything. And it's messy.

--"We stumbled onto a great little scam. You all know that tons and tons of toys come in in the fall for the Christmas season, mostly on container ships from China. We discovered that some of the toys sent to individuals, usually mom and pop stores, had packets of cocaine in them. Feliz Navidad, Merry Christmas, everyone.

--"We found one warehouse distributing to area schools, well, let's see, it was oranges. And they sent out ten pallet loads of oranges for nine actual schools, and the tenth pallet that didn't exist in the paperwork had some drugs the high-school seniors might have welcomed. It was intercepted.

--"Let me interject here that the drivers of these trucks may, or more likely, may not know what they're delivering, simply out of the loop. It's just another load to them. If the driver gets his bill of lading signed, well, that's that.

--"There are even bargains on the Internet, when customers request certain toys at pretty high fees, retrieve the hidden drugs, and obviously put the toys under the Christmas tree. All delivered by UPS or FedEx. Pretty, no?

--"We've also monitored those Internet sales, checking out why so and so keeps ordering such and such a toy. It's because the toys happen to come with guess-what inside.

--"Ever wonder what's in those vanilla beans from Norway? Or processed chocolate from France? Maybe some bags of cocaine or other drugs. It's all part of the cartel's doings. Happy hunting." And he sat down to applause.

Hampton returned to the podium. "Thank you, Tomas. He's becoming a real asset to us.

"Some of the runners we've picked up in our area say drugs are moving through local warehouses, but they offer no proof, give no addresses and, maybe to confuse us, could be making it up."

"Do you know how drugs come into Baltimore?" a major from the Eastern District asked.

"We believe that cocaine and heroin are coming here from New York and Florida. How? By truck, by ship, in containers, by rail, by cars. Somehow they get drugs into containers that have been sealed. I suspect some come in backpacks of motorcyclists, there's such a demand."

Capt. Dan Russo said, "We appreciated your providing information on a certain container we stumbled on that had been used to carry cocaine. We've made some connections involving that particular driver."

"Thank you, Dan. But you also asked some time back whether there was any container-tracking system so we could keep track of a particular container. We were lucky on that one you mentioned; one of our agents driving on the expressway actually recognized the container's numbers. But there's no competent system available yet for tracking containers. A lot of experiments, some very limited container tracking in a certain port, for example. But that's it.

"Any other questions?" He looked around. "Let's call it a day." And the officers and agents filed out.

An undercover detective

Russo and Wisniewski met privately with Hampton afterward and described their intention to plant an undercover detective in a particular warehouse. The two officers did not say which warehouse, and Hampton understood. He applauded the plan and asked to be kept informed. He admitted that he suspected that one or more of the police officers at the just-adjourned session was likely being paid by the cartel to pass along details from his briefing, and he complimented the two officers for not mentioning their plan at the gathering.

But he questioned their decision to have a new driver tag along with an experienced over-the-road trucker suspected of delivering containers carrying drugs. "I don't see any real value to this operation, other than you'll get an experienced trucker or a dead one. We now have several undercover operatives . . . "—Dan smiled on that phrase—". . . and we believe we should have some real results within three to six months."

Avoiding responding on that, Russo handed Hampton a sealed envelope. "We know who the men on the right and in the middle are, but do you have anything on the man on the left?"

"I'll run it through our photo bank," Hampton responded as he slit open the envelope. "We might just be able to help you. But he looks like an everyday Latino you might meet on the street, you know. But we'll check.

"We are really trying," Hampton continued, "to work with, coordinate and share information with local departments. We suspect that around the country criminal operators actually own trucking companies and shipping companies, and that there are certain officials, perhaps even in Customs, on the take."

The two officers—Russo and Wisniewski—shook hands with Hampton and left.

About two weeks later at the Patterson bowling alleys, Dan said: "Yep, we talked with the feds. Or rather, we listened."

Stach: "And they said we should keep our noses out, because whatever we do would jeopardize their undercover operations. Do we back off?"

"Hell, no. We do our own thing." He broke to bowl, followed by Stach.

Dan, when their conversation resumed: "You got a turkey going, not bad."

"I've had turkeys before, but never a four-bagger . . . So we go ahead. The major is OK with that."

"Good for him. I'll have Kenny stop by my office next week, OK?"

"Great. I'll have Sylvester Reed work up some ideas."

A week later at district headquarters, where Lt. Wisniewski's office is just off the roll-call room, a sergeant

rapped on the frame of the open door. "A Kenny Wisniewski here to see you, lieutenant. Friend of yours?"
"Worse, a relative. Come in Kenny, come in. You know Dan Russo?" Dan's office was on the second floor. He had come down for the meeting.
"Yes, sir. You talk about him quite a bit, Uncle Stach."
Dan: "Does he ever say anything good?"
"You don't have to answer that Kenny. Schooch has rarely said anything good about any Polack."
"I'll admit that—except your uncle, Kenny. How are you?" And they shook hands. "I'd like you to meet Lt. Sylvester Reed, my right-hand man," handshakes and nodded heads, "who has developed some ideas for us. Ah, you're living in Stach's old house now?"
"My grandparents' house. After they both died, we worked out a deal at the wake whereby my future wife and I would move in. Uncle Stach and Aunt Stephanie have moved over to their hardware store, and they're happy there."
"Your uncle says great things about you, and I've got a job that begs for a good truck driver."
Stach: "Have a seat Kenny." Kenny sat down. "I was telling Schooch and Syl that you used to drive tractor trailers in the Marine Corps."
"Yes, sir. We would be moving 'cattle cars,' er, personnel carriers, and would use MK-48s, sir. Sometimes we'd put a tank or a light armored vehicle on a flatbed and haul it to maneuvers or to an airport, whatever. The Corps has tractors just like the civilians, except they're painted for the Corps."
Sylvester: "And no 'call 1-800-whatever' on the back to complain about your driving?"
Kenny: "No, sir. We had NCOs taking on that role."
Sylvester, who served in the Navy: "I did, too."
Dan: "We asked you here, Kenny, because we'd like

you to make some runs from here to Savannah or Charleston and back. You're an inter-modal driver hauling containers?"

"Over to Philadelphia, down to Hampton Roads, up to Wilmington. That's why I bought the tractor."

"It wouldn't bother you to go south to Charleston or Savannah?"

"It's enough just dragging containers around without worrying about something else, you know. I'm pretty new in the business."

Stach: "Kenny, we want you to make these trips and just note what takes place, especially anything unusual. I could tell you, but . . . I won't," taking note of Kenny's concern mirrored in his face and then his relaxing on not knowing. "We just want to get some background on just how containers are moved up and down the coast."

Kenny: "I'll be checking on mine, that's for certain. And I want to get the feel of driving that far and back. If I see something that doesn't seem right, I'll just pass it along to Sylvester."

Sylvester: "My plan is to tag along in the background watching how everything happens. To start with, we're going to link you up with a very experienced driver for Rex Rossler Lines . . ." He stopped when he saw Kenny's smile.

"That's who Uncle Stach got me a contract with."

Sylvester: "Anyway, you would check with me from time to time on what's happening. You have a cell phone?"

"Yes, sir. I got it a couple weeks ago. It's the best way to keep tabs with the dispatcher."

"Sounds good. So come on up to my office and we'll go over the details." And the two men left.

Dan, turning to Stach: "I think we got our man. This should give us something to work with."

"Father wasn't in our lives"

Kenny followed Sylvester to the second floor detectives' office, and Sylvester found a free desk while he got out a file from his own desk, now being used by another detective who was questioning what looked like a spaced-out user.

"Detective work tough, sir?" Kenny asked.

"Drop the 'sir' business. You're no longer a Marine; I'm no longer a sailor. But in this job, you do see a lot of dead people, but I can't take it personally, 'cause it's not personal anymore. This job does take a lot of sympathy away from you."

"You got family? We got a lot of family along South Kenwood Avenue. It sure helps."

"You want family? My grandmother had seven girls and four boys. My mother grew up in a house of eleven kids. The girls did everything for the men in the house. My mother did everything for us, my brother, my sister and me. My father? He just wasn't in our lives."

"My mother and dad are into my life quite a bit, and Uncle Stach—well, you know him."

"A good man, Kenny, a very good man.

"You sound envious."

"I can't explain it, but a lot of black men, they want to make the babies, but they don't want to take care of them. Don't want the responsibility."

"Most of them?"

"No, I think the majority of black males take care of their kids. I believe that, but I didn't see a lot of it where I grew up." He paused for a different thought: "I don't believe a woman can raise a man. You have to have some kind of male figure in your life. I had my uncles, and that helped me . . ."

"Your uncles cops?"

"Nope. I'm the first in the family. You know, when I was growing up, I'd see folks dealing drugs all day long, but once I put on this uniform, if was different. Now I was supposed to stop 'em." He paused. "You married, Kenny?"

"Pretty soon. How about you?"

"Married a couple years. And she's just now accepting me being a cop."

"Too much worrying?"

"Yep."

"Mira's worried a little about my driving, but they regulate how many hours you can drive in a day. No need to worry about me."

"Yeh. Here's some things you might want to watch for on your drive to Savannah and back." He passed over several heavily typed index cards. "You can keep these in your pocket, or glove compartment, or wherever. No need to write down anything. I'll try to keep in touch with you throughout. And you can catch me at all times on your cell phone.

"And listen, how about you and Mira—did I get that right? —join Jasmine and Keeyse, our little girl, and me. We're going to the zoo a week from Thursday."

"I'm on call most every day, but, for some reason, I don't get as many calls on Thursdays as on other days."

"Fine, let's try for next Thursday. We can put together a great picnic basket, and . . .

"We'll bring the drinks."

"Great." Details were arranged, with Kenny cautioning that he might be called away. Syl said he was in trouble with his wife for often having to break off from an engagement.

Rehabbing in Canton

Most every night, weather permitting, the Wisniewskis, like the Russos on South Exeter and the Reeds on Darling

Avenue—at least the womenfolk—gathered on their front steps to talk, a practice slowing fading away.

Kenny and Mira live in his grandparents' house. Anna and George (Hawk), George Jr., nineteen, and Jimmy, seventeen, live next door to Kenny and Mira, and on the other side there are Aunt Irene—her husband Stanislaus, also known as Stach, died six years ago—and Aunt Sophia, who moved in with her after selling her house down the block profitably to a developer planning to redesign it.

He had bought the home for $48,000, estimated that he would spend about $90,000 improving the property, and figured to sell it for $234,000.

Another Canton rehabber, with his extended family as the work crew, pretty well gutted a row house built in 1910 to 1912 and ended up with two wider floors, and a deck on the roof, from which the sunbathers were able to see the Domino Sugars plant, but just the tops of the skyscrapers fronting on the Inner Harbor. However, he forecast a fantastic view of fireworks.

This rehabber, who had taught at Patterson High School and Dundalk Middle School, was coordinating all this for his sister and brother-in-law, who were putting in sweat equity. The rehabber estimated that the cost was comparable to the improvements scheduled for the row house that Aunt Sophia sold. He did have to hire in electricians and plumbers.

Stach and Stephanie Wisniewski reside over the hardware store that they bought with the extended family's help and a business loan from a Polish savings and loan shortly after they got married. She pretty much runs the store, with some hired help, retired carpenters and plumbers. Lt. Wisniewski and his three children, Ted, twelve, Kasia, seven, and Stella, five, tag along to hear the conversations on the front steps. Stephanie keeps the hardware store open until 9 p.m.

Anna, Betty, Mira, Irene and Sophia always sit around Anna and George's front steps, and Kenny—when he is not driving late—Stach, Junior and Hawk on the front steps of Kenny's place, with George Jr. and Jimmy stopping by from time to time, slowly getting away from the every-night talk.

Mira: "That's right, Anna, Kenny's gonna be going to Savannah, Georgia, and Charleston, South Carolina, instead of back and forth to Philadelphia and Wilmington. I think Uncle Stach has something to do with that."

Stach: "We are asking him to just sort of show us how those pickups and deliveries are made."

Stephanie: "Is Dan Russo in on this, dear?"

"Yep."

"Something to do with the Detective Bureau?"

"Sort of. I can't say any more than that."

Anna, frustrated in not knowing fully what was going on, turned to her nephew: "Do they pack up those big containers at a plant here and unload them in Philadelphia, Wilmington or Savannah, for example? How's that work, Kenny?"

"Aunt Anna, everything, or almost everything you buy today moves in big containers. Most are twenty or forty feet long, eight feet across, eight feet high. Actually most we pull around here are forty feet long."

Irene: "If they was using my foot, that wouldn't be too big."

"No, it's a standard measurement, Aunt Irene," said Anna, who opened her hands to a foot length, and got close enough that none of the men challenged her.

Kenny, going through the motions of his description: "Anyway, they'll pack up a container, overseas, like say in Germany, with machines or something, and they'll truck or rail it to a port, and winch it onto a special ship, and sail it across the Atlantic to Baltimore, and unload it with a humongous crane onto a truck chassis, just lock it in place, and, one-two-three, away it goes to a warehouse here in the U.S."

Sophia: "And one-two-three, away went the jobs of thousands of stevedores, like my grandson Roger. That's what happened to him. Now he has to go to that hiring hall on Oldham Street in Highlandtown (another section of Baltimore near Canton) to 'badge in' every day, work or no work. Sometimes there's only 60 jobs for 600 men. And they have to work so many hours a year to get their benefits."

"That's tough, Aunt Sophia."

"It sure is. One year they had more than 100 men taking five days to unload a ship. Now they tell me that eight do it in one day. Just like you said, Kenny, one-two-three."

Stach: "My grandfather worked as a stevedore, you know, Aunt Sophia. Well, sure you know. And the jobs are hard to get now. There were only maybe 150 people still working at the American National Can Company last year when it closed."

Sophia, not letting up on her grand nephew: "What's so good about these big boxes anyway, Kenny?"

"A lot of things, Aunt Sophia. For example, there's less damage to the cargo, and less loss, like from stealing . . ."

Stach: "That's a double-edged gain, Kenny, for now, instead of the gangs taking a bunch of computers, as many as they could carry to a getaway truck, now they steal the whole darn container."

Kenny: "I didn't know that, Uncle Stach. . . . But the containers just zip through the terminals. You know, they can unload a big ship in one day, load it the next, and it's off."

Sophia: "Well, it did take longer in the old days, but those men moved as fast as they could, and they put food on their tables for, what are they making now, nineteen dollars an hour . . . and those containers don't!"

From Conex boxes to forty-foot-long containers

After World War II, the U.S. armed services experimented with Conex boxes, small steel containers, to carry soldiers' personal belongings, mostly to cut down on thefts from break-bulk shipments. But history was made on April 26, 1956, when fifty-eight trailer truck bodies, detached from their axles and wheels, were lifted aboard a modified tanker, Ideal-X, by a crane moving along the dock in Newark, New Jersey. The ship sailed to Houston, where the truck bodies (in reality, containers) full of freight were off-loaded by cranes onto fifty-eight trucks on the docks and hauled to their destinations. The containers' modus operandi had been defined.

The mover and shaker behind this start was Malcom McLean—who in 1934 started a trucking company with one truck, by 1940 owned thirty, and by war's end had 162—when he encouraged veterans to take advantage of cheap government loans to become owner-operators and to haul freight for McLean Trucking, of course.

He and the experts he hired developed:
-- Containers thirty-three feet long to go aboard converted tankers from World War II.
-- Cranes with giant booms moving along tracks on top of reinforced docks that could take the weight of twenty-ton containers.
-- Spreader bars that could cover the length and width of the containers so they could be lifted on and off ships.

It wasn't until 1959 that containers were standardized at twenty or forty feet long, eight feet wide and eight feet high. And it wasn't until 1968 that vessels especially designed to carry containers, and only containers, began sailing the seas.

The Vietnam War provided Sea-Land and McLean the opportunity to turn the newly developed Cam Ranh Bay into a container port in November '67, thereby unsnarling the military services' supply chain.

By 1992, 80 percent of general overseas cargo trade moved in containers, millions of them. And by 1992, shippers had standardized a variety of these containers, boxes with strong, load-bearing corner posts that could be locked into the carrier, be it ship, truck or railroad car, or onto another container, above or below. They could be stacked four high—the limit then.

The majority moving through Baltimore are forty feet long. The forty-footer handles up to a gross weight of thirty long tons, and the twenty-footer, twenty long tons. The containers are built of aluminum, of steel, and of plywood and fiberglass combinations, each with its own special properties.

Some are insulated to handle temperature extremes, some heated, some equipped with refrigeration, some ventilated. They are all watertight.

In '92, the special container-carrying ships stretched for 700 feet and cruised at twenty-seven knots. Each carried more than 1,000 containers, many in the hold, many stacked on the decks. Above the water line, these new ships were wide and flat.

Trucking firms and railroads modified their equipment or built new to handle the containers once they reached port.

Mile-long trains were hauling containers filled with TV sets and clothes, for example, from the West Coast to the East Coast in three days. The cross-country trek was called a "land bridge," and it was cutting into the traffic from Asia through the Panama Canal. In fact these trains were bringing more containers to the East Coast than were ships crossing the Atlantic.

Incidentally, the competition between trucks and trains dates back to World War I when the trains and tracks of that day couldn't handle the munitions and supplies needed by U.S. forces, and truckers stepped in to help out. The roads of those days were hardly passable to begin with, and deteriorated dreadfully under the impact of the heavily loaded trucks.

In recent years, millions of dollars have been spent on both coasts:

-- to expand port terminals to provide the cranes, or shore gantries, to lift the containers off the specially-designed ships and onto trucks or trains at the container ports.

-- to build highway and railroad spurs to bring those trucks and trains up close to the container ships.

-- to clear hundreds of acres to store those containers before sending them on, in most cases along interstate highways.

The impact nationwide? By '92 more than seventeen million containers had been shipped through the United States.

The containers go from factory—where customs inspectors oversee the packing of the containers and their sealing—by truck to ship and on to port, and then back to truck or train, eventually to a warehouse for local distribution, when the seals are broken and they are opened—all under one bill of lading. This bill describes the cargo, lists its weight, notes special handling needed, and records the country of origin, the destination and the person or firm receiving it.

Port traffic in Baltimore

The port of Baltimore probably hit its high in 1985, handling more than 700,000 containers. By 1991, that had dropped to less than 500,000 containers, from almost 12 percent of the East Coast traffic to less than 8 percent, after the port lost three cargo lines to Hampton Roads, Virginia, weathered the impact of the recession nationwide, and, in 1990, was hurt by two short-term strikes by locals of the International Longshoreman's Association.

The strikers could not be replaced because of the national ILA contract with major ship lines. These "container rules" also prohibited the shippers from diverting container ships to other ports. The second strike ended when Local 953 agreed to work flexible shifts to allow the port terminals to run to midnight.

In 1991 the port of Baltimore handled 23,921,210 short tons of cargo, placing ninth among U.S. ports, right behind Long Beach, California. The Baltimore tonnage had a value of $16,615,188,000, also ninth among U.S. seaports. Baltimore's 1991 tonnage was 4 percent less than 1990, but only slightly less in value.

However, the opening of the Seagirt terminal in 1990 increased by 50 percent the port's capacity to handle containers, because container tonnage made up less than 20 percent of the total cargo moving through the port of Baltimore. The other 80 percent was in bulk shipments, like grains, coal, ores and petroleum.

In 1991, the top three countries receiving exports from Baltimore were Denmark, Germany and Japan, in tonnage, and Germany, Belgium-Luxembourg and Britain in dollar value. The top three exporters to Baltimore were Canada, Brazil and Venezuela in tonnage, and Japan, Germany and Britain in dollar value.

A total of 2,217 vessels called at the Port of Baltimore in 1991, down about 3 percent from the year before. But 1992 should show a slight increase in port calls because Overseas Container Line, lured to Hampton Roads in 1984, has returned to Baltimore.

(1991-2 port statistics courtesy of the Enoch Pratt Free Library's Maryland Room)

Many of the trucking firms pulling containers in and out of Baltimore don't go much beyond a 100- to 125-mile radius of the port, and they sometimes come back empty. But Rex Rossler Lines, like a few others, set up offices in such destinations at Akron, Ohio, Savannah, Georgia, and Charlotte, North Carolina, to develop return cargoes so their contracted trucks wouldn't have to dead-head home, at least most of the time.

A day at the zoo

Their day at the Maryland Zoo in Baltimore began when Kenny and Mira met Sylvester, Jasmine and Keeyse just inside the entrance and walked along toward the polar bear pit. Keeyse wanted most to see the lions, and the men thought they could watch her. The women elected to walk over to the giraffes' area.

Mira: "How old is Keeyse?"

"Four, I'm told. We're in the process of adopting her, and her parents' records were never found after they both were murdered."

"Murdered?"

"It's quite a story, and I can tell it while she's off with the men."

"There's a place to sit." And they settled onto a bench along the walk, with the giraffes to divert them.

"Perfect," said Jasmine, continuing, "Keeyse's parents never married, but I will give credit to her father. He didn't walk out. On the other hand, he was a worthless drug runner, and his mouthing off about one of the biggest drug dealers in the city cost him his life. And when his woman found out he had been killed, she lit out for the Inner Harbor, apparently wanting protection from the police or whomever."

"She didn't make it?"

"She did run into one of the members of our church, who took her into the church."

"The safest place around."

"Not for her. A couple of thugs working for some drug gang burst in and shot her to death in the closet where she was hiding. They didn't know about Keeyse, or they would have killed her, too."

"Why? A little one like that couldn't hurt anyone."

"Well, you might think so, but on an outing with Sylvester, little Keeyse pointed out a key drug dealer called Big Knife. My husband called in the department's tactical squad . . ."

". . . Oh, I saw the report on the television and read the story in *The Sun*. There was a shootout on the waterfront. One heck of a story, but there was nothing about a little girl, and I don't remember your husband being mentioned."

"For very good reason, Mira. The baby, and likely my husband, would be dead by now if the gang knew."

"They'd kill your husband out of revenge, I guess, but a little girl?"

"Her, too." Jasmine let the thought sink in. "In any case, Keeyse had no other relatives, at least none that would step forward, so we began the process to adopt her. We have her on temporary loan, you might say."

"Do you think . . ."

". . . that she'll turn out as bad as her parents?"

"Oh, I'm sorry. I shouldn't . . ."

Jasmine leaned over to pat Mira's knee. "Mira, that was the very first question I asked the placement official. Don't be embarrassed. She said that was always asked. And, no, she will not revert."

"Thank God."

"Oh, we have, we have," causing Mira to blush and say, "I've said the wrong thing."

"Never. But enough about our soon-to-be daughter. What do you do?"

"I work in the Central City Warehouse in the southern industrial section off Baltic Avenue."

"Doing?"

"The paperwork involved in keeping track of shipments, mostly from overseas in boxes, in crates, on pallets, even in twenty-foot-long and forty-foot-long containers."

"Which Kenny pulls."

"Why, yes. How did you know?"

"My husband fills me in on most of his doings, at least I hope it's most."

"What do you do, Jasmine?"

"Right now I'm on a break to watch Keeyse, but I'm a computer programmer for an insurance firm."

"Doesn't sound very exciting."

"It's not really, but it pays quite well. On the other hand, working in a warehouse . . ."

"Well, I'm a warehouse clerk, mainly concerned with receiving, storing, retrieving and shipping. I don't do all that lifting and sweating that 'working in a warehouse' usually means to people."

"You just didn't look the type, nor have the physique."

"Oh, we have some women like that, and they can handle the rude talk of the men. But they don't bother me, even though they do watch me whenever I come out of the office."

"I can understand that."

"But there's no dirty talk at all. Mr. Hansen, the operations manager, won't tolerate it, and he's fired a couple men, really just big boys, and that ended that. Also, when Kenny picks me up, from time to time, when my car is getting serviced and he's available, well, the men get the idea that I'm spoken for."

"What do you do all day?" Jasmine thought to herself that she was doing all the asking of someone who had a much less important and less interesting job, but then dismissed the thought as patronizing.

"Basically, I check what's coming in, where it's being stored, and when and where it's supposed to go. It's pretty good money for the moment, and I think I might just want to work up to assistant manager or manager. I graduated from Patterson Park High, and I'm taking classes at Catonsville (Community College) for an associate degree . . . " Jasmine tried without success to hide her surprise, but Mira didn't notice. ". . . and then we'll see. Kenny likes the idea even though he'd rather I didn't 'work in a warehouse.' But it's pretty good money, even now. . . . The other girls and I get along pretty well, and we get coffee breaks morning and afternoon, so it goes quickly. Once in a while it gets real interesting, and sometimes it's just plain puzzling."

"What's so interesting?" Jasmine said, though she really wasn't that interested herself.

"The stuff that comes in from all over the world. Like, oh, well, for example, the asparagus that comes fresh in eleven-pound boxes from Peru. Or the avocados that come in from Chile. Or the banana puree from Ecuador that they package in fifteen-gallon cans. And there's coffee from, well, a lot of countries in South America and even Africa. Take Lesotho, for example."

Jasmine blinked. She thought she knew her geography, but that was a stumper. "Lesotho?"

"It's a little country, about the size of Maryland—I looked it up, you know. And it's right on the bottom of Africa. We get footwear and some clothing from Lesotho.

"It's fascinating, isn't it? . . ." and Jasmine nodded in agreement, ". . . especially the late summer when we start building up for the Christmas rush."

"What's the puzzling part?" Jasmine admitted to herself that she had misjudged this young woman.

"Well, we get a lot of tea to store, some from here and there and some from Argentina, for example, or chocolate from France. Every so often, the operations manager, that's Mr. Hansen, well, he reports so many bags of tea have been damaged, just a few, mind you."

"I would guess you would have some damage like that, wouldn't you?"

"Yes, but just the tea or the chocolate? And yet, when I leave at night, I usually walk through the warehouse to my car, and I've just never seen a damaged bag in the waste."

"Just coincidence?"

"Could be. But I've seen other damaged bags, boxes, cartons, you know. But not for tea and chocolate. It's puzzling, don't you think?"

"Do you girls talk about it?"

"Not really. The other girl, the truck dispatcher, well, she's a company person. I wouldn't even suggest . . . Kenny says, 'Don't even think about it.'"

"And he's probably right. Doesn't sound like much."

"Yeh, you're probably right. So what do you do?"

Jasmine, relieved that she could describe what she considered much more important, began outlining her work. After an introduction that ran about five minutes, she became embarrassed for acting superior and glanced at her watch. "Isn't it about time for our men to be here, or should we start walking over to where they said they'd be?"

"You have a very challenging and interesting job," Mira said admiringly as she rose from the bench. She had maintained her interest, even though Jasmine suspected she had overwhelmed her.

The two women began walking toward the cheetah cases. Mira commented, "Both the guys probably are too engrossed with the lions to watch the time, or maybe even little Keeyse—have I remembered her name?"

"You have. My compliments. It's not Polish." And they both laughed.

"Kenny is only half-Polish, and my folks had to swallow pretty hard when I brought him home."

"Wisniewski? Now, did I pronounce that right?"

"Oh yes, and it's very Polish, but his mother is Scotch," Mira chuckled. And they smiled as they continued walking and finally saw their men coming toward them, with a beaming Keeyse bouncing along, anxious to tell her mother-to-be of the animals she had seen.

After the zoo outing, the Reeds drove home and Sylvester checked his phone messages to find that he could wait until tomorrow to respond to the four that were important. They got through dinner with a tired-out Keeyse nodding off from time to time. She was bathed and put to bed, and Jasmine finally had a chance to speak to Sylvester.

He anticipated her. "I know you're just busting to tell me something."

"That's not fair. How can you tell?"

"I'm not that naive, you know. And we've been married, for how many years?"

"Oh, all right." And she recounted her conversation with Mira Wisniewski, and he took notes. "This could be something," was all he would say. "I won't laden you with my suspicions, but it could be something big."

The next morning he met with Captain Dan Russo and Lt. Stach Wisniewski. "What do you think, Stach?" Dan asked.

"Dan, I've talked often with Mira, and she's a smart young woman, and I don't think I'm prejudiced when I say she's on to something, and, let me stress, we don't want to get her in any way involved. It could be very risky even to let her know how dangerous her suspicions could be."

Sylvester: "I'd like to suggest we somehow get someone in there who . . ."

Dan: ". . . who knows what to look for? You're talking about an undercover agent. Tom Hampton was telling us at the latest briefing that he suspects there is a warehouse in this area storing and transshipping drugs. We'd need an undercover agent . . ."

Stach: ". . . one that we recruit."

Dan: "Right. Especially when Tom said afterwards that his briefing probably had a turncoat or two among the listeners."

Sylvester: "Someone from around here might be recognized."

Stach: "It's got to be someone from outside."

Dan: "You think Pittsburgh's far enough?" Both men smiled and nodded. Dan recounted how, when he drove up to Pittsburgh to follow up on the crash that Stach's brother-in-law had been involved in, he had run into an old Marine buddy from Vietnam by the name of Lee Shantz, a sergeant on the narcotics squad, and Dan thought he might just be able to recruit someone from that station's detective bureau.

As the three men talked on, they decided that they would request a young detective willing to apply for a job at the Central City Warehouse off Bulgar Street with fake credentials giving his experience as a college student who worked at a warehouse in the Pittsburgh area and had transferred to Baltimore to make money for courses he wanted to take at one of the community colleges here.

His undercover role would be to work hard enough to gain the operations manager's attention, to take note of any illegal activities, if he saw them, and to install a recording device in Hansen's office. He would in no way talk or even look at Mira Wisniewski, so she would not be endangered. Sylvester would be his contact.

The next day Dan phoned Lee Shantz in Pittsburgh and got an invitation to visit with him and his superiors. "Off hand," Shantz said, "and I'm talking off the cuff here, Dan, I think you'd really like this new kid. Gaston Leal's his name, and he's eager, just begging to get some real experience. Hell, he could pass as a high school senior."

"With a name like that, he could pass for a cartel bigwig."

"Stereotyping, officer. He's as clean as me, perhaps even you."

"Sorry, Lee. But we believe we have Colombians running the local operation. And . . ."

". . . Dan, Dan, Dan. Why do Irish cops do best in Irish neighborhoods, and Italian cops in Italian . . ."

"I got the message. But I'd really want to talk with him some, see whether he'd want to relocate for a while, you know. Is he married?"

"Nope. No kids either."

"I might have assumed that. Caring for aging parents? That kind of restraint?"

"Nothing I know of. Come on up. Candace and I would love to show you around. The last time you were here you were in and out in such a hurry. And my two sons-in-law are making good money, so we can dine handsomely."

"I'm on my way. It's Tuesday. How about I drive up next Monday—if the weekend's not too crazy—and meet with this Latino, Gaston Leal. OK with you?"

"Be good to see you. And remember it's pronounced LEE-al."

"Gotchya."

'Just making history'

Capt. Russo was able to get away that Monday, and drove his gray '90 Ford Taurus up to Pittsburgh, following I-70 out of Baltimore onto I-68 through northern Maryland, taking a shortcut on West Virginia State Highway 7 to I-79 north of Morgantown, and on to I-279 into Pittsburgh proper. Which was about the same distance as if he had taken I-70 to the Pennsylvania Turnpike, a.k.a. I-76, and driven on to Pittsburgh—which he did the last time—but this time he avoided all those costly tolls.

He drove to the police station at 1014 Sheffield Street to meet with Sgt. Shantz, Capt. Ronald Pulaski, who heads the station's detective bureau, and Detective Gaston Leal, who had joined the force three years ago.

"Doggone it, Dan, it is so damn good to see you again," Shantz said as he gave the smaller Russo a bear hug.

"And damn it, Lee, you don't have to smother me, you know. You'd think we were back in 'Nam."

"How did we survive those twenty-six days?"

"We were never point. It's just that simple."

"No, Dan. I caught it once or twice, but luckily didn't get wounded bad. You got point, too, if I remember right."

"Yeh, I guess I did a couple times, too."

Capt. Pulaski: "What action were you two in?"

Dan: "You remember reading about the Tet Offensive?"

Pulaski: "Yep."

"Well, Lee and I and a darn few other Marines battled a whole bunch of North Vietnamese, most of whom filtered into the city, and drove them out of Hue, one of the most beautiful cities in Nam. And, because it was so pretty, the brass decided that we had to fight without air support . . ."

Lee: " . . . or long-range artillery . . ."

Dan: ". . . or naval guns."

Pulaski: "The U.S. lost that Tet Offensive business, right?"

Lee: "Hell, no, Captain. First we tore down the flag they had flown over Hue, and then we drove them the hell out of the city, and they went limping back into North Vietnam from Hue and from every other city they hit . . ."

Pulaski: ". . . including Saigon?"

Dan: "Including Saigon."

Pulaski: "Then how come . . ."

Dan: "The media. Plain and simple. The damn TV and news services. They just turned Americans into peace-lovers, pacifists, and LBJ lost his backbone."

Lee: "We could have marched into Hanoi, if they had let us."

Dan: "Yeh. But that's history, Lee. We were just making history, and counting bodies. On both sides."

Lee: "Yeh. And I can still see you stumbling back around some damn wall of that damned Citadel, and B-40 shells whacking the columns, and you hitting the deck. I thought you were a goner. But you just got up, a little bloody, or a lot bloody, and crawled under cover. My eyes were open, but I was praying so dern hard that you'd make it, and you did. Made me a better Catholic, I'll tell you that."

"Ah, hell, Lee, you were a pretty good Catholic long before that."

"Maybe. But I became a lot better one . . . and still am. But, damn it all, I'm sorry; this here's Captain Pulaski."

"Ron will do," as they shook hands formally. "Good to meet you, Dan Russo, and to see that you don't look like Superman after all. That's what I was expecting built on what Lee was telling me."

"Yeh, he does have an imagination. But he means well."

Capt. Pulaski: "And here's the guy you came for, or, at least, I hope you take him. Detective Gaston Leal."

The young man stood up to shake hands with the visiting chief of detectives from Baltimore. "Good to see you, sir. Seems you might have a job for me."

"Great. Let's talk about it. Are you OK with our borrowing your man for a while, Captain?"

"He can use some seasoning, but you seem to have a need for him. And maybe we could call on your department in some type of exchange. Can you tell us what's up?"

"A little while ago, a woman who works at a particular warehouse in the southern industrial zone of Baltimore just happened to be talking with the wife of one of our detectives—you know how women go on sometimes—and she was saying how curious it was that so many bags of tea had somehow got damaged, apparently after they arrived. The operations manager was having her note down the damage almost every week. Just curious, she said. But no other particular item was damaged on such a regular basis, although there had been some chocolate flour in bags that were damaged, too.

"The DIA tells us that there's at least one warehouse in our area that receives and passes along cocaine. They don't know who or where, but that's what they insist. So we thought . . ."

"Why not someone from your own department?"

"All our people are from Baltimore or its immediate suburbs. They might be recognized."

"Why not someone from the DIA?"

"Good question. I'm a little distrusting, and a little unwilling to lose control to the feds. . . . That's not a good answer, I'll admit . . ."

"Hmmm. Someone from a closer bureau?"

"I knew a great contact, right here," pointing to Shantz.

"But not Lee?"

"Too old to want to start working in a warehouse. That's tough work, even for this old fart."

"Who's an old fart?" Shantz interjected, chuckling. "But I'll pass on shoving big boxes around."

"And he had suggested Leal?"

"Yes."

"An excellent choice. You game, Gaston?"

"I'd love the chance, sir."

Pulaski: "What's involved, Captain Russo?"

"Simply work at the warehouse, try to gain the confidence of the operations manager, and keep your eyes open. We might want you to plant phone mikes here and there."

Leal: "I've never worked in a warehouse before, but I'm ready. Contrary to Mexican-American stereotypes, I've never worked in a field picking anything, and I've never made or served a meal at a Mexican restaurant, although I've dined in quite a few."

"Me, too," Dan commented.

"My grandparents emigrated here—well they probably snuck in—fifty-five years ago or so. And they did sweat in the fields of California, but they moved east and kept moving east, working when and where they could until they reached Pittsburgh. By that time they had obtained their citizenship, and, yes, I'm a second-generation American, Mexican-American if you want."

"What's your schooling?"

"Catholic Central High School on Fifth Avenue, here in Pittsburgh, and an associate degree in criminal justice from Central Pennsylvania College."

"Where's that?"

"Harrisburg."

"Well, I'm impressed. His record here, Captain?"

"Excellent, to date. He could use a break from

hounding low-level drug pushers. He's temporarily assigned to you, Captain."

Russo: "Welcome aboard, detective, and good luck."

A community police officer

That night Dan stayed overnight with the Shantzes and went out to a meal at a fancy Italian restaurant, where Lee's son-in-law, Bob Franklin, was well known to the waiters. The next morning Dan toured the city in a police cruiser with Lee.

"I'll tell you one thing that just might interest you," Lee said.

Dan: "Probably not."

"Ha, ha. You know there are times when I really believe you."

"Hell, I'm serious all the time, Lee. But what's so new?"

"I got me a new job. I'm now a community police officer . . ."

"Uh-huh."

"Well, I walk the beat . . ."

"You consider that a promotion?"

"Knock it off, Sarge. Oh, golly, you're a captain now. Anyway, sir, as I walk the beat, I talk with the people who live or work there . . ."

"Talking should be right down your alley."

"You got it. And I try to figure out what's bothering people, and I even go to neighborhood meetings, to sort of promote a police presence, and perhaps come up with a department response."

"Actually sounds like a good idea, Lee. Any results, so far?"

"Not much, really, but the people seem to notice me, even smile, wave a hand, stop me with some news of this or that. I think it could help bridge the suspicion some folks have of cops, you know."

"I don't think we have anything like that in Baltimore, but we do have good guys on the beats, and they help. You have this community police officer business throughout the city?"

"Slowly growing."

"Suppose I give you a call six months from now, maybe even invite you down to compensate for the great reception here, and see whether we might want to do that."

"And meet again that pretty wife of yours, Dan. Why so long?"

"Don't want you cutting in, good buddy," and they both chuckled.

After the city tour, the two old friends had lunch at a favorite of Lee's, on his beat, where they were interrupted four times by folks coming up to talk with Lee. He drove Dan back to the house so he could pick up his car and return to Baltimore.

Jest us good ole boys

The drive back should have been as uneventful as the drive up. But it wasn't.

Dan cruised into West Virginia on I-79 and turned down Highway 7, again to I-68 eastbound. He dropped down to forty-five miles an hour on the secondary road, when a dump truck loaded with rock roared by and pulled back in the lane, coming up on a Volkswagen Bug that had begun to slow down to get onto the shoulder for some reason—perhaps the driver wanted to get out his cell phone or find a tree to relieve himself.

Evidently the truck driver was not paying attention. He finally clamped down on his brakes, but not soon enough. The truck slammed into the Volks, sending it crashing through the retaining posts and down a ravine.

The Volks rolled over twice and hit a sturdy oak, which compacted the car. Dan stopped his car and climbed down the ravine to find the driver heavily bleeding and struggling to breathe, and pulled out his cell phone and called 911.

"You have any idea how close we are to I-68?" he asked the truck driver, who had stopped his vehicle a ways down the two-lane road and walked back.

"'Bout a mile or so," the driver responded, speaking close enough to Dan that he caught the heavy breath of beer.

Dan completed the call, and within three minutes they heard the siren of a police cruiser coming down Highway 7. It pulled up across from the truck, and a patrolman, apparently from a nearby town, walked up and saw the wreckage below.

"Damn, Henry, you do that?" A second siren was heard, and an ambulance pulled up opposite the crash scene.

"Oh, hell, Buzz. That little bug just stopped all of a sudden, and I couldn't swing around him. Had no time, you know, with the big load, you know."

Dan interjected, in an aside to the patrolman, "That truck went by me well over the limit, and if you'll get near this guy, you'll find he reeks of beer."

"Who asked you?" the patrolman shot back. "You from 'round here? I'd always trust my town's councilman, not some interloper from . . ." glancing back at the license plates. "Isn't that a Baltimore plate?"

"Yes, it is, and . . ."

"Go easy on him, Buzz," said Henry. "The bug's also from Maryland. They're probably 'lations, or somethin."

"You some relation of the guy in the Bug?" the patrolman continued, as the two emergency personnel crossed over, a man and a woman. Dan shook his head in disgust.

"Lo, Henry. How's business?" said the ambulance driver.

"Pretty good, Stew."

"You bump into this wreck?"

"Yep. He stopped too fast in front of me. Couldn't help it."

"Dose things happen. What's the verdict, Jestsie?"

"He's a goner," the woman called up from the wreckage.

"You sure?"

"Yep. Better call the coroner."

The patrolman, whose nametag read Homer Grouts, commented, "Well, we can't do anythin' for him. I'll ring up a wrecker. See you later, Henry. Those things happen." And the group broke up, with Dan heading back to his car.

"Hey, you," said the patrolman. "You got a name?"

"Yes. It's Daniel Russo."

"Address?"

"1424 South Exeter Street, Baltimore."

"OK. Now don't give us any trouble, OK. This looks like a regular accident. That's how I see it."

Dan said nothing as he got into his Taurus, thinking, 'There's gonna be a letter to the State Police tomorrow, boob, asking them to check out this garbage.'

He drove off, and glanced into his rearview window to see the patrolman taking down Dan's license plate number.

The next morning Dan stopped by Stach's office to recount the incident. "Would a letter to the State Police accomplish anything, do you think?"

"The beer breath would be gone by the time they check him out, and the patrolman would deny your observations."

"Suppose I suggest to them that they put this Henry guy—I don't know his last name—under surveillance? I could identify him as a dump truck driver who apparently has some office in a town near the accident site."

"Now that sounds like a better idea. They might also put a little fear into that patrolman."

About a month later, Dan got a short note from Captain William S. Baldwin of the West Virginia State Police:
Attention: Captain Russo,

Trucker Henry Prentice was pulled over two weeks ago on Interstate 79 just south of the Pennsylvania line for driving dangerously. He was examined by Trooper Robert McKenzie and failed several sobriety tests. He was arrested and charged with driving under the influence. Blood tests showed he was well over the legal limit in West Virginia.

He posted bail after he dried out; his trial will be in three weeks.

As a fellow lawman, I appreciate your tip. We have taken a very dangerous man off the highways, and intend to keep him off, if he doesn't sober up.

I talked with the town police chief whose deputy messed up, and the deputy has been dismissed. Hopefully, he'll find another job, and not in law enforcement.

I'm embarrassed that we had such an incident happen in West Virginia. Thank you, again, for your letter.

Some weeks later, Dan and Stach met at the Captain James Restaurant on Aliceanna Street for dinner with their wives. Stach got there about 7:00, Dan at 7:15. Both Stephanie and Tina worked, Stephanie at the hardware store and Tina at Biomedics Laboratory, where she was researching the synthesis of two agents believed capable of relieving pressure behind the eyes of people with head injuries.

Dan: "It's never easy talking with the feds. Frankly, they regard us as small potatoes. Anyway, Tom Hampton did admit that they suspect there are truck runs into and out of many cities like Baltimore carrying drugs. Some of this comes in containers loaded and sealed overseas."

"Is I-95 a regular drug conduit?"

"Yep, I'm pretty sure of that."

Just then, Tina and Stephanie arrived, and Tina, overhearing Dan's last remarks, expressed her reluctance for them to go outside federal agencies.

Stephanie: "What's with Sorensen, the deputy mayor?"

Dan: "He's over with Customs now. Which makes Stach and I suspect even more that some locally run trucking firm or shipping firm or importer is involved in running drugs."

Stach: "Kenny already drives for an inter-modal trucking firm, and now he's going to make some runs to port cities in the south. We actually got Rossler himself to add Kenny to his roster of drivers."

Tina: "How? He's got to have it in for you two."

Dan: "He married a very smart woman, and now she's really running the trucking firm, and he takes her advice. Her name is Janice Behrs."

"Your former wife?"

"None other. But I don't think he knows that."

Stephanie: "Didn't you have a girl?"

"She's twenty now, but Jan was so mad at me she changed Patsy's last name to Behrs a long time ago. Jan's also become very Jewish now, getting Rossler to contribute mucho dollars to one of those big temples in northwest Baltimore."

"St. Casmer's could use some help."

"So could St. Leo's."

St. Casimir's, called St. Casmer's by most everyone, was built in 1926 in a Renaissance style at South Kenwood Avenue and Hudson Street in Canton, only a couple blocks from where the Wisniewski clan settled. The church is 225 feet long, 70 feet wide and seats 1,450. In one of the two 110-foot-tall towers is the statue of St. Francis of Assisi, and in the other, a statue of St. Anthony of Padua, whom the members of St. Leo's the Great parish in Little Italy honor with a festival each year.

Construction of St. Leo's, named for a fifth-century pope, started in 1881 as a German parish, and it seats about 400. With its recreation hall and parish hall, St. Leo's, at Stiles and Exeter, is known as "the heart of Little Italy."

Part of the fallout from the drug-running case in the vicinity of Memorial Stadium in 1976 was the coming together of Jan and Rex Rossler. He had dumped his first wife after a Hawaiian vacation when he became tired of her. They had had no kids—her choice—and he had not pushed the matter.

The second, a trophy wife, was an airline stewardess he kept meeting on flights from BWI to St. Louis to see his ailing mother. But the flight attendant was overwhelmed by his associates. She was the center of attraction, of course, but she had nothing to say, nothing to contribute except a very sexy smile. She was a great bed partner, an embarrassment otherwise. Rex ditched her and cooled his heels.

At forty-three, he was having trouble keeping his weight down—it wanted to bulge around his middle—and needed someone to talk with, to argue with, to discuss the issues of the day, like Israel, the Palestinians, the presidency, the Democrats' hopes in the next election. He found that his chief aide, Jan Behrs, was precisely the one he needed, and he was delighted to learn that she had returned to the faith of her father, Judaism, specifically maturing Judaism.

Jan, mindful of all her conversations with her Aunt Rosie—who had given up on men when her only love dumped her—had passed up several anxious young men after Dan, for they were too interested in her body and not her mind. Patsy, her daughter by Dan, was growing up, with Jan's mother watching her after school, but Jan did want some company, and Rex Rossler's attentions seemed to be very appealing to her.

She took off two weeks to think about his apparent courting and found that she really missed him. And he found that he was hampered without her counsel. When she returned, he was at her desk by 9:15 a.m. asking her to join him for lunch at a nearby restaurant popular with truckers, and there he proposed, and she accepted him, and he presented her a two-carat solitaire in a platinum mounting and chain, along with a four-carat—total weight—platinum diamond bracelet. A jeweler at the Behrs-Rossler wedding, quizzed by his envious wife as they danced by, estimated that the set cost $30,000 to $35,000.

The wedding took place at a temple in northwest Baltimore, and her family, former coworkers from Sinai Hospital, and a couple other friends attended. Her mother came with Patsy, and there were nurses from the hospital where Jan had been a floor supervisor. Rossler had about fifteen to twenty business associates present. The reception followed in the heavily decorated gymnasium. And the noise and intellectual conversation were at deafening levels, as everyone crowded into everyone else and had to out-shout each other to be heard. Toasts were said, songs were sung, and dances were danced with more fervor than talent, and everyone had a joyous time.

Rex and Jan went off to Israel for three weeks, his fourth visit, her first, and they took along Patsy, showing her some of his favorite stops—the Western Wall, the Temple Mount, old and West Jerusalem, and, with Israeli soldiers guarding their party, Hebron, where they were cursed in Arabic by some Muslim women going in to pray.

The Rosslers also stopped at three kibbutzim, and Patsy, then twelve, was bitten by the kibbutz spirit. She would return four times to work at different kubbutzim on archaeological and defense projects.

'It's Judd.'

Inter-modal trucker William C. "Judd" Schmidt knocked twice and twice again on the door of the private entrance to the office of Felipe Sanchez on the fourteenth floor of the World Trade Center. Sanchez rose from his desk. He was a swarthy, nattily dressed forty-five- to fifty-year-old mustached man, wearing a light gray suit, a pastel grayish tie that matched, and a thin, solid gold cross that hung from his neck. His fingers were well manicured, his deodorant piney.

He stopped alongside the door, not directly in front of it. "Yes?"

Schmidt: "It's Judd."

Sanchez, as he opened the door and extended his hand: "You're early, Judd. Any reason for that?"

"Nope, jest early."

Sanchez, distracted by his phone flashing, returned to his desk and picked up the phone: "Send him right in." He hung up. "Sorensen. He'll have the right numbers for you." He got up to answer the door and shook hands with the former deputy mayor, Patrick Sorensen, crowding fifty, a thin, eager individual one might guess sold life insurance, dressed in a dark red sport jacket, light tan trousers, his off-red shirt opened at the throat.

"Good morning," Sanchez said. "You know Judd Schmidt." They acknowledged each other with slight nods. Sorensen did not like the trucker; Schmidt disliked most people.

Sorensen: "The container you will want on your return is AAY14600B2T. Here's a printout of its cargo. The carnet shows sugars, syrup products, honey, spices and leather."

Schmidt: "And sometin' not on a list?"

Sanchez: "Of course. There's about ten kilos shielded and buried in some leather rolls, according to my information."

He passed along the paperwork to Schmidt, who commented: "That's a hell of a lot of cocaine in one package."

Sorensen: "And that's one thing you do not have to worry about," staring down Schmidt. "No one ever checks, except the shippers, who are real fussy about the outsides of the containers, so that there's no damage to the cargo. Can you believe that?"

Getting no response, Sorensen continued, "I like it when they overload these containers down in San Paulo or wherever in Brazil, and the trucker comes back to the terminal here to unload a couple thousand pounds or so because he's overweight."

Schmidt: "What happen den?"

"Your boss asks me to go over and supervise what has to come off, and we place that on the side for separate delivery."

Sanchez: "Can you guess, Judd, what comes off? And who delivers it?"

"No shi'. But I don' think you'd want a do dagh too often . . ."

Sanchez: "No, I ring up the boys in San Paulo and chew ass. Then they'll overload a few clean containers before they come back to ours."

Schmidt, as he shuffled through the paperwork from Sorensen: "I'll be gettin' mos' a this from Rossler when I gegh to his office this afternoon. He'll have it from 'spatcher. He alway like to talk to the long-haul drivers. Give him a trill or a reason for being boss."

Sorensen: "Regular idiot. But he did marry well."

Sanchez: "She runs the company, and damn well. It's a great cover for us."

Schmidt: "I gaugh no complain', neither, long's she don' get too nosy about what's in dem c'tainers."

Sorensen, showing more interest than before: "You ever worry about being stopped?"

"Yeh, for lights or some shi' like tha', by the troopers who run I-95, but dem never open a box, jest check a seal."

Sorensen to Sanchez: "You know our Customs people check only 2 percent or less of those containers."

Sanchez: "Yeh, most people know that. And you're in a position to steer them away from our containers, right?"

Sorensen: "Hell, no need to. There's only a one-in-fifty chance. But yes, I do from time to time steer them to containers that are other folkses', or once in a while I'll actually suggest one of ours. . ." Sanchez, shocked, was about to comment. ". . . one of our clean ones. You have them, you know."

Sanchez smiled: "I would hope so. I have to pretend

this is a going business. But those are the ones that don't make much money for the firm, you know. Is there any criteria for searching the containers?"

Sorensen: "You'd assume port of origin, wouldn't you? And Cartagena (Colombia) would be a likely suspect, you'd say? And you might be right. We never disclose our reasons. But if you're right, I simply schedule a couple of your clean ones out of Cartagena to be inspected, and that establishes a clean pattern that legitimately puts off further inspections for a while."

Sanchez: "Makes sense."

Schmidt, breaking in: "It's hell on us drivers when you hold one of dem c'tainers, you know."

Sorensen, disdainfully: "How so?"

"Just tell 'im the 'cedure, dat's all."

Sorensen, turning to Sanchez: "Simple enough. When a particular container is picked by Customs, they move it to one of our docks and break the seal, unload it completely, search everything, document everything, reload the container and reseal it. We had a container, here from Italy, I believe, filled with chemicals we decided to check last month."

"How long da' take?"

"I think it was a week or more, if I remember rightly."

"And you guys did tha' to one of my c'tainers down in Charleston, and I had to kill two days 'fore I got another c'tainer to pull. Then I had to go back fer tha' one."

"Oh well," Sorensen commented, clearly indicating he could care less by turning to Sanchez and ignoring Schmidt, whose face began reddening and his eyes seemed to burn into Sorensen. "You know, it's kind of amazing in a way. They tell me that there used to be a lot of theft from the break-bulk cargos, but now the gangs are making off with the containers themselves. Somehow these gangs seem to buy off employees at the terminals or on the docks. It's so un-American, it is," and he and Sanchez smiled.

Schmidt was near exploding, but he tensed up and looked away. He thought how easily a couple well-placed daggers could carve up that overstuffed turkey. He clenched his teeth and rolled tightly the papers in his hands and said to himself, 'Dere's no sense killing the golden goose. Nough ye', bu' soon. Your day's comin' real soon.'

Sanchez, unaware that his driver was near going after Sorensen, said conversationally to the Customs official, "As long as we honest shippers keep talking about the need for swift delivery of all our perishable goods, Customs won't increase its checks."

Sorensen: "Oh, we're very sensitive to business as usual, very. It's the American way." He and Sanchez smiled. "I better get along. Can't give too much time to only one shipper."

"Even though his totals are way more than all the rest combined?"

"Especially because of that." But he shifted his eyes upward and toward Schmidt in such a manner that only Sanchez saw the move. And he picked up the cue.

"Hold on a minute. Judd, are you all set?"

Schmidt, glad to be away from these two, grunted and left through the door he had entered, without acknowledging Sorensen.

Sanchez, waiting until the door closed: "What's up?"

Sorensen: "There are no kilos on Schmidt's trailer. In fact, they're planting the first dirty one. And I got to confess that even you weren't supposed to know that."

"Oh, shit. Why not?"

"What difference does it make, all right? Now you know. I cover my friends."

"More like you need me."

"That, too." A pause as both men took stock of their changed situation, with Sorensen even more in control than before, but Sanchez with a valuable asset he didn't know yet. "This container will be brought right into the city, according to the paperwork that Vietnam-screwed-up Schmidt has. Incidentally, he's going to have an accident in a couple weeks or so after he gets back from this latest run. A fatal one. I won't tell you how, sort of saving up the surprise."

Sanchez was shocked: "He's been a good driver for me." Sanchez wasn't prepared to confess that his daughter, Alina, had run away with Schmidt nine years ago and their liaison, never made official in church or court, had led to Sanchez's three granddaughters. Sanchez brought Schmidt on board for extra income through the drug runs and was more than satisfied with the results.

"I've had him make special runs up to New York and over to Philly, and Pittsburgh, picking up or dropping off heroin," he said now to Sorensen. But Sanchez's training in Colombia had prepared him to take orders from the cartel, no matter what or who. "I'll really miss him." He said no more, not wanting to endanger his daughter or granddaughters by letting Sorensen suspect his concern.

"On the original bill of lading that I have here," Sorensen tapped an envelop in his sports coat pocket, "it's supposed to be delivered to your firm, parked at the back of your reserved lot over on Eastern Avenue, and just vegetate there until it's needed, so this means you won't be opening that cargo for some time, if ever." He paused. "They didn't give me any definite date. But it's likely some time off. I don't think they'd send these in all at one time. And I don't know how many places they have people in such critically important positions as you and me . . ."

"I'm not sure why you need me. You could just dump on me."

"When the time comes, I don't want to be in Baltimore, or even the Eastern Seaboard . . ."

"Holy shit. That wide an area?"

"Could be. I have no idea. In any case, you have a safe home to go to in Colombia, and we wouldn't want to miss seeing the TV reports, even if they're in Spanish. We'll be alive, and we'll have a great party. ?*Comprendes, amigo?*"

"*Si, el jefe.*" (Yes, boss)

Growing up in the barrios

Felipe Sanchez grew up in the barrios of Cartagena, Colombia, a child who aged quickly on the street, after his father, a lottery-ticket seller, was shot to death. He wouldn't allow his wife to be taken away from him by a lieutenant in the cartel. She was then raped by several cartel bodyguards and dumped off at a brothel.

At age six, Felipe was peddling marijuana for a minor dealer in the old quarter of the port city, and at ten he was helping mix coca powder with anything white, like chalk, that would extend the cocaine without changing its color or texture.

At age sixteen Felipe became a driver, moving cocaine from field to jungle laboratory.

Not long after, his British-style English having been modified into American by highly paid tutors, he was assigned by the Cali-type cartel to work in the United States—in his case, Baltimore—to handle and disperse the firm's main product, cocaine.

He dressed conservatively, even hanging a solid gold cross about his neck. He attended mass faithfully with his family at a Catholic church in the suburbs.

The workers in his office—three of them—were stalwart Americans, two white, one black, and their boss met all the U.S. and Maryland laws in their employment. Sanchez had been in the United States enough years to apply for and gain citizenship.

Incidentally he never used drugs himself, for he had too much going to blow it all, and drank a beer or wine only occasionally. He worked out each day in a neighborhood spa and maintained a 160-pound, lithe weight. He had the tan that went along with the body naturally.

He relished being rich, although he kept most of his earnings off shore, and his wife and two daughters never knew of that hidden wealth. His wife, Alina, had come from Cuba in one of the little boats that somehow made it to Florida.

The Sanchez family lived well, the rest of his family assuming that the income was from his importing business, and almost half of it actually was—he was a good retail operator. The cartel knew all about his family, even the relationship between Alina and Judd Schmidt, and the schools their girls—Sanchez's granddaughters—attended, so his loyalty was assured.

An opportunist

Patrick Sorensen was an opportunist, a lawyer with degrees from the University of Maryland and Virginia law school, who had gone south on legal ethics. He grew up north of Patterson Park in Baltimore, attended Patterson Park High School, and, in his senior year, volunteered to help the Democratic ward leaders get out the vote.

He was enthusiastic, persuasive and successful, increasing by 35 percent the turnout in the ward, with the result that some not-so-talented candidates were swept in with the good men and women. Sorensen's efforts were noted, and he got recommendations and placement in law school, thanks in part to fiercely Democratic alumni.

He came out still a very enthusiastic liberal, but owing fidelity to the alumni who had helped him. One was Jeffrey

Arbotnut, who ran a construction company employing nearly 100 men. He could hustle business, but he needed someone to keep everything legal. New attorney Sorensen showed he could do the job, and even fiddle a little with the paperwork and—with considerable money on the side—schmooze the right bureaucrats to acquire contracts from the city and the surrounding counties.

With a lot of influential people—office holders, contractors and ward leaders—in his debt, Sorensen decided to run for deputy mayor and was elected. But when he considered reelection, a *Sun* reporter began asking too many questions about Sorensen's pressures, and he decided to forego the reelection race and, through well-cultivated influence, transferred to the Customs Bureau, where with considerable outside pressures he climbed quickly to the number-two position. He is fifty-three, pudgy and not in good shape; nor does he care. He smokes, drinks and parties. He and his wife, Doreen, have no children, but she from time to time had suggested they adopt, and he responded with little or no enthusiasm, killing the idea.

On his rise to wealth and position, Sorensen ran into Felipe Sanchez, an up-and-coming importer, and they in quick time formed a partnership. Sanchez wanted the local connections to develop his legal importing business as a front for his drug running. Sorensen became the legal adviser for both the over- and under-the-counter operations. Incidentally, he wore a small gold cross in his coat lapel, supposedly as an active Catholic layman, but he rarely got to mass after his service as deputy mayor ended.

In the beginning, Sanchez called all the shots; he had the connections in Colombia and the debts owed him from his earlier days. But Sorensen met some visiting cartel officials and, somehow, no doubt taking full advantage of his ability to schmooze, was now regarded by them as number one in the Baltimore operation.

Judd and his 'Jeepster'

Judd Schmidt is a big man, six feet tall, weighing 225 pounds. He is forty-two years old, but is growing old fast. He loves to drive—it's a power thing—and he prizes being on the road, to see what is over the horizon. He has driven more than two million miles in his twenty-eight years on the road, without any serious accidents.

He grew up in Millbrook, a little town north of Montgomery, Alabama, not far off Interstate 65, and got through two years of high school before he gave up and started working in a garage full time. He idolized his father, an over-the-road trucker who was a dictator the couple days of the month when he was home, tormenting his wife and his four children.

Judd, the oldest of those children, enlisted into the Army on his eighteenth birthday, happy to get out of his father's hair yet following his father's example of serving his country. The father had been an infantryman in World War II. Judd accepted the discipline he got in the Army and welcomed the chance to fire something more lethal than the twelve-gauge shotgun his father owned. The year was 1968, and Judd was the drill sergeant's dream among a platoon of 90 percent draftees, of whom 30 percent were blacks, whom Judd hated with a passion.

He was a corporal when they shipped out to Vietnam and a sergeant within three months, taking credit in a little notepad he kept in his front pocket of seventeen kills in that period. He loved to kill gooks, he would tell the new recruits, whom he called twinks.

His squad hated him for willingly taking them into harm's way, even to double-check the body-count estimates. His squad was among the best in the company on body counts, and concomitantly its casualties were among the highest.

Schmidt loved the service, loved the fighting, and reupped for a second tour, even back to Vietnam. And he survived Vietnam, his razor-edged temper inherited from his father ready to lash out at the smallest challenge.

He gathered several combat medals, and might have earned a highly respected one for spraying 600 rounds a minute from a lightweight M60E3 machine gun over a company of NVA (North Vietnamese Army), killing at least thirty-two of them and wounding others, according to a subsequent body count, but as he swung the machine gun around, his appetite for killing at its highest, he also wiped out a green U.S. lieutenant who was leading a platoon into action. An investigation suggested that Schmidt might have intentionally done in the lieutenant, who was generally hated by the company, but Schmidt's record of kills outweighed the evidence. The lieutenant was given a minor medal posthumously.

Schmidt returned to "The World" without a desperate need for booze or drugs nor overcome by nightmares and flashbacks. But question him on what the purpose of the Vietnam War was and prepare for a lecture laced with curse words on how the war could have and should have been won, and a beating, if he felt it necessary.

When he got back to Alabama, his father and his hometown showed pride in his stripes and medals, and his father helped him put down a deposit on a black '68 Mack tractor. Judd proudly put his dog tags over his rearview mirror, and his medals soldered onto the dash.

Over the years Judd's temper has cooled somewhat. Yet it can flare up in a flash. But he doesn't challenge other drivers any more when Vietnam is discussed, for it rarely is, unless he brings it up, and few want to argue with him.

Still, it's been a hard life on the road, and he doesn't live well, even though he used to hunt some—he still wears his hunting boots—but he was getting too winded and had to give up hunting. He smokes heavily—Pall Malls; he doesn't eat well—way too much fat; and his stomach is beginning to bother him, despite the vastly improved air suspension cushioning his latest tractor, a 1986 Peterbilt with a 359 extended hood and a 425-horsepower Caterpillar diesel, a 13-speed transmission and twin-stacked.

On his doors, signs identify the tractor as "Judd's Jeepster." Those who ask find out that in all his time in Vietnam—not all in hunt-and-kill-and-count operations—he never rode in a Jeep, not even in Saigon, where his unit went in and out by truck. But he survived a number of terrifying helicopter rides.

He doesn't drink on or off the road, and doesn't dare, for he could be canned as a driver if the troopers found even a sealed bottle in his cab. A trucker can't even have alcohol-based cough syrup along, no matter how bad a cold he might have. But in his earlier years when he was pushing the limits—driving nearly ninety hours a week to pay off his truck—Judd used plenty of amphetamines to stay awake.

He tells new drivers at truck stops how he left Needles, California, right near the border with Arizona at 6 p.m. on a Friday and made it to Johnson, Pennsylvania, in thirty-two hours with no sleep. "Was it legal?" he says, and answers, "No way."

He continues telling the new men: "Running the road, you didn't get much sleep. And I don't care if you're a company driver or an owner-operator like me. Because at some places where you're picking up a container, they end up holding you there for six, seven hours, or they keep telling you to move here, move there. The next thing you know, you gaugh to be 1500 miles away to make the appointmen', an' if you don' make i' on time, you end up sittin' a longer time there."

Judd hates lawmen, local, state, whatever, mostly

because of an incident in his youth in suburban Montgomery when he was "taught a lesson" by a baton-wielding sheriff appropriately named Bubba for barreling through a residential street in the better part of town in a pickup Judd had "borrowed" at a shopping plaza.

Judd is heavily in debt on his relatively new Peterbilt, his third truck, but he's an independent owner-operator, and that's worth the debt that he's been able to meet all his years. Also, he's driving short-haul most of the time, meaning he doesn't have to cover all the tolls and fuel and wear on his tractor on long hauls. This run to Savannah and back is not his choice, nor was the assignment of the "kid" to travel along with him.

On the other hand, thanks to the drug runs that none of his trucker friends, associates or his woman or kids know about, Schmidt has built a substantial capital fund in an off-shore bank on an island to which he intends retiring pretty soon, with Alina and their three children, especially since Judd suspects that Sorensen hates him. Judd has been faithful to Alina, even though truckers who are on the road so much have exceptionally high divorce rates.

He's clearing $35,000 a year now—not including all that money on the side—but much of the $35,000 that he pays taxes on is going to retire his debts.

In his cab he carries his sleeping bag, CD rack, AM-FM radio, cassette tapes, Cokes for the caffeine, and cartons of Pall Malls, always having a pack in his pocket and another open and handy so he won't have to divert his attention to driving by opening it.

Ole Jim Poole

After his meeting with Sanchez and Sorensen, Schmidt drove his Peterbilt over to the diner at the Baltimore Port Truck Plaza at I-95's exit 57. A number of tractors were parked about. He savored the heady taste of cigarette smoke as he entered the restaurant, and, through the haze, looked about to see who was there. He gave small hand waves to some drivers, and relaxed his usual frown when he spotted Jim Poole, "Ole Jim," sitting at a table with a husky young man.

Schmidt walked over, pretending to give Alice, the waitress, a pat on her behind, which caused a few men nearby to chuckle and Alice to spin about. "Wha're you ep to, you . . . Oh, it's jest you, hon. . . . Well, you should knaugh bettern t'others."

"I do, Alice, I sure'n hell do," Schmidt returned, without smiling, and eased into a chair next to Poole. "How're you doin', good buddy?"

"Judd, Judd," slapping him on the back. "Alway good to see you, old man." He coughed. "Dis here's Kenny Wisniewski—didna I git tha' rite?—a new man wid a new bobtail for him, who's goin' on his first long trip 'morrow, and it's to Savanny, too. How 'bout tha'?" He coughed again.

"What say we 'low him to tag 'long? He got a rig that's new for 'im—he just startin' the payments . . ." he coughed, ". . . and he'll be runnin' a whole lo' harder than I 'ver did."

It wasn't unusual for drivers to meet at truck stops and drive together; there was no particular advantage, except that the drivers who do can keep each other's company talking back and forth on their CBs.

Schmidt: "Sure, Ole Jim. Boss Rossler told me someone new migh' be wantin' to go to Savanny, and I was sor' of supos' to watch over 'im." He reached over to shake hands with Kenny. "You want to get to Savanny? Righ' down I-95. Can't miss i'."

Kenny, puzzled by that comment: "Yes, sir."

"And it's a pretty ride, ain't it, Jim."

"Sure is, Judd."

Kenny: "Sounds great, sir."

"Kid, i' sounds to me, and i' looks to me, tha' you're militry, or were."

"Yes, sir. Marines, sir."

"Ain' tha' cute as shi', Judd?" Poole said, coughing several times.

Schmidt, waiting for Poole to breathe easier: "Army, m'sel', in Nam in '67 and '68, and then back again in '71. Seen a lota guys killed, 'n dey was the lucky ones, 'pared to those who goaugh home withou' a leg or arm or both, an' no eyesigh'. I don' know if I was damn lucky or naugh to ge' outta 'der alive."

"I was in Grenada, but that was a piece of cake compared to 'Nam."

"No shi', kid. Recess for kindegarters. I wouldn' c'nsider tha' anythin'. You migh' call i' a ligh' poleece action, or somethin'. Yeh, they took i' over. An they gaugh the 'mericans ou' and so forth. Dere's nothin' really dere to say i' was a war or somethin', jus' a sor' of a missmatched police action. Baby Marine. No singin' 'Hey, Blue' 'der."

Poole explained, "Tha's when one of the guys Judd served with bough' it, kid."

Judd: "Did you even see any one of your guys ge' blown apar' into little bitty pieces." Kenny shook his head. "Nah. You couldn'. You had to be in Nam. But tha' ge's to ya, kid. All the same, you know, Nam was fun, I'll tell yer, 'specially killin' those gooks."

Poole to Wisniewski: "You ough' to hear Judd tell about the 120 or so 'Gooks' he killed, along wit' some dumb green lieutenant.'"

Schmidt, quietly after looking at the nearest table: "The gooks deserved i', and so did tha' stupid 'tenan'."

Poole: "Tell the kid 'bou' the good time you guys had in Saigon."

Schmidt: "Oh yeh. It's a winner."

A Marine sniper

"Anyways, we was in 'dere for a little relaxin' and we had a Marine sniper along wid us, who had a hundred or more kills. We was stayin' on the third floor of a hotel and he gets out his sniper rifle and puts his feet out the window, and BOOM," a comment that caught the attention of four tables around them that Schmidt ignored, ". . . he had blowed a wire or somethin', and he laughed and laughed, an' sparks was flying all over.

"BOOM! Another bunch of sparks would fly. And he fires off 'bou' six or eight times, and then he says, 'Oh, I see somethin,' and he sho' the transformer off AF'nN. An', all of a sudden, the radio goes off. The Armed Forces Network wen' off the air. And the sniper says, 'It's time to go,' and we hauled butt out of dere."

Schmidt, savoring the impact he had on this new man, turned to Kenny, "So, kid Marine, you wan' to drive to Savanny and back. Will your fron' tires blow on the way, specially that lef' un, and you go barreling across the meeDEEon plumb into a minivan full of kids headin' north? Or will somethin' drop off a bridge righ' through your windshield—good bye, kid Marine. Or maybe you lose it goin' down a pretta good hill and your brakes catch fire, or maybe you jus' lose control, and no steerin' can save ya? So you wan' to drive to Savanny?" and he looked with pure disgust at Kenny.

"Yes, sir, I'm game," Kenny answered.

"Bu' the one thing you really gaugh to worry abou', kid Marine, is when you cross bridges." Ole Jim smiled, and Kenny caught that out of the corner of his eye. "Yep, when you're following either me or Jim here, you jest' watch whether my truck or his sways from side to side as i' crosses a bridge, for if i' does, and you're jus' too close, well, you'll never brake fas' 'nough', nosiree."

Wisniewski played along: "So what do I do then, Judd?"

Poole tried desperately not to laugh, but couldn't: "Kid, he's just shittin' you. You listen to Judd, you probly drive off tha' damn bridge into the river." He coughed four or five times. "Judd just likes to scare da rookies."

Kenny, in a comment that won over both veteran drivers: "Hell, Mr. Schmidt would have me leaning out the window watching the left front tire with one eye, the other watching him sway across some damn bridge, and one hand steering and the other up to catch whatever falls off the first overpass we come to."

Both veteran drivers laughed, the first Judd had in weeks.

Wisniewski waited for a minute or so for Poole to stop coughing: "I haven't driven like you guys, just short hauls back and forth to Pennsylvania and Wilmington mostly, but what bothers me most is that people driving cars just can't figure out that we go by momentum, not speed . . ." both men lifted their eyes to the ceiling at the revelation ". . . and we might go eighty down a hill and sixty up a hill when the limit's seventy, you know, and then I got this one guy who just boxed me off when I was trying to go around a slower truck on a hill, and . . . " he paused as he saw both men smiling. ". . . and the motorists like to swing out around you, cut you off and give you the finger."

Judd and Jim together: "Ben dere, son. Ben dere."

Schmidt: "You le' tha' stuff go. You don' keep track of i'."

Poole: "You'll likely never see 'em again."

Alice came by the table, asking Schmidt, "So, what'r you having, hon, just coffee, or what?"

Poole and Kenny had coffees and the remains of fresh biscuits in front of them. "The same as this vetran driver, here," motioning to Wisniewski.

Alice smiled at him as she walked away.

Kenny: "You been with Rex Rossler Lines for a while, sir?"

"Yep, ten year or so. Well, a same firm, same warehouse, bu' unner a differn name and boss man, well, now, a boss woman."

Poole: "Damn good one, too, 'cordin' to Judd."

"Yeh, you're righ'."

Kenny: "I've been driving short hauls, drop and hook, drop and hook, drop and hook, over to Philadelphia, Wilmington, and back. I guess you guys on long hauls drive truck stops to truck stops?"

Judd: "You live by the truck stops, kid." He had dropped the 'kid Marine' moniker. In fact, over-the-road truckers might spend up to eight hours a day at truck stops. "They gaugh' everthin' you need. Righ', ole Jim?"

Poole pursed his lips as he nodded: "You righ' der, Judd. We probly stop ah 'em three times a day."

"Yeh, they gaugh' diesel, food, smokes, ligh' bulbs, talkin' books, showers, Cokes, somewhere to sleep, hell, everthin' a trucker would need."

"Are they all pretty much the same, or do you have a favorite?"

"Deys all the same," Schmidt said.

"Yeh, I gaugh' one, tha' damn city by itsel' out in the Mid-wes', maybe Iowa, yeh near Illnoise." Poole hacked a couple timcs. "Tha's the bigges I know of. Dey gaugh' cobblers big as a cow dump," as he demonstrated with his hands.

Kenny: "This trip to Savannah will be the longest I've been on. Judd, have you had longer hauls?"

3200 to 3300 miles a week

"Yep. I was driving a company truck that time, a Freightliner, a mid-roof with a reefer unit (refrigerator). I had to pick up a container in Richmond, Virginia, and drive it to Irving, California. That's in Southern Calfornia, and I had to pick up a load of carrots, carrots or tomatoes, down by the border, and I had to run up to the market in New Jersey. Then I picked up in Newark and drove down to Jacksonville, Florida, to drop off. And then I ran back up to Altoona, Pennsylvany."

"Maybe 5,000 miles?" Kenny suggested.

"Maybe more, like 7,000 plus," Judd corrected.

"Usually driving my own truck, that '86 Peterbilt you see out there, I would run 3200 to 3300 miles a week on average, and then shut down for a couple days. But I'd eventually get home for a weekend, and head back on the road again Sunday around 5 or 6 p.m."

"I hope to do some long runs like that one day," said Kenny, glancing at his watch and adding, "Well, I better get going. My wife wants me to have dinner with her. See you in the morning."

The schedule for Savannah

Schmidt, quickly raising his hands to stop him: "Hold i', kid. In our world, 'der is no day, in terms of hours, kid Marine—like mornin', afternoon, nigh', so on. If you're goin' with us, and I don' care one way or t'other, but the boss wants me to wasth over you, I figure I'm gonna pick up my c'tainer at Dundalk about 4:30 p.m. today for this 600-odd-mile run to Savanny, den drive over to the truck stop in Jestsup for a nap, two, three hour or so, and den drive for five hour down to the truck stop jus' over the line in Nor' Caroliny—tha' way we miss the heavies' traffic

143

around D n C.—den have breakfis', and res' for about two hour, drive another five hour to lunch a' someplace probly in Sough Caroliny, maybe shower and sleep for six hour, den drive on for another four or five hour, when we should be at the Por' of Savanny."

"I thought we had to have an eight-hour break after every ten hours," Kenny said. "Mostly, delivering to Philly and Wilmington, I'd drive only eight to ten hours, back and forth a time or two or three, you know, no problem."

"Now, you listen, kid. Judd knaughs the rules . . . " Poole coughed and almost choked, ". . . real gough."

Schmidt: "You see, kid, from a logbook standin', a person jus' has to pu' eigh' hours in between those tens, bu' they legh you break i' up into as little as two-hour breaks. A guy like me can drive five hours, take off four, drive five, take off four, and drive five more, or fifteen hours or more out of twenty-three. A guy who leaves at 5 p.m. can be there the nex' afternoon legal. You can drive like tha' until you mee' the seventy-hour max a week. And the c'tainers don't mind one way or t'other."

"Well, thanks a lot, Judd," Kenny said, a little anxious to see Mira and get turned around. "I park my tractor here, so I'll see you at 4:30 over at the Dundalk terminal." Kenny couldn't park his tractor outside the row house on South Kenwood where he lived with his folks.

Schmidt: "You buy your fuel 'ere, too?"

"Yes, sir, a trade-off for the parking space. I got a parking permit in my window, too."

"And you'll wan' to star' stopping occasionally in other states," but Kenny was already up and gone. To Poole: "You sure tha' kid's old 'nough for a C'nDL (commercial driver's license)"?

Poole: "He's gotta be twenty-two, -three, -four, Judd."

Schmidt: "He sure'n hell don' look i'."

That same afternoon, Rex Rossler and Jan Behrs-Rossler were having lunch at a diner near the trucking firms.

Rex: "Did I tell you I agreed to sign on a Kenny Wisniewski as one of the long-haul drivers, a nice young man highly recommended by an old friend of yours?"

Jan: "The name Wisniewski is awfully familiar. A

Stach Wisniewski was a close friend of Dan Russo's, but I don't know any Kenny Wisniewski."

"A nephew of Stach Wisniewski's, I'm told."

"A police officer?"

"I wouldn't think so, but your former husband, now the police captain, recommended him."

"Both men are good policemen, as you well know. I'll bet the kid is following in his uncle's footsteps."

"Former Marine, I believe."

"As Dan would say, 'bingo!'"

"You know, on that wheel-chair mess, I thought I could pressure them, maybe even buy them off, I really did. I mean men coming from their neighborhoods, you know. Little Italy, Canton . . ."

"Never, never underestimate the Polish or the Italians in this working-man's city, dear, never, never . . . never."

"Think I should tell Judd Schmidt? He's going to Savannah, and I asked him to help Wisniewski adjust to the longer runs by letting him tag along for the experience."

"And never, never cross Russo or Wisniewski, dear. You don't know whether they have this man on Schmidt's tail." She didn't mention that a police lieutenant by the name of Sylvester Reed had stopped by her office a couple weeks back with questions about Schmidt, trips he had made and his record with the company, and had asked her not to mention his visit to anyone.

"I should just keep my hands off?"

"Absolutely."

"I'm offering him a little bonus for shepherding the young man."

"That's fine. He probably didn't expect it though. You might want to check with me next time."

"I get the message. . . . You want to see this Dan Russo again? The next time . . ."

" . . . Not really."

That afternoon, about 4:15, Judd Schmidt sought out Jim Poole and Kenny Wisniewski as they pulled into line to pick up their containers at Baltimore's Dundalk Marine Terminal. Jim Poole mirrors Schmidt in many ways, except Jim was drafted into the Army between Korea and Vietnam, grunting away but not having to duck any enemy fire—actually getting a charge out of driving ton-and-a half Army trucks, which led him to get into trucking when he completed his two years.

On the road, Jim preferred getting his caffeine from Pepsis and Mountain Dews rather than from Cokes. Schmidt got through two years of high school. Poole only made it into the ninth grade.

He has three wives in his past, seven kids he no longer knows. He is fifty-three, but looks fifteen years older, and his smoking is killing him. He is wearing an old, almost worn-out pair of cowboy boots, a tired Stetson and what might have been cow poke's shirts 100 or more truck-stop washings ago.

Ole Jim drives an '82 Peterbilt tractor. Its speedometer rolled over a million miles, and now shows about 500,000. But the truck is in sad condition. The seats are torn some, the headliner is loose in a couple places, fenders are dented, and there are cracks in the air deflector. There are dings in the front bumpers, and bent quarter panels missing in front of the back tire. Taillights are bent, and the tail lamp broken. Even the steps in the cab are bent some. And the windshields are pitted from sandstorms in Arizona. In back of the cabin is a well-worn double sleeper. The motor's been rebuilt, the transmission's been retuned, and there are enough clanks and rattles that other truckers appear to hold back and then scoot past him on the interstate.

On the driver's side door is painted "Chickmobile" in bright red letters on a dirty blue background, for Jim likes the women who frequent truck stops, and has his favorites as truck mates—who chatter away about going to Hollywood or Houston as he drives along until he stops for sex and sleep and a meal or a snack. She gets off the next day at another truck stop, to go on toward her professed career goal on the stage or as a model, or to backtrack and delay that career for a month or so, depending on the customer she accepts.

Wearing down from the hard ride of his rig, the smoking and the sexual adventures, Ole Jim now chooses the shorter trips. He was not going to Savannah with the other two, but taking a container down to Charleston, South Carolina, and picking up one there to return to Baltimore. He would tag along with the other men and would be waiting for them along the way when they returned from Savannah.

He doesn't drive for Rossler but for a relatively new firm, Carter Tman Trucking, also based in Baltimore.

Judd, leaning against Kenny's Freightliner as they waited for Jim to return from the rest room, said: "Ole Jim here knows this shi', but you're new here, Wisniewski, so pay 'tention. You say you drove in the militry?"

"Marines, sir."

"Sir? Naw. Let's knock off that shi'. Had enough of tha' in Nam. I'm Judd, tha' there's Ole Jim (who was walking slowly toward the two men). The only sir around here, in your'n and mine case, is Mr. Rossler, who runs the truckin' firm, and you're naugh likely to mee' him." He lit up a Pall Mall and took a heavy draw.

"Anyway, you'll follow me up to the booth here and give the guy there your pickup number and a card tellin' you where the damn c'tainer might just be. Your c'tainer will have a bunch of numbers, perhaps four alphas and six numbers and the prefix might be tied to a steamship line, like Evergreen EISU or EMCU, MAEU or SEAU, and you damn well better guard all tha' paper work. You'll also get a dock receip', or a bill of ladin', that will tell you exactly what you're carryin' . . ."

Poole, who just arrived: ". . . 'lessn it's drugs, you . . ."

Schmidt spun around: "What the hell you talkin' bough, Jim. I've never carried drugs, have you? I mean, damn i', I've never, never asked you wha' you were carrying, now have I? I've never asked any other trucker. An' I'm naugh gonna ask this pup, neither."

Poole, a little taken back by the sharpness of that comment, which caused him to start a long hacking spree, finally got his breath: "I'm sorry, Judd. I keep messin' up ever which way. Our company's as clean as yours, Judd. Jest tryin' to make conersation, you know."

"Yeh, sure, an' I'm sure you walked round that rundown tractor of yours, but did you see this young pup walk round his?"

"No, Judd, I don' think I did?" And he coughed nervously.

Wisniewski: "Afraid I didn't just now, Judd."

"Well, kid, you alway check, every damn time you stop, 'cause you don' know how fas' a problem can d'velop.

"Y'ever hear that song by Harry Chapin, called 'Twenty Tousand Pounds of 'nanas,' or somethin' like tha'?" Wisniewski looked blank, so Schmidt went on: "'Bout a driver los' his brakes going down a steep grade into some valley in Pennsylvany. He jest disingrates along with his tractor and load. . . . So you alway, alway check."

"Yes, sir." He almost saluted, and quickly walked around his tractor. "Looks clean."

"Now when you get your c'tainer, you alway, alway, check the damn chassis it's sittin' on."

Poole: "Alway look at the tires, kid. Make sure you don' gaugh any worn out."

"Like all your wives, eh Jim?"

"You got tha' . . ." he coughed for a minute or so, "righ', Judd." He paused. "You make sure you gough brakes. You gough no brakes, you gough twenty, thirty tons 'hind you that gonna flattin you an' your cab, kid." He coughed for about thirty seconds. "Jest' like dem damn 'nanas in Pennsylvany."

Schmidt, who waited for Poole to finish: "And the ligh's. Make sure they look good; make sure they all work. I alway carry a complete set of bulb in my cab, and you will, too, if you don' want the damn troopers 'rassin' you.

"Any one of those damn ligh's go ou', and those damn troopers have another reason to stop you."

Poole: "And that means money and time, son, time you're sittin' and not drivin'."

"I understand, Ole Jim."

Schmidt, leaning up against the door of Kenny's rig: "I know a lot of young punks get all fired up abou' truckin', and a lot of dem don' make it through the first year. Think you're game fur it?"

"I'm in for the long haul, Judd."

Poole, to relieve the tension, said: "Let's see the cab you have got 'ere, kid," and he climbed into the cab, and the energy caused him to cough some. "You got a pretty good one, kid, better'n the one I started with, tha's fer damn sure. Look like your woman pu' some goodies in here fer you. No smokes, though."

Kenny, standing outside the cab with Schmidt, who was looking in: "No, I never started."

Schmidt: "You probably will soon, kid. They keep you awake."

"Well, I don't know. I try to do a little running each morning, just to stay fit, and keep from getting leg cramps."

"Occupatial hazard, kid. You ge' them, too, no matter wha'. Jest' like headaches."

"Never heard of a trucker workin' out. You, Judd?"

"Not until now. Hell, you and me might jest have to star' runnin', too." And they both laughed heartily, with Poole coughing some, and even more ardently when Kenny added: "I'm really thinking about getting some dumbbells. Really."

Poole, through his laughs: "Damn i' all, kid," he coughed several times, "you just migh' make i'."

The trucker who had delayed them about fifteen minutes finally pulled away, and the three drivers moved ahead to the booth, where each gave his pickup number to a port worker, who handed over a printed TIR (trailer interchange report) and a slip showing where the box and chassis were on the lot, for example, alpha row, number twelve, and the right container would be there—or within a couple spaces one way or the other, usually.

Kenny found his container where it was supposed to be, and Schmidt watched skeptically as Wisniewski walked around the chassis, and all three drivers agreed that it was not road worthy. Schmidt had Wisniewski find a better chassis in the chassis pool. He brought it by, and Schmidt called the A-frame lift operator to come over to hoist the container from the poor chassis and put it down on its replacement.

Judd and Jim watched as Kenny flipped the lever on each corner that latched or pinned the container to the chassis, and then connected air and brake lines. "Ligh' look okay, tire look pretty good, air hose look good," Judd said as he walked around.

"Oh shi', here a bulb out. Okay, kid, here's a pack of them bulb, and you can pay me back later.

"And 'member, kid, at every stop, you fill out your damn log book, and you walk round this damn chassis, as well as your damn tractor, and you check every damn ligh', you listenin'?"

"I understand."

On the back of the chassis are two yellow lights at the front corners, two yellow in the middle, four red lights, two on each side, with three markers in the middle.

Off to Savannah

The three drivers drove back through the port gate for a final check and walk-around when each driver noted in his log book any damage to the container—dents, scratches—so that he would not be held responsible for them. They cleared the Dundalk Terminal about 5 p.m., climbed onto Dundalk Avenue and headed west on I-695 to I-95 south to the truck stop in Jessup for four hours of sleep. Schmidt had already paid a truck-stop worker to have three spaces kept for them, because truck stops along the East Coast, especially north of North Carolina, fill up early each night.

Schmidt said they'd weigh their loads first at the truck stop, before filling their tanks for the trip. Fuel figures into the weight—eight pounds a gallon. If the containers topped the 80,000-pound limit, with fuel tanks needing to be filled, the driver would return to a secure part of the Port of Baltimore terminal to unload enough from the sealed container to get below the limit.

But they all came up with 60,000 to 70,000 pounds, and could top off their tanks. The tractors could cover 1,200 to 1,300 miles before needing to be refueled, meaning another stop sometime on their return from Charleston and Savannah.

Judd, Ole Jim and Kenny climbed into their cabs and into their sleepers. Kenny, after waiting some time to allow the other two to drop off, dialed Lt. Reed.

"Yeh."

"It's me, Lt. Reed. Just checking in. Can you hear me OK?"

"You're sounding good. I saw you three pull in. What's the schedule?"

"We're sleeping here for four hours. Apparently Judd—he seems like a pretty good guy no matter that he's stiff as a board—got us some spaces or there'd be no room to park."

Then we'll be getting breakfast . . ."

"Breakfast?"

"Yep. I'm going to have to acclimate my stomach to this schedule."

"Okay. You don't mind if I have a burger though?"

"Whatever. I'd guess the restaurant serves them. How close will you be?"

"Close enough. I can't sit with the professionals (truck drivers), of course, but I'll be watching."

"Anyway, after that, we get to drive for five hours to whatever truck stop that is."

"Have fun, kid, and be careful. Looks like that would be in South Carolina. I'll check with you when you get there."

"Thanks, Lieutenant."

Early that evening, on South Exeter Street:

Angela: "So, Dan and Tina, you're going to Jamaica, I hear."

Rocco: "Really? How about that."

Angela: "Did I hear right?"

Tina: "You did, Angie. We'll be going in the spring, though, but it's a pretty good deal. We'll be flying."

Tooky: "All the way to Jamaica?"

Dan: "Yep. Take about four hours or so from D.C."

Angela: "So you'll be swimming, and what else?"

Tina: ". . . and dancing, and eating, food I haven't had to prepare, and floating down some river on a raft pushed along by some native, and . . ."

Dan: ". . . and some cool drinks, I hope."

Rocco: "What you should do—and I'm just suggesting this, you know. What you should do is write some notes describing yourselves and put it in a Coke bottle, or whatever, and cap it somehow, and toss it into the Caribbean and hope to hear where it wound up."

Dan: "Guess we'd have to put down our mailing address."

Rocco: "Be a starter. But you should also say something about your jobs and your kids, you know. And—this is important—ask whoever finds it to tell you where and when it landed."

Tina: "If I didn't know better, Rocco, I'd bet you just read something in the *Sun* about just that."

Rocco: "I sure did, but on a much bigger scale. See, there was this container ship sailing from Korea to our West Coast somewhere, and a huge wave came along and washed twenty or twenty-one of those shipping containers into the ocean."

Dan: "So?"

Rocco: "So five of those containers were carrying Nike shoes, you know, and four of those apparently burst open and freed thousands of Nike shoes."

Tina: "Thousands of shoes?"

Rocco: "Maybe 60,000."

Tooky: "Wow."

Rocco: "So, anyway, several months later, almost the next year, you know, people along the West Coast began finding Nike shoes washed up on the shores. All in pretty good shape."

Tina: "So a few folks got their Nikes free."

Rocco: "Well, the funny thing was that the shoes weren't tied in pairs, so they just floated all over the place by themselves, you know, one righty here, one lefty there."

Tooky: "Kinda like my closet."

Rocco: "So far beach combers have found almost a thousand."

Tina: "So you want us to go out and buy some Nikes and throw then into the Caribbean?"

Rocco: "Nah, I just think it might be pretty interesting to find out where your particular bottle went. They call that a drift bottle."

Dan: "We'll do it, and when we hear back from someone, if we ever do, well, we'll just call you over and you can see what happened. In fact, if we do get some response, I'll just have to buy you a beer, Rocco."

Rocco: "Or two. It was my idea."

Tina: "Hey, Rocco, we're flying down there and doing all the work writing all those instructions and putting it in that bottle and throwing that damn bottle into the Caribbean, you know."

"One beer's enough."

Tales of the Road

After four hours' shuteye—Judd and Old Jim had slept, but Kenny had tossed and turned, thinking of Mira and home—and breakfast of biscuits and sausage gravy and coffee, and their constitutional walks around their trucks, the three started up around 2 a.m. Judd said their first stop would be the truck stop at exit 105 off I-95, in Kenly, North Carolina.

As morning settled in they reached the Travel Plaza in Kenly, and the three men had a lunch of hot beef sandwiches and mashed potatoes, with beans on the side. The truck stops met the truckers' needs and desires, serving breakfast, lunch and dinner around the clock. Kenny chose milk, the others coffee, and they all had apple pie, a specialty at this diner, according to both Poole and Schmidt. Judd went to the rest room, and when he got back

Poole said, "Anyways, Judd, I was jest' tellin' the kid here about the worst scare I got on the road."

"In New Mexico, righ'?"

"Righ'."

"And this state trooper came cuttin' through the scrub brush . . ."

"Ah shi', Judd, it's my story."

"I've heard i' so offen, I though i' was mine."

"Well, it ain'." He coughed about five times, the last three heavier than the first two, until he was able to talk again. "Anyways, I was scootin' along pretty good in da fast lane—I was a lauh' younger then, you know—and this New Mexico state trooper just cuts through the scrub brush righ' in front of me, probly goin' after a speeder or somethin', and he zooms righ' up in my lane. Lucky I had just 'nuff room to swing to the righ' round him, or I'd a mashed that copper."

He coughed a couple times.

Schmidt waited: "Too damn bad you didn't."

"Well, he was pretty dumb, comin' up like tha'. I was a little shaky for a while, too, you know." And he coughed and drew his breath heavily. "If I'd a mashed him, somehow it woodaben my ass in the sling, ya know."

Schmidt, after taking a drag on his cigarette: "Yeh. I got a dumb cop story, too, kid. Out in Southrn Californy, cuttin' across from Bakersfield to Barstow on Stay' Highway 58, and goin' over this Techchoppy (Tehachapi) Pass, an it's late a nigh', an' the load was heavy, oranges, I think. Anyway i' had snowed some, an' i' was slushy. An' I come up on this Californy trooper drivin' a Mustang . . ."

"A Mustang in snow. Oh, shi'."

"You gaugh it, Ole Jim. Anway, he's doin' maybe twenty-five and slidin' all over the place, and I'm doin' forty, forty-five, in Mexican overdrive (putting tractor into neutral), so I jest' wen' around him, an' when I got further along where there was no more snow, well, up he comes, and he's goin' to write me up for goin' too fas' for 'ditions."

"No shi'."

"Yep. So I jest tole the dumb batard tha' I had plenty of weigh', I had snow tires on, an' I drive in snow a whole laugh' I was doin' a lo' of drivin' in the Midwes' then. An' den I said, 'hell, if I was drivin' a Mustang, then I'd be going twenty-five, too.'"

Kenny: "Sounds reasonable."

"We talked some more, you know. Bu' he never did give me a ticke'."

Killer Frogs

"Good for you, Judd," Poole said, and he coughed, almost gagged, and struggled for breath. "Tell 'im bou' dose killer frogs in Nam, Judd."

Judd nodded his head. "Dey was killers, all righ'. You touch dem, or even dey spi' on you, man, in no time ah' all, you are gonna be dead or insane.

"Like when we was on recon, an' we see entrances to a tunnel along da' Ho Chi Ming trail, you know, an' we jest' bring up some of those killer frogs. You wouldn't know nothin' of dem? Wal, if'n we found tunnels along da' Ho Chi Ming trail, and dey had a dead end, then we'd put dose damn frogs down dere among dose NVA (North Vietnamese Army) and North Korean irregulars."

Jim Poole: "You had to be real careful, Judd?"

"Damn righ'. We got dese frogs, an' we're wearing dese thick gloves, an' leather jackets an' hoods, 'cause if you just even touch dem, man, you are dead. An' we'd just toss dem frogs down those tunnel holes an' pretty soon you'd jest' hear dem NVAs whoopin' down dere, jest one scream and dey was gone, and we'd jest chuckle, and look for 'nother tunnel hole. Man, dat was fun, I tell ya."

He thought for a minute or so. "On recon in Nam, I didn' mind the snakes, but I don' like dose damn frogs." He got up, slammed a five-dollar bill on the table and stalked off, with Jim Poole and Kenny tagging along, and Kenny thinking to himself, 'In no way am I going to offend this Judd guy. He likes killing.'

Unless an over-the-road trucker picked up a girlfriend at a truck stop, as Ole Jim frequently did, sometimes more for the company than for the sex, he lived alone in his own world—his cab—where he was king. Inter-modal truckers didn't even have to check in with the home office more than once or twice a day, and they chose their own routes to their destinations—shooting the breeze with other drivers on their CB radios, listening to talking books, or tapes, or Rush Limbaugh on the radio, a favorite among OTR truckers, smoking, and drinking Cokes, Pepsis or Dr. Peppers.

On this Thursday, the three drivers pulled out about 8 a.m., and Kenny's cell phone rang.

"Yep."

Sylvester Reed: "How can you eat a hot beef sandwich for breakfast? And beans?"

"You hungry, it tastes pretty good. Remember that I was in the Marines. Where were you?"

"Just drifting around, kid. I didn't see any contacts there."

"Nor did I. Judd did go to the john though."

"Nothing there."

"You get around."

"What's the schedule?"

"We drive another five hours or so."

"Yeh. Be careful, kid."

"Hey, you, too, Lieutenant. This Judd guy, he don't like lieutenants and he don't like cops."

"He's a winner, all right."

Another sixty miles or so down the interstate, Judd closed on a slower tractor-trailer, probably company-owned with a governor, and a motorist slowed alongside him, boxing him in. Over the CB Kenny heard, "The four-wheeler needs a little push, kid."

Kenny swung over behind the '88 Cadillac, roared up behind and pounded his air horn, startling the motorist into hitting his accelerator. Kenny dropped back slightly, allowing Judd to sneak by. "Well, done, kid. You ain' so green affer all."

"No I ain't, Judd."

Ole Jim jumped in: "Amen, brothers, amen."

An Adult? Entertainment Area

On South Kenwood Avenue that night:

George (Hawk): "So what do you think? Will the city council close down the Block or not?" He was referring to the 400 block of East Baltimore Street, near the Inner Harbor, a so-called adult entertainment area.

Anna: "Well, we sure don't want all that garbage in our neighborhood, I'll tell you."

Sophia: "It's sinful, all right." And the men all smiled.

Junior, bravely: "Why do you say that, Aunt Sophia?"

Anna jumped in: "Well, just how many places are there, anyway?"

Stach: "I understand there's twenty-eight adult book stores . . ."

Anna interrupting: "Dirty book stores!"

Stach: ". . . and peep shows and strip bars."

George: "Is that all?"

Stach: "Well they outlawed nude dancing a couple years ago. "

Irene: "Good for them. I couldn't have done that anyway," she added, giving her left arm and leg a twist, "what with my 'ritis," causing most everyone to smile, and the younger men to laugh, wondering who would ever want to see Irene dancing in the nude.

Anna, struggling through laughs: "No, Aunt Irene, I don't think you could've."

Stach, recovering himself: "And we make more than 400 arrests a year in and around the Block for panhandling, public drunkenness, assaults and what have you."

Stephanie: "Compared with?"

"Oh, say, less than twenty-five or so in a year's time in the Inner Harbor and environs."

Sophia: "We don't want that here, that's for sure."

Junior: "Well, the *Sun* says that's what might happen if they close up the Block. The paper says they might move to South Baltimore, but to manufacturing zones."

George: "Not right here, anyway."

Anna: "Too close for comfort. We don't need those panhandlers and homeless here in Canton."

Junior: "Would you start up another neighborhood association, Anna?"

"One or more. Are you in, Steph?"

"For certain."

Betty, who rarely spoke out on the front steps: "Me, too." And her surprised husband, Junior, smiled with the other men.

George: "There they go again."

The three truckers were piling up miles down I-95. When they approached I-26 in South Carolina, Jim Poole called over his CB: "Guess I be seein' you boys later." He coughed. "Gaugh' to mee' my date down in the beUteeful city of Charleson."

Kenny radioed: "Have a safe trip."

"Preciate that, kid."

Judd: "Good huntin'."

"Oh, I got some tail waitin' for me. I don't need no blind."

"I figured."

Poole turned off on I-26 for the fifty-mile drive into Charleston, planning to stop in an industrial area to drop off the machinery that had come into Baltimore from Germany. He would then drive over to the Columbus Street Terminal to pick up a container from La Guaira, Venezuela, loaded with tropical fruits, coffee, cocoa and fish. He was not concerned about whether the container ship was on time or not; he could wait.

Charleston's Port Expansion

In the 1960s, the Charleston container terminal was expanded from fifteen acres to, by the 1980s, 300 acres. In 1991, the Port of Charleston handled 807,106 TEUs (traffic equivalent units), or twenty-foot containers, (the total includes forty-foot containers as two TEUs), up 3 percent from the previous year. The value of exports totaled $7.1 billion, and goods worth $6.8 billion were imported. Charleston's port handled 8,848,289 tons of goods. It ranked tenth in dollar value, right behind Baltimore, at $14,383,169 tons.

Charleston's top markets in 1991 for container trade were north Europe, 37 percent; Asia, 39 percent, and the Mediterranean, 11 percent. Latin America, surprisingly, accounted for only 4 percent of the traffic.

Poole said over his CB to Judd and Kenny as Ole Jim got onto I-26, "I'll try to be up at the truck stop five miles up I-an' 26 waitin' for you boys."

"We'll be lookin' for you," Judd responded, adding for Kenny's benefit, "Now that we got our anchor up, kid, let's see what's ahead." Over his CB, he said: "North-bound eighteen-wheelers on I-95, any smokies on the 'rizon?"

Someone responded: "Hello, south-bound. You got one with three little cubbies waitin' south of exit 33. Already got a reefer (refrigerated truck), a steel thermos (tanker truck), and a Jimmy (a GMC truck) all in a row sitting down."

"Preciate that, good buddy," Judd responded.

"No problem." And Judd pushed his truck up to eighty, with Kenny matching behind.

They drove on, slowed down when they got near exit 33, and, delayed a little by traffic around Savannah, arrived at side-by-side warehouses to drop off their containers. They presented the bills of lading to the warehouse official and wrote down the seal number for security reasons. The recipient watched as the driver cut the seal after writing down its number. Judd and Kenny then drove to Savannah's Containerport Terminal.

They pulled into a line of trucks waiting to pick up their containers from the ships that had come into Savannah. But when Schmidt got to the gate, he learned that the containers he and Wisniewski were to pick up were still aboard a ship that had been delayed about six hours in clearing the port of Cartagena, Columbia, and then was delayed once more at the container port in Balboa, Panama, and now it would have to jockey into position to get a slot, or berth, in Savannah.

Judd pulled out of the line, with Kenny following—"You don' wan' the gate people mad at you, kid. They can do more harm than good"—and parked under some bright lights at Savannah's harbor, intending to catch some shuteye.

Kenny followed, after alerting Lt. Sylvester Reed, who had stopped a mile outside the port. Schmidt saw Kenny talking on his cell phone, and shouted over, "Callin' home, kid?"

"Yep. Mira likes to know where I am."

"Jest tell her you're on the road, boy. She don' need to know nothin' more."

Kenny, diplomatically: "Yeh, you're right, Judd," and, to Syl: "Got to go." And hung up.

Georgia Ports Authority

In 1991, the Georgia Ports Authority moved 480,976 TEUs through the port of Savannah, with 235,759 in imports and 245,217 in exports, with the overall tonnage for 1991, including bulk shipments, of 8,406,215. That's pretty good, considering that Savannah didn't have its first container crane until 1970, when a number of other ports missed their chance to become container ports. And the first containerized cargo hadn't arrived in Savannah until 1965.

When Schmidt and Wisniewski woke up about 5 a.m., the two pulled back into line, with Judd scanning the harbor to see a number of container ships sitting in the bay. Frustrated that their ship might still be out there, and more than a little suspicious about Wisniewski's need to make calls all the time, Schmidt climbed out of his cab and strolled back to Kenny's, asking, "Call home often, boy?"

Kenny, cautiously: "Well, Mira wants me to check in once a day."

"Hmm? Kinda hen-pecked, huh?"

"Just married, more like it, Judd."

"Yeh, I suppose." But he didn't.

On South Exeter St. in Little Italy the night of Aug. 26

Rocco: "Tooky, did you see where Cal Ripken signed a contract for $30 million-plus for five years?"

"Indeed, indeed. Let's see, that's about $6 million a year, or about $5,970,000 odds more than me, I'd guess."

Angela: "You do very well, Tooky."

Rocco: "He's second highest in the majors, Cal is."

Antonio: "Who gets more?"

Rocco: "Ryne Sandberg, the Chicago Cubs second baseman."

Antonio: "Never heard of him. Bet he's missed more than a few games over the last twelve years. Bet you good money."

Dan: "Oh, I'm sure he has, Tooky. I'll save my money."

Antonio: "And how'd Cal do last night, Rocky?"

"Pretty poor if I remember. Let's see," looking up the box score in the *Sun*. "Yep, he went 0 for 4 and made an error in a loss to California."

Dan: "Everybody has a bad day now and then."

Antonio: "But not everyone makes $6 million every day, Schooch, good or bad."

"Not even the drug dealers, Tooky, not even the drug dealers."

Souvenirs for Mira

To help kill what turned out to be a fourteen-hour delay, Judd doubled back up Hwy. 21 to the truck stop at exit 19 of I-95, got a shower, shave and hair cut, and slept for two or three hours in his truck. Kenny elected to stay where he had parked overnight, called Sylvester Reed so he could keep track of Schmidt, took a two-hour nap in his sleeper, and walked over to Savannah's historic district and its visitor center, picking up some souvenirs for Mira—Georgia peach preserves and a Forrest Gump shrimp cookbook—though he was not certain that the cookbook would be appreciated. He looked at some teas, but passed on them, having no idea what Mira might like. He didn't think she had ever drunk tea on their dates, and he surmised that, even if he did remember, he would probably get the wrong stuff. He showed what he did buy to Schmidt, who had been waiting for him and was unimpressed.

"The wors' tha' can happen to inter-modal truckers," Schmidt complained, "is when the damn ship is late. Jest nothing worse. Then you got you-don-knaugh-how-long to wai', like us righ' now. Or you gaugh some messed-up paperwork, and you go' to go from this gate to tha' gate." He paused to drink some coffee from his thermos, and drew on his cigarette. "Or you get a chassis that's no damn good, and you gaugh to ge' i' fixed."

"What do you do?"

"You gaugh' to live wid i'. For example, you gaugh' an engine problem, and the maniac (trucker slang for mechanic), he don' give a shi' when you geh your load. He's working hours, naugh moves. So you try not to curse him, 'cause he migh' jest be able to help you, or he can go even slower. Jest live with i'." Then, turning back to his tractor, Judd said, "Let's try again."

The two drivers returned to the line at the gate at the Containerport Terminal and finally were able to pick up their containers. They headed out around 9 p.m., driving up Hwy. 21 to I-95 and getting off at exit 19 in Port Wentworth, Georgia, just short of the South Carolina line, to weigh their containers. Both were within limits. They didn't get fueled up then, for Schmidt explained: "I'm gonna top off in South Caroliny, when we mee' Ole Jim. We have to pay tax to South Caroliny anyway, you know."

Under the International Fuel Tax Agreement, if a trucker like Schmidt drove 1,000 miles in a state over several months, back and forth Baltimore to Savannah, Charleston, Jacksonville, whatever, and got five miles to the gallon, he would pay taxes on the 200 gallons of fuel he used. He owed the state $100, whether or not he bought any diesel in the state, so he'd occasionally fill up in that state, or at least top off, just to keep the current balance down.

Schmidt added that he was going into the truck stop to trade in some talking books for replacements, especially for what he considered a dull drive through South Carolina.

Kenny waited, and had his window opened slightly when he checked in with Lt. Reed. Judd, passing by, heard Kenny saying: "Nothing out of the ordinary, far as I . . ." Kenny noticed Schmidt coming up in his left side mirror. ". . . Yes, Mira, that's about right. I should be home about 8 p.m. tomorrow. We finally got our containers. Bye for now. Love ya."

Lt. Sylvester Reed smiled, recognizing Kenny's diversion.

Schmidt, who lived an anxious, seldom-rewarding life, suspected trouble and, on reaching his cab and pulling out onto the interstate followed by Wisniewski, called Felipe Sanchez on his private line: "I had ta call, boss. The kid's reportin' to someone, bes' I guess, and I don' think it's his new wife, either. Could he be a plan', unnercover or sometin'?"

"He doesn't suspect anything, does he?"

"Naugh' tha' I know of. He's pretty green."

"Well, if he don't know anything, that's fine, and we get what we want—with an escort. Hah, hah! On the other hand, accidents do happen."

"You want him to have an acciden'?"

"Hold off. Let me think about that for a few minutes. I can make a call or two. Where are you now?"

"Just crossed into South Caroliny, headin' north."

"Your next stop?"

"Well, let's see." He pulled up his road atlas from a pouch attached to his seat. "Should be at the truck stop five miles up I-26 from I-95. Meetin' an ole buddy, probably in a hour and a half."

"You stop that often?"

"Nope, usually go for five, six hours every time, but we're rendezvousing with an old buddy who's probably already there."

Sanchez: "That should give me enough time. I'll get back to you."

"I'll watch him real close."

"See if there's anyone else traveling with you. Was there a car that seemed to stay with you, or that showed up at the truck stops?"

"Non' tha' I 'member, but I'll be on lookou'. I'll wai' for your caw." And Judd thought and thought, but couldn't come up with anything or anybody unusual on the trip.

A cartel inspector?

Stach and Dan were bowling on their regular Thursday night at Patterson Bowling Center when Dan described the phone call from Bob Hampton of the Drug Investigations Agency.

Stach: "Helpful, or just BS?"

"Pretty helpful, really. Said he wasn't sure, the department wasn't sure, but some of his agents suspected the third man in the photos you gave him—you know, the guy we can't identify—could be an inspector for the cartel, traveling the country to see how things are going."

"And putting the fear of God into every drug figure, no doubt."

"I would think so. The rest of us, too, to have that organized an operation, kinda like a regular top-grade U.S.A-born corporation, except it doesn't trade on the stock market," said with a smile. "Hampton would like to get the guy under surveillance, but has no idea where he is now. They're circulating the photo—just him—to airport personnel to see where he's going or where he's been."

"Might scare him off."
"Not if they do it right."
"Hopefully."

Four hundred thirty miles to the south, Judd Schmidt and Kenny Wisniewski covered the miles to that truck stop up I-26 in an hour and twenty-five minutes, Judd mollified by the talking books that helped ease his mind a little at least about who really was driving the tractor behind him.

They came upon Ole Jim in the restaurant just as a well-worn woman of indefinite age, but likely crowding forty-five, left his table with a little hand wave, as she tucked some bills into the back pocket of her tight-fitting jeans. Ole Jim was smiling broadly when he welcomed Judd and Kenny: "Man, is she somethin', somethin', somethin', well, it's hard to deescribe."

Judd: "We got the message, Ole Jim, right, kid? The older the better."

"Yes, sir, I mean, you betcha," Kenny piped in, admiring the gait of the broad as she swayed off to the restroom. She returned to the cafeteria later to sit with another old customer, heading south, perhaps to Houston, where she hoped she might get a ride to the Hollywood of her imagination.

Back to the present. Judd: "Everythin' goin' well, Ole Jim?"

"No better, no better."

"You're not goin' to fade on us."

"I am 'vigorATEd, 'vigorATEd, Judd."

And they all ordered chicken fried steak, mashed potatoes and peas, with coffee. Following their meals, Kenny watched Jim check out his refrigerated container, for he was hauling apples and pineapples and he had to check the power cord and generator sets—the chassis has to have a generator built into it, which like the tractor itself runs on diesel fuel.

Judd watched Kenny as he inspected his own tractor and container for leaks and burned out bulbs. But Judd's meanness, strengthened in Vietnam, was getting the best of him.

I love you, too, Mir

After they pulled out, about midnight, Judd said over his CB radio that they would stop next in Ruther Glen, Virginia, exit 104 of I-95. It was almost 400 miles, and was a favorite truck stop for Judd. About 5:30 a.m., Kenny decided he'd wake up Mira on her birthday. He dialed their number and got a very sleepy "Hello."

"Hi, darling. It's me. Happy birthday."

"Well, hello, stranger. What time is it anyway?"

"Oh, 5:35 in the a.m., hon. You're missing a real pretty sunrise. First, there was just a hint of light, and you sorta guess that that's where the sun will come up. Then slowly the light grows some, just a little more, and you can start to see the outlines of the trees back from the Interstate, and the headlights on the trucks flying past aren't as bright, and slowly the light grows a little brighter, until it seems to spread ever so slowly over the landscape, and then there's the top edge of the sun just peeping over the horizon, and then it lifts itself up just a bit, and a bit more, and the truckers start turning off their lights, and it's a whole new day. Well, you just never see that on South Kenwood. It sure is pretty."

"Don't you ever sleep?"

"Mostly in the daytime, it seems. Four-hour shifts. And it's hard getting to sleep with the truck engines starting up all the time, and the traffic buzzing by. I guess I'll get used to it, but it might take some time."

"Where are you (a heavy yawn) anyway?"

"Headed north, home, that is. But right now we're

moving into southern Virginia."

"How's it going?"

"Pretty good, I guess. We dropped off the containers in Savannah, no problem. But we had to wait darn near a day and some to pick up our containers at the docks in Savannah. I got to do a little sightseeing."

"Well, good for you. About all I'm seeing here is my folks, the warehouse and South Kenwood Avenue."

"You'll see me later today. I don't know the schedule yet, but we should be in before sundown. I got to drop off this container at a warehouse in the southern industrial district somewhere. Maybe it's the one you work at?"

"Well, I'll be looking for you. You sound like you're really enjoying it."

"Yep. But I sure miss you. That's the downside."

"I miss you too, honey. It's just not very warm in this bed."

"Makes me want to push the pedal to the floor. But I got to stay behind Judd, on this run, at least."

"How is he, an old, experienced trucker?"

"His bark is worse that his bite. But he knows the road, he loves to drive, and I can put up with his barking. He's a Vietnam vet, you know, with no tolerance whatsoever of those of us who didn't serve there. . . . See you later today. And I'll make that happy birthday something to remember."

"OK, honey. Drive safe now. I love you."

"I love you, too, Mir."

The three trucks arrived at Ruther Glen around 6 a.m., moving a little slower because of Poole. This truck stop was a surging, droning gargantuan anthill of truckers and tractors, trailers and containers, behemoths of the interstate—Internationals, GMCs, Whites, Macks, Freightliners, Kenworths and Peterbilts, with an occasional four-wheeler (auto) sneaking through.

The big trucks normally fly along the interstates at seventy to seventy-five miles an hour, but here they crawl among the pumps and other tractor-trailers with inches to spare as they pause to refuel tractors and drivers—mostly white, but many black, even some women, some alone, and some sharing the steering wheel with their husbands. The tractor hoods and trailer sides glisten in blue and white, purple, green, the trailers displaying signs of movings, commodities, foods and beverages, and the containers offering labels that when translated identify origins in nations around the world.

Three firms—Petro, Pilot and Mr. Fuel—push fuel for the long-haul drivers headed north and south of Ruther Glen. Fuel tankers carrying up to 9,800 gallons of diesel and gasoline make deliveries at least ten times every day to satisfy the demands of the truckers, who keep managers of the truck stops standing at their cash registers for entire shifts to record the drivers' fill-ups and top-offs.

Wisniewski and Poole followed Schmidt into the Mr. Fuel area, and, because of the crowd, parked in different files deep in the lot. They had to walk quite a way to the restaurant, with Jim puffing away, and mechanically ordered biscuits with sausage gravy, coffee, and orange juice for Kenny. "Got to wash down those biscuits with something, you know," he explained apologetically. Schmidt looked Wisniewski over real close.

"Sleep good, kid?"

"Not bad, but that cab's not that big, you know. Well, I guess both you guys know that. . . . How often do you guys shower? So far I've usually been back home by dark."

Poole: "Ever' third day for me . . ."

". . . except when you have a rider."

"Yeh. Then it's ever' day. Need to 'fresh myself," and he chuckled, "ah, yes, indeed."

Not a 'chicken hauler'

At that moment, a well-seasoned OTR driver, garbed in fancy Stetson, freshly pressed cowboy shirt, jeans and well-polished boots, strolled over, grabbed Poole by the left shoulder: "Well, I'll be damned, if it ain't old Jim Poole. Damn it, Jim, it's been a long time." And he pulled Jim up to give him a bear hug, which got Jim coughing so hard he had to bend over. "Oh, hell, I'm sorry, good buddy," the newcomer said, lowering Jim back into his seat. "As you good old boys say down there in Alabama, 'You are a sight,' and that cough don't sound too good, you know."

Poole, after regaining his voice, said squeakily: "Tim Dooley, damn. It has been a long time. This here's Judd Schmidt, who had two turns in Viet Nam—I been taggin' wid him for ten year or so," they shook hands, "and Kenny Wisniewski, a rookie," who jumped up to shake hands with Dooley.

"Good to meet you both. I'll join yer, if yer don't mine," putting his Stetson down on a free chair.

Schmidt: "Hell, no."

Poole: "What you drivin' now, Tim?"

"A powerful, brand-new Kenworth, chromed stacks, and all. You can see her right out there," and he pointed to a shiny light blue tractor with extended hood, and its matching light-blue, forty-eight-foot refrigerated trailer right in front of the restaurant. "You can't see it from here, but I got 'Lone Star-Bound' scripted on my door."

Truckers would say, "The '92 KW has a 460-horse (horsepower) Cummins (diesel) and an eighteen-speed traney (transmission), aluminum wheels and lots of bells and whistles."

Schmidt commented: "You got enough ligh's on 'dere to star' an amusemen' park." He had been tempted to call it a 'chicken hauler' because of all the bulbs, but that nickname also suggested the driver worked for less money and his truck smelled like pig manure, and Schmidt wasn't real sure he could take Dooley.

"It gets noticed," Dooley agreed after taking a few seconds to decide that Judd's comment was not an insult. Tim had tamed a couple cowboys who had referred to his truck in his presence as a chicken hauler. So he took the easy road: "I get a lot of comments over the CB, you know, but most are just envious.

"That's why I came by this table, just so I could admire it and figure out what else I can put on her. Best friend I ever had. And there's a story about how I got that KW. You guys have some time?"

"Always have time for a good story," Ole Jim said. The two others nodded their agreement.

"Well, men, I was just getting by as a trucker, you know, and the wife, she wasn't that happy with me. We were livin' in Baltimore then—now she and the kids are in Texas. But then Lila was about to dump me. 'It's either me or the kids,' she says. And I says, 'Well, we got a little bit of money saved up, nothing much, you know. What'a we got to loose. Let's take a little amount out of the truck account that we got saved, and we go on up to Atlantic City and see what happens."

Schmidt: "Likely lost it all."

Dooley: "Ninety-nine percent of the time, Judd, you're right. But we didn't know what to do, right or wrong, so I asked one of the floor bosses 'what's the best slots?' He makes his suggestion, and I stuck a twenty-dollar bill in, and I just started hitting buttons, and the next thing you know, we hit."

Poole: "How much, Tim?"

"Well, I'm not going to give you any exact figures, you know, but we got a big down payment on that truck you see sitting out there, and I got my Maryland inspection, some small repairs, got tags, filled the fuel tanks, and still had $260 in my pocket."

"Whooee," Ole Jim said, and the two other drivers seconded the motion.

Dooley continued, "The next week I went to the trucking firm where I was a company driver, and told the dispatcher, 'Hey, I got the money for my truck. Would you hire me as an owner/operator?' And he says, 'Sure.'"

Poole: "That's one good story. But you had 'nother, going north from Baltimore . . ."

Dooley: "That's another story that happened after we had relocated to Texas, and I remember that story, too. I was coming out of Golden Ring, up here in Baltimore, and I had to get to some place in New Jersey and be there by 9 p.m. I had driven all day, slept about an hour or two. And a lady in a black car was coming off the ramp to get onto I-95 northbound, and she and a black truck driven by a man were fighting for pole position, I guess. And he cut her off, and she was right there in front of me, and I laid the truck and trailer right across 95. I jackknifed it."

"Whoa," said Judd.

Tim: "Believe it or not, I didn't hit anyone, and no one hit me." He paused, "And the only damage was to the air bags on the back of the sleeper. The brackets just snapped off."

Schmidt: "Whooey. That is a story."

Dooley admired his tractor some more as he drank down half his Coke, and turned to Poole: "What are you driving now, Ole Jim?"

"You won' believe i', Tim, bu' the same damn '53 Peterbil' 441 I was chasin' you back and forth along I-10."

"Not that old bucket of bolts. What the hell's holding her together? Hell, how many miles has she got by now?"

"1.9 mill, derabou'."

"My god, Ole Jim, that thing must be as worn out as you look. And, I hate to ask, but are you still chasin' the girlies?"

Poole, who started in a series of coughs: "Yeh. But they're gettin' harder to ca . . . " He coughed seriously for a minute or more, during which Dooley, flexing his fingers, quietly ordered his biscuits with sausage gravy from the waitress, while still looking at Poole.

". . . tch, Tim."

Dooley gulped down some of his coffee, looked at Schmidt and hitched his thumb toward Wisniewski: "You teachin' this here boy?"

"He don't seem to be too interested. Newly married, you know."

"Good for you, kid," Dooley said, clapping

175

Wisniewski on the back. He forked a piece of biscuit and sausage with gravy into his mouth. "This kitchen is good, I'll tell you. I had it down in my logbook, and it's as good as it was before. What are you driving, Judd Schmidt, and where are you headed?"

Judd: "An '86 Peterbil', and we're headed north to BaltEmore, where I'm based. Took one c'tainer down to Savanny. Heading back with 'nother."

"And you're chasing him?" said to Wisniewski, who nodded. "How about you, Jim?"

"Up to BaltEmore. Been to Charl . . ." he coughed for a minute ". . . son, Tim. Whare you headed now?"

Dooley controlled his emotions and said evenly: "Off to Beantown (Boston) this trip, Jim. Then be heading west to the Space Needle (Seattle), and down to the big dome (Houston), where I'll see my wife and kids for a couple days or so. That's a shame, but it's a great country, ain't it?" And he settled in to devour his meal, with a couple donuts on the side, and turned toward Schmidt: "You were in Vietnam. See any heavy action?"

Schmidt: "Yeh, a little. You 'member i'. You can't ferge' i'."

Poole: "Tell 'im 'bout dose natives over dere, Judd."

Kenny: "They were on our side, weren't they?"

Schmidt: "Sure as hell wouldn't want them agin us. Like we would go into one of dere villages, and they had poles all around this village, connected with wire. And they would sneak out at night and grab a NVA (North Vietnamese) or a Chink (Chinese), and they'd take a hot wire and poke it through one ear and come ou' t'other . . .

". . . You lookin' a little squeemish, kid?" And Kenny was.

"Anyhow," Judd continued, "they'd take this guy and stick a wire into one ear and out the other, and hang him on those poles. They would scream for 'bout an hour and den die."

"That's some story," Dooley admitted, "almost hard to believe."

Schmidt, giving Dooley a fast look: "I don't make up stories like dat."

Dooley flatly: "I guess I'll have to believe you."

"Yeh," said Schmidt, about ready to floor the trucker. Looking at the others, he added, "The only way to get by over dere was to count up their dead, subtract ours from 'dem and claim victory."

Poole, hoping to ease the tension: "How 'bou' tha' guy you met from 'bama, Judd."

Schmidt: "This ain't so bad," he said, looking haughtily at Dooley. "See, I heard dere was a guy from a town near mine in 'Abama, so I goes over dere, an' I finely find him. He'd been dere only a couple months—not a twink (new recruit in Vietnam), you know, bu' naugh much better. An' he says, 'Less go down in the bunker and ge' some chow.' So we did, An' we were talkin' an' talkin', me eatin' my chow on a stump and him sittin' up a little higher on a downed tree trunk, you know, from all the artillery fired 'round dere. An' every onct in a while a mortar round goes over us. You don' pay much 'tention to da', you know. And then in comes a rocke' and wham! Man, I duck, and here comes a head rollin' down right beside me, an' I look up, and dere's the guy I was just talkin' wid, and he's keeled over and he ain't got no head." Schmidt paused for about fifteen seconds and added, "Oooh, oooh, did I geh' sick. . . . Bu' you jest find an empty body bag or two . . ."

Then he turned to Kenny, a little awkwardly: "So, kid, did you check in with your wife again?"

Kenny, who was looking at his remaining food wondering whether he could get it down or keep down what he had just swallowed, sensed Schmidt's suspicions and tried unsuccessfully to appear cool: "Yeh, Judd." He looked up for a second, trying and failing to appear nonchalant, but quickly bringing his eyes back to his plate he forced another chunk of biscuit into his mouth, and said, "She's pretty worried, I guess," although he hadn't called her but once since he left home. An idea finally came into his head. He looked up and straight at Schmidt: "She's thinking she may be pregnant."

Ole Jim jumped in: "Well, hope it looks like you, kid. Right, Judd?" and Jim chuckled. Judd forced a smile.

Dooley, happy to be done with Schmidt's gory stories, took the cue: "Keep 'em barefoot and pregnant, that's what I say. Eh, Jim?"

"Good for you, eh, Judd," Poole said, and he coughed, almost gagged, and struggled for breath. "I know Tim has a similar story."

"I do?" Dooley said. "Oh yeh, on the New Jersey Turnpike. I'd almost forgotten that. But it goes this way.

"It was a Friday night, I remember now, and I was headed up New Jersey on 695, right up there by White Moss, and I was blessed," he looked toward Schmidt—"to have a police officer right behind me, believe that or not.

"Anyway, this guy come up alongside me on the right and suddenly he made a left turn right into my trailer, and I drug him for maybe 500 to 600 feet before I was able to stop. And I stayed in my lane, and the police officer who saw it all right behind me said I did a good job in stopping my tractor and trailer.

"Actually there were two guys in that car, but we didn't see the passenger, because he was squashed down in the passenger side, and they had to cut him out."

Poole: "How many kids you got now, Tim?"

Tim held up one hand counting off five as he bolted down a donut with the other, took a final slug of coffee, and got up, shook hands all around, "See you boys next time. Got to hit the trail." Threw five dollars on the table and strode off to the cash register, the clicking of his silver-tipped cowboy boots muffled by the chatter of drivers on cell phones and on the regular phones provided by the truck stop.

The other three men watched silently as Dooley walked outdoors, and observed him as he checked out the refrigerator unit on his trailer, walked around his tractor and trailer, and climbed into his rig, slowly eased back the rig, and pulled into the truck stop's exit lane, tipping his hat to his audience. He thought to himself, 'I could have matched that lunatic's stories one by one. I could have talked about the NVA's underwater bridges. Yeh, that might have confused him.

'Or how those little North Viets pushed a bike down the Ho Chi Ming trail with 500 pounds of this and that, and dumped off that stuff under cover and rode those bikes back up the trail. Now, that is a story.'

As he eased through the traffic lanes in the truck stop, he thought some more. 'I suspect this Schmidt guy could be one of those who loved body counts. Should have asked him about those. But even he would have had to agree they were a lot of hooey. On the other hand, that guy probably multiplied the "silly count" by three or four.

Tim had explained to his father, a World War II infantry veteran, "We didn't intentionally mess those body counts up, but we weren't given the chance to get them right. Everything was happening so fast."

'But back to this Schmidt guy,' Dooley thought to himself as he threaded his way through the labyrinth of trucks and trailers. 'He apparently came back to the world with the hope of impressing folks.

'Oh, let me think. Yeh, for some heavy action, I could have described driving up Highway 9 under all sorts of fire, carrying equipment for an Engineers Bridge Company, while the North Viet soldiers encircled Khe Sanh, but I don't get into those "can you top this" games. And I could never ever come close to being as gruesome as that Schmidt. I pity the poor kid. He looked like he was about to lose his lunch. But he'll grow accustomed somewhat over time to injury and death on the interstates; it happens.

'I could have helped him a little by telling how apes were throwing rocks at Marines, near Khe Sang. Nah, nobody believes that one but the guys who were there. They swear by it. The kid would have liked that one.'

'And Ole Jim. Damn it all. I suppose that's the last time I'll ever see him. He looks so bad, and sounds worse. Not a bad guy, really. A driver of the old school.' And Tim grimaced.

He slid his gloved hands around the steering wheel and, as he pulled onto the friendly Interstate, looked to the left, started shifting gears, and said quietly to the throbbing engine, "Next stop, good buddy—Beantown. Oh yeh, you'll need a little fuel along the way. I won't forget you."

Back in the diner, Lt. Sylvester Reed took note that this was the first time he had seen anyone approach the three drivers he was watching. At Ruther Glen, Reed had been observing their table from a booth in the non-professionals section, and, though he had not been close enough to hear anything more than the "Boom" shouted by Schmidt, decided he ought to check out the stranger. He followed Dooley out, memorized his plate numbers and some details about the snazzy truck and trailer, and walked back to his car, which took about ten minutes or more—it was so far back away among all those trucks—to phone Capt. Dan Russo.

"Yes?"

"It's me, Schooch. We did have a contact here at the truck stop in Ruther Glen, Virginia. Seemed innocent enough, but it's the first time I've seen anyone approach

Schmidt or the others. Actually, the new guy seemed to know Poole better."

"We'll check it out. What can you tell us?"

Reed described the truck and the plates, and reviewed what little he had observed at the table.

Still at the table in the diner, Kenny was pondering why Judd was so suspicious, for this was only to be a trial run for him, just for experience. Was one of these three trucks carrying drugs? Perhaps his? The thoughts flashed through his mind. But he could not bring up from his subconscious any incident on this trip nor could he remember any suggestion of trouble during his briefing—a knack his Uncle Stach had. Nothing popped into Kenny's mind.

Ole Jim broke into Kenny's concentration: "What'r your marchin' orders, Judd?"

"You both check your vehicles. You know we've been damn lucky drivin' to Savanny and Charleson and headin' back without even one tire blowin' all 'cause of our Southern hea' and 'midity. We been luckier than shi'. But if one goes out unner the cab—you prepared for tha', Wisnew whatever?"

"Happens in the Corps, too, sir. We just held on for dear life, especially if it's on the cab."

"Hmmph. Likely get you killed, kid."

They finished up their breakfast with a second round of coffees. Ole Jim looked about for a pretty rider for his scheduled trip to Hampton Roads, Virginia, tomorrow, but shied away from the only girl who smiled at him—she looked like she might have been fifteen or sixteen. Jail bait, he thought. And even if she were old enough, she'd probably fall asleep on the road, he thought, and have nothing to say worth listening to, except maybe, 'Are you sure you can do it, grandpa?' And he'd show her. But she was just too damned young.

Poole returned to the two men he was driving with: "I 'member one cute chick I picked up here." He coughed three or four times. "Damn, she made off wid my walle'. I los' $2,500 from the credy card 'fore I could cancel i' ou'."

Judd's cell phone sounded. He answered, said, "Hold on," and got up quick, telling Poole, "Cover me here. I gaugh' to check this ou'."

Schmidt left the restaurant, walked along the sidewalk in front of the restaurant and leaned back against the window: "What's up?"

Sanchez: "We got possible trouble. I checked with my sources in the police department, and they believe you got the nephew of a real officer following you who's a good friend of the captain in charge of the Northern District's detective bureau."

"I don' think he suspec's nothin'."

"It's not a federal thing. I had Sorensen try his contacts, and they have nothing in the works just now, and he has sources who know what the DIA is doing before they even think about doing it, so it's either the Highway Patrol and the city PD, or the city PD on its own. My people say this Wisniewski's uncle is in the Northern District, too, and he's a pal of Captain Russo, head of the detective bureau. Those two don't mind going it alone, and they've been a problem in the past—cost me one of my best men, who just disappeared ten or twelve years ago."

"I can take care of the kid."

"I'm just warning you. I'd just as soon you forgot about that kid and delivered your container as scheduled. It would probably be better that way. We don't want to get the cops stirred up any more than they already are. And if you do something dumb . . ."

"You really don' wan' the kid taken ou'?"

"No, let him be. You just deliver your container, and park it, as scheduled." But Sanchez had a second thought, which he would later regret. "Could this kid be eliminated cleanly?"

"No swea'."

"No, no. That would be stupid. They've got nothing on us, and I don't mind walking on the edge of a precipice."

"You never drove a ligh'-loaded, high-profile eighteen-wheeler in a wind storm, boss. Tha's for sure. You hold on or die."

"No, no. Ignore the kid. You hear me. You just bring your container home to where it's supposed to be dropped off, Eastern Avenue, isn't it? That's worth more to us right now."

"You're the boss." And he closed his cell phone and put it in his shirt pocket, but his anger continued to swell against Wisniewski. Schmidt looked back into the restaurant to see that their table now was empty, and turned, just as Poole and Wisniewski came out the door. "You owe me $10.50, boss," Ole Jim said.

"Big tip to Doris, eh?"

"'Course. You're a big-time tipper, Judd," and Poole chuckled and then coughed.

A tire bully

As they walked toward their trucks, Judd, trying to keep his climbing anger under control, said with menace he couldn't disguise, "Kid Marine, I didn't like the look of one of your tires, that front right one under the chassis. Jim, why not grab a coffee for you and me for the road, and the kid an' me'll see to the tire. Thas your truck over there a ways," pointing to the far left. "Well, we'll mee' you at your truck."

"Righ', boss."

Judd's anger in suspecting he was being watched by a police team was growing more furious by the second, and the fury that had helped him survive in firefights in Vietnam had taken control of him as it had cost dozens of Vietnamese soldiers their lives. "Dig out your tire bully, kid," he told Kenny rather sharply, Kenny thought.

He walked around to the left tractor door to reach in past the fire extinguisher under his seat to grab the tire bully—which resembles a large hammer—and met Schmidt at the right front tire. "Want me to pound it?" Kenny asked Judd.

No, I'll do it," and he grabbed it as he knelt down on one knee. "See the problem is, kid Marine, if this tire were to blow, the chassis would star' swaying, and probly swing you out of control, or flatten you, one or t'other. Now listen to the hum. That sounds right. Let see if it 'tinue all da way 'round."

Kenny leaned in, and Judd tapped the tire, and continued around the tire, which was standard procedure, but he glanced from side to side to see whether anyone was in sight along the double row of semis. And no one was.

Then as he bounced the tire bully off the tire, he suddenly whipped about and, with a two-handed swing Kenny could never have foreseen, cracked Kenny in the forehead before he could react. Kenny winced, before collapsing backwards in a heap.

Judd glanced around—still no one in sight along the double row of semis—and felt for Wisniewski's pulse. He was alive, so Judd whacked him twice aside the head with the bully, and the pulse speeded up, ebbed and stopped. "Good friken riddance," Schmidt mumbled as he wiped off the bully's handle with his glove, dropped it by Wisniewski, rolled him over to pull the wallet out of his back pocket, let the body fall back, and walked off. He took the money out of the wallet and dropped the wallet in the first trashcan he passed.

"He needed killin'," Schmidt said loudly to himself.

He walked along the line to his cab, only four trucks along, started up and drove through the lines to where Poole was standing beside his truck, which he had kept idling for the refrigeration in his trailer. He handed Schmidt his coffee. Looking behind Judd's trailer, Poole asked, "Where's the kid?"

"Had a problem with one of his tires. He's gonna have to replace i'. We go on. He knows the way."

"What'r you say, boss. He's a nice kid, doh. You thin' so?" And he climbed into his cab.

"Yeh, right," Schmidt said, but Ole Jim didn't hear him.

The two pulled out and were a half-mile up I-95 when two drivers walking between the lines of trucks saw a body huddled on the ground, came up to it, and could not awaken it. The older man waited while the younger trotted back to the fuel station to alert authorities. "Some son of a bitch has killed one of our drivers for his money!" he shouted to the clerk at the cash register, who mechanically placed some change in her register with her right hand and picked up a phone with her left and dialed 911.

Judd and Jim were about two miles up I-95 when a state patrol car roared by on the opposite lanes. "Look at Johnny Law go, boss," Jim said over the radio to Judd, who didn't answer.

By the time the first state trooper arrived at the truck stop, about twenty to twenty-five drivers were milling around at the back and the front of the double-parked trucks, mostly white men, but also five blacks, including one who didn't appear to be a trucker. Only three truckers had started up and driven off, and they were at the end of one of the lines. The rest felt they had to stay with their fallen comrade, even if it delayed them.

Trooper Alan Henderson, who pushed his way through the truckers to Wisniewski, leaned over and confirmed that the man was dead: "Any of you men see anything?"

One trucker, Bobby Somers, from Meridian, Mississippi, said, "Yes, sir. Me and Robbie here," he pointed with his thumb to the man standing next to him, "well, we were jest walkin' back from lunch, you know, and we seen this guy layin' there. We though' maybe he fell down or passed ou' or somethin', you know, but then we found he wasn' breathin' none, and there was some vicious-lookin' stuff oozing from his head."

"Was this," the officer pointed to the ground, "ah, what do you call it?"

Several men spoke up, "Tire bully."

"Was this tire bully lying like this when you got here?"

Somers: "Yep, we didn' touch i' or nothin'."

"And, as far as you know, you were the first here."

"Yes, sir. I sent Robbie back to the station to tell them, and they called you."

Just then, as a second state police cruiser pulled up, one of the black men at the back pushed his way through the truckers. "Trooper," as he showed his badge and ID, "I can identify this man for you, but I believe we should clear the area, if that's all right with you."

"Certainly, Lieutenant . . . Reed. All right, men. We'll handle this. I appreciate your concern, but if any of you has something else he can add . . ."

One trucker: "Yeh, I seen him eatin' with three other guys in the diner, trooper. But," as he looked around, "I don't see none of 'em here now."

Trooper Henderson: "Please stay for a minute. You other men—did anyone else see anything?"

Another trucker: "Seems like I saw this guy in there, too."

The trooper: "You stay, too. We'll try to be quick about this. I know you all have schedules to meet." And that reminder helped the others to move off to their trucks, assured somewhat that authorities were responding properly, with something they could discuss for days over their CBs and at the truck stops along the interstates.

Trooper Henderson, Lieutenant Reed and the two truckers who provided information about the victim's last meal moved to the back of Kenny's truck attempting to talk and listen as a dozen or more semis started up and began moving on, some north, some south. The newly arrived trooper, Don Marino, secured the area with crime-scene tape and radioed for an ambulance and the department's crime-scene investigators.

Henderson opened the cab—Kenny had left it open—and reached for the bill of lading, logbook, and a phone number for Rex Rossler Lines.

"You obviously knew this man, Lieutenant," he said to Sylvester Reed.

"He was a good kid, a nephew of a police friend of . . ." he broke.

"It must be hard . . ."

"I ben seein' people getting shot and killed for some time now, since I joined the force in Baltimore, but mostly they probably deserved it. You have to learn it's part of the job. I . . ."

"You get a lot of murders in the city?"

"When I first started, I had this seventeen-year-old kid, and all he wanted to do was make it. He just said, 'Please, help me make it,' and I'm like talkin' to him, and then he died in my arms. That kinda . . . Well, I just had to do the job."

Trooper Reed waited a minute. "No doubt someone was after money. We found his wal . . ."

"Nope, I think he was done in by the lead driver, a Judd Schmidt, who we think is running drugs. I was supposed to keep watch over the kid, but I was off talking on the cell phone with my boss. This hurts pretty bad."

"We need to question this Schmidt, that's for sure."

"I can give you some information, and you might want to radio ahead to a driver by the name of, ah, let's see now," as he flipped through his notebook, "ah, Tim Dooley, an over-the-road driver. You might ask the truckers to call ahead. He was heading north. I got some notes on that," as he reached into his back pocket. "And then there's another driver, a James Poole, driving a rickety old Peterbilt."

"I'll do that," the trooper said, and he turned to a couple drivers whose trucks were next to Wisniewski's and were waiting to pull out. The trooper waved them on. Meanwhile, the state police crime scene team arrived for photos. They also checked for fingerprints on the tire bully. They subsequently released the body to representatives of a nearby mortuary temporarily until the family could be alerted and could make their wishes known.

On the road ahead, Judd quickly realized he had a real problem, not in dealing with the police but in handling Sanchez. For as soon as Judd called in, a furious Sanchez would send out killers to eliminate him.

First he had to call Alina and get her and the girls out of the way and beyond the grasp of her father. For as soon as he found out about the killing, he would have his men watching Alina's apartment and their three daughters just in case Schmidt tried to reach them. Even Sanchez didn't know that they had been under surveillance for some time.

Judd decided that first he better get off the interstate quickly. He radioed back to Ole Jim, "I'm gonna turn off the next exit, Jim. I got a broad that's really hot for my body, and her man's off on a trip to Phoenix, and I'll stop for a half-hour or more, if that's all righ' with you. You could slow down and see if the kid catches up, or go righ' on in."

"I'll go on. See you den, Judd. Have fun."

"Righ'." And Schmidt turned off at exit 130, thinking to himself that there was a Wal-Mart here somewhere. He drove onto U.S. Hwy 3 headed west, and, at a light, pulled out his state map.

A tractor-trailer can't start fast, and it can't stop fast. It can't outrun a patrol car. It can run over one; it can run one off the road, but eventually the tractor-trailer will be stopped, probably by troopers putting down spikes to flatten the tires.

The light changed and Schmidt started up again and smiled as he saw a sign advertising a Wal-Mart in two miles, but at the same instant he saw in his rear-view mirror a police car closing fast.

Deputy Murdock Pinot had noticed a flickering taillight on Schmidt's chassis and saw an easy ticket to impress Sheriff Bryan Cupples, who had only yesterday chewed Pinot out for issuing so few tickets. But as Pinot pulled alongside, he got a call from headquarters about someone collapsing at a strip mall down on Hwy 3 east of I-95, and pulled away, making a sharp U-turn through traffic.

Schmidt told himself that maybe there was no alert on him, not yet, anyway. He drove on, observing the speed limit, and, as he turned left into the Wal-Mart parking lot, saw another patrol car coming fast, but roaring by.

He drove slowly through the parking area to the right side of the store, where containers were parked, backed his truck into an open slot and climbed out of his cab, disconnecting the chassis. He left the container there, its numbers facing to the rear. No one paid the least attention; containers were coming and going constantly at such big box stores.

Schmidt drove off in his tractor, down back roads back toward Fredericksburg, looking for parked trucks—a garage, a small truck stop, a diner. He guessed that, for a while at least, the cops would be looking for a tractor pulling a container, not a bobtail. He intended ditching his tractor as soon as possible, but first he needed different plates on it. There were no plates—just an identifying code—on the container he dropped off. There were plates on the chassis when he picked it up, and he left them on.

As he drove down one street, he saw a tractor parked outside a warehouse. He slowed and parked. No one was around. Within three minutes he had removed the plates from the parked tractor and replaced them with his.

Soon he reached I-95 and turned north, going three miles or less to Exit 133 and Highway 17 west, crossing over I-95. He was looking for a cheap motel. He found one in seven miles, stopped outside the door. "Need a room for the nigh'," he explained to the old man he woke up when Schmidt banged open the front door to the lobby.

"Yeh, sure. Thirty-five dollars up front. Number eight along the side. Here."

Schmidt took the key. "Okay I park the truck around back? Wouldn' want anyone breaking in."

"No problem." The old man just wanted to go back to sleep. He couldn't care where the tractor got parked.

Schmidt started up the tractor and drove it around back. He grabbed some clothes, cigarettes, the coffee Jim Poole had bought him—it was still warm—and walked back to the room, pretty clean, but well worn. 'Kinda like Ole Jim,' Judd thought.

He decided to call Alina and pulled out his cell phone.

"*Como estas?*"

"*Estoy* pretty bad. I got myself in a jam?"

"What have you done this time? You lose your temper again?"

"Yeh, I killed a trucker. But I can get out of it, and you, and the girls. But you gotta act fast."

"I know. We've already picked out the goons who

have been watching us for some time. We'll get away. So what do we do?"

"First, get out."

"*Adios.*" Alina had expected something like this for years. She hung up, called the girls together, and they followed a plan they had thought out. They called a taxi, and they all drove off into downtown Baltimore.

Alina, in the front seat, told the driver, "We're being followed. I have a hundred-dollar bill in my purse—she brought it out—and I want you to lose that car that is trailing us. It's a matter of life or death, our deaths, and maybe yours, too." She turned to the girls." Which one is it?"

"The blue Mazda," the youngest said.

The taxi driver, Alberto, said, "I see him. One car back of that Buick?"

"Yes."

"Hold on."

What Alina did not know was that Alberto had trained on the streets of New York City. He swerved from one street to another, and glancing around to see whether any police officer was at the corner, swung right, through a red light, drove the wrong way on a one-way street, turned through three corners, and pulled into a parking lot. The pursuing blue Mazda flew past. Alberto wove through the parking lot and onto a parallel street, going south, then west, south several blocks and finally east.

Alina: "Have we lost him, girls?"

Alberto: "I don't see him."

The youngest daughter: "You lost him easy."

Alina: "Then I guess it would be best to get out of town, however you wish. We want to get to the Dover Mall on U.S. Route 13 in Delaware."

"You're paying the bill. But if the guy chasing us somehow got my number and has an *amigo* who calls ahead?"

Alina: "You, *amigo*, call your best friend-driver, and we'll switch to his car *pronto*, and he gets a hundred dollars, too."

Alberto: "We're on our way." He pulled out his cell and called his friend. The switch was planned in southern Baltimore. And the three girls and their mother, who gave $100 to Alberto, piled into the second car, a Pontiac Grand Prix, and onto I-895, through the Baltimore Harbor Tunnel, and onto I-95 bound north.

Checking in with the Boss

Finally Schmidt decided he better phone Sanchez before too much time had passed. He should be happy just to get that damn trailer, Schmidt thought. "The cop spy is history—plain and simple," he announced when Sanchez picked up his phone.

"What are you talking about? What the hell happened?"

"I womped him with a tire bully. It did the trick. Cleaned out his wallet and drove off."

"You killed the kid?"

"Yep. At a truck stop in Virginia."

"Anybody see you."

"Nope. He needed killin.'"

"So what did you do then?"

"Jest left him dere."

"And?"

"I skeedaddled."

"Why the hell did you kill the kid? Maybe I can understand that, but why the hell did you run? They might not have tied it to you, you know. You could have stumbled onto the body, you know."

"I don't know, boss. I hated that kid so much, onct I knew he was cop kin. I'd probably have told the cops, 'Hell, yes. I killed the son of a bitch. He was no good living.'"

"You could have lied," Sanchez said, realizing that Schmidt had become a major liability now and not a week or two from now, as Sorensen had announced only a few days ago.

Schmidt: "Don' they have dem lie 'tectors?"

"Well it's too late now. You can't turn around and say it was an accident." A long pause.

Schmidt: "I'd better ditch the trailer. I'll have Ole Jim Poole continue, and I can bullshi' him 'bout needing to visit some broad along the way. He'll buy . . ."

"Hold on! That container goes to Eastern Avenue. You can't just abandon the load. Just where are you now?"

Schmidt: "I'll let you know." And he hung up, realizing he had offended someone who had helped him get rich and now could have him wasted, no matter that he was father of Sanchez's grandchildren.

An hour and a half later, Alina and the girls walked into the Dover Mall in Dover, and Alina called from a restroom.

Schmidt took the cell phone call in his hotel room. "Where are you now?"

"At the big shopping center in Dover, Delaware."

"Yeh, I dropped off c'tainers there a few times. Anyhow, I don't know whether I can bee' this. So here's how you geh away, and the girls, too. You should probly rent a car. There's a lawyer with an office in Highlandtown. His name is Benedito Alvarez; I've told you about him. And I showed you his office once oft Eastern."

Alina: "I remember."

Judd: "You have to go to his office. Leave the girls in Dover. They should be fine. When you get to Alvarez, ask him to get you all the money in our offshore account. If I can make it, we're going to South America."

Alina: "He'll never give me that money without you being there."

Judd: "We have a certain code that will free the funds, and you're registered as a co-partner, and Alvarez gets a cool $10,000 for getting all the money to you. Got a pencil?"

Alina: "Hold on. OK."

Schmidt gave her a series of letters and numbers. "OK, read that back." And Alina did. "There should be no problem," Judd said. "The process might take an hour or two. And he'll give you the funds as soon as he receives it. I'm going to try to geh a ride into the city with Ole Jim Poole, and I'll find a place to geh together with y'all."

Alina: "You in real trouble?"

Judd: "Yeh."

Alina: "What do I do then?"

Judd: "If I can't get to you, you and the girls jest have fun with the money, OK?"

Alina: "You'll make it. You always do." But he had hung up.

Schmidt decided he had better contact Sanchez once more.

When he answered, Judd said, "I parked the c'tainer at a Wal-Mart off Route 3 west of Fredericksburg, Virginia."

Sanchez: "You were supposed to take it to my reserved space off Eastern. But it should be safe until I can get someone to clean it out."

Schmidt: "I don't think the cops will even think of that for a week or more."

Sanchez, thinking that he had to call his woman contact immediately for a contract on Schmidt: "We'll have to break into that container real soon. Where are you now?"

"I put that c'tainer pretty much at the back of the lot out of the lights."

"Well, you're very hot now, especially since you ran

away from that kid. Can you dump the tractor somewhere? Where are you now?"

"I'll try, boss. Right now I'm . . ." cutting off his phone and thinking to himself that he'd be dead if Sanchez knew exactly where he was. He probably shouldn't have told him where he had dumped the container, for that wasn't too far away from where he was right now. But it was too late to worry about that now.

As trucks left the Ruther Glen truck stop heading north and south, the CBs crackled with the news of the killing, and within fifteen minutes Tim Dooley heard it as he circled Washington, D.C. He couldn't believe it, and called 911. "Yeh, this is a trucker heading north on I-95, and I can add some info to that killing at the truck stop in Ruther Glen in Virginia." He gave his cell phone number, and the person answering the call said he would alert the state police. A state trooper called within a minute, and took down all the information Dooley could provide, and his assertion that he believed this Judd Schmidt was certainly able and willing to kill the kid, for good reason or none.

The toughest phone call

Back at the truck stop, the crime-scene team was checking out the origin not only of Kenneth Wisniewski's tractor but also of the container it was pulling. They checked out his paperwork. They made sure he had been pulling the container he had signed out in Savannah. Each container has a SCAC (standard carrier alpha code), plus other numbers showing dimensions, owner, and country of origin. The box has a paper trail leading back to its construction, but most of that is in paper and filed away each year.

Lt. Sylvester Reed decided he was the one who had to notify Lt. Stach Wisniewski of his nephew's death, assuming Stach would want to be the first to tell Kenny's parents, his widow, Mira Wisniewski, and the rest of the family. This would not be easy, but he had to do it. He called Captain Dan Russo.

"Yes. That you, Syl?"

"Yes, and I need to talk to Stach."

"Hold on. He's just finishing roll call."

"I can wait. You'll probably want to listen in, Dan."

Russo: "Stach, Sylvester Reed wants to talk to you."

"Stach here. What's up?"

"Maybe you better sit down, Stach."

"What's happened?"

"Your nephew has been murdered."

There was a long pause. Stach was looking querulously at Dan Russo, who took a couple steps over to Stach and put his hands on Stach's shoulders. Finally, "What happened, Syl?"

"Kenny was killed with a tire bully, Stach."

"A what?"

"It's much like a long-handle hammer, Stach, and truckers use them to check the pressure in their tires from time to time."

"And . . . ?"

"Some truckers found him lying alongside his truck. He wasn't breathing then, they said, and his head was oozing badly. Apparently someone bashed him with this tire bully, took his wallet—it was found in a nearby trash basket, no money in it."

"Who . . . " Stach paused for a few seconds. "Who did it?"

"I'm not sure, but I'm guessing Judd Schmidt."

"But you were watching these guys . . ."

"Not at that time. And I am real shook up. I was back in my car talking with Captain Russo when it happened. See, the three of them, Schmidt, a crony of his, Jim Poole, and Kenny were at a table in the truck stop diner—Ruther Glen exit off I-95—and another trucker joined them for a while. He seemed to know Poole the best of the three, but I was not that close to pick up much. Anyway, I trailed this other guy out and took down all the details I could of his truck, license and such—it was parked right in front of the diner—and then, real stupid like, I walked back to my car to write down my notes and to call Captain Russo."

"And?"

"I heard a police siren and then saw some truckers running, and I asked one of them what happened, and he said that a trucker had been attacked. I hustled over there, the state police were on the scene. Kenny was crumbled on the pavement. I gave the troopers all the information I had, and they've put out bulletins to all their people."

"Have they got this Schmidt?"

"Not yet. But you can't hide a tractor and trailer like that."

"Thanks, Syl."

"I feel really bad, Stach. I should have been there . . ."

"No, Syl. I can't blame you. We never expected this kind of reaction. Right, Dan?" who nodded. "Here, I'll give you to Captain Russo."

His voice cloudy, Wisniewski stood up and said to Russo, "I have to go over to South Kenwood and break the news to Mira and the rest of the family. She should be home from work at the warehouse by now." He paused, then said quietly, "God in heaven, give me the right words to say."

Dan, holding the phone but not speaking into it, "It's my fault, Stach, for even allowing Kenny to go."

"No, Dan. We never expected this." And Lt. Stanislaus Wisniewski walked slowly from his office, nodding slightly to officers getting ready for their shifts but hearing nothing.

About a half-hour later, the phone rang at Rex Rossler Lines trucking firm in southern Baltimore. Mike Vitris, the dispatcher, passed the call along to the boss, identifying the caller as Virginia State Trooper Henderson.

"This is Jan Behrs-Rossler of Rex Rossler Lines. How may I help you, Trooper Henderson?"

"Ms. Rossler. I'm afraid we have some bad news for you." He paused. "One of your drivers—a Kenneth Wisniewski, twenty-nine, of South Kenwood Avenue in Baltimore—has been found dead at the Interstate 95 truck stop in Ruther Glen, Virginia. We suspect it's a homicide, that he was bludgeoned for his wallet," giving the cover story that Lt. Reed had suggested.

"Whatever you want or need will be made available to you immediately, Trooper Henderson. Will you be alerting the city's police department so that they can alert his family?"

"Yes, that was taken care of by a Lieutenant Reed. Can you confirm what Wisniewski's cargo was and what his destination was?"

"Please hold for a minute while I get that information." She put Henderson on hold and dialed Vitris. "What was the new young driver, Kenneth Wisniewski, pulling, and to where?"

"Hold on." After a minute. "The manifest shows textiles and garments, printed materials, pharmaceuticals and semi-precious stones, from Colombia, ordered by Sanchez Imports but being driven to a warehouse in the southern industrial area—the Central City Warehouse."

"Thank you." She clicked off, and passed the information along.

Henderson: "Thank you. Now, was Wisniewski driving, caravaning you might say, with any other drivers? One of the truckers said he saw him eating with three other truckers at the restaurant at the I-95 truck stop."

Ms. Rossler responded, "I believe so, but let me check. Please hold."

Vitris: "Yes, ma'am. You probably know Judd Schmidt was supposed to be shepherding Wisniewski, kind of showing him the ropes on the long runs to Savannah and back, and I seem to remember Ole Jim Poole, who drives for another OTR firm, usually tags along with Schmidt. They're both OTR veterans."

Mrs. Rossler passed along the report, and Henderson said, "That confirms information we have. And you might as well tell me what they were pulling."

Vitris relayed the information: "Schmidt was supposed to pick up a container carrying the same type of load as Wisniewski, also for Sanchez Importers, which was to be dropped off at a lot off Eastern Avenue near the Inner Harbor.

"I wouldn't know about Poole, if he was the third driver, for he drove for another firm, and I'm not sure, but it could be Carter TMan Lines. That's a new firm. Don't know if anyone else would hire him. He has some health problems.

"Schmidt and Wisniewski picked up containers at the Port of Savannah, Mrs. Rossler. I don't know about the third truck. Ole Jim doesn't like to make long runs anymore now, I seem to remember."

She passed along this information to State Trooper Henderson and then confirmed the plate numbers and truck numbers, as well as the numbers on the containers they were pulling. She passed these along and pledged whatever more help she could. She also said she would have someone from the firm—probably both she and her husband—seek out Wisniewski's family to express condolences.

A time to mourn

As he drove over to South Kenwood, Stach decided to go by St. Casimir's to see whether Father Miczelowski might be in. He was, and he agreed that he should go along with Stach to pray with Mira and her parents. Her father, Emil, had been and still was a pillar in the church.

Lt. Wisniewski knocked on the door at 847 South Kenwood Avenue, and Mira came bustling out. "Uncle Stach and Father Miczelowski, how great to see you," and she urged them into the parlor, while she bubbled along: "I'm just starting to put dinner together. I got off early from work. Kenny should be getting here any minute now. It's been his longest trip so far." Stach tried to interrupt her but was unable as she hurried on. "He called when the sun was just coming up this morning. Oh, it's been such a great day. And he said he had some souvenirs from Savannah, and . . ." She stopped. "Oh, Father, did you want to see my dad?"

Father Miczelowski: "Yes, it would be good if we could talk to your father, and your mother and you, Mira."

She stiffened. "Something's wrong. Uncle Stach, is something wrong? Oh no. It's Kenny," and she exclaimed, "Oh, my God!" and then screamed, bringing her father, mother and sister running from other rooms into the parlor.

Emil: "What is happening? Mira, why are you screaming? Oh, Stach, good to see you. Father? Is there something wrong at St. Casmers?"

Father: "I think it would be better if Stanislaus spoke first. Then I'll speak, Emil. Please sit down, all of you."

Stach: "I asked Father to come over with me. I have some very sad news. Kenny was killed . . ."

Mira screamed, "No! No! No!"

Her father and mother quickly rose to comfort her. But she could not stop, until they both hugged her.

"Let's hear Stach out," her mother said through sobs, as neighbor ladies responding to the screams rushed to the front door.

Mira's crying eased to sobbing, for she could not be comforted, and she trembled and sobbed on throughout the evening, as the families, neighbors and friends quickly gathered.

Stach, taking her hand: "We should invite Junior and Betty over. I'll get them." And he left to go three doors down and to bring Betty over. Junior was still on a painting job, and had called about an hour ago that he probably wouldn't be home until dark.

Father Miczelowski: "Emil. I don't know the facts yet, but it apparently was a murder."

Emil: "Who in hell, oh, I'm sorry, Father, but who would want to kill that young man."

Danuta interjected, her arms around her daughter, trying somehow to stop the shuddering: "It's unbelievable, Father. How could this happen? He was such a nice boy, and about to become a father," a comment that spurred Mira into even more shuddering and sobbing.

Stach and Betty entered the home and turned into the parlor, Betty tearing but going over to Mira to share her misery.

Stach spoke slowly: "I've told Betty a little, but this is all that I know at the moment. Kenny was killed by someone wielding a tire bully, which is something like a long-handled hammer. This happened at a truck stop in southern Virginia. He was found by other truckers lying on the pavement alongside his truck. His wallet had been taken and tossed into a garbage barrel, with no money in it.

"We're not sure who did it, but we suspect one of the other two drivers that he was traveling with. Captain Daniel Russo is in contact with Virginia State Police, who have issued a thirteen-state alarm for both of the other drivers.

"We don't know why he was killed, but we suspect that one of the other two drivers was secretly conveying drugs into Baltimore, and Kenny somehow found out." He stopped.

Father Miczelwoski jumped in: "Let us pray." He spoke quietly and firmly as tears ran down the eyes of all gathered there, with Mira's sobbing ebbing and flowing, and all there knew for certain that Father was being prompted by God in the words he chose. And he continued on for more than ten minutes. He said later that night to a fellow priest at St. Casimir's that he felt he had truly been coached from above.

Emil was so moved that he hugged the priest, embarrassing both of them. But then he did it again. "Thank you, Father. Thank you."

The front door to the row house had not been shut when Stach and Betty entered, so a growing group of neighbors had assembled, alerted not only by Mira's screams but also by Father Miczelwoski's presence, and they filtered in, the women to cry with Mira, Betty and Danuta, and the men to shake hands and share shoulder embraces with Emil, who lost his voice, and Stach, who accepted the condolences in what he hoped was a manly fashion. As evening settled in, Junior arrived, and he cried openly and unashamedly and hugged the women who came by, and the men, too. He needed the consoling.

Father left about 10 p.m. after visiting with each of the family, assuring Emil and Danuta, Junior and Betty that he would return the next day to help plan the funeral. Mira had dozed off thanks to the sedatives her girlfriends had urged her to take.

The hunt begins

Meanwhile, Capt. Dan Russo called Rossler Lines and was routed to Jan. He chatted politely for a minute with

Jan, asking about Patsy, and then asked that the firm develop as full a history as it could on both Schmidt and the containers he had pulled. She called two shipping clerks from their dinners to get back to the office to develop the information from the company's files.

Virginia State Police put out advisories to stop all Peterbilts headed north and south on I-95, and they completed this task, now fully armed with the numbers on Schmidt's container and his license plates. Trooper Henderson had talked to Tim Dooley, who, now in New Jersey headed to New York, described the Peterbilt Jim Poole had driven while following Dooley for eight years or more.

Within five minutes of this last advisory, Poole was slowing down and pulling onto the side of I-95 escorted by two Virginia state patrol cars. He reached for his logbook and his CDL, and waited for the troopers to come up, assuming he had committed some minor transgression.

Poole, from his cab: "Well, officers, what have I gon' and don' now? A light burn out?"

State Trooper Dan Murphy: "We just want to question you. Please step down."

Poole: "Whatever." And he did.

"Did you just stop at the truck stop in Ruther Glen?"

"Yep. Had a meal there."

"You alone?"

"Nope. Der was three of us."

"Their names."

"Sure. Judd Schmidt—I ben drivin' with 'im fer ten years now, but I'm not sure that's his first name—and a new kid, Kenny Wiz-somethin'." He coughed a little. "Oh, and Tim Dooley, an old driving buddy of mine. He stopped by for a while."

"Were you in some sort of a convoy?"

"Sorta. But not Tim. Now Judd and the kid was comin'

back from Savanny, and me from Charleson, and I jest' waited for Judd to stop at the truck stop north of I-95 on I-26, and then tag along. Oh, yeh, Tim Dooley, another trucker, he stopped by. It was good to see him." Poole coughed several times. "We ate at that truck stop you mentioned. Then Judd said the kid had a tire problem and had to have a tire fixed or replaced or somethin', so we wen' and lef' him at the truck stop." He coughed more heavily, ". . . and Judd, well, he got off a ways back to see one of his, ah, girlfriends."

"The younger man, this Kenneth Wisniewski, was found dead beside his truck at Ruther Glen. Could you . . ."

Poole: "Dead! Oh shi'." And he coughed and coughed for several minutes, before leaning against his truck and getting his breath back He whispered harshly, "How the hell'd he die? That's a rough place, 'specially at night." And he coughed again.

Trooper Murphy, who waited: "You're going to have to come with us, Mr. Poole. Lock up your truck. But first get whatever you have in there about yourself, your truck and your cargo. You said this Judd Schmidt got off the Interstate? Where was that?"

"Shi'. Let's see. Yeh, I know. He got off at Highway 17. Yeh, that was it."

"When?"

"Mebbe fifteen minutes 'go, I guess, but I didn't look at . . ." He coughed extensively, ". . . my watch."

"You know which direction he took on Highway 17."

"Nope. Weren't interested. But I got to keep this refrigerated container going, troopers. I can't leave it. If it's all righ' with you, I'll follow along."

"I understand. Fine, we'll escort you and turn around over the next overpass."

The two troopers started up, one ahead of Poole, the

other behind, and Murphy radioed in the information Poole had provided to the State Police district in Virginia.

In Baltimore, *The Baltimore Sun*'s wires desk picked up the news service report from Ruther Glen, Virginia, on Kenneth Wisniewski, and a reporter was immediately assigned to dig into Wisniewski's background, to develop a sidebar to the main story, which would be filed by a Washington-based reporter now on his way to the truck stop. The victim's name probably meant the trucker came from Canton or Highlandtown, the assigning editor surmised. *The Baltimore Sun* accents its pages with news stories and features about ethnic neighborhoods.

Jeff Allen, who was assigned the sidebar, had worked the police beat for several years and immediately called Lt. Stach Wisniewski, an old friend, on his cell phone. Stach was going back to the Kowalski household, but passed along what little information he had, a passionate remembrance of Kenny and also some leads to some of his friends, who might give Allen the color he really sought. But the lieutenant could not relay any details yet of exactly what had happened at the truck stop in Virginia. He suggested Allen call Capt. Dan Russo.

But Allen headed to Canton to follow up Stach Wisniewski's leads. Two young Polish-American women, one married, the other divorced, sobbed in remembering the young man they had been unable to catch, but Stan Petrovski, who was walking down South Kenwood when Allen spotted him, provided precisely what Allen was looking for.

Petrovski, now an accountant, had grown up in a Canton row house a block or two east from South Kenwood and had been a close buddy of Kenny's. In fact, the two had enlisted in the Marines together, had gone through basic together at Parris Island, and were assigned to the

1,900-member 22nd Marine Amphibious Unit (22d MAU in service talk) that in October 1983 was sailing to Lebanon, with maneuvers on the way in Spain.

Or so they thought, until President Ronald Reagan intervened. In an address to the nation, the president spoke about the safety of 600 American students at an offshore medical school on the little known Caribbean island of Grenada, and a communist leader's ascension to power in Grenada by having the prime minister, also a communist, executed. It was later determined that the Reagan administration really wanted to show that the United States would not tolerate communist Cuba's escalating influence in the Caribbean.

Anyway, Petrovski and Wisniewski, with many other green hands in their company, but with well-seasoned non-coms, were suddenly briefed on Grenada by officers who knew little of the island and were not too clear on what they would do when they got there.

"We had just heard that 241 gyrenes had been killed by a truckload of explosives in Lebanon, so we were ready for a fight," Petrovski told Allen.

But Petrovski's comments that caught the attention of Polish-Americans in Canton, Highlandtown and the eastern suburbs of Baltimore, where many Polish-Americans moved from the city, centered on Kenny and a mutual friend they had at Mount St. Joseph's, a foreign exchange student.

Petrovski said, "We were on amphibs which landed at Grand Mal, about 7 p.m. And there we waited for hours until another company coptered down to join us. We were to rescue some English official from Government House. This was really an English island somehow. Don't know whether they appreciated our invading. . . . Anyway, the Grenadian force bailed out from the Government House, and we rescued Sir somebody or other (Scoon, Grenada's governor-general)."

"We were then assigned to take a Fort Adolphus, and we found out later that our colonel could have called in planes or ship batteries to level the place. Don't really know whether he was actually considering that. Officers don't consult with us grunts, you know."

But Kenny's friendship with a foreign student at Mount St. Joseph saved what could have been an international incident, no doubt damning the whole operation, according to Petrovski.

"(Kenny) told the sergeant, who passed the word up through channels, that the flag flying over the fort, which nobody else could identify, was Venezuelan. Damned if it didn't turn out to be the Venezuelan Embassy! I don't think Kenny ever got credit for that, but it was something he did.

"So instead of maybe blasting the fort into rubble, the colonel ordered us to scout it out, and, sure enough, it was the embassy. Man, that was close."

Allen's feature, as a sidebar to the news story on Kenny's death, fueled Polish-American passion throughout the area, causing several Polish-American veterans of Korea and Vietnam to organize a contingent to escort Kenny's body to the cemetery, and the snowball just started rolling and growing. The ethnic groups of Baltimore have a history of parading, for example, the Polish Constitution Day Parade, the St. Gabriel's and St. Anthony's parades through Little Italy, and the I Am An American Day Parade by Italians, Poles, Czechs, Greeks, Ukrainians and others.

Kenny Returns Home

On the day after Kenny was killed, a mortuary from Baltimore sent its vehicle to the funeral home in Fredericksburg to pick up Kenny's body. The coroner confirmed that blows to the skull, likely from the tire bully, had killed the young man. He said there had been bleeding into the brain and some epidural hematoma.

Mira was able to choose the suit he would wear, which was actually the only one he owned, a light brown suit he put on when going to church on major festivals. Mira was unable to do much more than that; her nerves were shot; her appetite was gone. She went through the day in a stupor, chaperoned and consoled constantly by girlfriends, her mother and her mother-in-law.

Father Misczelowski returned to work out the funeral details, and Emil, Mira's father, pretty well accepted what Father suggested. Mira heard all the details, but understood nothing. The funeral would be in two days. Her father and mother went to the nearby funeral home to see, with Junior and Betty, Kenny's parents, that the body was ready. They all rode in the funeral home limousine in front of the hearse that delivered the body to South Kendall Avenue.

Mira suddenly rushed out with two girlfriends at her side to see the coffin lifted out by the attendants and to place her hand on the coffin as it was carried up the five steps and into the parlor of the row house she and Kenny had purchased. When the coffin was opened, she saw her husband in his brown suit, broke into heavy tears and collapsed into the arms of her girlfriends.

About 2 p.m. that day the extended families began arriving, the Wisniewskis and the Kowalskis. Most knelt down to pray beside the coffin and then to speak softly with Junior and Betty, Kenny's parents, and Stacy and Lynn, his two younger sisters, and with Emil and Danuta, Mira's father and mother. The women hugged Mira for as long as she allowed, and cried with her.

Father Miczelowski came by twice, once for about a half-hour in the morning and again about 3 p.m. Like everyone, he partook of the buffet offered in the kitchen, where everyone gathered and spoke softly after praying at the coffin. The soft, respectful talking carried on into the night.

Wal-Mart Pickup

On the next day, the day before Kenny's funeral, three men on Felipe Sanchez's under-the-counter payroll but wearing Wal-Mart aprons drove a rented delivery truck to the Wal-Mart on Route 3 west of Fredericksburg, Virginia, and parked near the trailers.

One walked around to see whether there was any security about, found none and signaled to a second man, who went to the back of the store to take possession of a forklift. He drove it to the side of the container they had been looking for. The first man then attached a small explosive to the locks sealing the container. One of the men checked to ensure that no one was near enough to hear, and signaled the second man, who detonated the explosive, which made a quick and fairly quiet puff. The two then opened the doors, and the third drove up the forklift.

All of this was observed by two Fredericksburg police officers who were the second relief officers as stakeouts to the men who had discovered the van. The two relief men were lying prone in bush beneath some trees. Wal-Mart personnel had been instructed to leave a forklift available and to keep clear of the back of the store until further notice.

The two staked-out officers hiding in woods across Maple Grove Drive behind the Wal-Mart quietly alerted their headquarters to the latest development, where Virginia State Police waited to coordinate the assault. They immediately rushed to the scene in police cruisers, no sirens sounding nor emergency lights flashing, rendezvousing at a gas station about a mile from the Wal-Mart.

Meanwhile, the Sanchez men were picking up cartons from the container and transferring them by forklift to their trailer. They had been given the numbers on the boxes that Sanchez wanted and their location—he had never suggested there was anything but drugs for the three-member team to retrieve—but they were getting edgy about taking much more time than they anticipated getting to the right carton, and the man waiting in the truck was the most anxious. He studied every car entering and parking in the Wal-Mart lot.

The staked-out officers kept their headquarters alerted, and a desk officer radioed the policemen and troopers at the assembly point at the service station.

Fredericksburg Chief Jonathan Alkron suggested, and the state troopers agreed, that most of their men should transfer to civilian vehicles to enter the parking lot, with drivers of patrol cars parking along the exit lanes awaiting orders.

Policemen then drove to the Wal-Mart, parked in various lots nearby, and then stopped several cars, pickups and minivans entering the lot. The policemen explained that they were responding to a drill and needed to enter the parking lot unseen. The citizens bought the idea, promising not to get in the way, and each parked—guided by the officers—in an irregular semicircle around the container and parked truck, with everyone but the officers getting out and walking casually toward the Wal-Mart. They looked about, as almost anyone in that situation would, but luckily for the police the third man, who had been sitting on the forklift, had climbed into the container to hurry the other two along. He returned to the cab, but saw only one or maybe two of the minivans pull up and park, and watched the civilians leave, but could not see the officers remaining in those vehicles.

Chief Alkron and his second-in-command entered the lot in the back of a Dodge Grand Caravan driven by a young woman with two infants, who had to take each boy from his car seat and transfer him into what she made a two-passenger cart. She said she would probably take about forty-five minutes for her shopping. The chief suggested that she try to wait a good hour, and she agreed that she could feed the little ones with snacks she had bought. She wished the officers success in their drill.

All the men in vehicles partly encircling the truck were in contact with walkie-talkies and checked in with the chief. The two staked-out Fredericksburg officers relayed information from time to time.

"We'll likely wait until they get whatever they are going for," Chief Alkron said to his chief aide in the back of the Grand Caravan parked about forty yards from the trailer. His orders were to shoot to kill if the men fired on police officers. He assumed they would.

"Think they're important?" Lt. Bob Tansey, the second in command, asked as he cradled his rifle in his lap.

"Whatever weapons they're carrying might just help us resolve a number of drug-related killings here and elsewhere, I would guess. I don't think they're minor people, by any means. But I assume that what they're after is much more important than the three of them put together."

"No way we can take them without a shootout?" Tansey asked.

Chief Alkorn: "I don't want to risk our men. Here's something," he added as his phone bleeped. "Uh-huh." He turned to Tansey. "The stakeouts say it looks like they're getting ready to pull out."

The state and city police officers were alerted to the imminence of gunfire, with one squad ordered to stop all traffic entering the lot, and several officers prepared to stall shoppers and workers trying to leave the store.

A small pickup to the right of the chief's minivan started up as the three men exited the container and began

211

to close the doors. The unidentified vehicle suddenly doused the three in two strong spotlights, and chief Alkron shouted over a loud-speaker from the Dodge Caravan: "This is the police! Stop what you're doing! Drop what you're carrying! Don't go for your guns! Put your hands up!"

But all three men had brought out revolvers to shoot out the spotlights and whomever they could see, and did knock out one spotlight before Chief Alkron shouted into his microphone, "Open fire!" And a barrage of arms let loose, tearing the three men to shreds.

"Enough!" the chief commanded within thirty seconds, and the firing ceased. One of the men was still moving on the ground. A number of officers ran toward the truck, including the two staked-out patrolmen. But the man still moving on the ground gained control of his revolver, and one of the staked-out officers, the nearest to him, fired three times, killing him before he could reach the trigger.

"Cordon off the area," Chief Alkron commanded, and several officers holstered their weapons and played out crime-scene tape. Other officers checked to see whether any bystanders had been hit, and they did find an old man, who had been walking to his car at least 150 yards away, down from a chance bullet hitting him in the thigh.

"OK, let's get the crime-scene people in here, pronto," the chief said, and the tactical squads secured the container, the forklift, the rental truck and the trailer. And he ordered officers to allow traffic to resume, both vehicle and pedestrian.

Unnoticed by all the officers on the scene, a blue '92 Acura Legend coupe slowly pulled out of the now-open exit of the Wal-Mart parking lot and drove within the speed limits back toward a condo overlooking Baltimore's Inner Harbor. Bo Jager had seen the police officers gathering, and assumed now that he would have a different contract.

He was to have eliminated the three henchmen and taken over their rental truck after they drove off the lot.

He was listening to the radio report as he drove. He had not connected their contract with the killings at the hospital. It was just another contract to him. 'Oh well,' he thought, 'just a little ride in the country.'

Sanchez was having a second Corona at Sorensen's condo when the radio news reported a shootout involving police at a Wal-Mart near Fredericksburg, Virginia. Both men put down their bottles and sat up, and Sorensen turned the sound louder and flipped on the TV to WBAL, but it had not switched to its newsroom. He turned down the TV sound, and the two men concentrated on the radio report.

Sorensen: "I'll assume our hit man wasn't able to wipe out the three."

"No indication of that yet." Both listened as the radio announcer gave a very preliminary report. "Let's wait to see what develops before getting on the phone again."

Back at the Wal-Mart, the bodies of the three men were taken to a local mortuary, where state and federal officials checked for fingerprints. In addition, the weapons recovered were given to the FBI to see whether they could be linked to other crimes.

State and city officials then called in a local trucker to pull the container and back it into a nearby firehouse, and had another trucker drive the rental truck to the same location. These movements were made not only to allow the DIA and local and state police officials to check out what was in the rental truck and in the container that Schmidt dropped without a crowd of gawking locals watching, but also to accommodate Wal-Mart officials, who wanted to get back to business. They had some of their workmen wash down the area where the rental truck and trailer had been.

Fredericksburg Police Chief Alkron had already been briefed by Baltimore police officials on what they suspected was aboard the container—they said drugs, specifically cocaine—and Chief Alkron had decided to invite DIA agents to help check out the cargo. He expected that this process would last up to three days as agents carefully opened and searched each box and each barrel.

The DIA agents and police detectives started with the cargo that had been moved into the rental truck and, in less than an hour, Chief Alkron called in the FBI.

And Baltimore Capt. Dan Russo suggested to Virginia State Police and the local DIA office that they also ought to double-check everything aboard the container Kenny Wisniewski had been pulling. Taking into account Wisniewski's murder, the Baltimore police officials suggested that there could have been drugs on that container as well.

Kenny's Funeral

The next day was the day of Kenneth Wisniewski's funeral, and the young new widow tried to control her tears.

She had slept little during the three-days wake in the Wisniewski home. Her eyes would indicate she was listening attentively, but she was hearing absolutely nothing from the many good women, young and old, who sat down with her to console her, to hold her hand, to wipe away her and their tears, and to maintain their own composure to help her get through. The younger women—Mira's girlfriends over the years—mainly hugged her for what seemed like hours, unashamedly allowing tears to flow down their faces.

The men mostly nodded, perhaps shook her hand, mumbled something, and went along to talk with Junior or Emil or her brothers about Kenny, and drugs, and baseball, and bowling and politics. That appeared to be the progression. Capt. Dan Russo and his wife, Tina, stopped by, he to talk with Stach Wisniewski and she to visit with Mira and her mother, Danuta.

Also stopping by were Rex and Jan Rossler, he the owner of Rossler Lines, she the actual boss. He spoke briefly with Junior and Emil; she consoled Mira, Danuta and Betty, who throughout characteristically said very little.

The phone rang from time to time with outstate relatives asking about funeral plans. One call was passed along to Stach. "Yes," he said.

"Stach, this is Tom Hampton, and I just want to convey my condolences to you, Kenneth's parents and his widow. I'm sorry things ended like that."

"Well, you were against this plan, and we ignored you, and you were right. Lieutenant Reed foresaw nothing out of the usual."

"I've been wrong more times than right, it seems. I'm real sorry I was right this time. How are his folks taking it?"

"Predictably."

"I guess I would be that way, too. Anything new on the case?"

"We're still looking for the driver Kenny was sort of shadowing."

"You apparently were dealing with a seasoned killer."

"Dan Russo is asking the FBI to get his military record. According to an over-the-road trucker who had lunch with the three of them apparently just before the murder, this Judd Schmidt had some gruesome stories from Vietnam."

"Whenever we can be of help . . ."

"Thank you, Tom. I really appreciate your call and I'll pass along your condolences."

"Thank you and good day."

There were no real estate deals considered at the wake—which frequently occurred for old folks who had died—for Mira and Kenny were already living in the row house on South Kenwood that he inherited from his grandparents in a deal approved by the extended Wisniewski family.

By the hundreds

That night, the third of the wake, Mira finally dropped off to sleep as her mother rubbed her back. For breakfast, she had a toasted cheese sandwich and some juice, got dressed in a dark pant suit and followed her parents out the door, only to see hundreds of folks, all dressed in their finery, heading for St. Casimir's.

'Did alla these people know Kenny?' she thought. 'This is overwhelming,' and she slumped against her father, who grabbed her about the shoulder. Actually someone known as a *clepsydra*, rather like a town crier, had shouted the details of the funeral at corners throughout Canton, Highlandtown and other points of Baltimore's own Polonia. And Polish-Americans, whose loyalties just needed to be touched ever so slightly, responded.

"We'll walk to St. Casimir's," Emil said. "Looks like everyone else is," which caused Mira to bury her face in her hankie.

The crowd silenced itself and walked more slowly to allow the family to pass through. Her mother kept her head high and looked ahead, but her father nodded without smiling to people he knew. However, he didn't appear to know more than half those going toward the church. 'Surely it won't hold them all,' he thought. 'It only seats 1400.' He would learn later that besides packing the church beyond its capacity, the crowd had encircled the building, built in 1926 of Renaissance design, 225 feet long, 70 feet wide.

In response to the predicted overflow attendance, speakers had been rented and set up outside. *The Sun* estimated that more than 1,000 people stood outside for the funeral mass, with another 1,500 inside.

The extended Wisniewski and Kowalski families took up the first two rows on both sides of the aisle, and, after being seated for a minute or two, stood, looking toward the back of the church, causing the rest of the congregation to rise and look as well.

There waited Father Miczelowski. The organist began playing "On Eagle's Wings," and Father Miczelowski nodded to three waiting cross bearers. They raised their crosses and slowly began walking toward the altar, followed by twelve pallbearers, each holding a handle of the gantry on which the covered casket lay. Then came Mira, with her father and mother, and Junior and Betty, Kenny's parents, and his two sisters. They had been standing in back.

The pallbearers, all Polish-Americans, were two truckers, two police officers, two U.S. Marines, two members of St. Casimir's Church Council, with symbols of their office, and four high school friends of Kenny wearing the purple and cream colors of Mount St. Joseph High School, including Miguel Santos, the Venezuelan friend, now an attorney, who had a tiny flag of his country stuck in his vest pocket.

Mira had started our fairly calmly from the back of the huge church, but the sobbing of the women as she walked along broke her down, and caused a flow of tears all along the aisle. Men smothered their grief by holding their breaths, the old men turning a bright red in the effort. The younger men studied St. Casimir's reproduction of the altar of St. Anthony in Padua, Italy, with its thirty sculptures.

When the casket reached the altar, Father Miczelowski sprinkled the casket with holy water and invited a representative from each family—Lt. Stranislaus Wisniewski, in uniform, and Ted Piasecki, Mira's cousin—to assist him in placing a white pall over the casket, a ceremony tieing Kenny's death back to his baptism, when he also was dressed in white, Father Miczelowski explained to the congregation.

Father then said the church was filled with the family and friends of the deceased, "and I'm told all around our church, to praise and thank God for Jesus's victory over sin and death. And to commend Kenny to God's mercy and passion."

Father then read an opening prayer, and the liturgy of the Word. He led Psalm 23, alternating with the congregation.

Tadeusz, Kenny's cousin, was invited to the lectern to read from the New Testament lesson from 1 John 3: "Behold what manner of love the Father hath bestowed upon us, that we should be called the sons of God; therefore the world knoweth us not, because it knew him not. Beloved, now are we the sons of God, and it doth not yet appear what we shall be, but we know that, when he shall appear, we shall be like him, for we shall see him as he is. And every man that hath this hope in him purifieth himself, even as he is pure."

A gospel acclamation was sung, and Father Miczelowski read the familiar John 14: ". . . in my house are many mansions . . ."

'Not row houses,' Mira thought as she listened.

"And whither I go ye know, and the way ye know."

She remembered Kenny's proposal, and his promise: "Mir, I'm not good at talking about love and all that, but I really love you. And I won't ever stop loving you." He had paused to catch his breath. "Yep. That's it."

And she came back to reality to catch Father saying, ". . . God's love embraces you now, especially you, the widow, and the parents, both of the deceased and of his widow. God will provide. He is always ready to listen. And you will go on, with the faith he inspires. As the words of the most familiar psalm say, 'you are walking through the valley of the shadow of death,' but you will get through."

Mira thought to herself that Kenny had been more than a good man. He had suffered without complaint the silly engagement business her parents had demanded of him and the silliness at the reception. 'There weren't all those people out that day. What a happy day! Now it's over, and the little one growing in me will never know his father. What a good man.' And the tears flowed, and the priest stopped in his homily, but continued on: ". . . by the family. Please stand."

And he said a Prayer of the Faithful, and moved into the liturgy of the Eucharist. The Kowalskis brought up gifts of bread and wine for the Eucharist, and Mira thought to herself, 'Will they ever stop? And answered herself, 'No, they won't.'

The communion went forward and lasted for almost an hour, as people filed into the church from outside, and then back, each turning to nod toward the first rows, and touch the casket as he or she passed by. Pallbearers shook their heads ever so slightly to discourage those who would have kneeled beside the casket. Such prayers could have caused the service to run into the evening hours.

The celebrant then announced that James Magurno, one of the pallbearers and a close friend of Kenny's at Mount St. Joseph, would deliver a brief eulogy. Many people in the congregation frowned on learning that a non-Polish American had been chosen.

Magurno took the lectern: "It is very difficult . . . " He stopped as his throat seemed to dry out, but recovered, ". . .

to speak of your best friend in the past tense. But, Mira, I assure you that Ken lives in my mind, and will never die there.

"I know that he was a credit to his family and to his church. It will be only right for me to walk to the cemetery (a three-mile hike), as I suspect many of you plan to do." Many who hadn't even thought of that decided in a flash that they would. "Captain Daniel Russo, chief of the detective bureau at the Northern District, told me before the service that the marching band from St. Leo's Church, which we both belong to, has volunteered to march at the very end of the column and play in honor of Ken."

A ripple of claps grew into a crescendo in appreciation of the significant gesture from a fellow Catholic community. As the applause quieted, Magurno resumed: "Ken Wisniewski grew up in Canton, son of Junior and Betty Wisniewski, older brother of Stacey and Lynn. Seven months ago he married a beautiful young lady, Mira Kowalski, in this very church, and I was honored to be one of the groomsmen. I add today that her beauty is enhanced even more by her expecting their child." Mira flushed, and lowered her watering eyes.

"Ken graduated from Mount St. Joseph's—where we were close friends—he having starred on the purple and cream's soccer teams. But he would not brag, even though *The Baltimore Sun* called him the school's greatest striker.

"It was his idea, but Kenny, Stan Petrovsky (Magurno nodded to Petrovsky) and I enlisted together into the Marine Corps, and saw action in Grenada. You read in the paper how he avoided an international incident. I suspect that even you did not know that, Mira." She nodded her head slightly. "He was a very modest man.

"In his second enlistment, he learned how to drive big trucks in the Marines, and he turned that knowledge into a career. He made a few dozen runs to Philadelphia,

Washington, Harrisburg, Pennsylvania, and Cleveland, pulling those huge containers that come into Baltimore by ship from overseas.

"Many of you read the great story reporter Jeff Allen did in *The Sun* about Kenny. Stan really helped on that," and he nodded again to Petrovsky. "Yesterday, Jeff Allen got a letter from Havertown, Pennsylvania. I had called him for some help on this talk—I'm not much good at it—and he shared this letter.

"This woman, who didn't want her name used, said she recognized Kenny from the photo in *The Sun*, and she wanted to tell his wife of how he had stopped to help her and her two children when they had been rear-ended on the interstate south of Philadelphia. The other driver, an older man, had had a heart attack just before the traffic slowed, and his car had rammed her car into a delivery truck ahead. She said she couldn't open her door, and couldn't get to her children who were screaming in their car seats in the back.

"She wrote, 'But this man stopped his big tractor-trailer on the side of the road behind us and ran up with some kind of a bar and wrenched open my door, and he and another man who stopped were able to get the children out. He then checked on the man in the car that rammed me, but he was unconscious. And he waited with me and the children until police and the ambulance arrived, and then left, never even giving his name.

"His stopping and helping showed me there really are good people in this world," she wrote, adding, "Please tell Mrs. Wisniewski that we suffer with her in the loss of this good person."

Once more applause sounded throughout the church, echoed outside by those listening to the loud speakers.

Magurno continued, "Captain Russo, who heads the detective bureau at the Northern District, told me that he and Lieutenant Wisniewski, Ken's uncle, had asked Ken a couple months back whether he would be willing to caravan with a driver they suspected of trafficking in drugs. This is a scourge of Baltimore, an illicit business that ruins young people. Ken never hesitated in saying he would help in any way he could. According to Captain Russo, it appears that Ken was surprised by a drug-trafficking driver and killed." Magurno paused, taking a deep breath. "His death stunned us. How could anybody hate this man?" He paused.

"As fellow Catholics, you and I know that Ken is now awaiting the glory of the resurrection. I thank you, Ken Wisniewski, for being in my life, and I salute you." James saluted the casket. "God bless you," he added quietly, and tears appeared in his eyes as he started down from the lectern. The applause was deafening as the congregation rose to its feet. Mira, in heavy tears, was steadied by her father.

Father Miczelowski allowed the applause to run its course, and everyone to sit, before incensing the casket and saying over it the prayer that commended Kenny's soul to God. Father then walked down to the family, who rose, as they waited for the casket to be turned by the pallbearers. The congregation rose as the casket headed out, and followed the family.

Outside, hundreds of people parted on O'Donnell Street to allow the funeral procession to form. Following three police cruisers that led the procession were three boys carrying crucifixes and candles, which had to be relit from time to time by one of the boy's fathers, who walked along the sidewalk as the boys walked down the center.

Then came Father Miczelowski and two assistants in smocks. Then the casket, on an old farm wagon that dated back to when Stach Wisniewski's grandparents had worked in the fields way out Eastern. The wagon had been specially decorated and was escorted by the twelve pallbearers.

Following were Mira and her sister, Kasia, and parents, then the extended Wisniewski family—including aunts Sophia and Irene, who walked all the way despite her arthritis, and never complained—and the extended Kowalski family. The Polish-American veterans had provided a type of soft shoe that women could use to walk to the cemetery. Most like Mira had been wearing high heels, and followed her example in switching to the soft shoes.

Next were the children of St. Casimir's schools, led by those wearing the special outfits their parents had bought for first communion; the Holy Name Society; the Junior Holy Name Society; the Young Ladies Sodality, even a few of the Beautiful Years Club (the old timers), and three cars full of those old timers who couldn't walk that far.

Then came the friends, most every one of Polish-American descent in the city and suburbs, and others. *The Sun* estimated the total at 3,000. Hardly anyone disputed the figure, although Emil said later that he thought there were at least 5,000 people marching. At the back was St. Leo's band.

The procession followed O'Donnell Street east under I-895 and I-95 to pick up Boston Street, turning into Saint Stanislaus Cemetery. It took twenty minutes for the column to inundate the burial sight. Volunteers had set up tents with water and benches for those who wearied, and Johnny-on-the-Spots along the route.

Finally, Father Miczelowski heard St. Leo's band turning in, then toning down the instruments to a single drum, which in turn stopped. All the two extended families were seated or standing under three tents placed next to each other, Mira and her immediate family in the center along with Betty and Junior and their daughters opposite the grave.

Father explained that this rite of committal would be the final act of this vast community of faith on behalf of

Kenneth Wisniewski. In this ceremony, Father explained, speaking directly to Mira but with a microphone that echoed throughout the cemetery, this community of faith was expressing the hope that, like others who have gone before him, Kenny awaited the glory of the resurrection. "He is passing with the farewell prayers of this vast community of believers," Father said, extending his arms over one of the largest gatherings he had seen at a funeral, "into the welcoming company of those who already see God face to face."

The casket was lowered into the grave, and Mira rose and stepped forward to drop the flowers she had carried from the church. The rest of the immediate families filed by, and then everyone else decided they should, too. Head held high, her tears in check, Mira then began the walk back, shaking her head when her father suggested that she ride back in a funeral home car. She felt that she needed to exhaust herself.

Almost everyone else decided that they, too, would walk the three miles back, even those who had made different arrangements, but a few of the old timers, including Aunts Sophia and Irene, wisely puffed over to cars and minivans to make the trip back.

Why such a response?

In an op-ed piece in *The Baltimore Sun* the day after Kenny Wisniewski's funeral, editorial writer George V. Abington discussed the procession that had accompanied the body to the cemetery and then walked back. "What was it that prompted such a turnout?" he asked, and he theorized that a number of factors were involved:

-- The city, with its ethnic neighborhoods, has a history of parades and processions, many by such churches as St. Casimir's and St. Leo's. Abington also cited the I Am An

American Day Parade, with such participants as Italians, Polish, Czechs, Greeks, Ukrainians, and others, and the Polish Constitution Day Parade.

-- The appeal not only of a young man who had a faultless background, who was trying to do his job, who was cut down in a savage death, but also of a young woman, his wife, carrying his child, who chose to walk the six miles to and from the cemetery in his honor. And the hundreds who walked for him, for her.

-- The episode from the eulogy of Wisniewski's portraying the Good Samaritan when the ex-Marine helped a mother get to her two small children whose car had been smashed.

-- The fact that Marine Cpl. Wisniewski had alerted his superiors to the Venezuelan flag in Grenada, saving the United States and President Ronald Reagan from what could have been a major international embarrassment.

-- The unleashing of patriotism in a city that has held back recently in welcoming home its heroes from the Gulf War and the Vietnam War.

-- And finally, Polish pride, plain and simple.

Heavy security at firehouse

Three days after Kenneth Wisniewski's funeral, Captain Dan Russo, Lt. Stach Wisniewski and other detectives gathered at Northern District headquarters to hear what the DIA agents had discovered and what the heavy security was all about in Fredericksburg, Virginia.

Russo said he had asked, but Fredericksburg police had declined his offer to send a Baltimore contingent to assist them and Virginia state troopers whenever anyone attempted to open the container. "But they have kept us informed.

"And now they've moved the container and the rental truck into a firehouse nearby in order to thoroughly check out both. And I suspect to accommodate Wal-Mart.

"In fact, the Fredericksburg's police chief called just an hour or so ago that they had decided to call in FBI agents, not because they had already found drugs—we had suspected cocaine, as you know, and none has been found, so far—but because they had made an even bigger discovery, and they weren't really certain just what it was."

That prompted a number of questions, and then Major Bentzen suggested "a dirty bomb," which scared everyone.

Guessing out loud

He stressed that he was only guessing, but reasoned out loud, "The state troopers and the Fredericksburg P.D. could have conducted their full operation, and quickly, simply by cordoning off the area and keeping folks away. But let's consider my suggestion of a dirty bomb.

"Now that would help explain why they've moved both the container and the rental truck to a firehouse: A) they can complete their work without having everyone, especially the press, looking over their shoulders, B)—and this is a big one, men—if they don't hush that up they could spur an evacuation of the city and who knows how much more if there's even a hint of radiation." Each officer nodded to himself.

"Realize, men, that what I'm saying is off the record, way off the record. And I'm strictly guessing. Got that?" And everyone nodded.

"So, for us at this time, let's keep a close watch on Signor Felipe Sanchez and Mr. Patrick Sorensen, who apparently have had some type of illicit link with truck driver Judd Schmidt, who dropped off that container. And I'm guessing Schmidt didn't even know what was in it."

Captain Dan Russo said, "This Schmidt was supposed to have driven his container to a Sanchez Importers' lot off

Eastern Avenue and drop it there. I'm guessing that Kenny stumbled onto something really big.

"Now, we've checked with security at the World Trade Center, and a guard disclosed that Sorensen, the former deputy mayor, as you know, and now Customs official, had stopped by Sanchez's office several times in the last few days.

Major Bentzen: "We know Schmidt drives for Rossler Lines. What about Rex Rossler?"

Stach Wisniewski: "Dumb, but clean. He's just a front. The real boss is his wife."

Bentzen: "Your former wife, Dan?"

"Smart enough to dump me."

"She runs the firm?"

"That's what the truckers say, and does it well. Kenny met with Rossler, and his wife, separately, and visited with some other truckers. She knows what she's doing."

"Rossler smart enough to work behind her back?"

"Hell, no.

"How about our undercover agent at the warehouse?"

"Gaston Leal. And that ties in very neatly with our suspicions. Because Kenny Wisniewski was supposed to drop his container off at the warehouse where Leal is working."

Lt. Wisniewski: "Really? Then that means—boy, this is a real bummer—that Kenny's container had drugs aboard. And Schmidt's must have carried something else—we don't know what yet—but the major's suggestion holds water with me."

Capt. Russo: "Should we raid that warehouse before the crooks clean it out.

Bentzen: "What's your thought, Stach?"

"First, I'd get Sanchez out of his office in the World Trade Building, and I'd go through everything, quietly, and off the cuff."

"We have no warrant. The feds aren't interested, at this point in time. We can't do that."

"You never heard me even suggest that."

"I absolutely never did."

"Suppose someone does it for us?"

"I didn't hear that either."

Russo: "It's all right if we keep watch on both those players, just to make sure they stay around?"

Bentzen: "You think they might take off?"

"I'd bet on it, once they feel the heat."

Wisniewski: "And that might just be today, tomorrow, the next day."

Bentzen: "No problem with the surveillance. Go for it. . . . But I don't want either of you eager beavers," looking from Russo to Wisniewski, "going down to Fredericksburg."

Russo: "How about the warehouse?"

Bentzen: "Let's ask the DIA to help in the raid. We can give them the information Gaston Leal has developed. Make sure he's fully debriefed and off on vacation or holiday or whatever."

Russo: "Yes, sir. And we'll move immediately."

Undercover agent at work

What had Detective Gaston Leal (or his alias Jim Jamieson) of the Pittsburgh Police Department found out? First of all, he discovered in Pittsburgh that he would never work harder in his life.

He prepped for the Baltimore assignment by spending a month working an overnight shift at a downtown Pittsburgh warehouse. The warehouse measured 250 feet deep, 600 feet across, and it rose 32 feet high. Fifteen men worked at the plant, plus clerks and management. Several of the men were hoping to get jobs at steel mills—the warehouse experience qualified them, and the money was much better. Others with lesser skills made a career of warehousing.

The building was both a food grade and industrial warehouse, giving Jim experience with both.

For example, food grade meant the warehouse had passed FDA (Food and Drug Administration) and USDA (U.S. Department of Agriculture) inspections. The warehouse workers had to maintain basically good housekeeping. There could be no bugs anywhere. The food was not refrigerated, but included such varied items as soda, bottled water, chocolate, tea in eighty-pound bags, even cigarettes.

Industrial referred, for example, to the storage of paint pigments, zinc oxide and pallets of shrink-wrapped car wheels, equipment and supplies being housed for nearby industries—which were becoming fewer by the year in Pittsburgh and almost extinct in Baltimore.

In addition, just recently the London Metal Exchange began storing some of its six metals in industrial warehouses in Baltimore: aluminum, copper, zinc, lead, tin and nickel. It just sits there until someone wants it, when it may be reloaded on ships to take it to some other country.

The food and industrial pallets were different in size, and, in fact, the food pallets had four-way entries. Cigarettes, which could be crushed by weight, were not placed on pallets.

Leal was only five foot eight, but he was stocky and muscular. He was twenty-three years old, although his forged driver's license had him identified as James Jamieson, twenty, and his other forged documents supported that.

He told the manager, Fred Ferguson, that he was going to a junior college in suburban Pittsburgh daytimes, and that was the truth, but the first two days after working the night shifts he spent sleeping heavy, getting into the rhythm. By the third night, he could get back to his morning classes and still match the pace set by the worker appointed his supervisor at the warehouse, and Jim kept it up for the month he spent there.

He started out as a "lumper," unloading trucks and stacking boxes by hand. As a practical matter, a lumper had to be able to hand-load, lift and stack a weight of fifty pounds or more throughout the eight-hour shift.

Jim, in the first week, also was kept away from anything fragile. He was allowed to load boxes of pantsuits from China onto trucks; he unloaded boxes of hats and ties from Ecuador from trucks, bringing them out from the front to the back and easing them onto pallets for forklift drivers to pick up. After two weeks on the job, the operations manager, taking note of his enthusiasm and strength, allowed Jim to drive a forklift, under the eye of an experienced man, Bill Hinckle. But Hinckle, anxious about keeping his own job, allowed Jim to get too close to a stack of pallets, crunching in the corner of a twenty-four-foot-high tower of boxes. Jim had to lift, slide and wrestle about twenty-five boxes of bottled goods, each weighing between sixty and sixty-five pounds, onto the forklift to fit back into the stack—one of the best lessons he learned in his time at the Pittsburgh warehouse.

His knees ached when he lifted, and his shoulders hurt when he pushed up over his head. But Jamieson kept on. He didn't try to make friends; it wasn't his style. But, meeting with one of his superiors in the police department, he was told bluntly that he would likely learn more from these guys experienced in warehouse work—there were a couple women—than he would going it alone. And Jim found out the advice was right:

-- Tom—last names were seldom offered—showed him how best to handle the quirks of the three forklifts available to him. Tom's face spoke better than he himself. A grimace saved him fifteen words. A grunt meant stop. A growl—well, Jim never figured out what that meant, but guessed it sufficed for a sentence of swear words.

-- Luke, a 225-pound high school senior hoping to be a lineman for a suburban college, who loved to handle the hot, dusty, eighty-pound bags of tea, maintained that Jim could use the sweat work.

-- David, a heavy, pleasant, Bible-quoting black, suggested that Jim buy a different brand of steel-toed shoes.

-- Jeanine, a fairly pretty, older woman, recommended that he nibble chocolate bars for energy, and keep bottles of water handy.

-- Bernie, who admitted being forty-five but looked much older, explained how critical the bill of lading was, and how it had to be on every box or sack.

-- Jasper, a high-strung veteran of Vietnam, still dropped to the deck any time a box fell, sounding like a shot, sometimes intentionally dropped. But that stopped after he went through a week of nightmares and the jitters and gained the sympathy of his tormentors. They had had their fun.

-- and Lois, a clerk, who said simply: "We live by numbers. Locator bay numbers, for example. If it's moved, we call it relocation; we have to know exactly where it is. 'Cause, when we got to ship it, and we don't know where it is, well, all hell breaks loose. And if you're to blame, we probably won't see you again."

Jim made it through the month without losing any pallet, or dropping any box, admitting to Allen Anderson, the Pittsburgh police lieutenant he was assigned to, that the last week had gone pretty well, and he actually felt in better physical shape than when he started. He shared with Lt. Anderson the recommendation from Fred Ferguson, the warehouse manager, on his good work at the warehouse, that he'd be welcomed back whenever. Jim had explained to Ferguson that he was switching to a community college near Baltimore and hoped to get a job at a warehouse there.

On to Baltimore

Jim was then briefed on what to look for at the suspected warehouse in Baltimore, mostly information developed by Lt. Sylvester Reed from what his wife, Jasmine, relayed from Mira Wisniewski, without her realizing she was being pumped.

Jim was given three days to get his apartment or rented room there, to acquaint himself with the city and to be fully advised by the triumvirate of Captain Dan Russo, Lt. Stach Wisniewski and Lt. Sylvester Reed, who would be his contact. Jim then applied for the job at the Central City Warehouse, a freight consolidation and distribution depot off Bulgar Street in Baltimore's southern industrial zone. Sylvester found Jim Jamieson a well-worn '75 Dodge acquired from a drug seizure to drive about.

On Sept. 8, Jamieson drove down to the warehouse, walked by the clerical offices, glancing at a comely young lady he would later learn was Mira Wisniewski, and entered the office of Winston Hansen, the warehouse manager.

"So, have you ever worked in a warehouse before?" Hansen said before he began looking through the resume Jamieson proffered. Jim explained that he was going to be taking classes at Dundalk Community College to complete work on an associate's degree in business administration and management. Hansen showed little interest in that. His simple qualification for a warehouseman was: Can he write legibly? Can he read? Does he know basic math, like add and subtract? To him, these skills were more important than being able to load or unload a truck.

So Hansen was very impressed by, and somewhat suspicious of, the reference given by the Pittsburgh warehouse manager. Hansen immediately had a clerk get the phone number for the warehouse, talked to Fred Ferguson to confirm the recommendation, especially about Jamieson's driving a forklift, and promptly hired him. Hansen suggested that Jim start work on Monday—four days away—reporting at 4 p.m. for a shift that would end at midnight. "I'll be there," Jamieson said, putting out his hand, guessing he could take day classes after all. He had planned to attend night sessions. He figured now that he would try to get in as many classes as possible just to protect his cover, and to profit from the instruction as well.

"Hold on. Let's show you around," Hansen intruded on Jamieson's thoughts. He led him through the offices, introducing him to the two clerks, Maggie McDonald, the truck dispatcher, and Mira Wisniewski, the warehouse clerk, and into the warehouse, a huge rectangular building.

"You warehouse tea like they do in Pittsburgh?" Jim asked.

"Yep," Hansen said. "Finally in bags. They used to ship them in beautifully built mahogany boxes with tin strips around them. So I called—some place in Africa—and asked why they couldn't ship a lot less weight and make it a lot easier for us here, without those damn heavy boxes. Well, they said tea was their number-one industry. Can you guess what was number two?"

"Making those boxes?"

"You got it." Hansen was impressed. He had used that story often on new men and few had guessed, and none correctly. Some didn't understand the question.

Jamieson was introduced to the workers, almost all of them men. The exception was Sarah, who drove a forklift. She was well built and quite pretty, probably in her early thirties. As they walked along, Jim commented, "We didn't have any women as cute as her, and not driving a forklift."

"She's well qualified, I'll tell you that," Hansen said, and chuckled. "One time she was out back, where the trucks come in, and one of the senior men, oh, Bob—you remember him?" Jim nodded. "Well, he got a little worried about her, and he went back there with another man. And they found a real slimy, slicked-up driver up against his truck with one of the forks right against his belly. 'Look, you SOB,' says Sarah, sitting on that fork lift, its motor running, 'you say one more word to me and you're dead.' 'We turned around and come back,' Bob told me. 'We didn't worry about her no more.'"

"I can see why," Jim volunteered.

"We have two shifts now. Sometimes we have three, like when we're repackaging," which triggered a suspicion Jim's new police advisers had passed along. "The day shift runs seven to four, with a half-hour for lunch. You'll be starting on the swing shift, just to get used to it. And that starts at four, but you come in at three thirty to set up. It runs to midnight, with that half-hour for lunch. OK?"

"Fine." He waited for thirty seconds as they walked along, and then broached the issue that the Baltimore officers would like him to explore: "We didn't repackage anything at the Pittsburgh warehouse."

"That should be no problem for you. We'll turn here, and you can see what that's all about."

They walked beyond some full bays, to see a small force of fifteen men, a few women. Hansen nodded to the foreman. "Just briefing a new man, out of Pittsburgh. Jim Jamieson. Tony Cabrini." They nodded at each other.

Hansen explained, "You got these pallets here of shampoo, what, maybe thirty cases of 100 each," said questioningly, with Cabrini immediately nodding his head. "Anyway, you also got a pallet of sponges—something called loofahs—it's a gourd with a bunch of fibers from Central America somewhere. And you combine the bottles of some liquid soap on a little tray, with the sponges, and then run them through a heat-sealing machine—see it over there—into a little package, and that's it. Put 'em in boxes and they put them up in a grocery."

"How do you keep track?" Jim queried, a question that prompted more suspicion on Hansen's part. He turned to Cabrini.

"We set up a pallet of the shampoo that's got a count of thirty cases of 100 each, so you got 3,000 of those. Then you got so many bags of the sponges, and you count them coming up, and then you count your units coming off at the end. It's not hard."

Hansen interrupted: "We just re-paletize it for shipment. It's just assembling a package, much like you'd assemble a car." And he studied Jamieson to see whether he was satisfied. Jim nodded his head enthusiastically.

"Also, we rent space to a crew that assembles papers, like stuff they might hand out at conventions here, near the Inner Harbor, and they got to put the pages in the right order and put them into an envelope."

"Mostly temps?"

"Yep, but I guess the guy in charge tries to get people who have been there before."

"Makes sense."

"Some of the warehouse is racked," Hansen continued, "because we haven't converted yet, and that makes for hand-stacking onto pallets, and so forth. But most of the warehouse is in bays twenty feet wide, sixty feet deep, thirty-two feet high. Similar in Pittsburgh?"

"Mostly bays, some ninety feet deep, hardly any racks."

"You work with these paint pigments?"

"Some."

"These come in from Germany, Great big bags—like you see there, super bags. Weigh 2,000 to 4,000 pounds. They're on pallets, with these straps the forklifts can use. They come in in containers."

They walked along to where a couple men were unloading a pallet by hand onto a rack. "I'm impressed that your boss in Pittsburgh said you can handle a forklift, but there's also some hand work overnight, like unloading some containers. That bother you?"

"No problem."

"And there's still one of our forklifts that has no rollover cage."

"We had three of those in Pittsburgh. Got to keep alert."

That reassured Hansen some. "You do any records keeping?"

"Well, in the sense of moving stuff, like into a different bay. One of the clerks would give us a code and we'd stick it on whatever and move it to the new bay. And we'd keep track of it that way."

"Records keeping is a big part of warehousing. You got to keep the records straight. We double-check our inventory every month. Basically, we got square feet to lease out, man hours to account for."

Monotonous work

The next Monday afternoon, Jim Jamieson reported in on time. He was briefed by the swing-shift boss, Angelo "Angie" Napolitano, one generation removed from Naples, Italy. "First thing, kid, is you got to unload those cigarette bales from Venezuela (from a truck backed into the dock), stack 'em three high so the forklift driver can clamp 'em and put 'em on a rack inside. You want to have those stacks ready whenever he is. Got it?"

For Jim it was easy work. Monotonous but easy, and his muscles relaxed as he lifted the bales and stacked them, moving effortlessly. A radio played rock off in the warehouse somewhere, and Jim responded to the beat. From time to time Angie looked him over. He was satisfied.

Lunch provided a break, and Jim waited until most everyone had chosen his chair at the table, and took a seat, bringing out a brown sandwich bag and bottle of water, one of three he carried in his backpack, along with some chocolate bars.

Angie mouthed introductions, alternating with bites of his cheese sandwich. "This guy's Jim. That's Alex, Bill, Swenson—you got a first name?"

"Sakarias."

"Okay. Swede will do. I guess you get called Swede, too?" Swenson nodded. "Rob. Jerry. Paul. Buzz. Shorty. Hell, he's almost taller 'n you. How about that? And Lou."

Shorty spoke up: "Where you from, Jim?"

"Pittsburgh. I worked in a warehouse there, too."

"You going to colledge?"

"Yeh, community college, Dundalk."

"Figures."

"How so?"

Jerry: "You speak differnt, man, differnt. You know?"

"Sorry 'bout that."

Angie: "No problem, kid. We get college students from time to time. Some are really in shape, playin' football, you know. But you're too small for that."

"Just trying to make money to get through college."

Shorty: "Wha'er you hopin' to do?"

"I'd like to get into business."

"Yer own?"

"Probably not. I don't have the cash for that. But maybe one day . . ."

"You won't get rich working here, that's for sure," Shorty said, and the other men laughed, and offered a variety of grunts of agreement.

"As long as it gets me through college, I'm happy."

"Good luck, kid," said Swenson.

After two weeks on the job, Jim was allowed to run a forklift when one of the regular drivers called in sick. He showed he could handle it, and Angie mentioned to the operations manager, Hansen, that the kid was doing fine.

The next morning, about ten, Jim was called to the area's district police headquarters to meet with Major Jeff Bentzen, Capt. Dan Russo, Lt. Stach Wisniewski and Lt. Sylvester Reed, along with Bob Hampton of the DIA and a couple agents from the DIA.

Hampton was demanding, in a hurry as usual. "So what have you found out? That clerk's suspicions pan out?"

Capt. Russo: "I doubt he's learned much, but I would guess, based on what Mira Wisniewski said to Syl's wife, that cocaine is coming in, and somehow it's going out. Goro?"

"I've been on the swing shift, which gives me some time to watch those products she mentioned, tea and chocolate—the chocolate from France, incidentally—and I've never seen any that would have to be thrown away. So someone has to be replacing the tea or chocolate . . ."

Hampton interrupted: "Frankly, I don't see what good it is having you working there. But I've said that before. There can't be too many trucks leaving from that warehouse every day. You know, kid?"

"At night sometimes four, sometimes five. One guy told me there's twice as many on the day shifts."

Hampton: "Fifteen in one day. Suppose we hit them all one day, John (Ristau)," the DIA agent sitting in, "how many men would we need?"

"Five agents, maybe more. The dogs, of course."

"Suppose we hit them all one day. What do you think, Russo, Reed?"

Capt. Russo: "I'd like to have Goro get on the day shift and see what's happening there."

Reed: "We got to let him see what's what."

Major Bentzen: "It seems to me, Bob, that we should give Goro some time to take note of what's going on during the daytime . . ."

Hampton: ". . . I'll give you people two weeks. If you don't see anything to change my mind, I'm going to order our people to stop every single truck leaving that warehouse on a certain day. Can we cover them all, John?"

"We could use help from the locals, sir." John said. "As you know, sir, we have had cases where the drugs are coming in in shipments like in flowers, but going out by mail in toys, for example, to mom-and-pop stores."

Hampton, turning to Gaston Leal: "Do you have those individual shipments?"

"Yes, sir, usually by FedEx or UPS. The warehouse uses both."

Hampton thought for a moment: "John, we'd have to intercept all those too, I guess."

John: "We'd have to intercept those trucks, too, sir. How many a day do you see, Goro?"

"I've seen a couple overnight. I don't know how many come in by day."

Hampton: "Let us know in a couple weeks what the pattern is, and we'll include them in the stops and searches. We'll make it a complete sweep of everything that moves out of that warehouse."

Dan Russo: "We'll be ready, but I think you're giving us very little time . . ."

Hampton: ". . . I really don't like this undercover bit at all, especially with such an inexperienced detective, but either we get the cocaine by stopping every vehicle leaving that warehouse, or we'll just get out of it and let you follow up as you will." And Hampton, agent John Ristau, and the second man, who had not been introduced, got up to go. The Baltimore officers nodded.

As the door closed, Dan looked at Stach. "You didn't help much."

Stach: "We'll see what Goro can do on dayside. Snoop around as much as you're able, but don't get caught looking too suspicious. I really think we can delay Hampton, but we need to have something to go on. We need evidence, Goro."

Goro: "If the cocaine's coming in, as the DIA certainly believes, then it has to go out somehow. I'll try to find out . . ."

Sylvester: ". . . without getting caught."

Goro: ". . . without getting caught."

The meeting recessed, and Leal got a chance to catch some shuteye before reporting for the swing shift—his last at night.

The morning after, he reported at 7:30 and was assigned to help rebuild a stack of boxes of chocolate powder, some of which had been damaged. It was heavy lifting, and the operations manager, Winston Hansen, was always about, monitoring just about everything that was done in the warehouse, and appearing over every worker's shoulder.

A rotten life

Hansen had had a rotten life. He grew up in Philadelphia, getting through high school and being caught up in the draft. He learned how to survive in Korea, especially the retreat forced by Chinese forces, by taking care of himself and whoever could help him.

When he returned from Korea, he walked out on the only woman who could stand him—his mother—and he hadn't returned home, written or called since. He never married, and went from sweat job to sweat job until he came to the warehouse, somehow gained the confidence of the owner, a World War II veteran, and, following a suspicious accident that crippled the previous operations manager, was named to replace him.

Now fifty-one, Hansen, always serious, never trusting, cynically doubted that the hard workers actually enjoyed their work. But he held women in high estate, probably based on his mother, whom he worshiped from afar, which explains why he had fired two men who tried to move on Mira Wisniewski.

Hansen took his lunch in his air-conditioned office, so the men had their lunch break free to bitch about him, which consumed a great deal each day of the half-hour around the worn wooden table in an empty bay.

"Where're you from?" Tom—again no last names—asked through huge bites from a ham and cheese sandwich. He was a burly man, in his forties, perhaps the hardest worker in the warehouse, able to out-hustle the football linemen.

"Pittsburgh. Name's Jim, Jim Jamieson," and he extended his hand. Tom clamped down on his hand, almost crushing it. Jim smiled. "Good grip. When I need help, I'll know where to go."

"Colledge kid?" Tom asked.

"Yep."

"I'da guessed that," said a sallow man, perhaps thirty-five, wiry, tall and lanky, and he shook hands across the table. "If Tom can't help you, and that ain't happened yet, I'll be glad to. I'm Hank. What'd you do in Pittsburgh?"

"Grew up, mostly. Was going to community college when I ran short of money, so I got a job in a warehouse there, then decided to switch to a community college here,

Dundalk, . . ." which caused three or four heads to nod, ". . . and needed some dough. So I'm here."

Tom: "Pay's not too great. Work ain't too hard, onct you git used to it. You'll larn to put up with Hansen. He ain't too bad."

"If you get through the first week with him, you'll make it OK," said a graying man, light of build, always serious.

"Name's Joe." And he shook hands with Jim.

"Me, I'm Gustav," said a Swedish-looking man across the table. "And Ben," said a middle-aged black man, extending his hand. "Best job I ever had. Got six kids, three of them girls, to feed and house."

"You making it?" Jim asked, surprising Ben.

"You better believe it." And he nodded his head, thinking to himself, 'this is a good one.'

The men at the second table were into their own discussion, mostly Orioles talk and predictions of pennants and series. Hansen appeared at exactly noon, and the men got up and returned to their jobs.

Jim's first week went slowly, with Hansen always around and always criticizing someone, often Jim. When he met Saturday afternoon with Sylvester Reed, Goro was unable to report anything suspicious. "I saw nothing out of the ordinary. Should I try to talk to this Mira?"

"No way. We don't want to put her in any danger knowing you, and you might get fired by your friendly operations manager, which would undo our whole effort. My wife, Jasmine, recruited Mira to join a young women's group, which meets weekly, so she kind of incidentally, and accidentally, keeps tabs on what's happening, trying real hard not to alarm Mira."

"Hope I find a woman like that one day."

"One in a million. But good luck."

The next day Goro had a message on his phone to call

Sylvester Reed. "Goro here. What's up?"

"You got anything to report?"

"Nope. Just another day at the sweat shop."

"Well, Mira told Jasmine at some women's group meeting that six more bags of tea from Argentina were damaged and had to be discarded. She just shook her head, adding that she would never mention anything to Hansen. Jasmine amen'd that."

"I'll just have to watch that tea from Argentina and chocolate from France whenever I can. I'm not often in that section of the warehouse, but if I see anything . . ."

"Be careful. This guy plays hardball, and he probably has a killer organization behind him. If he's as dangerous as we suspect, you can be sure of that."

"Anything else?"

"Nope. Good luck."

And Jim's luck changed. Bill Henry, a forklift driver, called in sick, actually from a hospital where he was taken after breaking his leg in a play at second base in a softball game. He would be out for three weeks, maybe more.

Hansen was fuming, at Henry, when he ordered Jim to take over the forklift. He watched as Jamieson climbed up, adjusted the seat to match his height—Bill was six foot one—and started it up.

"Start moving those pallets over there," Hansen ordered, pointing to pallets of bottled soda from Canada. "Now, Jamieson, we want them in the bay over there, 15A. Got it?"

"Yes, sir."

"You have to put the new labels on them. Make sure each pallet has the right label."

And so the morning went, with Hansen watching every motion for at least an hour. This didn't bother Jim, who had had to adapt to this forklift. It wasn't as new as the ones he had driven in Pittsburgh, and it surged when he wasn't expecting it. But he caught on, and Hansen drifted off to other sections of the warehouse to reassure himself that no one was goofing off.

When Jim finished moving the soda, it was almost lunchtime, but he figured he had better get his orders from Hansen before sitting down to eat. The operations manager appreciated that. "After lunch, I want you to use the clamps to move some tea around. And be very careful. We often lose some of those bags simply due to driver error."

'Bingo,' Jim thought. 'That's one way to get the bags damaged.' So he spent the lunch hour talking with Tom about the forklift and its peculiarities.

"Sometimes it just surges. You got to feel it out, and slow it down. Them clamps is reliable, but it seems whenever Hansen's 'round, they smash up those bags, or at least that's what he says. So be careful, specially when he's around."

"Appreciate your help."

The lunch talk centered on Ben, a talker who started every story, "Well, by golly, I'll tell you," and the rest of the workers just smiled, and corrected him when he varied even the tiniest bit from the last time, perhaps only last week, when he had told the same story. In these tales he described his family, his wife, who was always nagging him, his three daughters, who had inherited her genes, his neighborhood, which apparently was overrun by kooks, the shops that overcharged him, the different beers he had tasted. "Well, by damn, I'll tell you," he began, "we was in transit to Germany, well, West Germany then, you know, and we had this layover in England, for a couple a days. Well, we go on down to London. Hoo, that there is one big city. And we went into this big train station, Kings somethin', and we thought we'd have to have a couple beers, you know." And everybody nodded. "And would you believe it, dey was warm, damn near hot."

"No," said the Swede.

"Yes, by damn, dey was warm, warm as my hand here."

"Could you drink it?" Swede asked.

"Well, by damn, I'll tell you, I haven't found a beer yet I couldn't drink. But it took some doing, I'll tell you."

"Why didn't you get some ice?" Swede asked, as he always did in this story.

"'Cause you don't put ice in beer, you dumb Swede," Ben responded, as he always did, and everyone chuckled, as they always did for that story.

Hansen appeared, and the meal broke up. "Jamieson, let's see how you move this tea. Seems even Henry, who's the best we have, just clamps that tea too hard. But I'll be watching."

Jim was especially cautious as he clamped the first three cartons and moved them gingerly to the rack the label had instructed. "Keep that slow, and we'll be here all night," Hansen commented loud enough to be heard over the forklift.

So Jim speeded up a little, but still hesitated as the clamps took hold, insuring there would be no damage. The third effort prompted Hansen to look carefully at the bags. "Put her down here," he ordered. When Jim unloosened the clamps and backed off, Hansen studied the tea bags and pulled out three in all. "You squeezed these too hard. We're going to have to discard these. Let's be more careful. Keep going. I'll be watching you."

And he walked away with the three "damaged" bags, turning to see that Jamieson was continuing his work. "Go easy, now, damn it," he shouted.

Jim had to give up any hope of seeing where Hansen placed the bags. He was back in about a half-hour, and there were no more incidents that day.

But on Thursday, the fourth day for Jamieson driving the forklift, he was scolded once more for damaging some bags of chocolate from France. "Damn it, kid, you just got to go easier. Get the feel of that forklift. I sure don't want you wrecking the place."

Jim couldn't figure out an answer, so continued his work, noting that whenever he handled other cargo, he didn't seem to smash it up. Except for one pallet that had been stacked improperly, so that when the pallet was lifted, about ten boxes of soda came sliding off. "Damn it, kid." scolded Hansen. "There's no excuse for that. You should have looked at it before you started. So get it stacked right." And he walked away.

DIA Interceptions

When Goro reported to Sylvester that night, he relayed the information to Capt. Dan Russo. After checking with Major Jeff Bentzen, Dan called Bob Hampton, and he was hot to go.

"They're going to load that stuff onto a truck immediately and get it to the drug lords," Hampton predicted. "So starting at midnight tonight we're going to stop every damn truck that leaves that warehouse, and we'll go through it with a fine-tooth comb, and by God we'll find that cocaine. I can just feel it in my bones."

"You don't think we should wait for some more evidence?" Dan asked.

"The faster we intercept that cocaine, the faster we shut down that damn warehouse, the more impact we have on the cartels," Hampton responded. "We go tomorrow. Can you help us?"

"Let me doublecheck with the major. I'll get right back to you." And he hung up before Hampton could respond.

Major Bentzen, Dan, Stach, and Syl met quickly with Goro. He relayed how the operations manager discovered the damaged bags, and how he believed the drugs got into the warehouse. But he had no idea how they got out. He assumed they went out in regular truckloads, or were sent parcel post or carried by UPS and FedEx to mom-and-pop stores.

The first question the major asked was, "Are we sure this is drugs that the operations manager is covering up, or just poorly shipped tea and chocolate. I'm very uncomfortable about this. Drugs do come in by containers, I'll admit that, but you haven't seen any, have you, Goro?"

"No, sir."

"No hint from any of the other warehousemen?"

"No sir."

"I think this is a no go. I'm going to lean heavily on Tom Hampton. l) He could make asses of all of us and become a joke in the city and state. 2) None of our sources has been breached. We just don't know yet, or even reasonably suspect, that there are drugs there.

"Goro, keep up the good work. This guy Hansen is certainly suspicious, but we can't go crazy over suspicions. Dan?"

"I'd keep Goro there for another month if that's all right. Let me clear it with your bosses in Pittsburgh?"

Major Bentzen: "Yes, I really suspect this Hansen person is moving drugs, but we can't stop all those trucks in the wild hope that we find some. There's not enough to go on. Stach?"

"I'd keep Goro working for us for another month. I'm too loyal to my nephew's widow not to keep going. I think we're on the brink."

"Sylvester?"

"I'm with Dan and Stach."

Goro: "I'm game, sir. I'm beginning to enjoy the work. I might just make a career our of working in a warehouse."

All the men chuckled, and Bentzen picked up his phone to call Hampton to try to stop him, and the men filed out.

Sylvester, his arm around Goro's shoulders: "Keep up the good work. The kind of stop and search Hampton wants could make us the laughing stock of the East Coast. Another month on the job won't hurt."

Goro: "Easy for you to say." And the men smiled as they went their different ways.

But Major Bentzen was persuasive, hinting that a bust would ruin Hampton's hopes of going on to Washington some day, and he decided not to unleash his troops on stops and searches that night.

Almost a month passed without any new development, not even a clue to follow. Goro (Jim) was in his last scheduled week at Central City Warehouse off Bulgar Street. He would not give his notice until he was ready to walk out the door, for the others at the lunch table had in conversation noted how a good worker, in their opinion, had given two-weeks notice and was fired immediately.

Jim had tried to watch Hansen, and, by this time, knew well how the cocaine was coming in. The bags of tea and boxes of chocolate that evidently contained cocaine had been marked in some way—a coded stamp, an X marks the spot, something stuck on—he was never sure. He didn't have an opportunity to study the bags while he drove the forklift.

On Monday of the last week that he intended working, he was clamping cartons of tea, three at a time, when a fourth stuck to the other three, and he had to get down off the forklift. He slid his hand under the fourth bale to loosen it, and noticed that the label had a tiny star in the upper right corner, which he had not noticed before. He let the bale ease downward and returned to his work, just as Winston Hansen came by, cautioned Jamieson on moving the bales and studied the ones still to be moved. As Jim backed away, he chanced to see the operations manager fingering that fourth bale. Sure enough, the next time he picked up bales, Hansen explained that that bag of tea had been damaged, along with three others, which he had Jim place on the side, then walked off to the office to report the damage to the clerks.

Pockets full of cookies

The next day, Jim happened to come walking up on the operations manager, a police sergeant, who looked fiercely at Jim, and the middle-aged man who twice a week brought in tanks filled with propane for the forklifts, and took out the empty ones. Hansen was handing one of the tanks to the deliveryman, who almost dropped it, he was so shaken by Jim's presence. All three looked like children caught with their pockets full of cookies.

Hansen grunted, "Jamieson? I thought you were stacking boxes over in Bay 14?"

Jim: "I have to replace the label for this box," showing Hansen a badly ripped label for some bottled soda. "Somehow it got ripped off, and I was going to the girls to get a blank label, and get them to put on the right numbers."

"OK, OK. Don't be all day about it," Hansen said acidly, and he turned back to the other men. He barked at Jamieson, "Oh, let Mrs. Wisniewski know that we had six more packets of tea damaged. Can you remember that?"

"Yes, sir," Jim responded, and walked a little faster into the office area, feeling the eyes that were following him. 'By golly,' Goro thought to himself. 'What a perfect way to move that cocaine out. Those propane tanks must have false bottoms. That delivery guy almost said it out loud?'

Jim stopped before Mira Wisniewski's desk. "I need a label for a box of bottled soda in this sequence. It got lost somehow." And he gave her the numbers from the adjacent boxes. "Oh, Mr. Hansen wanted me to tell you there were six more bags of tea damaged," and he caught the querulous look in Mira's eyes, but quickly turned away.

She took down that information, pulled out a pack of labels, and typed out the information he needed. He did not watch what she was doing, but thanked her with a nod when she handed him the label. Then she pulled out a drawer, picked up a heavy file, and added the six more bags of tea. But Jim had already left the office area.

Late that afternoon, after returning to his apartment, he phoned Lt. Sylvester Reed and left a request to call him. Syl called back three hours later as Goro was falling off to sleep.

"Sylvester here. Guess what's up?"

"The DIA about to stop every vehicle leaving that warehouse?"

"How'd you know? As of 7 a.m. tomorrow. Full force. Stops and searches throughout the area."

"I'm for it. There were six more bags of tea damaged today. Let them stop and search every truck that leaves the docks, UPS, FedEx whatever. If they come up with nothing, and that's what I think they'll get, I know how it's going out."

"So let's plug that gap."

"Better to assure it's not what the DIA thinks."

"Your last week, right? And you don't want to go out empty-handed?"

"True. That's why I'm not against cooperating with the DIA on the stops and searches. I suspect they're not going to get anything at all, because there was a police sergeant visiting with Hansen today, and I'll bet . . . "

". . . that we got a snitch? Damn it. Damn it all. A sergeant should be getting enough pay to get by without working for the cartel. But you never know. They could be threatening his family, you know. Get his name?"

"Nope. I couldn't gawk, but I got a look at his face, perhaps eastern European, so if you came up with a book of photos of cops . . ."

"We'll get to that in due time."

"Anyway, that's not the big news. I could be wrong on this, Syl, and those DIA stops and searches will cover all the rest of the traffic. But here's what I think you should do: You and a couple of your best men should check out the guy who brings in filled propane tanks twice a week and takes out the empty ones—including one or more that I suspect, now listen to this. I suspect some of them have false bottoms, and I'll bet there's cocaine in there, or there was and the dogs can tell you."

"Damn it, that's good. I love it, Goro. I love it. Can you tell me much about our delivery man?"

"He drives a Ford pickup with Baltimore Propane Delivery on the door, and he comes by twice a week, usually around 3 p.m. each Monday and Thursday. Middle aged, white, bearded, always wears a scrubby Colts cap."

"I'm on it. But we'll stay clear of the DIA operation in case they find something first. Then we'll check out the tanks. You want in on the kill."

"I'll be at work at 7:30 a.m. tomorrow. In case I'm wrong, I don't want to lose my week's wages. Happy hunting."

"You've made my day."

Sylvester put down the phone, signed a thumbs up to his wife, who had just turned over in bed, and began dialing the detectives who were not already recruited by the DIA. But all the dogs had been reserved for Tom Hampton and his stops and searches, so Lt. Reed had to call down to Annapolis to a friend in its canine corps, who got up from his bed, woke up his dog, and drove up to meet Reed at the Jessup truck stop.

Stop and Search

At 8:15 a.m. Wednesday, the DIA-led, Baltimore county and city police-backed stop-and-search campaign began at the Central City Warehouse off Bulgar Street. The first truck stopped, a mile from leaving the warehouse, was a UPS brown truck, and its driver was directed to present his mailing list and to bring out whatever was being sent out from the warehouse. There were three small boxes to three different hobby shops, and the dogs weren't interested.

A DIA agent was observing the traffic into and out of the warehouse from a window in a nearby industrial building and alerting officers in the area.

The second truck out was FedEx, and the results were the same.

The first regular truck, loaded with pallets of bottled soda for delivery to Wilmington, was stopped at 10:14 a.m. The driver was instructed to pull into a nearby parking lot, and an agent experienced with forklifts began unloading, pallet by pallet, rebuilding on the pavement the truck load, with aisles between the rows of pallets.

Tom Hampton and Major Jeff Bentzen were there. The dogs found nothing. So the truck was reloaded, and the driver began calling ahead to explain why he'd be an hour late at the ten mom-and-pop groceries and the two supermarkets destined to receive the cargo.

"It won't be long," Major Bentzen said, "before the warehouse people realize everything's being stopped. We have told our man there to watch to see, if he can, whether any cargos are being unloaded or packages being taken off the docks. So we should know whether any diversions take place."

Hampton: "Good plan. They might just do that, and we can then go into the warehouse. Meanwhile, we'll just do this throughout the day and evening. I'm sure we'll get a haul. I'm absolutely certain."

It was probably around 1:30 p.m. before the driver of one of the trucks, after being stopped and emptied, decided to ignore the DIA agents' warnings not to contact the warehouse. He didn't call, figuring the phones might be tapped. But he did stop one of his company's trucks heading to the warehouse to deliver a container and asked him to pass along the news. Operations manager Winston Hansen then officially learned about the stops at 1:55 p.m. from that driver—he already knew, thanks to the police sergeant, of course—and went into an act, storming through the office area and out into the warehouse floor, shouting for all to know that his warehouse was suspected of having drugs, and every truck leaving the plant was being stopped, and damning the whole police department and Drug Investigations Agency, and whoever else he could think of.

Mira Wisniewski would later tell her father, "Mr. Hansen was swearing right and left about the Drug Investigations Agency stopping everything leaving his warehouse. 'Those damn agents are unloading every damn pallet off the trucks and letting dogs sniff them. Of course, they won't find anything. Because we don't have any drugs here, and never have, and never will. But the publicity will hurt us.' He roared into his office, saying he would call the owner. He was so furious."

But Hansen didn't call the owner first. His first call was to Jonathan Belkron, owner and operator of Baltimore Propane Delivery. "Jon. We have a problem here, some type of backup, and the forklifts are not moving. So we won't need to have the tanks replaced for a while."

He listened for a minute.

"That's right. Skip delivery this Thursday, and I'll let you know about next week."

Another pause as he listened to Belkron. "I damn well do say so. And don't you go blabbing anywhere, hear."

And he hung up the phone.

Raid on propane delivery store

That telephone conversation was monitored by Lt. Sylvester Reed as he and other detectives arrived in the vicinity of the small storefront office in the Central City Warehouse neighborhood. Jim Jamieson, several days ago, on one of the very few times that Hansen had invited him into his office, had neatly stuck a phone bug under the chair he was sitting on.

The officers got out of the patrol car, with Reed and Paul Simmons and his dog from Annapolis, heading for the front door of the Baltimore Propane Delivery office, and the third man, detective Robert Shaw, walked around the back to see the door suddenly pushed open and a middle-aged white man wearing a well-worn Orioles cap come rushing out.

"Sorry, the office's closed, and I got to go. It's an emergency," Belkron said, but stopped when Shaw pulled out his badge and announced that he was a detective, about the same time as Reed and Simmons and his dog came in behind Belkron.

"Mr. Belkron, am I correct?" Reed asked. The man nodded his head. Sylvester continued, "I am Lieutenant Sylvester Reed of the Baltimore Police Department, and these are two detectives, Paul Simmons, and his dog Jupiter, from Annapolis, and Robert Shaw, also from Baltimore. You've apparently already met Detective Shaw.

"We have some important questions to ask you. You may refuse to answer them. You may have an attorney present."

Belkron didn't speak.

"Is that your truck?"

Belkron nodded.

"Note that the suspect nodded his affirmation. You want to just walk around it, Paul?" And Paul did, and the dog's tail began wagging when he passed by the bed on one side and then the other.

"At this point, Mr. Belkron, I am telling you that anything you say will be held against you in court. This dog responds to cocaine. Do you wish to say anything now, or do you want an attorney present?"

Belkron looked hopelessly at Reed and Shaw. He tried to speak but couldn't say anything. His eyes watered. He was actually crying. Reed noted in his notebook that he did not answer.

"Would you allow us to have our dog walk through your shop?"

Belkron nodded dejectedly. He didn't stop. He may have forgotten the question.

"He nodded," Reed said, and wrote in his notebook.

He motioned for Simmons to go through the shop and have the dog sniff throughout. Its tail wagged as it entered, and the dog went crazy as it came upon some propane tanks piled in the corner.

Reed motioned to Shaw to cuff Belkron and got out his cell phone to call Capt. Dan Russo.

"Captain Russo here."

"Dan? Sylvester. We hit pay dirt. Our borrowed dog is going crazy at this guy's truck and in his office. Goro had it right. This guy Belkron's crying real tears, but he's not talking. Will we need warrants to look into those propane tanks?"

"No question. Secure everything there, and we'll get the major to approve our request for warrants. Give me the address. Think you'll need more officers?"

"You know it. We could be hit by the cartel goons at any moment. You just don't know. I don't know his delivery routine, whether he was supposed to be here for a pickup or was to make a run. But you know the cartel is not going to take this lying down. And they'll get wind of this real soon." Russo: "*The Sun*'s on to something, and the radio and TV stations have already reported on the DIA stops, of course. We're watching to make sure Winston Hansen, the operations manager at the Central City Warehouse, doesn't try to skip out. With your information we'll take him into protective custody. And I'll get Goro out of there, just to be safe.

Reed: "He's certainly earned his pay today. Send us help *pronto*. It looks like we already have company." And Sylvester dashed back into the shop as two small pickups drove into the small parking lot behind the storefront and skidded and squealed to stops.

Reed signaled the two other officers to take cover, and got down behind one of the show cases. Belkron stood helplessly behind the counter, his hands cuffed behind him and being held in place by Lt. Reed, as two men, one white and short, the other black, medium build, got out of the first pickup and came toward the back door.

The first man to enter, seeing Belkron standing there, said calmly, "We're here for the pickup. The boss is real upset over all those truck . . ." He stopped when he realized Belkron was shaking his head and moving his eyes in a manner designed to point out the officers in the shop.

"You look sick," said the man, later identified as Denver Preston. "Oh shit," he added as the three police officers rose, their weapons drawn. He went for his, as did the black man, identified later as Absolom Powell, and both were brought down by the officers' pistol shots. Before he collapsed, Powell got off a shot that wounded Belkron.

The driver of the second pickup jammed it into first gear, swung around past the open back door, and his sidekick sprayed the storefront with a machine pistol. The truck sped off, as sirens sounded and grew louder coming from the north.

"Everyone OK?" Sylvester asked as he rose up from behind the counter.

"Okay, here," Shaw said, looking around from a box, "but Simmons has had it."

Belkron was down on the floor, too, but he appeared to be alive, shivering as he attempted to bite his way through the floor. The officer from Annapolis had been severely wounded, with blood pouring from his head. His dog also had been hit.

Within a minute, two police cruisers slammed to stops in front of the storefront, while two others took off in pursuit of the pickup speeding south. Four police officers rushed into the storefront, weapons drawn. One stopped to call in ambulances.

"Are you all right?" Sgt. Will Brockmann asked, first Reed, then Shaw, and finally Belkron, who had to have help to get up with his hands handcuffed behind him.

"We might have lost a good friend of mine, Detective Paul Simmons from Annapolis," Sylvester said. He pointed to the man behind a shattered display case. "I really regret bringing him up here."

"He was where the action was," Sgt. Brockmann commented. "He would have wanted to be here." He looked around at the pockmarks from the weapons fired. "What's this all about, anyway?"

"Unless we're very mistaken, Sergeant," Lt. Sylvester Reed said, "some of those propane tanks in that pile there have false bottoms full of cocaine. There could be twenty, thirty, forty pounds or more."

"Oh, wow!" said Sgt. Brockmann.

The arrest of operations manager Winston Hansen at the Central City Warehouse turned out to be routine. Police officers, led by Capt. Dan Russo, quietly pulled up to the front door. Two remained there. Russo and three sergeants entered the main entrance, went up to the office complex and asked for Hansen. A secretary—it turned out to be Mira Wisniewski—pointed toward his office and motioned with her hands to indicate he might be in the closet. Dan entered the office, went up to the closet, reached over for the door handle without putting his body in front of the door, and pulled the door open. Hansen stepped out.

"Oh, I'm sorry, gentlemen. I was looking for a report. What can I do for you? Who are you?"

"I'm Captain Dan Russo of the Baltimore Police Department, and these are three officers in our bureau. We have some questions for you. You should know that you have the right to remain silent. You don't have to answer them, and you have the right to call an attorney."

Hansen nodded his head. "I certainly don't need any lawyer, because I haven't done anything to be concerned about. I'll answer all your questions, Captain."

"Thank you. Now, you are Winston Hansen, operations manager of this warehouse, am I correct?"

"That's right. Been the operations manager for seventeen years."

"Have you heard about the interception by the Drug Investigations Agency of all the trucks that left this warehouse today?"

"Yes, and I was quite curious about that. We have never had drugs on the premises, to my knowledge, so I'm sure you didn't find any in the trucks you intercepted today."

"Well, you're right on that. We haven't found any drugs in any of the trucks we stopped today."

Hansen smiled. "So what can I do for you officers? You seem to have been misled by someone, probably a disgruntled worker. They'll try anything, you know."

"But we're in the process of opening some propane tanks . . ." Hansen's smile faded, ". . . at the storefront of the Baltimore Propane Delivery where a Mr. Jonathan Beltron . . ."

"And that's the son of a bitch I would have guessed. He's not a worker here, you know that, Captain. He brings in the tanks filled with propane and takes out the tanks when they're empty. If there's any chicanery . . ."

"Mr. Hansen, as I said before, you do not have to answer my questions, and you have the right to speak to an attorney."

"Because of the nonsense that you've come in here with, Captain, I will indeed call my attorney," and he turned to reach his phone.

"Just a minute, sir," Dan said as he placed his hands on the desk phone and indicated to two of the sergeants that Hansen should be cuffed. "You'll have the opportunity to make that call from the police station. We believe you may be in very serious trouble, with likely the possibility that the cartel might want you eliminated, so we'll take you safely to the station and allow you to make your call." Hansen was about to speak. "And you need not talk now. You'll have your moment."

The five officers guided the handcuffed operations manager from his office through the office complex, where Mira and the other clerk watched in shock, and out the front door, with a few of the warehouse workers watching. There were no comments of sympathy, just a concern as to who was in charge now.

Hansen spoke as if he were still in control: "Tom, you take charge until I get back. This is a major mistake, and I should be free before the day ends." And in true Hansen style, he looked over to some men who were watching and snarled: "The rest of you, get back to work!"

Russo smiled, and opened the door for the three

officers and the operations manager. The other officers had waited outside to provide cover. Two patrol cars brought Hansen to the police district headquarters without incident.

Police sergeant identified

While all this was taking place, Gaston Leal went down by cruiser to police headquarters to look through books of photos of police officers, and in about an hour and a half identified Sgt. Wexel Novaki of the Northern District.

He was home in the Highlandtown section of Baltimore having a late lunch when Lt. Stach Wisniewski and two patrolmen stopped by the row house. The steps looked freshly washed, and a highly polished, dark red '92 Ford Mustang two-door hatchback was parked right in front of the row house, a "Policemen Are Your Friends" sticker in the back window.

Lt. Wisniewski knocked on the door, and a woman, later identified as Novakl's wife, Bette, came to the door. "Oh, sure, he's in the kitchen having lunch, Lieutenant."

Wexel Novaki looked up in surprise when Paul entered, with two officers behind him.

"What's up, Lieutenant?"

"I'm afraid you'll have to come with us down to headquarters, Sergeant," and Novaki sprang to his feet as if he might reach for his revolver. But the two officers behind Wisniewski already had their revolvers drawn, and Novaki backed off. "I'll relieve you of the weapon," Lt. Wisniewski said calmly. "We don't want anyone getting hurt."

Lt. Wisniewski turned to the woman, whose eyes were wide with fright: "Ma'am, we'll be going down to the police station for a while. We'll let you know where Sergeant Novaki is so you may visit him."

"Wexel, are you in trouble?" she asked.

He just looked at her stupefied, and Lt. Wisniewski said calmly, "We just don't know yet, ma'am. But we'll find out real soon and let you know."

"I'll get ready quick and go with him," she said, as she turned to get her sweater. "The kids are in school, and I can . . ."

"No, ma'am. He'll be going alone, but we'll call you later today, or you can call the station, say about 6 p.m., and the duty officer will tell you where your husband is."

She stopped, looked down, and back up to her husband. "It's that big money you got, isn't it?"

"Shut up, woman! Shut up!" he said quickly.

"I knew it would bring us trouble. I knew it, and now it has, and now we don't have any money. I knew it. I knew it. But we got that fancy damn car." And she sat down at the kitchen table, pushed her half-finished lunch aside and cried into a kitchen towel. "I knew it, I knew it. But you said you would never get caught. I knew it, I knew it, I knew it. And what do I tell your son? He looks up to you. And your daughter? She won't understand. But I'm gonna get me a hammer from your workbench and I'm gonna work over that fancy car of yours . . ."

Lt. Wisniewski nodded to the two officers escorting Sgt. Novaki and they walked out of the kitchen, with each officer holding firmly one of Novaki's arms.

Stach went to the front door to peak out through the curtains. "Uh-oh, we got trouble. Better keep him down on that sofa over there," he said as he backed away from the window and pulled out his cell phone.

"Yeah, Dan. I may be wrong, but I think we got trouble here. We're on Conkling Street with Sergeant Novaki. You know the case. We're pretty sure we got the right guy. But when I looked out the front door, it appears to me that we could be ambushed. I also glanced at our cruiser, and the tires have been flattened.

"I'll get patrol cars to come in from both directions, Whiz. Do you think they'll try to bust in?"

"I would doubt it, but I would guess that when they hear the sirens coming they'll look for cover. Can we get an ambulance, back it in here and get him in that? And we'll need some roadside assistance, the tires and all."

"Everything will be on its way in minutes. Keep your heads down, and good luck."

Stach waited with the three other officers, still hearing Wexel's wife lamenting at the kitchen table. Finally one of the patrolmen said, "There's the sirens . . . " and Stach added, "And there go our snipers. They're on foot." He watched as three men ran off into the neighborhood.

A patrol car pulled up from the left, with the officers bouncing out when they came to Conkling. "You okay in there?" one hollered.

"We're good, officer. Lieutenant Wisniewski here. We'll wait inside for an ambulance. It's gonna give us more cover."

A second police cruiser came in from the right. Then, within two more minutes, as the officers outside took their places, an ambulance arrived, and with that cover, and the other officers looking in all directions—much like Secret Service agents guarding the president—a well-shaken Sgt. Wexel Novaki was escorted from his home, past his car, as he worried about what his wife might do to the Mustang, into an ambulance and conveyed to the Southeast District Police Headquarters, where he later was placed in a lineup and identified by Gaston Leal. The questioning would go into the wee hours of the morning, but around 4 a.m. Sgt. Novaki had told enough lies to confuse himself and he confessed that he was working for the cartel and identified two low-level enforcers who had threatened his children. His wife had not called.

Around 10 a.m. the next day, a policewoman called the Novaki house and left a message that the sergeant was being temporarily held in a cell at the Southeast District headquarters.

A policeman making a run past the home around noon found a dark red 1992 Mustang two-door hatchback with all its side windows broken, the windshield badly cracked, the tires flat, and the hood and doors apparently smashed with a hammer. He called in to headquarters, "There's a beat-up car right outside Sergeant Novaki's home. Didn't he have a red Mustang?"

"Yep," the desk sergeant replied. "And he's just been picked up and charged with working for the cartel. The officers who picked him up said his wife was just furious about that car that he must have bought with the tainted dough. Bet you money his wife did that."

"Always liked that Mustang," the officer, sitting in his cruiser behind the ruined car, commented. "Not worth much now, though."

The desk sergeant commented, "He likely won't be needing it. The brass are worked up pretty good on this one."

"Poor Wexel. He wasn't a bad sergeant, you know."

"Little you knew, officer."

The officer decided he had said more than he should have and pulled his cruiser around the ruined Mustang and continued on his rounds.

The News at 10

The stops and searches that Sergeant Novaki had alerted warehouse operations manager Winston Hansen about continued throughout the day and into the evening, until Tom Hampton, under pressure from his superiors in the DIA, called it quits. Nothing suspicious had been found.

He had been pressed by *The Baltimore Sun*'s reporters and the TV anchors for statements throughout the day, and had put them all off with comments like: "We don't want to endanger anybody at this time. . . . We don't want to prejudice any actions. . . . We'll be ready to talk when the stops and searches end."

They ended about 9:30 p.m., and Hampton called a press conference for 10:00, perfect for the nightly TV news programs, but at the Southeast Police District's headquarters, and not Central District, which surprised most of the reporters who had to scramble to be there.

At 10:05, Hampton walked into the roll-call room with Major Pivac of the Southeast District. Hampton took the mike.

"Good evening. Thank you for coming. Today, fourteen trucks were stopped leaving the Central City Warehouse off Bulgar Street. Five of them were UPS and FedEx trucks. Nine were trucks from various lines that picked up full or partial loads at the same warehouse. We suspected that cocaine was being smuggled out of the warehouse. We were certain that cocaine had been brought into this warehouse.

"However, we found no drugs on any of the trucks in any of our stops and searches." He paused, then continued. "I will now turn the microphone over to Major Jeff Bentzen. Jeff."

"Thank you, Tom. And thank you for the diversionary actions that helped us unravel the actual method that the cartel used to smuggle cocaine out of that warehouse. Yes, the warehouse had been a distribution center. And yes, the man who runs the warehouse had been tipped off, unfortunately by a Baltimore police officer. He has not yet been charged, so I cannot give you a name yet.

"Also, I will not identify who, but I will say that we had an undercover detective working in that warehouse for some time, and he sniffed out not only how the cocaine was delivered but also how it was moved out of the warehouse.

"We anticipate bringing charges against several persons, only one of whom worked in the warehouse. I want to make that perfectly clear. We will bring charges against only one person who actually worked in the warehouse. And you'll have to wait until those charges are made tomorrow to have all the names. I'm sorry. I'm sorry."

"The others facing charges include the individual, a middle-aged man, who delivered propane tanks to the warehouse and took out empty propane tanks. They are used to propel the three to five forklifts usually in use in the warehouse. That sounds perfectly legal, doesn't it? And it is.

"However, we have discovered, having first obtained warrants, that some of these tanks had false bottoms, and we were able to seize today in those tanks with false bottoms more than twenty pounds of cocaine. Tom Hampton estimates that could be worth about $200,000 on the streets of Baltimore.

"As some of you know, our officers also had a shoot-out at the storefront where the propane tanks were delivered, with the result that two men, whose identities we don't know yet, who we suspect were there to pick up the cocaine for delivery, were killed when they drew on three police officers, two from Baltimore and a volunteer canine officer from the Annapolis Police Department, who brought along his dog to check for cocaine. That officer, Detective Paul Simmons, was seriously wounded, as was the dog, and the man who delivered and picked up the propane tanks.

"Two more men whom we believe also were high up in the cartel drove by our officers at the storefront and sprayed the store with a machine pistol. They were injured, disarmed and arrested when their pickup overturned on Chesapeake and St. Helena in southern Baltimore pursued by two of our cruisers. They have been taken to an area hospital—I won't say where so as not to jeopardize their lives—and we intend to question them further. And we'll have more than adequate security this time," alluding to the killings after the Inner Harbor water taxi shootings. Veteran police reporters present smiled.

"One thing further. One of the reasons all those stops and searches didn't find any drugs is that a Baltimore police sergeant knew about the raids beforehand and tipped off the warehouse person we intend charging. That sergeant was paid by the drug cartel to provide information. He has been arrested, and will be formally charged in the morning.

"I'm going to ask Tom Hampton of the DIA to return to the microphone." Several questions were shouted from the floor, and Bentzen ignored them.

Hampton: "I want to go out of my way to complement the Baltimore Police Department, its Southeast District, and the undercover man from another jurisdiction who gave us the clues that solved this case. Our figures show that twenty pounds of cocaine would command about $200,000 when sold on the street corners of our city.

"I also want to say that as the cartels come up with other devious ways of getting their drugs into the United States and to dealers in this city and elsewhere, we will be watching and will infiltrate and conduct such actions as undercover agents and stops-and-searches until these cartels have to fold. Thank you."

He stepped away from the microphone, ignoring the flurry of questions fired at him, and shook the hand of Major Jeff Bentzen, and raised it high like a prize fighter might, which played well on the ten o'clock TV news.

"Major, just a few questions."

"Jim (Abbot of *The Baltimore Sun*), I can always handle a question or two."

"Major, it appears that the hero of the day is the undercover agent. You don't intend giving his name . . ." Major Bentzen nodded, "but can you at least tell us where he's from, or what experience he has."

"Jim, I can tell you that he is a detective in a different city. I can't tell you any more, because that would jeopardize his life if the cartel knew who."

"He gets no recognition?"

"He just gets to know that he did some excellent work for us, for which we're extremely grateful. It would be a disservice to him to make his name known or his home city."

"Was there anyone else who helped you zero in on the Central City Warehouse?"

Major Bentzen put up his hands, which also made the 10 p.m. news broadcasts. He looked around for another question.

"Does this portend the end to drug trafficking in Baltimore?" the very attractive, but not too sharp, Dottie Runyon of KBAL-TV asked.

"I wish," the major responded, noting to himself that that might have been the dumbest question he had been asked this month. "But it does slow it down some, Dottie, and the rest of the people involved know we can and will penetrate their networks, and they'll be the big losers, as several of them found out today. I think that's all I can say tonight. Thank you." And he stepped away from the microphone and listened to a number of questions from print journalists, put up his hands in an I-can't-answer-that manner, and returned to his office.

When he closed the door, he smiled at the men gathered there, and went over to Detective Gaston Leal of the Pittsburgh Police Department and gave him a big hug, as the other officers, Captain Dan Russo, Lt. Stach Wisniewski and Lt. Sylvester Reed, applauded.

Bentzen: "That was beautiful, Goro, or should I call you Jim?"

"Thank you, sir. Goro will do." He sat down again. "I just got lucky when I came on Hansen and the police sergeant and the propane-tanks man. They just looked so damn guilty, especially the poor slob who delivered the tanks. He just gave it away."

Reed: "That bug you planted in Hansen's office confirmed your suspicions and ours, and sent us hustling over to Belkron's store."

Leal: "Lucky Hansen doesn't look under his chairs too often."

Russo: "I think he really had no idea we were on to him. He was real feisty about the stops and searches when I first confronted him. But when I mentioned propane tanks, he just went white. Goro, that was beautiful."

Wisniewski: "How did Tom Hampton take it?"

Bentzen: "As you saw in the news conference, he admitted he goofed, but he thought the stops and searches may have helped disturb both Hansen and Belkron. On the other hand, men, we need the DIA in this war as much as they need us. Never forget it. We're on the same side. We had our moment. They'll have theirs, plenty of them. Let's get some sleep. Goro, what're your plans?"

"I get two weeks off, and I'm flying to South Padre Island, get a tan, and show off my muscles earned working in a warehouse . . ." He demonstrated for the amused officers. ". . . and have a few beers. Then it's back to work in Pittsburgh, as a detective."

And the men applauded, and each shook his hand or gave him a shoulder embrace. Sylvester waited until all the reporters and cameramen had cleared the area before driving Goro to BWI, the Baltimore-Washington airport.

All this is a recapitulation of what happened shortly before and then almost parallel to Kenny Wisniewski's killing in Virgina and his funeral in Baltimore. Mira Wisniewski returned to work at the Central City Warehouse about a week later and never discovered that her talks with Jasmine Reed had led to the breaking of the drug case. When Hansen was arrested, she was chosen by the warehouse owners to become temporary manager. After delivering a fine little boy, whom she would name Kenny Jr., Mira completed study for her master's degree from the University of Maryland and took over as operations manager at Central City Warehouse.

What about Judd?

Judd Schmidt saw the news report on Kenny Wisniewski's funeral on a flickering black and white TV in the little old motel about thirty miles west of Fredericksburg, which was costing him thirty-five dollars a day. He might have been the only viewer who was unmoved.

Partway through, he turned off the TV and walked down to a small, well-aged grocery for some donuts for his breakfast, rather bland coffee, and a sub for lunch with a Coke. He also walked to a hardware store, where he bought some metallic paint and a couple brushes to change the color of his tractor. With tools from his toolbox, he removed some of the chrome he had added. He decided to try to call Jim Poole again.

The day after the killing, Ole Jim had been sequestered in a motel in Fredericksburg, instructed to stay there and not to phone out. But he had been allowed to check on his refrigeration unit from time to time, under surveillance, and to call his trucking company in the morning to explain the delay. Virginia State Police detectives had stopped by his motel room for about two hours the first day and twice this day to complete their questioning. He had turned off his cell phone to deter Schmidt, if he did try, from calling when the cops were there.

They gave him permission, finally, to return to work, with Trooper Murphy sending him off. "Sorry that we had to inconvenience you, Mr. Poole."

"You got your jobs. I unnerstand." And he coughed some. "I sure am sorry for that kid—he was a nice kid—and I donn know how or whether Judd is involved." He coughed several times, and, regaining his voice, added: "It sure donn seem like him, you know."

"We'll get to the bottom of it, probably when we find him, or he turns himself in."

Poole checked out the refrigeration unit as he walked around his rig, started up his truck, entered the time and date in his log book, with some notes on the day before and the day before that, and started off, noting that the troopers had waited for him to leave.

Ole Jim had about an hour to drive to turn in his container, he thought, having double-checked where he was going to make that drop. He checked his fuel gauge and decided that he had enough for the dropoff.

About ten minutes later his cell phone rang. "Yeh, hello."

Schmidt: "Hey, good buddy. How goes it?"

"Judd, Judd, it's good to hear ya. Hey, tell me the tooth, Judd. You didn't kill the kid, did ya?"

"Never. Like I told you, the kid had some problem with his tire. That's the las' I seen a 'im."

"Why'd ya run, Judd?"

"I heard about that killin' over the CB, after I left you, good buddy, 'n' I though', shi', they're gonna blame me, and sure 'nuff that's wha' I hear now."

"Yeh, they wan' to talk to you real bad."

"I'll come in, don' worry, Ole Jim, but I need your help to geh' to my lawyer. Where're you now?"

"I'm circling D and C."

Schmidt, with forced laughter: "An' putt-puttin' a' dis time of da day."

"Well, I got stopped some fifteen minutes after you turned off, you know, too far up I-95 to double back to 295."

"Yeh, I guess." Paused to think. "I need you to pick me up, but not today. You takin' a c'tainer out tomorrow?"

"Supposed to. Hampton Roads."

"That'll do. What time you figure you'll be heading ou'?"

"'Bou' ten in the a.m., I would guess."

"I'll call you sometime after. Good talkin' to you, good buddy."

"Catch you later." And Poole turned off his cell phone, still loyal to his old friend, but puzzled why he was wasting time before turning himself in.

Poole was in stop-and-go traffic, which made it relatively easy for a blue '88 Ford Taurus driven by Lt. Sylvester Reed to stay a couple vehicles behind.

Capt. Russo had asked Lt. Reed to tail Poole without being seen, suspecting that Judd Schmidt might contact him.

And Reed followed Poole to where he dropped off his container, and then drove down to the Inner Harbor truck stop for dinner. Poole slept in his truck that night.

The next morning Poole woke up around seven and, after showering and shaving at the truck stop, had breakfast and drove over to his truck company down Boston Street. He was told to stop by the owner's office to review the Wisniewski incident, which he explained in considerable detail, and considerable coughing. He was advised to stay

271

well clear of Judd Schmidt, and Jim promised that he would.

Jim then got his paperwork and drove over to the Sea Girt container park, checked with the gate, and had to choose a new chassis for the park crew to put on his container for Hampton Roads. The paperwork showed he would be pulling coils and tubing from Eastern Europe for eventual use in Panama. In Hampton Roads, he would pick up a container from Poland loaded with kitty litter and dog food for a Philadelphia warehouse.

He left the container park about 10:15 a.m., cleared Baltimore, weighed and topped off his tank at the truck stop in Jessup, Maryland, and headed down I-95, when the cell phone rang.

"How's it goin'?" Judd asked.

"Not bad, Judd. I ben lectured up and down, I'll tell you, not to have nothin' to do wit' you." He coughed several times. "Johnny Law sure wants your ass. But, hey, you didn't think I was gonna leave you out there floatin?"

"No way, Ole Jim."

"Like you say, Judd, cops are shi'."

"You got that righ'."

"So what's up with you?"

"Where er' you headed?"

"Hampton Road, like I figured."

"I'll meet you there. Somewhere. But if not before, I'll climb on board while you're having lunch on da way back, like tha' truck stop at exit 200 off I-64. You wouldn't mind leaving your cab open, onct? You have a girlfriend lined up?

"Tenative."

"Probably have to break tha' date."

"Ah shi'. I do need the divertin', Judd." He coughed. "But no probem."

"I'll see you then, good buddy."

"Keep you head down."

"No shi'."

And Jim turned off his cell phone.

Hampton Roads

Poole continued down I-95, around the I-295 bypass of Washington, D.C., and he never noticed the '88 blue Ford Taurus, keeping about three vehicles back. Ole Jim was too busy wondering what Judd Schmidt wanted.

Poole swung over to I-64 and drove on into Norfolk to a warehouse to drop off his container from Eastern Europe. He then drove over to pick up a container at the Norfolk International Terminal, got his paperwork at the gate, and picked up another chassis carrying his container from Poland. It was quicker to truck these containers along the U.S. eastern sea coast port to port than to have the container ships stop at the various ports to unload at each. The ship that brought in Poole's container two days before was already headed back to Europe loaded with containers filled in the United States and driven to Hampton Roads.

Actually there is no town or city of Hampton Roads, but there is the port, which is run by the Virginia Port Authority on behalf of twenty-odd public and private terminals mostly in the communities of Chesapeake, Hampton, Newport News, Norfolk, Portsmouth, Suffolk, and Virginia Beach, an area already heavy with U.S. Navy installations.

In 1991 the port handled 855,219 TEUs, which includes twenty- and forty-foot containers, second to New York/New Jersey in tonnage on the East Coast, but likely to surpass New York/New Jersey in 1992 in tonnage, but not in dollar value. Charleston was seventh in that ranking, and Savannah eleventh.

Poole wrote all the information about his new container down in his logbook, keeping it accurate, for he assumed the state troopers would be especially interested in him now if he were stopped again. Before, he had accepted truckers' slang that the logbook was really a comic book, fictionalized as needed to meet state and federal law. Now he drove off, pretty hungry, pushing it a little bit so he could have a late lunch at that truck stop Judd had mentioned.

He dropped off his container at a warehouse, which didn't take too long, and picked up a new container from the yards where chassis were parked. He got to the truck stop about 3 p.m., parked, remembered not to lock the door—after he had already done so, and had to retrace his steps—and went into the restaurant for a hamburger steak with mashed potatoes, green beans, and coffee, looking about but not seeing Judd nor taking any note of a black man in a windbreaker standing in the corner reading a paper.

Poole went to the john and, coming out, ran into Jeannie, who had just arrived at the restaurant carrying a small bag. "Hey, Ole Jim, I'm ready to ride. Are you?" said with as fetching a smile as she could muster for a young woman growing older quickly, who was still headed to Hollywood, one day.

Poole: "Oh, damn it all, Jeannie," he broke off to cough some. "You look so good, you know, but I just can't do it today. Got the smokies over my shoulder, an' I donn wan' a get you in any big trouble, you know?" And he coughed a few more times.

Jeannie, coming in before he had stopped: "Oh shi', but, hey, maybe next time," and she walked away exaggerating the sway of her butt to sit down at the counter, light up a cigarette, and check out any other prospective customers, smiling fetchingly at Sylvester Reed, who smiled back but moved his hands and fingers in a way that indicated he didn't have much money.

Poole wasn't happy as he paid his bill, walked out of the restaurant and tried to unlock his cab door, forgetting that he had left it unlocked, then climbed into his cab and slammed the door.

"Hey, man, how's a trucker 'pos' to git any sleep?" Schmidt whispered from the sleeper.

Poole spun around in his seat. "Judd, Judd, you son of a bi." He coughed several times, slapping the wheel to make himself stop. "I had to forego a girlfriend just for you, you know."

"T.S., good buddy. I'll make it up to you one day, but I gaugh to have help today."

"I'm listenin'. You didn' think I was gonna leave you out there floatin'?"

"Nah, Ole Jim, I jest need to get back to BalTEEmore, so you migh' jus' as well get rollin'." He waited while Poole started up the truck and headed out of the lot onto the Richmond bypass.

Poole, having moved up through his gears: "On the road again, as Willie likes to say."

"Got your poin', Jim. I'd like to get ou' of this sleeper as soon as you think it's safe."

Poole: "No one here but me an' you, Judd."

Schmidt: "Well, let me know when you get onto I-95. There'll be a lo' more traffic. I'll jest' doze here a little."

"OK." And Poole drove on, turning on his CB where truckers were chuckling back and forth about Rush Limbaugh's latest commentary on the upcoming election. About thirty minutes later, when he had gone a ways on I-95, he said: "We're on I n' 95, Judd."

Schmidt pulled himself up and over into the seat alongside Poole: "I'm amazed you got enough room in there for your chicks. You ever sleep?"

"It's comfy. Good to see you," and he reached over to shake hands with Schmidt.

"Me, too, good buddy. I got my KW (Kenworth) stashed in back a motel wes' of 'ere. I painte' i' up some, and have some borrowed plates—you know wha' I mean." He waited for Jim to stop a coughing fit. "Now I gaugh' to mee' face to face with a lawyer man in BalTEEmore."

"If you had notin' to do wid that kid's death, why you runnin'?"

"'Cause you know how much I hate smokies, and someone on a phone call tole me that kid was kin to a police lieutenan' in BalTEEmore, and if the cops would ask me, even now, I'd probly say, 'Hell, yes, I killed him,' and, you know, I don' even know how he gaugh' killed.''

"With a tire bully, the troopers said. Guess he was testin' his tires an' some punk snuck up on him. Took his money ou' an' dumped his walle' in a trash barrel, they said. He was a pretty big guy though, you know." And he began another coughing spree.

Schmidt waited patiently: "Yeh, too bad. Not a bad kid, I guess."

They drove on, listening to the CB chatter.

About three vehicles behind, Lt. Sylvester Reed was on his cell phone to Capt. Dan Russo: "Glad you got back to me. At the last truck stop this Poole guy just ran off a girl hustler who seemed to have had a date with him, and that's pretty peculiar."

"That's not what we would expect him to do. He's supposed to be a real Don Juan."

"And . . . whoa!"

"What's up?"

"You shudda seen that, Schooch. A black Acura Legend coupe just roared by me doing what must have been ninety-five or more. That's sure a pretty car."

"It's a sure sign there's no troopers around."

"You got that right, Captain. They'd love to chase that car for a while, I'll bet, just for the fun of it."

It had been two days since Bo Jager had gotten his latest contract: to eliminate Judd Schmidt. He also had the word on Jim Poole and had trailed him out of Baltimore—taking note of the blue Ford Taurus, which he assumed was a police undercover agent also on the trail—to Hampton Roads and back to the truck stop on I-64. Unlike Lt. Reed, who got out of the Taurus and followed Poole into the restaurant, Jager had remained in his car outside the restaurant and had seen someone he assumed was Judd Schmidt climb into Poole's tractor.

Jager had then allowed the Taurus to follow Poole's trailer and had held back until they got onto I-95, then roared past the truck to confirm that two people were in the cab and continued on for about five miles at that speed to finally find an overpass. He slowed a little to make the exit, and drove up onto the bridge, slamming to a stop, jumping out, opening his truck and pulling out a five-foot-long block of cement he had taken from a construction site after he got the phone call from his woman contact. He crossed the bridge quickly to the other side and waited, the block tilted up in front of him. Only two cars passed over the bridge while he was on the bridge, and neither driver took note of him or his block of cement.

Jim Poole and Judd Schmidt also had seen the fancy sports car roar past. "Whew. Look at tha' batard go. Ole Jim, how'd you like to barrel along at tha' speed?"

"Get down to Hampton Roads . . . " he coughed twice ". . . and back in one morning. Hell, he's 'ready out of sigh'. Can' believe there's no smokies around."

"Those batards only worry about truckers."

"What'er you gonna do in BalTEEmore?"

"Got to find this lawyer I know; he owes me a favor. But jest' let me off in Jessup, and I'll go in mysel'. Show your CDL and you can usually get a ride somewhere or t'other."

"You gonna keep on the run?"

"For the momen.' Hey, you have any Cokes in this cooler? I'm thirsty as hell."

"Help yurself."

Schmidt opened up the cooler to dig out a cool Pepsi. "Never liked this shi', but if tha's all you gough'." He uncorked the lid with a can opener tied to a door handle, and drank down about one third of the Pepsi, looking out the side window for the first time; he had been fixated on the road ahead, just as if he had been driving himself. "You know, I can't 'member the last time I rode on the passenger side. Mebbe twenty, twenty-five years ago, when I started drivin' for an OTR firm that had . . . " He saw someone on the overpass ahead pulling up what looked like a big block of cement. "Oh shi', Jim, INCOMING! SWING LEF'!" and he shoved into Poole, "IN . . ."

Lt. Sylvester Reed saw Poole's trailer suddenly weave and the tractor stagger to the left and drift through the fast lane toward the median. He also saw out of the corner of his eye someone on the bridge watching the trailer weave. He punched his phone as he swerved off the interstate onto the exit. Capt. Dan Russo answered, "Yeh, I'm here."

"We got trouble, Captain. . . . I'm off I-95, exit 92, I think . . . going after some son of a bitch . . . who has wiped out the truck and trailer with Poole and I'd guess Schmidt inside. They're careening through the median . . . and into oncoming traffic. Oh, hell. The cars are piling up. . . . Call the state police. I got to get the killer."

As Reed sped up the overpass, he saw the Legend take off to the north. Dan over the phone: "Where the hell are you?"

Reed, screeching around the corner to come onto the bridge, "Crossing the overpass of exit 92 . . . on Highway . . . 54, I think," as he glanced at a road sign. "Try to get somebody ahead of me. I'll never catch that Acura."

278

"Can do. Take care. I'll alert Virginia state troopers. Take care, Syl."

Jager was astonished that the blue Taurus had driven up onto the overpass. "Stupid cop should have stopped for the accident," he said aloud as he floored the accelerator of his Acura on Highway 54 for less than a mile, swung right, peeling rubber onto U.S. Highway 1, sped in and out of traffic, and cut left in front of a delivery truck, which braked into a drainage ditch as Jager whipped left onto a two-lane blacktop, Archie Canyon Road, swinging right and left as the road twisted. He flew over railroad tracks and sped on for a while, coming to a T, glancing into his rearview mirror to ensure that the pursuing Taurus was not in sight, and slowed to swing left, without leaving tire marks, into the lesser-used road, which wove into the countryside of small homes, small pastures and small truck gardens.

Back on Highway 1, Reed was losing the race to keep the Acura in sight. He had no siren, no way to get cars out of his way except to sound his horn. He saw Jager far ahead swing left onto a side road, but Reed had to wait for traffic to clear before he could follow, and the Acura was nowhere in sight as he drove the two-lane, slowing when he reached the T. He looked both ways and elected to go with the heavier-trafficked road.

Behind him, a Virginia state trooper, alerted by several 911 calls, arrived from the south at the I-95 crash scene and immediately called in ambulances and fire trucks. It was carnage that Trooper Jeanie Bradley had not seen in her seven years on the force. With a breaking voice, she radioed in that a northbound tractor-trailer had crossed the median and two lanes of the southbound I-95, and that two cars had smashed into the trailer, and at least five other cars had driven into the crash debris. She didn't know yet that south-bound truckers, alerted over CBs by north-bound drivers who had pulled over to help, had slowed enough to block the highway enough to bring the carnage to a halt.

"We got wreckage and . . . bodies . . . here for a couple hundred feet," Bradley reported to headquarters.

"Help is on the way—more troopers, paramedics, fire engines. Just stay calm."

"Thanks. I'll try to find . . . people . . . still alive," she said, but the last words were lost as she scrambled out of her cruiser.

Bo Jager was flying down the two-lane, looking for a safe road. A sign indicated a turnoff to the right ahead a mile. He slowed a little, studied his rearview mirror to see no blue Ford Taurus there yet and cut quickly to the right.

Lt. Sylvester Reed was still barreling along in his Taurus, hoping that local police had been alerted to set up roadblocks. He wondered how they would stop the Acura; they probably wouldn't have tire shredders.

On the cell phone, he called Dan: "I've lost the Acura, but I think he's still ahead of me. If not, then he must have gone the other way at a T I passed about three miles back. I thought I saw some dust when I turned the other way at the T."

"Take care. This guy must be a hired killer, and a hell of a good one at that, from what you're saying."

"I hated to leave that crash scene, but there wasn't anything I could have done there except call for help. I heard a series of crashes as I flew over the overpass."

"You did right, Syl. You did right."

Back at the crash scene, before the first ambulance arrived, Trooper Bradley reported to her regional office that one doctor, aided by a couple truck drivers, was treating at least two people, but that six people were dead or nearly so, and three others seriously hurt.

She added ominously: "This was no accident. The driver of the tractor-trailer and his passenger were killed by a block of concrete apparently dropped from the overpass through their windshield." She based that on what a couple northbound truckers told her. They had been behind the truck that crossed the median, and showed her what was in the damaged cab of the tractor-trailer. The State Police regional office immediately dispatched a crime-scene team.

Meanwhile, the first of six ambulances arrived, along with more state troopers and firemen, who doused two gasoline fires. The paramedics quickly triaged the injured, confirmed seven deaths at the scene and sent those seriously injured to the nearest hospital. Five were in those ambulances, and two of them would reach the hospital DOA.

Capt. Dan Russo called the Virginia State Police regional office to follow up on what Sylvester Reed had told him about the chase. Russo had earlier called in on the crash itself. With the latest news, state troopers were dispatched to Cedar Fork and Chitesburg, Virginia, and local forces were alerted to stop—if they could—a speeding sports car.

Off to Colombia

Over the last four days, Patrick Sorensen and Felipe Sanchez had been trying to work normally, but on the sly they were both getting cash together to bail out for Colombia. Both had been rattled, first by Big Knife's death some time ago—the two bodyguards were of no consequence—but especially by Schmidt's murder of "the kid."

The shootout at the Wal-Mart the day before had Sanchez completely unraveled, but Sorensen explained that, if found by the police but not handled extremely carefully, the dangerous cargo hidden in the container Schmidt dropped off at the Wal-Mart would either get into the atmosphere and cause who knows what, or dissolve into something benign—he had been assured by cartel officials, who in fact were accepting some guesswork provided by a terrorist group in southeast Asia. Sanchez was somewhat assuaged.

Admittedly Sorensen was on edge, but he was more concerned at the moment about Schmidt. The Customs official had always believed Schmidt should not have known about the illegal drugs he carted, but Sorensen also knew that Schmidt and Sanchez went back fifteen years or more, and Sanchez had explained that he trusted the cranky trucker throughout, getting first-class service from a gear-jockey who was paid well—off the cuff.

Sorensen was in Sanchez's office around 2:30 p.m. when the phone call came through. "Your contract has been fulfilled," was all the woman on the phone said. "And we have the money."

Sanchez's reaction to the call prompted Sorensen to give a thumb's up with questioning eyes. Sanchez hung up, and said quietly, "He's dead."

Sorensen said brightly: "You have any idea how he was taken out?"

"I never ask. I don't even know how they ran him down. From what we've seen on TV, the cops had no clue where he was. They'll know now."

"And that bothers me," Sorensen said. "They want him for the kid's murder. And the cops apparently were shadowing Schmidt to and from Savannah, so our sources say. They somehow were on to him. And he was to drop off this container at your reserved lot. That should have prompted them to question you? And yet they haven't, have they?"

Sanchez, waving his hands about: "No bugs in this office, I assure you. And nobody's been in here talking to me."

"Then why haven't they questioned you? That Russo-Wisniewski combination is not sleeping. It seems to me that with Schmidt gone—when they find out about it—they would definitely want to talk with you. They'll also begin to check out that container . . ." The phone rang.

"Yes." Sanchez listened attentively, grimacing at Sorensen, and hung up.

"What's up?"

"Pedro."

"Oh, shit."

"We got to get the hell out of here, both of us. They want to see us in Bogota tonight, or tomorrow morning at the absolute latest. I sure as hell don't like the thought of that."

"Will we live?"

"Calvano assured me we'd both live, but we can't run. He already has men around both your family and mine waiting for his orders. He wants us in Bogota today."

"We can't even call our wives?"

"I wouldn't try. They might try to get away. They don't know anything—at least my wife . . ."

"Nor mine."

"So let's get to the airport and hope for the best."

"I've got my bag in my car."

Sanchez, not surprised by Sorensen's preparations: "Mine's in the closest. We'll use the back way out, just in case. Check out this schedule," and he flipped over a schedule of flights on Air Jamaica as he rose to get his bag.

Sorensen, glancing at the schedule: "How's 5:30 p.m. for you, *amigo*."

"*Vamos, el jefe.*"

They left through the door that Schmidt had entered not too long ago, taking a back elevator to the ground floor and walking a block to Sorensen's car, taking no note of a staked-out officer in civilian clothes who was doing the

283

tourist bit of shooting pictures of the boat traffic in the Inner Harbor.

They drove east a block on Pratt Street, followed by a police detective in his private car, turned left on President and left again on Lombard, left on Light, right on Conway, and left in front of Oriole Park at Camden Yards onto I-395, where an unmarked police car picked up their trail, and onto I-95 southbound, where a second unmarked police car carrying Lt. Stach Wisniewski and four members of an elite squad pulled in to take over the pursuit.

Neither Sorensen nor Sanchez spotted the shadowing police officers as they drove, about five miles over the limit, to BWI.

Stach was talking on his cell phone to Schooch, who had just reached the scene of the tractor-trailer crash down I-95 at exit 92.

Dan: "Yep, it's Judd Schmidt. The other guy, Poole, just might have survived, but a state trooper here said the paramedics suggested that he choked to death. They even thought that Schmidt was trying to save Poole's life. You never know. You just never know."

"Right now we're tailing our two key suspects down I-95."

"To the airport?"

"I'd bet on it. Where would they be flying to do you think?"

"Sanchez is originally from Colombia. That would be my guess."

"Mine, too. But we'll do whatever is necessary to delay them."

"You'd never believe who I just got a call from?"

"The killer on the loose?"

"Nope, Bob Hampton of the DIA. He's on to what we're doing, and he wants in."

Stach: "No way."

Scooch: "Oh, way, way, way. He's got some scans of Felipe Sanchez's paper transfers sending money offshore, some little island in the Bermuda chain, and bringing it back, just before those two punks in the water-taxi shootout were eliminated."

"That's great."

"That's not all. They also have gotten short-term warrants for wiretaps on Sanchez and Sorensen. And one of the three clerks in Sanchez's office is an undercover agent. Hampton wants us to delay Sanchez and Sorensen today so that he can get warrants for their arrest."

Stach, doing a Mighty Mouse imitation, sang flatly: "Here he comes, to save the day."

Scooch: "We both win. The major wasn't about to get us any warrants based on what we had."

Stach: "Can we stop those two? I've got Malinovski with me."

Scooch: "Beautiful! Marvelous! Wish I'd thought of him."

"But we can stop only one. I need help in holding up the airplanes."

"Hampton volunteered to help."

"Great, great. Heard from Sylvester Reed?"

"Nope, and I'm worried like hell."

"Sorensen and Sanchez are turning onto the access road. It's BWI as we suspected."

"Check with you later. Good hunting."

Bo Jager escape

Sylvester Reed was pushing his Taurus to eighty-five mile per hour as he roared up the back road. He knew the black Acura Legend Coupe was well out in front of him, or at least he hoped so. But he did not know that, well behind him, Bo Jager had already turned off onto a farm road and driven a mile and a half to a small truck farm where an old farmer was just coming in from his small pasture for lunch. Jager drove right onto the place and around to the back of the barn to get his Acura out of sight. He then bounded out and dove for the ground, rolled over and fired shots faster than he could count from his machine pistol at the old man in coveralls who was coming on and just bringing down his 30.30 rifle. Hit several times in the chest and head, he collapsed in a heap, the rifle falling from his hands, and his wife screamed from the doorway of their farmhouse. She rushed out to help her husband of forty-seven years and was immediately shot several times by Jager, falling dead before she reached her husband's body.

Jager ran to the house, checked to see that there were no other people there, grabbed some clothes, including a hat from the kitchen, and returned to the yard, pulling the two bodies into the barn, and driving the Acura in there, too.

He checked out a worn 1978 Chevy pickup parked beside the house; the keys were in the ignition, as he expected. He then donned the farmer's clothes, located a drum of gasoline, and backed his Acura into the back of the barn. He filed down the car's VIN with a file from the farmer's tool box, pulled off the license plates, spilled gasoline all over the vehicle and around the barn, including the tractors parked in there, wrapped up a stick with some rags wet with gasoline, went outside, lit the torch, threw it into the barn, climbed into the pickup and drove casually down the farm road and to the blacktop, turning back the way he had come.

Lt. Reed had finally reached the end of the hardtop, and roared onto Highway 54, where, in less than a mile, he had to slam on his brakes to stop from running into two police cars parked across the highway. He got out with his hands up, yelling, "Police Officer! Police Officer!"

The town's police chief and deputy had their pistols

out and pointed at Reed as he asked to be allowed to show his ID. The chief studied it before allowing his deputy to holster his weapon.

"You chasing that Acura sports car?" asked Chief Warren Brandell.

"I couldn't keep up with it. I was a good half-mile or more behind, but I thought he had come this way. Maybe he took a left at a T back there. Can you check with the department, is it Montpelier?"

"Nope, none there, but I'll try Bumpass." And he returned to his police car and called. He said through the car's open window, "They've put up a roadblock east of Bumpass where it branches, but no black Acura Legend. Someone who stopped said they had seen a blue Taurus—would guess that was yours—tearing up Hwy 54, but not any other sports car."

"Then he's gotten off somewhere. Can you stay here with your two cars, and the deputy come along with me, and we'll check out the side roads?"

"Well, Shawn's a good man, and he knows all the folks who live round here. So, yeh. Shawn, you want to ride with this city cop?"

Deputy Shawn Pepper, with a little skepticism: "Hell, I migh' even larn somethin', why naugh'?"

"You'll be a big help to me." Syl shook hands with the deputy, and they pulled out in Syl's Taurus, back the way he had come, but at a much slower speed.

There had been a slight rain early that morning, so Deputy Pepper said, "You can pretty well tell in some of these roads and trails, really, whether any vehicle has gone in there, sports car or whatever. They'd leave tire tracks pretty clear."

"You're a big help already to this city boy." And they drove along, slowing at each side road and driveway for a mile or two, with none indicating traffic that morning.

Then pointing to the southwest, Deputy Pepper said: "Now, who the hell is burning stuff? Damn, that's big enough, it could be a house or a barn. We better get the hell over there."

Lt. Reed pushed his Taurus up to seventy, driving through the other wing of the T, and slowing when Pepper pointed to the side road leading to the fire. "It's Max Andrews' driveway. We'll check it out before we call in the fire brigade. They couldn't get here for a good half hour, anyway, and maybe Andrews's just burning brush."

"I hope so. I hope our Acura driver hasn't come onto the place, for he's a sure killer." Reed then recounted for the deputy the crash on the interstate.

When they turned a corner to see the farm place, Deputy Pepper said, "Oh, shit. The whole damn barn is ablaze. You want to call the fire brigade?"

Reed quickly dialed 911 and passed the phone to Pepper, who alerted the emergency personnel as Sylvester drove as close as he dared to the fire.

They got out, Deputy Pepper rushing to the farm house to find no one, and Lt. Reed circling the barn in an attempt to see what was inside. The flames and smoke were too intense to pick out anything, but it appeared that a car, perhaps the one he had been chasing, was now fully ablaze.

Deputy Pepper: "No one in the house. There was some food in the oven apparently warming for lunch, I'd guess, but nobody around. What's your guess?"

"How soon do you think your fire brigade will be here?"

"Probly fifteen to twenty minutes, and thar ain't much they're gonna be able to do 'bout this, but maybe hose down the outsides so we don't get a forest fire going."

"Could they sprinkle some inside so we can see what's in there?"

"Suppose they could try."

Just then, another pickup pulled into the farm place, and a middle-aged farmer, Bill Higgins, got out and walked over to the two officers.

"You know, I just passed Andrews' pickup going down the road, and whoever the hell was driving waved to me, and you know that old son of a bitch ain't never waved to anyone in the last forty years."

Lt. Reed: "How long ago did you see him? And how far down the road?"

"Oh, fifteen, twenty minutes ago, mebbe ten, twelve miles down the highway, almost to the interstate."

"I'll bet our killer has abducted or shot Andrews . . ."

Deputy Pepper interrupted: ". . . and his wife."

"Hadn't thought of that. Or they could be in there." Reed pointed to the raging fire, causing the two other men to grimace.

Higgins: "Even for Andrews, it's a hell of a way to go. Roasted even 'fore he gets to hell."

Lt. Reed: "I'll try to call in the word on our killer. Will you describe that pickup for me?"

"Sure. '78 Chevy pickup, green onct, but now mostly rust. But it could still go. Don't 'member the plates, though."

Lt. Reed called in this information to Capt. Dan Russo, who relayed it to the Virginia State Police. Dan was at the site of the Exit 92 crash.

Lt. Reed told Higgins: "I guess you better stay here to wait for the fire brigade, and the deputy and I'll go down the highway and see if we can catch up with the killer, whoever he is."

"Mind if I check in with the chief. He should know what's going on, you know."

"Sure. Give him a buzz." And he waited until Deputy Pepper had described for Sheriff Brandell the latest developments. Brandell told Pepper to stay with the barn.

On the loose

A half-hour ahead Bo Jager had turned north on U.S. Highway 1, a road that had once been the main highway along the Eastern Seaboard. Now 90 percent of the traffic that once puttered past diners, motels, gas stations and drive-in movie theaters flies along parallel I-95.

Highway 1, which ran from Fort Kent, Maine, to Key West, Florida, pretty well followed the fall line east of the Appalachians. That's the point where coastal plain meets plateau, where falls and rapids provided waterpower to the founders of cities like Philadelphia and Baltimore.

But Jager had no need for that knowledge. Right now he required a different vehicle. He figured someone would see that fire fairly soon and wonder where the farmer's old pickup was.

He was looking for a diner, and Highway 1 still had some dating back to those glory days. He saw a gas station ahead with a diner alongside, worn out signs advertising burgers, hot dogs, fried eggs and grits. A few cars were parked in no particular pattern around the diner, a throwback itself to another era.

Jager pulled in, parked and entered the gas station, encountering a kid, perhaps sixteen, wearing coveralls, and asked where the "can" was.

"Ou' back," the teen said, pointing out the direction to walk.

Jager ambled around back, past the outhouse, its door with traditional half-moon banging in the breeze, with historic smell to match, and strolled past the back of the restaurant and up the outside. He found an '88 Buick Sabre open and climbed into the back, pulling a blanket he found down over him as he lay on the floor. And waited.

He heard individuals walking to their vehicles and starting them up, a couple arguing about the generous tip the man had left for the apparently young, blonde waitress, and finally someone coming to the Buick, whistling a Beatles tune and climbing into the front seat. The car started up, the radio came on blasting "golden oldies," and the driver pulled out on Highway 1, heading north, Jager hoped.

He waited through five "golden oldies" woven in among three commercials, and popped up, his pistol cold against the back of the driver's neck. The man, short and stocky, winced, glanced into his rearview mirror and returned his eyes to the road ahead in time to correct his car from running off the pavement.

"Just keep driving," Jager said. "Don't try anything funny, and you won't get hurt." He shifted his pistol to his left hand—he was wearing light tan gloves—climbed over the seat into the front passenger's seat, and with the pistol still pointed at the man, pulled on his seat belt. "Now, that's comfy. You won't try to crash me into the dashboard, and I can put this aside for a while," returning the pistol to a holster slung under his left arm. He had his right hand at the ready, as it were, to grab the pistol.

The driver had not said anything yet, and Jager assumed he was thinking too much. "What's your job?"

"Salesman. I sell janitor services, mainly to schools."

Jager, matter of factly: "How's business?"

"Could be better, but I get by."

"Got a family?"

"A wife, three kids, one in college."

"What college?"

"Community college, really. Catonsville Community College outside Baltimore."

Jager knew the college, but decided against giving any information about himself: "What's the kid there for?"

"Don't really know. Talks about print journalism, but who knows. Keeps him out of trouble, I guess."

"Wife work?"

"Yep, in real estate."

"And you drive a lot."

"Yep."

A Virginia State Police cruiser roared by heading south, its siren whining.

"He looking for you?"

"I'll ask the questions. Where were you headed?"

"Woodbridge. Got an appointment there, and the chief financial officer will be real concerned if I'm not there on time. He'll probably . . ."

"I make all the threats, too. Got that? And I need you for a day or so. Sorry about that."

The driver winced.

Jager glanced at highway signs and turned back to the driver. "When you come up to that Highway 17, let's go west to . . . Hartwood," glancing back at the sign.

"Whatever you say."

"And don't worry. You keep cool and you live. It's that simple."

"I'm cool."

Jager smiled. "I thought you might say that." Paused, but then remembered that he had to keep the driver occupied. "What's your name?"

"Bob Brophy."

"And who do you work for, Bob Brophy?"

"East Coast Janitorial Services, Inc., from Baltimore to Savannah."

"And how do you sell janitorial services?" hoping the salesman would launch into a detailed description of his work, which, like most people who enjoy their work and are used to talking, he did. Jager tried to look interested, and from time to time said "uh-huh," or "really," or "that's good." But he was not listening; he was just figuring out how he would reach "Sandra Dee," the code name for the young woman who passed on his contracts. How was he going to call her with this stupid salesman on his hands?

For his part, Brophy figured that if he was still talking, he was still breathing. So he painted a picture of a dedicated, hard-driving salesman whose family needed him, and who without question deserved to live.

Twenty minutes into Brophy's soliloquy, Jager said suddenly: "Pull in over there," pointing to the right side, "just onto the side of the road. And stop. . . . That's good. Now pass me the keys," and he brought out his pistol. "Now, you just stay where you are, and don't attempt to jump out or anything, hear, and I'm going to make a quick phone call. I don't want you to hear, so I'm going to step out of the car, and, while I'm looking straight at you, I'm going to make that phone call. Understand?"

Brophy nodded his head. His confidence in living through the next hour was suddenly shaken. But now he could think of what he might do, given the opportunity.

Jager returned his pistol to its holster, and keeping his right hand at the ready, reached back with his left hand to unsnap the seat belt, grasp the door handle, and let himself out of the car, shutting the door and backing five steps from the car. Watching Brophy carefully through the car's window, he dialed "Sandra Dee's" number.

"I'm here," said a young woman with a sweet voice.

"I've had to ditch my car, and I need another. Park one with the keys over the visor in Marshall, Virginia, perhaps near the post office. Anything but a black sports car or a Buick. And I'll need new plates, too."

"How soon?" said the woman with the sweet voice.

"Two hours. No more."

"I'll call when it's there."

Shootout at the terminal

"Yeh, I heard you," George Mihok said to his wife, Anna, "but I got to go, now. The plane takes off in an hour and a half."

"Mr. Folks must be giving you the best customers if you have to keep flying about," Anna said.

"Yeh, he does, and the flying sure beats driving."

"And you even got your exercises in this morning. You're looking better every day, hon. You really are."

"You, too, my love," and he kissed his wife, who gave him a big hug that almost tempted him to skip the flight. He glanced at the photos of their two boys on the wall and headed out to his car, parked on South Kendall Avenue, before driving off to BWI for his flight to Chicago. He was smiling, and breathing. The meal Anna made was great. They had made very satisfying love last night, and that's always good. His smoking and drinking days were history. Life had been hard; he had made it that way, but God was good.

Sorensen parked his car in a long-term parking lot, and he and Sanchez climbed onto a small bus over to the BWI terminal. Ahead of them, Lt. Stach Wisniewski, Detective Stefan Malinovski, and two other detectives got off at the front door, each in civilian clothes carrying suitcases or brief cases, and Officer Bill Dowding parked the car in a short-term lot.

The officers were in place when Sorensen and Sanchez got off the parking-lot bus to enter the terminal, turning to the international airline ticket counters. There was a pretty heavy crowd going in all directions, and two of Wisniewski's officers in a heated argument walked right into Sorensen and Sanchez, giving Stefan Malinovski the opportunity he needed to relieve Sorensen of his passport.

Finally Sanchez and Sorensen, having cursed the two who had bumped into them, reached the international ticket counter. "Two tickets to Bogota, Columbia, and return," Sanchez said. "Yes," the charming ticket seller said through a pretty smile. "You'll have to go through Washington, D.C., you understand. Your credit cards and passports, please."

Sorensen dug out his wallet and pulled out his credit card, but couldn't find his passport in his inside coat pocket. He went through his pockets again, without success. He then rifled through his briefcase and suitcase.

Sanchez smiled. Sorensen studied him carefully. "You really didn't want me to come with you, did you?"

Sanchez did not erase the smile, completed the purchase of his ticket and guided Sorensen away from the ticket counter.

"No. I didn't lose your passport. You did. Or someone pick-pocketed you when we got bumped coming in here, and that's trouble for both of us."

"More for me."

"You can get a replacement passport in a day or two. No problem. But you might better get out of town if you're the victim of a shyster who might just be a cop or agent."

"Would you wait a couple days, *amigo*?"

"Sorry. I'm heading out today. I have my passport and my orders. There's just too much coming down just now. You know, I don't think you lost that passport. I think someone doesn't want you to go."

"Let's grab those chairs over there between those two moms with kids."

Sanchez looked, and saw the advantage: they would be able to talk without being heard by anyone but the young mothers, who were already worn out by the screaming little ones.

Lt. Wisniewski observed the two walking to the open chairs. He motioned to his officers to spread out. He had anticipated that Sorensen and Sanchez would figure out they had been had. Stach sat down with his back to the two, talking with Malinovski, also with his back to the two. A third officer seated with them was keeping the two suspects under surveillance through a slit in his newspaper.

Sorensen, after the two took their seats: "Well, if there are police or FBI agents or CIA or whatever watching us, got any suggestions?"

"I'm taking off. Call me when you get to Bogota."

"I'm off to wherever I have to to get a replacement passport in a hurry—like Chicago—and fly out of there. I'll call you when I get to Bogota, and, unless we're intercepted, we'll know for certain there's no feds involved, just that damn combo of Wisniewski and Russo."

"You got any files they could rifle through for evidence."

"I've nothing at Customs. You?"

"There'll be nothing important for Wisniewski, Russo and friends to find," he said forcefully. Actually he had paperwork and his computer in his office that could be incriminating. "There's nothing at the house, except the computer and the offshore investments," he assured Sorensen.

"That could implicate you."

"I doubt it, but I better get going. Hope to see you in Bogota." He got up to leave, and Sorensen shook hands with him and walked off to visit with a ticket agent and see how he could get a replacement passport. The agent was happy to get a last-minute customer to fill the plane to Chicago.

Lt. Stach Wisniewski was on his cell phone telling one of his officers tailing Sorensen: "Get in line behind him and buy a ticket to the same place, whereever. You got enough on you?"

Officer Ben Bedwell: "Not if it's to the West Coast, I don't. But my credit card should cover me."

"Keep me posted." Stach hung up and looked to his third officer, Benjamin Cutter.

"Where's Sanchez headed?"

"To the ticket counter for international flights. You want me to tail him?"

"No, I'll have Hummel." And he dialed Detective Lawrence Hummel, who was watching Sanchez pass him by at the moment, and fell in behind him.

Sanchez glanced back to see Sorensen disappearing around a corner, headed for a domestic ticket counter, and Sanchez pulled out his cell phone and dialed. Hummel tried to get close enough to hear the conversation but failed.

A woman answered: "Yes."

"I have a contract."

"Yes."

"A passenger on a Southwest Airlines flight from BWI to Chicago. Name is Patrick Sorensen, fifty-three or thereabouts. He's still here, but when he gets there he'll be going from O'Hare to the State Department office for a passport. He's wearing a light green shirt, darker green jacket, and brown slacks. He needs to be eliminated."

"Expenses involved will mean doubling the contract of the last person."

"Doubling?"

"Yes."

"All right. I'll get the money as soon as I can." He would transfer it from an offshore account.

"We can wait." She hung up.

Sanchez dialed again, one of his assistants in his office in the World Trade Center building, and gave him the address and the amount he wanted sent, made out to Holy Holidays Inc. He explained to the clerk that he was planning a trip to Israel. The amount, when it moved within twelve minutes, was duly noted by DIA agents monitoring electronic transfers from the importing agency.

Sorensen got into line at the Southwest Airlines ticket counter behind someone carrying a display case with his suitcase. The man ahead turned and asked: "Headed to the Windy City, too, eh?"

Sorensen, who was not interested in bantering with a sales rep: "Yea."

However, the salesman, George Mihok, was too wired to be put off: "I love that city. Just can't get enough of it. But I got a couple of demanding appointments. You on business?"

"Yes, private business."

"Sorry." Hawk was disappointed. He had discovered that giving up smoking and drinking had given him a lot more energy and free time than he needed, and he just had to do something, for example, talk: "You go to Chicago often?"

Sorensen ignored the question for a while, but finally answered: "Yes, quite a few times."

"Me, I get there nine, ten times a year. Sell toys, expensive toys, with lots of computer chips in them, great slot cars. And we got a couple hobby store managers who eat them up. Well, let me show you the leading model." And he opened up his display case for the highly annoyed and impatient Sorensen.

"Right at that next turn."

After Bo Jager hung up after calling "Sandra Dee," he got back into the car, with nothing showing on his face that would give salesman Bob Brophy any clue as to his fate.

Jager gave Brophy the keys back and put on his seat belt using his left hand, keeping his right hand at the ready. "Let's go. Just keep driving up Route 17. I'll probably have you turn off sooner or later," and he watched as Brophy started up and returned to the highway.

Jager: "Just pick up where you left off, describing that important work that you do." And he settled back to listen, occasionally, and to watch for a side road.

Brophy had to think for a minute, but then picked up with the steps he usually took in approaching a prospective client—checking in with the school office and asking whether he might talk first with the janitors before his appointment with the school bureaucrat actually responsible for the contracts. And he droned on and on . . .

Brophy's heart beat faster as he slowed to make the turn. "Take the turn slowly," Jager commanded. "We wouldn't want to slide out of control," said rather sinisterly.

Brophy slowed and turned into a one-lane dirt road, his soliloquy ended, as he glanced at the menacing stranger. He drove on silently and slowly over the rough road, his concern mounting as the minutes passed. The sweat built on his temples and started to work down his sideburns. He wiped away a drop, causing a quick turn by his unwanted passenger. He drove on.

"Stop here," Jager said, bringing the pistol out. Brophy stopped and said to himself once again the prayer he had composed in the first minutes of their encounter. "Now, leave the keys in the ignition, and get out on your side." Brophy took off his seat belt, as did Jager, and both stepped outside. Brophy considered running, but Jager anticipated him: "Don't run. Just start walking straight ahead. I'll tell you when to stop."

Brophy repeated the end of the prayer to himself, and repeated the entire entreaty three times—it wasn't that long—before he heard Jager yell, "Just keep on walking! Just keep on walking! And don't look back."

Brophy walked just a little faster, until he heard the car door slam and his car start up. He kept on walking, and heard the car moving. Was it coming this way? He kept on walking and listening. The car appeared to be going the other way. He kept on walking, a little faster now, and the car sounded farther and farther off. He was still too scared to look back. And then the car seemed like it was so far away, he stopped and listened, and glanced to each side, and decided to walk some more, around the next corner. And he did, and he strolled closer and closer to the right side of the road and then ran into the woods and flattened himself against a cottonwood, and sunk to his knees, with a final thanks to God.

Brophy guessed he was five or six miles along this dirt road, but he smiled, for he was still alive. He was excited enough that he had to relieve himself, and then he mopped his brow with his handkerchief and sat down by the side of the road, the pounding in his chest and head slowly easing. He glanced at his watch—it was almost 2 p.m.—and he wondered whether he should just go on, or whether he should walk back to the highway. He decided to walk farther along the road, hoping to find a home or farmstead.

Bo Jager did not enjoy driving the Buick Sabre, and he pushed it up to forty-five on the rutted back road. He hoped that the car he would pick up in Marshall would have some life in it; he thought about losing his black '92 Acura Legend coupe. He thought to himself that he could have been roaring along the interstate in the coupe rather than bouncing about in this junk if that damned cop hadn't interfered.

After twenty minutes or so, he made Highway 17 and turned west, keeping to the speed limit and figuring he had about a half-hour or more to go. He pushed various buttons to find something better than "golden oldies" and eventually came back to the original station after fifteen choices of country western.

The traffic was light, mostly headed east. He saw no police cars, but didn't know whether that was good or bad.

After twenty-five or thirty "golden oldies" and eight commercials, he reached Marshall, crossing over I-66. He drove into town, what there was of it, to look for an American flag to point out the post office. His cell phone rang.

Jager: "Yes."

"Sandra Dee": "The car waiting for you is a 1988 red Sable, with Michigan plates."

Jager, sensing she had more to say: "What else?"

"You have another contract—at BWI, a Patrick Sorensen, in his fifties, business type, wearing a green sports jacket over light green shirt and brown trousers, planning to fly to Chicago. I have further information if you miss him."

"Is this the former deputy mayor?"

"I would assume so."

"Price was doubled, yes?"

"Yes. And it's been received and properly sent along (into a secret offshore account)."

"Well done." And he hung up.

He drove the Buick slowly into Marshall, stopped for a red light on Main Street, looked left and saw an American flag, signaling the post office. He drove by the post office and the red Sable parked in front, pulled into a grocery parking lot, placed the keys under the floor mat, walked back to Main Street, past the Sable, which had current Michigan plates, and into the post office, where he picked up a flyer as he looked up and down the street. He came back to the Sable, climbed in, reached up for the keys over the visor, and started up, turning at the end of town to reach I-66 eastbound.

He figured he had about eighty miles to BWI, or an hour and a half, he guessed. He'd stay pretty close to the speed limit, but speed up if any tractor-trailers passed him, indicating there were no speed traps ahead.

Salesman Bob Brophy walked briskly along the dirt road whistling to himself, and then loudly to the animals of the woods. He mopped his brow with his handkerchief and eased his pace. He began to consider whether he could rescue today's appointments with the staff at Woodbridge Middle School. He could not remember an appointment he hadn't made on time in the last fifteen years. Usually he was early.

'But who cares,' he said to himself. 'I think I'm gonna go into the nearest town and have a beer, and maybe buy a beer for everyone in the bar. Or maybe just enjoy that beer all by myself, and then I'll call the principal, and . . .

'Wait a minute. I don't have a car, or my briefcase. All I have is the clothes on my back.' And he breathed deeply.

'Well, guess I'd better pick it up and see whether this road goes anywhere. The road's pretty well worn, so there must be some traffic.' He marched along, and once more felt the need to relieve himself. Getting behind a tree off the road, he spotted what appeared to be a trail into the heavy forest. He decided for some reason or other—for he had never walked through woods before—to walk a little up the trail, and about 100 yards or so off the road saw through the trees what appeared to be a small farmhouse, two-story, perhaps six rooms, likely an outhouse out back, he thought to himself. He walked up to the door. It had been painted brown in some bygone day. He rapped, and from inside came a strong voice. "All right. I hear you. Just walk right in."

And Bob did, right into the sights of what he found out later was a 30-30 Winchester rifle. His face went white, and he almost fainted.

"Oh sorry," said the young man seated at a small wooden table with the 30-30 aimed right at Brophy. "I was just cleaning my hunting rifle. Sorry to scare you. We don't get too many, what ere you, book salesman, preacher, wanderer, surely not here to save my soul."

Bob Brophy's voice came back to him. "You wouldn't point that gun away," he said weakly, pointing to either side.

"No problem," said the armed man, as he locked a shell into the rifle and laid it across the table, still pointed in a general direction toward Brophy. "What can I do for you, stranger? Not many folks ever come up that trail."

"I'm Bob Brophy, and I've been looking into the sights of a special pistol of some kind or other held by a guy who stole my car, and I just about passed out when I saw your rifle."

"Tell me your story, Bob Brophy. Have a seat," as he pointed to a wooden chair at the head of the table and out of the direct aim of his rifle. "You sure don't look like you live 'round here, specially not walking back in this here part of the woods in those clothes. I'm sorry if I scared you. You never know, you know."

"I'm a salesman. You were right about that. But all I sell is janitorial services to schools."

"Not sure I really need a janitor, Bob Brophy," the young man said. "My wife's out back in the garden. She does most of that, you know."

Bob thought to himself that she apparently didn't do much in this room. Then he explained, "About noon today I stopped at a small diner off Highway 1, and when I came out and got into my car some guy put a pistol to my head and said keep on driving north on Highway 1. Then he had me turn off on this dirt road and stopped and made a phone call, and then had me drive some more, and then ordered me out of the car after I had to hand over my keys."

"Bet you you thought you were a goner."

"Sure did," Brophy admitted with a noticeable breath. "But he said to start walking and not turn back, and I did."

"Prayed some, too, I'd wager."

"A whole lot as I kept walking and walking and finally heard the car start up, and then he must have turned around . . ."

"You didn't look back?"

"No way. I just kept walking. And it seemed the car was going in the other direction. And I kept on walking. And walking, and I had to take a leak and saw what I thought was a trail and saw your place through the trees."

"You want me to saddle up and go after this guy?"

"No, I'd just like to call the police and get my car back."

"Well, I guess we can help you somewhat. I don't think my chasing him on horseback would help much if he got back on the paved roads. We ain't got a car, and we ain't got a phone, but we do have a couple horses, and we can ride a piece to Cab Webber's place, cause I think he has a phone. That suit you, Bob Brophy?"

"I'm in your debt."

"No sweat. Maybe a ten or a twenty dollars would help our economy." And Bob quickly pulled out his wallet, and dug out a twenty.

The young man said as he pocketed the bill, "Let me put this rifle away for the moment, and I'll tell Jeannie, and put the two horses in harness, and we'll be on our way."

"How far is it to Webber's place?"

"Probably eight miles. It won't take too long."

"I'm in no hurry. But I would like the cops to know, and I would like to get my car back, you know."

"Think you'll be a better salesman after this episode, Bob Brophy?"

Bob thought about that for a while. "Now that's a question I wouldn't have expected. But I guess it's better to be a live salesman than a dead salesman. So, yes, I think I'll be a better salesman. Never did get your name, you know."

"Yeh. You don't need it. The gendarmes might just want to look me up, you know. I'll drop you off about a half mile from Webber's, and you can walk over to the road and then to the house. They're good people. And they got a phone, I think. You never met me, you know."

"Let's Saddle Up."

"Fine. Let me tell Jeannie, and we'll be off." The young man picked up his rifle and closed the back door as he walked back to the scraggly garden with its lettuce, watermelons, corn and beans. His wife was scrawny, ungraceful, in well-worn jeans and torn shirt.

"Somebody came walking into our place. Says he was threatened by a guy with a pistol who took his car. Can you believe that?" She didn't speak. Her man continued: "He wants to reach civilization, probably to have the cops look for his car. Said I'd ride with him down to Cab Webber's place. Any objections?"

She shook her head no and turned back to hoeing. He clicked his teeth and walked back to the house and his salesman guest. "Guess we'll be going, soon as I get out the saddles. Ever ridden before?"

"Never. Drive a car."

"We'll be goin' a lot slower over a back trail, but it beats walkin'."

And the men climbed into the saddles, Brophy needing a push to make it, and started at a slow walk to Webber's. For Brophy it was part of an adventure, and he decided he might just as well enjoy it. The thought crossed his mind that this nameless young man might just shoot him in the woods and no one would know the better. But that apparently was part of the adventure, and he was now thinking positively.

They moved along at a walk, and Bob felt the rock and roll of the horse, and enjoyed it. He tried a number of moves in the saddle to find a placement of his butt that wouldn't hurt, but he couldn't, so he just kept moving this way and that and hoping they would reach Webber's place soon.

He studied the woods on both sides, and almost fell out of the saddle when a doe dashed off to his left.

"Just a doe," his companion said. "Lucky she had no fawn with her—not the time of year—or she might have given you or the horse, more likely you, a swift kick."

"I don't think I've ever been in deep woods like this before," Brophy said.

"Might as well enjoy it," said his companion. "Not much of a market here for janitorial services, you know."

Brophy smiled. "I appreciate your humor, and your help."

"Yeh, well, we'll be there in no time, and you'll miss all this fun." He paused. "You got a day to remember, Bob Brophy. You married, got kids?"

"Yes, both."

"You'll have a great story to tell them, and it won't be about selling custodial services."

"Yeh," and Brophy chuckled. "You impress me as someone who's had some education beyond high school."

"Yep. Try not to atrophy here in the woods. Jeannie, she don't say much. So it's a good day for me to talk with you, Bob Brophy. I'll miss you."

"Really appreciate your help."

And they continued on for another hour, until the young man stopped. "I'll let you off here, Bob Brophy, and point you in the direction of the road. You walk straight this way and you'll hit it. Probably best to follow the remnants of a trail. When you get to the road, turn left. I'd say east, but you might not know your directions. You should get to Webber's place in less than a half hour."

"Sure appreciate your help," Brophy said as his companion helped him down from the horse. He offered to shake the man's hand. "Don't mention it, or me. That's all I ask, brother," and the unknown man turned his horse and took the reigns of the other and started back up the trail.

Brophy watched, then turned in the direction shown him and stumbled along, staggered a few times, pushed aside boughs, and in about forty-five minutes saw the road through the trees, climbed down to it and turned left, heading toward Webber's place.

You gotta keep trying

Police Lt. Sylvester Reed was extremely depressed. In the immediate past he had had nothing but rotten luck multiplied over and over again. He had been on the cell phone to Captain Russo when Kenny Wisniewski, a real nice kid, was killed. And Syl didn't get back to the scene at the truck stop until Schmidt and the other driver had driven off. And then he chased the man in the Acura Legend that caused the tractor trailer to stutter across the interstate, killing and maiming for life who knows how many, but Syl had lost the car, guessing wrong at that damn T where the killer must have lost him. And then at least one more person had gotten killed at the farm, and he hadn't stopped that.

And the damn murderer was still on the loose, and Syl had no idea where the hell he was, who he was, where he was going, or whether he had dumped off that farmer's pickup. He did get a description of the farmer's truck from the neighbor and had radioed that information to Captain Russo, who relayed that to Virginia authorities.

Lt. Reed really didn't know which way to turn now. 'I guess I'll head on home. Not much more I can do here.'

He called Captain Russo, who had to admit, "Syl, I guess you could drive around, perhaps up Highway 1 and see if you can find that truck. That would help. But that's a wild goose chase, and I have no idea where he's headed. I would guess he would burrow under somewhere and let the air settle. We should let the locals worry about him. But you just don't know whether he's gotten another target, perhaps one of those two that Stach suspects. Where are you now?"

"Heading up Hwy 1, just puttin' along. Maybe I'll see that farm truck, or maybe that Acura will reincarnate itself. I'd love to give it a run again."

"Yeh, right."

When planes don't fly

At BWI George Mihok was right behind Patrick Sorensen in the line boarding the Southwest Airlines flight to Chicago when the clerk at the boarding gate got on the loud speaker. "Attention, passengers boarding or preparing to board this Southwest Airlines Flight to Chicago, there has been a delay, and we will have to ask you to return to the concourse. We don't yet know when we'll have the mechanical problem solved, but we hope to be airborne in a matter of minutes or more."

Sorensen: "Damn, damn," and another "damn," said under his breath when George Mihok commented: "Well, better late than never, I say. There are a couple seats over there."

Sorensen thought to himself that he might just as well sit down with this dumb salesman; he wouldn't have to talk, just listen, and the time would pass, eventually. "Just wait a minute, I want to check with the girl over there."

He walked over to the ticket counter. "Hello, I'm deputy director of the U.S. Customs Division for the Port of Baltimore," and presented his credentials.

"Yes, sir."

"Just what is the problem?"

The girl, following the exact directions she had just been given by her senior, who got them from Bob Hampton of the DIA: "The copilot has come down with a serious kidney problem, and we have to call in a replacement. It shouldn't be long, sir."

"Thank you, young lady." And he made his way over to the seat held for him by Mihok, who asked: "Find anything out?"

"Yes. They are waiting for a replacement for the copilot, who got sick."

"Haven't heard that one before, but those things happen." And he pulled out his display case: "Did I show you this slot car called the Bill Clinton Special. You can see the Arkansas state flag on the hood, and even a likeness of Hillary on the passenger window. It's a pretty good seller."

"You vote for Clinton?"

"Whatever Democrat's running gets my vote. South Kenwood Avenue, in fact most of Canton, has always voted Democrat."

Sorensen: "But aren't you getting a whole bunch of rehabbing young people in Canton, and most of them will vote Republican."

"The world's made up of all kinds. We'll have to deal with them, I guess. Might convert them into Polish-Americans, you know," and they both laughed.

Then Sorensen settled back, and Mihok, happy to have an audience, launched into a soliloquy about world issues, interrupted occasionally by his one-man audience:

--Restaurants always placing grape jelly packets on their tables, because nobody likes grape.

--Why mothers do a better job than men of raising sons, bringing in his wife and two sons.

--The advantage of working with exercise tapes over workout machinery. This was something he had just discovered, what with his new exercise routine.

--The time saved by going to mass on Saturday night rather than Sunday, even though the Saturday night preacher is duller.

--The reason Hawk never calls his wife Anna by her nickname, which he didn't explain further.

On and on and on, until he finally stopped, but only for a minute, before Sorenson, who had enough on his mind to figure out, even noticed, and then going on: "Well, at least I got my Powerball ticket today. That means I can win, how much is it, hmmm . . ." He glanced at the ticket he had brought out, ". . . $72 million; well, I guess that's enough."

"I'd hope so," Sorensen said—his first words in what must have been an hour or more.

"Actually more. Because what I'll do when I win—and I'll take the whole amount over twenty years, not just the quick payout—I'll just rush down to the nearest Chinese restaurant, let's see, that would be the one over on Aliceana, I think, and I'd cut a deal . . ."

". . . with a Chinese restaurant?"

"You're damn right. Now listen. You ever eat in a Chinese restaurant?"

"Once in a while, mostly buffet."

"Makes no difference. Either meals or buffet, the restaurant will give you fortune cookies, right?"

"Of course, with those silly tables of animals and who you should marry. And the numbers are meaningless."

"You're right, of course. But, here's the deal. After I win the lottery, I'll go to the owner of the Chinese restaurant, you see, and I'll say, 'Look, I've just won the lottery.' Now I actually got a quick pick from the gas station on Eastern, but I'll tell him that I got the numbers from one of his fortune cookies. And all I'll want is, oh, say, 20 percent of the extra business that comment draws when it gets in *The Baltimore Sun* or on the TV.

"Now, if the garage owner protests that I got the ticket from the garage, *The Sun* will run a correction, but nobody ever reads those, and I'll apologize, but I'll still contend that I got the numbers from the Chinese place, and they won't be able to challenge that. I can say it was just a mistake on my part. I'll bet the Chinaman will be taking in extra cash for at least a year or more, just like that gas station, but I won't get anything from the station."

"Brilliant, my man, brilliant," and Sorensen patted George on his shoulder. "I'll have to buy a lottery ticket."

"And start eating Chinese," George suggested.

A hike through the woods

Bob Brophy walked as fast as he was able, but probably took an hour or more to reach a two-story house alongside the road, with an all-terrain vehicle in front. It was getting long in the day. He took a deep breath and walked up to the home as a tall man, perhaps sixty-five, maybe seventy, stood up from a rocker on the front porch, and said abruptly: "Who ere you and where in hell you'd come from?"

"I'm Bob Brophy out of Baltimore, Maryland, which is up north from here, and someone got into my car when I was having lunch and then pulled a pistol on me and stole my car and dropped me off on this road some miles back."

"Whooee, that is a good story. I'll believe you, brother, but that is a good-un. You're not a revenuer by chance? Cause I don't care, cause I ain't got no stills. But that is a story. What does Bob Brophy out of Baltimore do for a living?"

"I sell custodial services for schools. And I was headed to Woodridge for an appointment this afternoon."

"If you were walkin' along this road for some miles, how come you got some stickers on your clothes? Just checking, you know."

"I'm not accustomed to relieving myself on the road, so I'd go into the woods a little to do that."

"Sounds reasonable, Bob Brophy out of Baltimore. And I'm a reasonable man. Name's Caleb Webber," as he got up from his rocker and reached out to shake hands. "Guess you're looking for help."

Taking into account the caution expressed by his young friend, Brophy said, "I'm hoping you can help me. Maybe drive me along this road, or maybe you might have a phone?"

"I ain't got no phone, but you can climb up behind me on this handy AT'n'V and I'll take you to a store a few miles along where they might just help you. Be sure you tell the same story now, because I'll be listening."

"I won't change one word."

At BWI, Lt. Stach Wisniewski on his cell phone to Capt. Dan Russo, who was at the accident scene in Virgina: "We have both targets under surveillance. Both flights have been detained."

"Any chance they'll see each other and figure out that something might be amiss."

"They're in different parts of the airport. That's not likely."

"They could call each other."

"They haven't yet, at least. I guess I could have Malinowski pick off one of their cell phones."

"That would be far too suspicious and put them on their guard. We shouldn't have to wait very long for those warrants with Bob Hampton pushing the prosecuting attorney."

"Well, we can restrain them, I guess, for one reason or another. Oh, I almost forgot. You'll never guess who's been talking to Sorensen—Hawk, my brother-in-law."

"Judd Mihok? That's beautiful. Just hope he doesn't

get in the way."

"Oh, I'd holler if he did. Just hope he doesn't spot me and start bragging to Sorensen. He's been talking nonstop for a couple hours now. It's like he broke out in talk once he quit drinking and smoking."

"Keep your head down."

The wheels of justice grind slowly, even when the DIA gets involved, and Circuit Court Judge Amnon Wintersfield was miffed that he had been pulled away from his oldest granddaughter's birthday party. After a half hour's briefing by a DIA lawyer, the judge acceded to the arrest warrants sought.

About three hours had passed from the time Sorensen and Sanchez entered the airport terminal. George Mihok was still talking. He had moved from merchandising to politics to labor relations to truck traffic on the interstates, and back to his toy cars. And he still needed to talk.

Sylvester Reed needed to think, needed to walk, needed his wife and daughter, needed to be among people. He didn't need to go to BWI; there were enough there. He had called Stach, who suggested that Syl take a break, for Stach and his men had that operation under control. Syl drove into the city, parked at the Italian parking lot off Eastern and walked slowly over to the Inner Harbor, calling his wife Jasmine on his cell phone—she was just home from work—and inviting her to bring Keeyse down for an outing.

"What a great idea," she exclaimed. "We should be there in, oh, twenty-five minutes?"

"Great. Tell you what. I'll meet you at the fudge place. We can wait until the workers start singing, and Keeyze will be jubilant. Our last visit here wasn't that great for her. If you're on, see you there."

Reed put his cell phone away as he approached the World Trade Center, and stopped at a fence overlooking the harbor traffic. He saw the water taxis passing and remembered the shootout, for which he had been commended, and felt a little bit better. He leaned on the fence and watched the tourists coming and going. It was nearing dinnertime and some workers were hurrying from their offices to home. He felt extremely guilty about Kenny Wisniewski's death, contending that he should have been backstopping him. He felt equally bad about losing the driver of that '92 Acura and his car. He was disappointed with himself, and just plain tired.

He looked in the other direction toward the pedestrian bridge in front of the Hard Rock Cafe. He noted three Latino types walking along in their light summer suits. He turned back to the Inner Harbor, and suddenly realized that one of the three Latinos, the one in the middle, was the third man in Lt. Stach Wisniewski's photo on the bulletin board at the Northern District's roll-call room. He thought to himself: 'yes, black mustache; wasn't that a scar on his left cheek?'

Lt. Sylvester Reed froze. He reasoned that he could not look back at the three for fear of showing too much interest, so he kept looking over the harbor, waiting for them to pass. He glanced back to see them heading toward the twenty-seven-story World Trade Center building, and immediately turned away and pulled out his cell phone, calling Capt. Dan Russo.

"Yes?"

"Dan, Sylvester here. I just saw the third man in Stach's photos from the stadium, and he's just entered the World Trade Center with two *compadres*."

"They're probably going to clean out Felipe Sanchez's office on the fourteenth floor. Let me think. . . . It should take them some time to do whatever they're planning to do. Let me get you some help, maybe even the DIA?"

"It's your call, but I think we could manage with five or six of the tactical squad."

"OK, but I'll alert the DIA anyway, since they were helpful on this guy, Pedro something or other, probably not his real name. Supposed to be an inspector of sorts for a Colombian cartel. Maybe we can get that Tomas—who's that singer, oh yeh—Estafan who talked at a recent briefing."

"An inspector sounds important."

"You better believe it. . . . Let me see. . . . I'll get some plain clothes people from the Southeast District and invite some people from the DIA, especially Estafan, since he speaks the language."

"I'd need them now, or within ten or fifteen minutes."

"Right. I'll have them check with you. What are you wearing?"

"Light tan wind-breaker, blue Maryland crabs cap."

"Great. Stay near the front door, and they'll check in with you. Then place them facing the elevators and stairways, and get the jump on this cartel official and his *amigos* as soon as you can.

"Better clear out civilians from the first floor. You won't be able to clear the building. And don't start shooting if they happen to exit the elevators with a bunch of civilians. It would be better to grab them outside in that case. So have three or four of our people on the outside, ready, in case."

"Roger. I'll be just inside the front doors on the left."

"Good luck. You should start getting your people in ten minutes or so. Think up some diversion, just in case the trio comes down early. Now let me see. There's another officer, oh yeh, Sergeant Breckenridge. He used to do security there. I'll send him along."

"The more experienced the better," Reed said, and he signed off.

Bo Jager drove his Sable into the short-term parking lot at BWI and made his way into the terminal. He needed another victim, and he saw one, an airport workman, probably one of those men who load and unload planes or clean up the cabins, walking into a rest room. The rest was simple, and Jager walked out five minutes later wearing the gagged and trussed worker's uniform.

Jager cleared security easily, even with his pistol and silencer in his specially modified and baffled briefcase, simply by diverting the guard's attention while he passed through. He then studied the departure board, finding a number of flights to Chicago on various airlines, some duplicating each other.

But he stopped when he saw a Southwest Airlines flight delayed, and he walked toward that gate. Sure enough, there was a man in his forties, business type, wearing a green sports jacket and brown trousers, sitting alongside a salesman hustling, ah, looked like slot cars? 'Oh well,' he thought.

He walked about the terminal to plan his escape route.

Within ten minutes of Sylvester's call to Capt. Russo, four detectives had reported in to Lt. Sylvester Reed and were strategically placed around the bottom floor of the World Trade Center. Next came two agents from the DIA, Estafan and an older man, and the older man was assigned to help intercept the three suspects as soon as they exited the elevators, while Syl asked Estafan to join him.

The next three detectives from the Southeast District were ordered to work with security in clearing the bottom floor of all civilians, asking them to move quickly without sounding any alarm, and to walk quickly for cover in the retail and restaurant offerings just a few steps from the World Trade Center.

None of the detectives and agents on the scene was in uniform, but all were heavily armed. And they waited for about thirty-five to forty minutes, watching each delivery of elevator loads to the bottom floor.

The detectives from Southeast District and the DIA agents had brought along copies of Lt. Wisniewski's photo of Pedro Calvano to share, and they all tensed immediately when they spotted him and his two associates coming off the elevator pushing three file cabinets piled high with folders, along with five other people, including two women. As the detectives and DIA agents moved toward the open elevator, Calvano immediately saw the threat, pushed his two aides forward with their file cabinets, and dove back into the elevator, reaching up to close the door and ascend.

The DIA agent and three of the Southwest District detectives charged into the jumble of people and floored the two bodyguards, disoriented by being shoved by Calvano, before they could draw their weapons. Other civilians were roughly shoved aside. Apologies were made later.

"Hold the two goons!" Reed shouted, as he, Estafan and two other officers ran toward the stairs. "Just keep this exit covered, and we'll go up the stairs!"

Calvano's two bodyguards had tried to grab civilians as shields, but the officers had been on them too quickly. They were relieved of their handguns. Lt. Reed was alerted by phone on the weapons the aides carried, machine pistols.

The building's security officers helped the civilians get outside, where the buildup of police officers was continuing. Calvano's bodyguards, who turned out to be from New York, were immediately cuffed and pushed into police cruisers for a trip to the Southeast District headquarters. The files and folders were secured by the DIA for analysis.

Lt. Reed had two detectives from Southeast District, Moses Green and John Abcock, and DIA agent Estafan chugging up the stairs with him. Reed alerted officers on the bottom floor that they should begin sending up officers to close off the landings on the other floors as quickly as possible. A security officer in the tower reported by phone to Reed that the elevator had made stops on the sixth and seventh floors before someone had ordered him to shut down the elevator's power, stalling the elevator between the eighth and ninth floors.

Capt. Russo also alerted Lt. Reed about the stopped elevator. He and the people with him assumed Calvano was still aboard, but they weren't sure.

Bob Brophy was tired. He was happy; he was still alive; the adventure was still going on, but he was tired. "How long . . ." he said loud enough to be heard.

"'Most there, oh, couple hundred yards or so, I'd guess," said the driver of the ATV, Caleb Webber. "Your butt starting to wear a little."

"Yeh, somewhat."

"Well, looks like we're here," as the ATV turned a corner and came upon a store, or what might have been a store in the not-so-distant past. When they entered, Bob Brophy saw some groceries, some sodas, and, 'ah, there it was,' a phone on the wall. He asked the older woman behind the counter, "How much for a phone call?"

"Two quarters."

"Here."

"To reach the police, do I call 911?"

"Yep. What's the problem?"

"It's a long story."

Bob Brophy dialed 911 and explained his day to a clerk at what was the nearest police station. She took down his name, home address, the make of his car and the license number, details of his adventure, and promised that the information would be passed along to the Virginia State Police and the regional and local police forces.

Bob took a seat at the counter and asked for a beer, whatever was cold.

"All we got is Budweiser," said the older woman, "but it's cold."

There were only five other folks in the grocery-bar, and Bob gallantly bought one for each person, and sipped his ever so slowly, smacking his lips.

He repeated his story for all of them—they had heard most of it while he spoke on the phone—and ordered another round. He answered a number of questions about his day, his work and his family. In the middle of his description of the culprit, the phone rang. "Yes, he's right here," said the older woman, and turned to Brophy: "It's for you."

"For me?" And he took the phone to hear from the Virginia State Police that a town officer in Marshall, Virginia, had found his car at a grocery, with the keys under the mat, and the car apparently in good shape.

"Yes, there was a briefcase there." Another question. "I guess I'll get up there somehow. I sure appreciate the fast response." And he hung up and relayed the good news.

The older woman said, "Well, Mr. Brophy, I reckon my son can drive you up to Marshal. We don't want to give Virginia a bad name, you know."

Perhaps inspired by the two beers, or the quick response by the police, or the kind offer to drive him up to Marshal, or just the strain of the day, Bob Brophy teared up and said huskily to everyone, "Thank you. I really appreciate all you've done." And he brought out his handkerchief and wiped the tears out of his eyes, and said, "Before I go," he shouted, "ONE MORE ROUND!"

A hero of his own making

At BWI airport, meanwhile, Bo Jager sat down and opened his brief case, looking about to see who was looking at him, if anyone. He saw no one concerned. He did not know that three police officers and Lt. Stach Wisniewski in civilian clothes were watching Patrick Sorensen and George Mihok, although Stach glanced at Jager a couple times.

Jager had had sufficient time to decide on his escape route. He slipped the silencer on his pistol in the briefcase, and then pulled it under his left arm and into his coat, stood up and walked toward Sorensen.

". . . but you didn't get that sale," Sorensen said, looking directly at George Mihok, ignoring the man walking toward his seat.

"Not yet," Mihok said, glancing at the man walking toward him, and noticing that his right hand was inside his shirt. It appeared to George that the stranger might be in the middle of a heart attack.

"What's wrong?" George asked as he rose, his display case in his hands, about to put it in the next seat when he saw the man's hand come out with the weapon. Mihok shouted, "Look out!" and lunged at the gunman, slamming his display case into the man's middle section, causing a bullet to split through the man's left shoulder and snap into a ceiling tile.

Sorensen also jumped up, but was immediately slammed back into his seat by police officers, who piled over him and onto Mihok and the unknown assailant.

Jager, a U.S. Ranger-trained and Vietnam-experienced veteran who worked out at a gym daily, could have taken any one of the police officers alone, and maybe two of them, but he was overmatched by the three of them—two had kept up their Marines physical training when they joined the police force—and crashed to the floor, with Mihok directly on top of Jager, and Jager's finger finally pulled off the pistol's trigger, after a second volley skittered across the floor and into a suitcase in a row across the concourse. One shell narrowly missing a three-year-old boy playing with a toy dog next to his mother.

"Look, Mommy. See the hole in Daddy's suitcase."

The officers, now aided by Malinowski and Wisniewski, wrestled Mihok off the assailant. One of the officers kneed Jager in the back, while the other two struggled to pull the man's arms back so that Wisniewski could put the cuffs on. The struggle was intense, but the lawmen won as Mihok crawled away.

Airport security officers were on the scene by this time, and Wisniewski had two security guards chase down Sorensen, who had quickly walked away.

World Trade Center Standoff

Back at the World Trade Center, Reed, Estafan and the two detectives from the Southeast District slowed their ascent, partly because they were becoming cautious and partly because they were getting bushed. They were on the fourth floor, and Reed thought they had better get some more officers and begin prowling through every floor. They still suspected that Pedro Calvano was trapped in the stalled elevator, but they had to ensure that he hadn't gotten off before the elevator was shut down. Sylvester called Capt. Russo, who ordered five more officers to ascend the tower.

When they arrived on the fourth floor, Reed and the three others began searching to the right, and the four additional officers prowled to the left. Everyone working on the level being searched was instructed to walk down the stairs; they were told that the elevator was permanently stalled and a killer was on the loose. No one argued, and the descent began, with the folks instructed to leave the building and gather in nearby retail stores or restaurants.

A janitor was called up to open some of the closet doors, and he did, quickly jumping back whenever he pulled the door open, with the officers over his shoulder, their weapons drawn and aimed inside. Progress was slow.

The fifth floor was cleared, and then the sixth. At the seventh, Reed and his detectives found one office door locked, and the janitor got behind a wall and reached over to place the key in the lock. As it rattled in the lock, a volley of shots rang out; the janitor screamed and fainted—his arm had been shattered. A detective standing far behind was hit in the leg. Everyone else ducked even farther down for cover.

Lt. Reed called Capt. Russo: "He's holed up in a travel agency on the seventh floor, Dan. A janitor we were using to open locks has had his arm pretty well shot up. Calvano shot through the door, possibly with an Uzi, and he wounded one of our detectives."

"Does he have hostages?"

"Don't know yet. I would guess so. We're emptying the rest of this floor and shooing the folks back upstairs who were coming down. Hold on."

Reed turned to a secretary hurrying by. "Can you tell me much about this travel agency? Who's in there? First, let's get you behind some cover." And he escorted her into an office not in line with the closed door.

"I don't know whether there were any customers in there, you know," said Jeanne Reiter, an executive secretary to an imports company on the eighth floor. "They have Mr. Bartholomew—he's the boss—and his wife works there, too. And there's John Enright, Bill Winters, and some new guy—they're all salesman types. And they just put on a new girl, rather pretty, but I don't know her name."

"So we're talking about at least six people."

"If they were all there. That I don't know."

"In any case. I'll call down and see if we can find any of those, John Enright, Bill Williams, a Mr. Bartholomew and his wife, and the new guy and the new girl. And we'll go from there. Thank you. Walk carefully toward the stairs behind these cabinets we've placed as sort of cover."

Ms. Reiter stooped low to get behind the cabinets and descended the stairs. Sylvester called down to have her escorted outside to see whether she could find any of the people she had named.

Reed checked with Estafan: "All the other rooms cleared?"

"Yes, Lieutenant. We had to force a couple doors without the janitor, but the rest of the floor is clear. How about upstairs?"

"Later. Let's take care of Calvano. Who else would be blasting through that door?"

"Yes, sir. We'll keep the people from trying to come down."

Lt. Sylvester Reed on the phone: "Dan, can we loosen that elevator, take it down and bring up something we can use to break through that door. We can't knock it down now without taking a lot of casualties."

"I'll see what the state police can provide us. Don't they have some remote they've been testing? But it will likely take a while."

"We're not going anywhere. We've got the upper levels sealed off, not allowing anyone to come down. Don't want any more casualties. And we're in good shape here, covering all sides. Calvano will likely . . . "

"Hold on." Capt. Russo was being signaled by the

chief of security for the World Trade Center building. About three minutes later, he called Lt. Reed back.

"Syl, Calvano has just told the chief of security here that he's coming out. He's going to have people in front of him and behind him. He'll take them all out if he sees anybody on the floor. He wants the seventh floor completely clear of police officers. He's giving you and your men five minutes. He wants the elevator started up and brought down to the seventh floor within five minutes.

"He can wipe out all the people—he's holding eight, he says—and he will if he's crossed."

"I'm on it. Thanks, Dan. Wish me luck."

Reed called the other officers together, assigned three of his men to hiding places in the outer offices on the seventh floor, had the rest hide down the steps, and he and Tomas Estafan went up the stairs around the corner out of sight. They all waited.

The elevator returned to the seventh floor. When the five minutes were up, the locked door to the office clicked open, and a crying woman slowly pushed it open.

"Anyone there?" she was asked by a person with a heavy Latino accent.

"No one. It's empty," she replied honestly, for she saw no one.

The Latino: "Everyone move forward slowly to the elevator. You know I will keell all of you if you don't do exactly as I say."

All holding hands, the party slowly crossed the floor, each one searching the corners, looking for help, the first woman still crying. "Shut up," she was told. "Push the button."

The door opened. Calvano dropped to his knees, his weapon pointed between the office workers toward the elevator car, but there was no one on it. "Everyone in," he said. "Push the button for the second floor." He looked around, saw no one, and stepped back onto the floor as the elevator door closed. He heard the sound of people running up the stairs. He turned quickly to the stairs going farther up, and right into the sights of .38-calibre pistols aimed by Lt. Sylvester Reed and DIA Agent Tomas Estafan.

Reed commanded, "Don't even think . . ." but Calvano fired his Uzi as he raised it, tattooing the steps right below Reed and Estavan. But the cartel inspector's weapon dropped as he was stopped cold by shots from both men, one going through his heart, followed by three more through his body. He collapsed to the floor, shuddered and died, as the other police officers reached the seventh floor, followed by the detectives hiding on the seventh floor.

"Well done, Lieutenant. A great plan," said the first agent to Reed. "That stomping on the stairs"—they had not ascended until the shots were fired—"did the trick."

"It's been a long day," said Lt. Sylvester Reed as he carefully removed with his handkerchief the Uzi from Calvano's hands. "It's been a long day."

He took out his phone and dialed Capt. Dan Russo. "We got him, Dan. 'Fraid he won't be able to testify."

"Well done. Well done. We'll be up shortly. The DIA got a lot of stuff to look through from the briefcases the bodyguards were carrying and the files they were pushing. That should seal the case. Ah, here are the hostages." Applause could be heard. "They look a little peeked."

The woman first off passed out, and was caught and steadied by two of the waiting officers.

Firehouse Headquarters

In Fredericksburg, Baltimore Police Major Jeff Bentzen, having ordered everyone else to keep clear of the Fredericksburg's metropolitan center, arrrived at the firehouse that now sheltered the rental truck and container

325

from the Wal-Mart shootout. On the way was the container Kenny Wisniewski had been pulling. His tractor was examined by DIA and FBI agents and released. It was driven back to Baltimore by a state trooper who had been an OTR trucker. The extended Wisniewski family decided to meet on its future. Likely they would ask Sam Zaleski to help get the best price; he had been along when Kenny took the tractor for a spin before buying it.

Along with the tractor came some of Kenny's clothes that Mira had put together in a small satchel, and some Georgia peach preserves and a Forrest Gump shrimp cookbook. Mira burst into tears when she saw the souvenirs Kenny had brought for her—his last gifts.

And at Fredericksburg, a police sergeant, after clearing with Chief Alkron, reluctantly allowed Major Bentzen to park outside the firehouse and walk into the building and introduce himself to the chief.

"So you're Major Bentzen?" the chief said. "You got any good idea on what we have here?"

"Well, you know that we thought it was cocaine," Bentzen said as he sat down.

Chief Alkron: "Yep, we were going on that, too, but when we brought in the dogs trained to pick up the cocaine, we got no response, at least around all the boxes that were unloaded from the first container. We presume the men sent to do that—their bodies have been taken to a mortuary in town—would have been instructed on specifically what they were to remove."

"Then they didn't unload the whole trailer?"

"Nope. They took off fourteen boxes. Now, they were pretty heavy, so they had this forklift they borrowed going pretty strong. We had made sure there was a forklift available. Anyway, when they closed up shop, as it were, we assumed they had what they were supposed to get. But the dogs trained to sniff out cocaine found nothing suspicious in any of those fourteen boxes."

"They missed the drugs?"

"Maybe they're hidden extremely well, and the FBI agents are double checking that, opening everything up. By the bye, the FBI have not yet come up with identities on the three guys sent to pick up the boxes, but the weapons have been linked to a couple cartel killings—the elimination of some fairly important officials.

"But back to the boxes. Maybe we're being set up. So we discussed it with the DIA agents, and decided together that we'd ask the FBI to help out."

Major Bentzen: "Suppose there's nothing dangerous in there? On the other hand, the driver was supposed to park that container right in the heart of Baltimore, in Little Italy. Could it have some hazardous materials? I recently heard a presentation on the possibilities of what's called a 'dirty bomb.' By definition, that's a regular bomb with some radioactive material thrown in." Chief Alkron nodded his head, letting Bentzen know he was familiar with the subject. The major continued, "Could some foreign power, actually subservient to the cartels—like Colombia or Afghanistan—be planting these around the United States?"

Chief Alkorn: "That very much concerns us, I'll admit. But there's been no trace of radiation . . . yet."

"Can you cover with the press why you brought in the FBI as well as the DIA?"

"I'm working on that. The press is really hounding everyone. I'll come up with some answer, maybe that I didn't feel confident in such a publicized case. I may look like a loony on page one, but that's part of the job. We are called to protect the city and its people."

"And if there really is a dirty bomb, or what might have been such a thing . . .?"

"We'll simply say it was drugs. Your cocaine will do. The FBI wants us to be sure not even to suggest it was anything that would cause mass hysteria or an evacuation, unnerving everyone, especially the politicians in Washington. We're just not that ready as a nation for that. I'm not sure we'll ever be ready."

"Is there anything I can do now that I'm here?"

"Want to sit and wait, and help me with the press? We'll have the other container brought in here this afternoon. Perhaps the drugs you're warning us about will be in that container."

"Well, one thing I'm absolutely certain about," Major Bentzen said, "and that's that Kenny Wisniewski, the young man driving that truck, who was killed at the truck stop, knew absolutely nothing about carrying any drugs. In fact, we had asked him to convoy with this Judd Schmidt just to see whether there was anything unusual. . . . On the other hand, Kenny's container was supposed to be taken to a warehouse in southern Baltimore that figured in some major drug arrests in the last two days. So I wouldn't be surprised if you do find cocaine in that container somewhere."

Chief Alkorn: "There's got to be good reasons for three people being killed . . .

Major Bentzen: "We've had some more killings in Baltimore tied in with all this—a cartel inspector and two distributors, and some others injured in a car crash. And we had to arrest one of our sergeants."

"Is it out of control, Major?"

"For the moment."

Chief Alkorn: "But why would the drug cartel want to get involved in that, you might ask. And I've no answer, unless it's a long-range thing. Consider this: Suppose there is a dirty bomb in there?

"This driver, Judd Schmidt, was supposed to drop that container off on a lot pretty central to Baltimore. Now he might know if he were pulling drugs, but not about any dirty bomb, so, after he killed Kenny, Schmidt would just get rid of the trailer wherever he could, and a Wal-Mart sounds like a good place. Trailers being parked there every day and night. That makes sense."

Bentzen: "Yeh. Now suppose the cartel—which is extremely rich—just happens to be really a front for some worldwide terrorist group?

"It's fanciful, isn't it? But the cartel knows what was in Schmidt's container and what was in Wisniewski's. You're also protecting both those containers by parking them in firehouses."

Alkorn: "We need the protection, that's for certain. In any case, Major Bentzen, we're not going to be talking about any dirty bombs, I can tell you that. Both the DIA and the FBI want no mention of that, no suggestion. . . . Can you imagine . . . well, if that got out, folks would be deserting Fredericksburg in one big hurry."

"Terrified?"

"Yep. We're not going to do that. We're going to say there were drugs in there, no matter what we find. The FBI boys tell me that they can neutralize whatever is in there."

"And if they trigger it? Just suggesting?"

"They won't." He looked down at his hands. "What else can I say, Major?" And the police chief, who honestly believed that his city could be wiped out, if he were wrong, clenched his fists and his jaw, and looked down at the paperwork on his desk

"May God help us," Major Bentzen said quietly.

"Amen," his host added just as quietly.

At the BWI terminal, Patrick Sorensen, when he was brought back before Lt. Wisniewski, said with authority, "I'm Patrick Sorensen, deputy director of the U.S. Customs Office in the port of Baltimore," pulling out his credentials, "and this son of a bitch tried to assassinate me. You saw it, and I thank you, especially this man, George Mihok—if I remember correctly."

"Yes, I'm Lieutenant Stanislaus Wisniewski, and I saw everything, Mr. Sorensen. But where were you going now?"

"Getting the hell out of here. If there's one assassin, there could be more."

"Well, just a minute. I'd like to know why you thought you might be a target. The real target could have been Mr. Mihok."

George was just getting up off the floor and picking up the remains of his display case. "I'm sure as hell glad to see you. I sure as hell am," he said to Lt. Wisniewski.

"Hawk, that was some stunt you pulled. You could have been killed," and he gave his brother-in-law a big hug.

"You know each other. Is this a frame-up?"

Lt. Wisniewski pulled out his cell phone as it rang: "Yes." And he listened for about two minutes, motioning twice to his officers to make Sorensen stand where he was. "Well, Sylvester sure did it right, didn't he?" He listened some more. "Great for Syl. We've had some action here, but we'll pick up the two suspects immediately." He ignored Sorensen as he dialed Officer Donald Simpson. "Pick up Sanchez," Wisniewski said. "We have the warrants."

He put his cell phone back in his shirt pocket and turned to Sorensen. "Patrick Sorensen, you are under arrest, charged with aiding and abetting drug trafficking into and through the port and city of Baltimore. A warrant for your arrest has just been approved by Circuit Court Judge Amnon Wintersfield. You're entitled to a lawyer. Anything you say from now on can be held against you. You'll have your day in court, Mr. Sorensen, thanks to my brother-in-law, George Mihok, who stumbled into this case, and miraculously saved your life."

Sorensen, recovering his composure, shook hands with Mihok: "I thank you, sir, for saving my life. This," he indicated Bo Jager just being lifted to his feet with cuffs on his wrists and his ankles, "this assassin obviously was hired to kill me, and I think I know who hired him."

Lt. Wisniewski: "As I said, you're entitled to a lawyer. Anything you say from now on can be held against you." His phone sounded again: "Yes . . . great . . . thank you. We'll keep them separate. Take him to the county jail."

He turned back to Sorensen: "Felipe Sanchez, an importer with offices in the World Trade Center building, has just been arrested on the same charges as you as he was attempting to drive out of the airport. Apparently he had a different route to Colombia. We'll be very interested in what you might want to say about him."

Wisniewski turned to Jager, who was being held on both sides by officers, even with cuffs on his wrists and ankles: "And where is your black '92 Acura Legend coupe, sir?" prompting Jager to blink. "We have quite a lot to ask you about. Yessirree, shootings at the hospital, a tractor-trailer crash in Virginia, and perhaps Mr. Sorensen might help us."

Sorensen was about to say something when Wisniewski cut in. "You'll have your time. Don't worry."

Police officers aided by security guards took Sorensen, Sanchez and Jager off in cuffs. Stach turned to his brother-in-law: "Come on, Hawk. Let's go home. You've had a big day," as he put his arm around George's shoulder, and the airline passengers, air crews and airport personnel made way, applauding George as he walked out, George smiling broadly from side to side. A flash went off, causing George to blink.

The colored photo on page one of *The Baltimore Sun* the next morning showed salesman George Mihok carrying his crushed display case, with his brother-in-law's arm over his shoulder, and airport personnel applauding, under the headline in thirty-six-point bold type:

Slot-Car Salesman Outwits Assassin at BWI

The eighteen-point subheads read:

2 Cartel Front Men Seized, Another Slain At WTC

and the twelve-point jump head said inside:

FBI Reports Cocaine Found in Containers Pulled by Slain Truckers

Deep in the story by Stuart Allderney of *The Baltimore Sun*, he wrote: "Fredericksburg Police Chief Jonathan Alkron reported that FBI agents had found cocaine hidden in both containers, one dropped off by Judd Schmidt at the Wal-Mart outside Fredericksburg and one that had been driven by Kenneth Wisniewski that was to have been dropped off at a warehouse in south Baltimore.

Chief Alkron said he was certain that Wisniewski never knew there were drugs in the container he was pulling, but the chief suspected that Schmidt probably did. Alkron was quite sure that Schmidt killed Wisniewski, probably because Wisniewski had somehow given away his role of shadowing Schmidt. 'That's my read on it,' the chief said, 'but the FBI and the DIA are thoroughly involved in the investigation, and I believe they'll have all the angles wrapped up in a week or so.'"

According to Allderney's story, Virginia State Police reported that the container pulled by James Poole, who was traveling with the two other truckers, was clean. There were no drugs or anything suspicious in that container, which was refrigerated to carry food.

Poole and Schmidt were killed when a concrete block was dropped from an overpass through Poole's windshield. Nine persons were killed in all when Poole's tractor and refrigerated container crossed the I-95 median north of Richmond and was struck by several cars. FBI and DIA agents involved in the case declined to return phone calls, Allderney wrote.